PLAYING THE

BADGER

GAME

Robert Henson

DEDICATION

In memory of my wonderful son Stuart.

.

CONTENTS

Preface

According to the *Oxford English Dictionary*, the verb 'to badger' is to bait, hound, subject to persistent harassment or persecution; repeated and irritating requests to do something.

The term 'Badger Game' is colloquially used by professional criminals to describe a situation where embarrassing and damaging information about a person with influence could be used as leverage for their advantage. Organised criminal gangs function through strict tiers of hierarchy, with such information often traded between criminals as favours, or by those seeking advancement within their organisations. Once the victims have been made aware of their indiscretions, contacts with them become more frequent and threatening. The aggravation of this harassment becomes blackmail, especially where the demands are dishonestly made, with menaces.

Many of the victims are married men, often tricked into compromising situations involving a secretive relationship with another, thereby leaving them vulnerable to blackmail. This is normally referred to in the media as extortion, the courts define it as blackmail, whilst criminals call it the Badger Game. Perpetrators of the Badger Game are known in criminal circles and the police as 'players'. Whatever the name, in law it carries a maximum sentence of ten years' imprisonment, thus elevating it to amongst the most serious of offences on the criminal statute.

Often connected closely to this practice is prostitution.

Renowned as one of the oldest professions in history, in recent times it has attracted a criminal element attracting the social distaste of the wider community.

Within the United Kingdom, prostitution is not a criminal offence in itself, but attracts legal punishment when it is solicited or offered in public. Aggravated offences of living off these 'immoral' earnings and proceeds (pimping) or allowing premises to be used for such purposes (keeping a brothel) have always been vigorously pursued by the police and keenly prosecuted in the criminal courts.

Brothels were commonplace in the ancient urban landscape, often nestling amongst other civil amenities such as public baths, libraries and market places. However, their activities became increasingly obscure after the Regency period in the early nineteenth century, soon becoming a dichotomy to the rise of Victorian values and attitudes. They were referred to as houses of ill repute, a scourge on the morality of a civilised society.

However, brothels still existed, and they continued to flourish as private gentlemen's clubs particularly in London, Bristol, Manchester and Birmingham. Membership was strictly by invitation only, their clientele usually consisting of either professionally qualified men or those wealthy and influential enough to protect the club's activities from public scrutiny. Secrecy and discretion were the cornerstones of their existence.

Women who operated in these premises were often self-employed and gave a percentage of their earnings to the proprietor for the use of the room and the club's facilities. They usually received large financial rewards and operated in a relatively safe environment. The members attended on an appointment only basis, hiring a woman's services and room, rarely seeing anyone else. Most clubs were large houses in private grounds, hidden from the public gaze. Authorities, even the police, were usually aware of their presence but turned a blind eye, accepting they served a purpose of sorts and caused little or no offence to the community, provided they remained discreet.

Other than the occasional scandal involving perhaps a member of the clergy, a politician or someone of public interest whose ruination featured in the News of the World, this remained the status quo until the Profumo affair in 1963. After that, everything changed. It was widely speculated that Badger Game players were indirectly responsible for the demise of Harold Macmillan's Conservative Government.

During the following years, these private clubs became more exclusive, seen as secret societies, and robustly repulsing any unwarranted attention. They simply went underground.

Even with the emergence of a more tolerant and liberal view of sex outside wedlock during the 1970s, these clubs remained hidden. Occasionally the press had their scoops. Indiscretions by people in the public eye were exposed and they paid the ultimate price. Careers were ruined and they were humiliated, in common disgrace.

Cynthia Payne, perhaps the most notorious woman in the late twentieth century sex industry, once said, 'Vicars, MPs and lawyers were amongst those who considered me to be the best hostess in London.'

However, towards the close of the seventies, organised criminal gangs began to turn their attention towards more lucrative enterprises, such as the large-scale importation of narcotics from South America, the Middle East, Pakistan and Afghanistan. This migration from extortion to the importation and supply of drugs occurred quickly, with those gangs failing to move with the times, losing their territorial control and power. The old criminal codes of practice disappeared.

Now, there were no rules. Only the ruthless and well-disciplined gangs survived.

1

On a bleak winter's night in January 1983, Gordon Black retired to his private rooms in the grace and favour flat in central London where he planned to stay for the weekend. He was sixty-two years old and a Circuit Court judge. A quiet and private man, widowed for nearly twenty years, he had no family and lived a solitary and lonely life, never socialising with his fellow judges or other members of the legal justice system. His career was his life, specialising in family and domestic law in the Crown and County Courts. He enjoyed great respect from all corners of the legal profession, from Law Chambers through to the Lord Chief Justice's Office.

Tonight, in the Judges' Lodgings, he sat on a green leather Chesterfield sofa peering into a roaring fire; the flames flickering brightly before disappearing up the large chimney.

Once again, he studied the photographs lying on the carpet before him. How could he have been so stupid? How gullible to believe a woman young enough to be his granddaughter loved him and only wanted a warm and secure relationship. There was no fool like an old fool. The photographs now clearly showed the brutality of being duped. The sight of his old body intertwined with the young woman's filled his heart with anger and acute embarrassment.

He ignored the veiled threatening message accompanying the pictures. He knew there was only one escape as he began throwing them separately into the fire where they instantly ignited and were reduced to ash. He turned to the Scotch whisky in the crystal tumbler and the white pills set out neatly next to it. For a moment he hesitated, thinking of his late wife and those glorious years they had enjoyed together before she was so cruelly taken away. Perhaps they could be together again. Perhaps.

Suddenly he scooped the white tablets up with one of his clammy hands and dropped them to the back of his mouth, then he took a large mouthful of the spirit. With both mixed, he swallowed them down and poured another whisky. He continued to drink, emptying five measures in succession before relaxing back into the sofa. He knew that any further drink would make him vomit and cancel out his efforts. Nature must now be allowed to take its own course.

Gradually he began to relax, his memories of a younger life returned. All the anxiety of recent weeks subsided, his inability to cope with the menacing demands disappeared. He relaxed further, unaware of his incontinence, the glass dropping onto the floor. His breathing became shallower as he started to fall away. With no one to mourn his passing, no letter was written as he gently left this world.

His Lordship would remain undisturbed for several days until found by Monica, the domestic cleaner. His death would cause consternation and bewilderment. Why should a successful and much respected Circuit Court judge take his own life? Undoubtedly the police would investigate the circumstances, but his motive would forever remain a mystery.

2

John Evans had recently celebrated his forty-forth birthday with his wife Charlotte at an exclusive restaurant in Highgate, London. They had been married for the past seven years and lived nearby in Hampstead in a modest town house. She was a semi-retired accountant working as a director in the City and always preferred to be known as Charlie. She was a few years younger than John and looking forward to working part time so they could spend more time with each other. However, the recent turmoil of the financial markets had placed a temporary halt on these arrangements.

John was a freelance investigative journalist. He was in good physical health for his age, although signs of overindulging had begun to appear on his slowly expanding waistline. Eight years previously he had resigned from the West Yorkshire Police as a Chief Inspector, bitterly disillusioned by the failure of the Chief Constable and the Home Office to expose serious corruptive practices involving senior police officers. He was in effect the subject of a 'gagging order' imposed by the Government that would remain in place in perpetuity.

His resignation had attracted the attention of several national newspapers, followed by offers of employment to investigate miscarriages of justice or suspected scandals involving public bodies and their officials. Gradually, he gained a reputation for identifying the facts, being wholly objective and unbiased, never failing in reporting the truth. He always double-checked the authenticity of his facts, sometimes at a painstaking pace, never rushing.

Fortunately, Charlie's business had become commercially sound. Her personal wealth had accumulated considerably. She had often urged John to consider going freelance as they were now financially secure enough to enjoy a more leisurely life style. After all, they had spent too much of their earlier lives in different unhappy relationships. The clock was ticking.

Twelve months ago, John had been approached by several news-media companies, including the BBC, to examine a number of current affairs issues that were emerging from both domestic and foreign sources. After agreeing on fixed contracts, he accepted two assignments, one from an independent press association and the other from an agency connected with the BBC. He commenced both simultaneously, allowing himself a period of six months to investigate them.

His first enquiry centred on the suspicious circumstances surrounding the hanging of Roberto Calvi, Chairman of Banco Ambrosiano, beneath Blackfriars Bridge in London in June the previous year. The case was still being investigated by the Metropolitan Police and was commonly known as the murder of God's Banker. Although several theories had been considered, no real progress had been accomplished to explain the bizarre death. Calvi was connected to the Vatican Bank and had suggested links with the Mafia, and rumours that his death was suspicious abounded. John was invited to re-examine the case discreetly, concentrating on Calvi's personal life.

The second investigation was less dramatic. It considered the possible involvement of radical left-wing Merseyside politicians in infiltrating the Labour Party's National Executive Committee. Although some stories had previously identified the political turmoil, a whisper had reached John's ear of inappropriate withdrawals of funds and expenditure by a local councillor.

Both cases were going to prove challenging and potentially hazardous but they were the very essence of John's professional curiosity. He had developed a sixth sense for identifying corruptive practices, knowing that the human failings of greed and ambition were central to them.

Progress on his first case began to pick up pace after he received information about Calvi's business interests in Rome, involving hearsay evidence connecting a suspected money laundering merchant bank to the Vatican Overseas Aid Department. However, the second case in Merseyside appeared to flounder from the start, with local politicians and their activists closing ranks, keeping tight-lipped.

Since becoming freelance, John had set up his office at home, converting the large attic into a spacious and light-filled area. Serviced by two external telephones, one green, the other grey, and the latest telex system, he was able to keep current with both domestic and foreign news as it broke. His connections with fellow journalists and the wider media were well established. Whilst he trusted some unconditionally there were many he would not. Those with only self-promoting motives, a quick story for a 'quick buck', he avoided, only exchanging news and information with his trusted sources.

Whilst examining the latest incoming reports from Reuters on the deteriorating relations between the British Government and the National Union of Coal Miners, his green telephone rang. Its number was only given to his trusted circle of friends.

'Evans.'

'Good morning, John, Yvonne here. How are you and Charlie?'

'We're good, thanks. How are you? It's been a long time.'

'Yes, I'm OK. Listen, John, I need to speak to you about something very delicate. I think you'll be interested in this one. There's very little to go on. No complainants as such, no identifiable offences and only a smidgeon of intelligence against some people in your profession and mine. It's just that I've got a bad feeling about it. Still interested?'

'Of course. Come around for dinner tonight if you can. We can talk about it then.'

'Brilliant. Say about seven thirty?'

'Yes. Look forward to seeing you then.'

3

Yvonne Hall was a senior police officer with the Metropolitan Police. Within twelve years of joining the Service, at the age of thirty-three, she had attained the rank of DCI. Like John, she had previously served in the West Yorkshire Police. A highly self-motivated officer, she had been identified for high command, anticipated to attain a chief officer post within the next decade.

Her present role was heading a department trialling a new evidence collecting and reference computer, recently introduced to hold a magnitude of data, allowing information to be retrieved instantly.

She lived alone in a flat overlooking Vauxhall Bridge. Although she had enjoyed several serious relationships in the past, her private life did not mirror her successful professional career. She was a lesbian and such sexuality and gender issues were still frowned on by the Establishment; she was a woman sometimes described as 'before her time'. There had been little movement towards the equality of the sexes, despite recent legislation, and even less regarding same sex relationships. Although not overtly demonstrated by the Service, a deep prejudice existed just below the surface on both fronts. Being a woman with rank was enough to contend with, but openly gay was too much for her male colleagues to accept. Her natural assertion and leadership skills were never questioned, yet her sexuality remained deeply hidden. It was singularly the only characteristic she deliberately kept secret, often acquiescing uncomfortably to safeguard her career. Although rumours had circulated amongst her colleagues, she doggedly kept her private life detached from her career.

Her closest friends were John and Charlie Evans. They had shown true affection, without prejudice, often encouraging her to pursue her goals in the police, even in the face of a male and homophobic domination.

*

Two weeks previously, she had been summoned to New Scotland Yard by the Deputy Commissioner, Sir John Simpson, where, behind closed doors, he had assigned to her an unusual project. Recently he had become aware of unconnected and uncorroborated rumours that a number of men in high profile positions had been compromised by young women, probably sex workers, and subjected to unwarranted demands and blackmail. Some of these rumours emanated from the Home Office and other Whitehall departments.

The Deputy Commissioner had chosen Yvonne because he suspected she had some prior knowledge of these incidents due of her personal connections. This was because, by chance, her father Sir Edward Hall, was the Permanent Under Secretary to the Department of Trade and Industry (DTI). She informed the Deputy Commissioner that her father had confidentially spoken to her about the recent behaviour of an MP who was being blackmailed. But Sir Edward was aware of this and a much wider picture. This information coincided with several rumours circulating through the corridors of Scotland Yard and recent information leaking from the Attorney General's Office. Together, these whispers referred to the alleged scandalous sexual behaviour of people usually in the public eye, including politicians and even a Circuit judge who had recently committed suicide. Was there any connection? If so, why were these being targeted and by whom? And perhaps more disturbingly, where had all this information, true or otherwise, come from?

He was aware of Yvonne's inside connections through her father and wanted to combine her knowledge with his. After all, she had a short cut to the centre of Government, whilst he had taken years to foster his sources. But her career was in its ascendancy, whilst his was on the wane, facing retirement in two years' time.

Having collated their accounts, a clearer picture began to emerge. Prostitution and blackmail were the common elements in all these rumours. A particular journalist was being supplied with damaging and scandalous material.

Sir John Simpson said, 'DCI Hall, I smell a leak coming from within our ranks. Go and sort it out.'

So that had been her assignment. Tonight, she would be seeing her friends and hopefully convince John Evans to come on board with her.

4

As the hallway clock struck seven thirty, a figure appeared through the front door opaque glass. John was ready. Opening the door briskly before she had the chance to ring the bell, he welcomed Yvonne with open arms. 'How lovely to see you again. Come inside. Charlie is just finishing preparing dinner.'

She stepped inside, holding her large service black leather handbag. It was bulging with papers, more like a child's satchel than a fashion accessory.

She gave him a polite kiss on his cheek and continued through the hallway. 'Good, I'm starving. Hell, that smells great. Roast lamb, my favourite.'

They walked into the kitchen where Charlie hurriedly took her apron off and embraced their visitor. 'Yvonne, it's been too long. You look as though you're in need of a good meal.'

They both smiled and embraced again.

'Well, I've come to the right place. Looks like your cooking hasn't been wasted on John.' She gently pressed a finger into his stomach.

'All muscle, you cheeky sod.'

Charlie smiled. 'Your very good health,' she said, as they sat at the table and raised their glasses. Yvonne glanced through the patio doors towards the modest back garden, where Charlie spent so much of her spare time. She was envious; she had nowhere to sit outside her flat. Turning to face them, she was reminded just how close and deeply in love they were. Although immersed in their own separate professional lives, John and Charlie spent as much time together as possible.

By contrast, she lived alone, hoping someone would step into her life in the future and provide an opportunity for a loving and stable relationship. Then her thoughts went back to when they first met.

Eight years previously, John had been a Police Inspector and Yvonne a Detective Constable in the West Yorkshire Police. They had been investigating the suspicious death of Charlie's mother who had been killed by a car, driven by an off-duty Police Superintendent. In attempting to cover up the crime, the Superintendent later conspired with other senior officers to frame John for the theft of ten thousand pounds from her mother's flat. Yvonne's involvement in the case proved John's innocence and led to the introduction of Charlie into his life. After being completely exonerated, John resigned from the force and he and Charlie married soon afterwards.

Yvonne sighed. 'Oh, it's really good to see you both again.'

'How's the world of the high flyer?' asked John.

'To be honest, it's not all what it's cracked up to be at times. But I'm not complaining. God, Charlie this meat is fantastic.'

After their meal and two further glasses of wine, John said, 'Well, Yvonne, let's get to the serious business of your visit, before we continue with this good wine.'

Charlie stood up to leave, but Yvonne beckoned her back. 'No, Charlie, I trust you just as much as I do John. But what I'm about to tell you is very secret. John, I'm going to offer you a proposition, I'll try to keep it brief, but it seems to become more complex every time I re-examine all the information. All of what I'm about to tell you is a mixed bag; some of it are true facts but much is fundamentally conjecture and hearsay. Preliminary investigations have been ambiguous yet compelling.'

John and Charlie sat forward, their curiosity whetted; this sounded intriguing. Yvonne took another gulp of wine.

'Right, here goes. You may recall a couple of months ago, a circuit judge called Gordon Black was found dead in the Judges' Lodgings close to Whitehall. Apparently, he had taken an overdose of a cocktail of barbiturates and with no signs of foul play, the Coroner ruled at his inquest he had taken his own life. Although there was no letter, a thorough search of his flat revealed a number of photographs had been burnt in the open fire in front of the chair where he was found. All these photos were destroyed, apart from one that had slipped out of the fire onto the hearth. I have a copy of that image here for you to look at.'

Yvonne reached into her large handbag and produced a sizeable folder of papers, clipped together in a brown cover. She placed it on the dinner table and pushed a sheet of paper forward for them to look at. They peered at a copy of a black and white photograph. Burnt down the right side, only a third of the original image remained. It showed a woman in her early twenties with short dark hair looking directly at the camera. She was slim and naked to the waist, holding a cigarette in her right hand. Her skin appeared very pale, with a small tattoo of a swallow bird above her left breast. The scene appeared to be in a bedroom, possibly a hotel. There was little further detail apart from the woman.

Yvonne continued, 'The initial investigating officer, a Detective Constable Jones, seized this photograph and submitted it along with his report to the Coroner for the impending inquest. The post-mortem revealed barbiturate poisoning, no signs of other interference; a simple case of suicide. The verdict was recorded as 'Gordon Black took his own life.' This was unchallenged and that's where it remained for a couple of weeks. Then out of the blue, the naked body of a young woman was found floating down the Thames towards Dartford in Kent. She had been in the water for some considerable time and her body was in a dreadful condition. No facial features, teeth missing so no dental records available, no jewellery. Nothing. The only recognisable feature on her whole body was a small tattoo of a swallow bird above her left breast.'

Charlie reached forward and took another look at the image before taking a sip of wine.

John said impatiently, 'Hell, get on with it, Yvonne. You've really got my full attention now.'

'Mine too,' said Charlie.

'Well, DC Jones read this report of the unidentified dead woman, circulated by the Kent Police to all the neighbouring forces. He remembered the partially burnt image taken from Judge Black's fireplace and contacted the Kent Police. Their enquiries were more successful. Within three days of asking in the right places, they had established her true identity. Apparently, her parents had recently reported her missing, the tattoo being the defining identification.'

'Who was she?' asked John.

'Her name was Julie Brecon. She was twenty-three years old, originally from Harlow but moved to Islington in London, where she became a sex worker in the King's Cross area. She had told her parents she had been cautioned by the Vice Squad for soliciting in the streets several months ago but had recently found a job as an escort in a Soho club. Although they attempted to persuade her to look for alternative ways of making a living, it seems she had tasted the good life of easy money, fancy clothes and expensive jewellery. But when she returned home, according to them, she had changed. She was a broken woman, recovering from a beating and emotionally disturbed, petrified of returning back to London. Something had seriously gone wrong. She refused to tell them what had happened to her, but they were convinced she was in hiding. Then one night, about a week later, she told them she was slipping down to the off-licence for some cigarettes. And that was the last time they saw her alive. The following day they reported her missing to the local police.'

'OK, but this sounds like a straight forward murder enquiry' replied John.

'Yes but let me finish.'

'Sorry, carry on.'

'Well, now we had Julie Brecon identified in Kent, we cross-referenced cases involving other women discovered in similar circumstances and found another had met with a similar fate four weeks previously. She was called Vicky Thompson, also found in the Thames. Although their deaths were treated initially as suspicious, there was nothing to connect them, until now.'

'And what's that?' asked John.

'They were prostitutes, operating within the King's Cross area. Both had been arrested at various times by a DC Barry Taylor of the local Vice Squad. Unfortunately, this officer resigned last month, and all his official diaries and duty pocket note books have since vanished.'

'Can't you go and speak to him?'

'Not really, he's disappeared too. The house he lived in was rented, but it's now empty and apparently enquiries with his neighbours suggest he has gone abroad, possibly Spain.' She leant forward. 'There's something else you must know.' The suspense increased.

'This is to do with my father.'

'Hell, Yvonne I'm so sorry' said Charlie.

Oh no, not in any bad way. Let me explain. Are you aware that my Dad works in Whitehall?'

'I only know he is a civil servant, but I have no knowledge what he actually does.'

'Well, he's a little more than that. He's actually the Permanent Under Secretary in the Department of Trade and Industry.'

'Bloody hell Yvonne. We didn't know that' said John.'

'Yes, now he is a real high flyer. Anyway, in his position he hears many things, mostly gossip and rumours, but occasionally information comes to his notice that requires his attention. A Member of Parliament called Jason Moore who works as a junior minister in that Department, approached him about a request for a temporary import permit for a small quantity of crops from Pakistan. Apparently, this was to facilitate some research purposes connected with several food manufacturers in the UK. But Dad dismissed this request, citing it was highly irregular to import such goods without a European Directive and clearance from the Ministry for Agriculture.

Jason Moore asked him several times again to reconsider, but Dad was adamant and dismissed his claims on each occasion. Eventually, the MP mentioned a journalist called Alex Gilmour who had uncovered a seedy story involving him with a prostitute in a Mayfair hotel. He further mentioned that if an interim approval was given to the importation of such crops from Pakistan, the matter of his indiscretion would disappear. Naturally, Dad went into an absolute rage and threw him out of his office.'

John said 'I've heard of this Gilmour; he's someone I avoid at all costs. He usually preys on those who keep a high public profile, exposing them through the cheap tabloids. Frankly I think he's a little shit. But that's just my opinion.'

'Yes, that's the one' replied Yvonne.

Charlie asked, 'Since your father threw his MP out of his office, what happened then?'

'Three days ago, Moore tried to overdose himself at his country home. Although he lives there alone, he is still married, with three grown-up children. He left a letter addressed to my Dad, apologising for his unprofessional and compromising request for the special import permit, saying how stupid he was for allowing himself to be hoodwinked into thinking a woman less than half his age was serious about a relationship with him. He had tried to contact the woman, but she had disappeared.'

Yvonne drank some more wine and continued. 'Dad received a package yesterday through the internal post from Moore. It must have been stuck in some office for a couple of days. When he opened it, he found images of Moore and a woman in bed, together with some letters. Once he had read them, he contacted the local police in Gloucestershire who broke into Moore's house and found him in a deep coma. He was rushed to hospital where they managed to save him. His condition was described as serious, but stable. The early neurological tests indicated brain activity, but the prognosis was uncertain. Until he regains consciousness, nothing else can be predicted. The circumstances of him attempting to kill himself have not been publically released, other than he is presently unwell and taking a long holiday.'

'That's horrible,' said Charlie.

'Yes. And that's why my Dad decided to let me know about all this.'

'Hell, that was a lucky break. I bet this wasn't the first time a leading politician or civil servant has been compromised like this,' said John.

'You're right, and I bet such inappropriate behaviour when it surfaced, was always conveniently swept under the carpet.'

'So what's the significance of this permit? It must be important.'

'Yes, I think it is. I think these crops from Pakistan are just a decoy. They in fact represent quantities of high-grade heroin or other narcotics.'

'Well it's coming from the right part of the world.'

'Anyway, have a look at the package my father received. The first letter is the one Moore received first. The second is his response to Dad.'

Yvonne passed the note sent to Moore first. It was typed on cheap white notepaper.

17

Mr Jason Moore

As you can see we have a collection of embarrassing photographs of you and a young lady taken recently inside the bedroom of the Belle Vue Hotel, Mayfair. Whilst I do not wish to cause you any further political harm, I really would appreciate it if you could arrange for the issue of a temporary special import licence, allowing a small quantity of crops for research purposes to be brought into the UK from Pakistan. Once you have arranged this, please place an advert in the Times stating, 'Pakistani grains and pulses ready for research.' Include alongside it, a post office box number so you may be contacted later. When I have seen this, I shall arrange a meeting. If you ignore this request, I shall hand these photographs over to the press and you can face the consequences.

She then passed Jason Moore's note over.

Sir Graham

Please forgive me for my unprofessional manner at our last meeting, where I realise now I attempted to coerce from you the impossible. Unfortunately, I have committed a serious breach of the standards expected of a person in my position and my conduct may cause embarrassment to you, the Department and myself. In short, I'm being blackmailed for an indiscretion I committed with a young lady who I honestly believed was genuine in her feelings towards me. These are the photographs of me and the letter I received, which show the extent of this sordid affair. By the time you read this I hope to have left this world and ended all my painful shame. Please accept my apologies once again.

Jason Moore MP

John read the letters again, then sat back. 'Do you know who the woman is in the photo?'

'Good question. Yes, she's one of the women I've just mentioned, Vicky Thompson.; found in the Thames last month.'

'Right. It's now starting to make some confusing sense.'

'Isn't that an oxymoron?' enquired Charlie.

John smiled. 'You're probably right, but there does appear to be a picture emerging connecting these people. Let's just recap. So, you have two dead women, known to be sex workers, found in the river, whose causes of death are unknown due to the condition of their bodies, the apparent suicide of a judge and the attempted suicide of an MP, a junior minister within the Government.'

Yvonne replied, 'Yes, that's right John. The two men appeared to have been victims of the old honey trap set-up, both middle-aged men at the peak of their careers with some considerable influence.'

'Although I know of this man journalist Gilmour, I'm intrigued as to where he fits into these suspicious deaths?'

'I've put some feelers out about him. It would appear he is a close friend of the police officer in charge of the King's Cross Vice Squad, a certain Detective Sergeant George Morley. Apparently, DS Morley and Gilmour go back a long time. My source mentioned that one of them is the godfather to the other's daughter. It's all very cosy. Ex-DC Barry Taylor has perhaps jumped ship because it was getting too messy. Now, I can't prove any of this, but my hunch is that DS Morley is feeding Gilmour with material about men caught in embarrassing circumstances, who if exposed, stand to lose a great deal. And when they are made aware of this from Gilmour, they are vulnerable to losing a great deal of money by keeping it out of the papers.'

'This sounds like blackmail,' said Charlie.

'Yes, it is.'

'Clever, it's the old badger game approach.' John replied.

'Looks like it.'

'What does that mean John?' asked Charlie.

'I'll explain later.'

'Alright.'

'Carry on Yvonne.'

'There's no paperwork available at the Vice Squad office on any of these women. All reports, including intelligence gathering, photographs and surveillance logs have disappeared. I smell a rat.'

'Dead bloody right there.' John agreed.

'It's my belief the judge and the MP were being badgered and blackmailed. And those are the only two we're aware of. There must be others. Now, I don't know who for certain, but I think Alex Gilmour and DS Morley may hold the key to all of this.'

'So what do you want me to do?'

'Being a journalist yourself, I'd like you to find out more about Gilmour. What circles he operates in. Dig into the newspaper archives to see what features he's written and the sort of people he's exposed relating to the sex trade.'

'OK but what else. I suspect you could do all that without me Yvonne?'

'Hell John! You're astute. OK, this is the rub.

'Remember in the letter sent to Moore, it mentioned something about placing an advert in *The Times* once he had successfully procured the permit.'

'Yes.'

'Well, if we the police, do that, it will be seen by the courts as acting as an 'agent provocateur' but if, a private individual was to make that move, well that's different. And if that person brought evidence to the attention of the police after posting the advert, a prosecution would more likely succeed, even though keenly challenged.'

'What exactly are you asking me to do, Yvonne?'

'This why it's all very hush-hush. It's my belief we're dealing with people who understand the law as well as we do, and they'll find every loophole possible to save their skins. Of course, this conversation never happened; it could be viewed legally as a conspiracy to pervert the course of justice by not following the rules of evidence code. But the stakes are too high. I believe there are some serious attempts of blackmailing people in public high office in order to obtain favours that are not in the public interest. If you agree, I can officially hire your services. I've got the Deputy Commissioner's approval to offer you three hundred pounds per day plus reasonable expenses, provided you sign the necessary "gagging order" forms.'

John interrupted, 'But you must know Yvonne I won't do anything that is illegal. I've built my reputation on my integrity. And it's cost me dearly too.'

'I know that and so does the Deputy. We're not asking you do anything illegal, perhaps a little unlawful. But if you're uncomfortable about it, I fully understand.'

John's mind also wandered back eight years. It was the primary reason for his resignation from the police; he was prevented by the authorities from exposing the truth about the criminal activities of several serving senior officers. Was this case any different?

'OK, I'll think about it. But can't you just remove DS Morley from the Vice Squad?'

'Yes, we could. But the Deputy thinks we'll miss an opportunity to root out a wider bed of corruption. That's why he's keen on you having a look first.'

'Why me?'

'He asked me if I could recommend someone who we could trust outside the police. I mentioned you by name and he remembered what you did in Yorkshire. Although not publicly acknowledged, your reputation for taking a stance against the Establishment became almost folklore in the Service, especially after your resignation. He told me you were a good choice.'

'Friends in high places, eh.'

'Yes, it would appear you do. Now, John, will you take this assignment on, or would you like more time to think about it?'

'Would I get free access to DS Morley's personal records and those who work closely with him?'

'Yes, but's that not official. You will be given the authority of a serving Special Constable and the administrative rank of a Police Inspector for the Met for the duration of the contract. This and other permits will be set out in the confidentiality clause. Basically, John, you will be a serving police officer again and we need you right now.'

'There's one other condition I would have to insist on if I agreed to take this on.'

'Go on, I'm listening.'

'I would need our old friend Phil Smith to come on board too. He's got the necessary skills to get fast results.'

'OK, but I know Phil. He operates in the shadows and sometimes his work ethic is questionable, if not downright unlawful. If he joins us, you must take full responsibility, John. Remember, the Met are still recovering from the fallout of Countryman.'[1]

'Of course. He'll be fine.'

Yvonne looked at John. She was not convinced.

'If you do agree and uncover enough intelligence, we may want you to place the advert in *The Times* together with the post box address on behalf of Jason Moore. Then wait until we see what happens. But we must keep this tight. Very tight. Only four of us

---

[1] Operation Countryman was an investigation into police corruption between 1978 and 1982.

would know of all this. Sorry, Charlie, I mean five.'

Charlie smiled and looked at John. He was in deep thought. Then he turned to Yvonne and asked, 'Can I let you know tomorrow? I must discuss this with Charlie. I also have to consider my other commitments.'

'Yes, of course, come and see me in the morning at the office with your answer. Meanwhile, is there any more of that cheeky claret left, before I get my taxi home?'

5

Twelve months earlier

Sammy Clarke was a likeable young man who engaged with everyone he came into contact with. He was twenty-three years old and the youngest and smallest of five brothers. Only five feet three inches tall, he had always been conscious of his height. All the family had immigrated from St Kitts in 1969 and settled in east London. His father, a strict disciplinarian by nature and a devout Christian by faith, had worked tirelessly on the London Underground to provide a comfortable life for his family, until his untimely death at the age of forty-six. His wife, Martha, was left to manage for her five sons alone.

Within weeks of the funeral, all had become beyond her control, apart from Sammy. They had resorted to crime for their livelihoods. Unlike his brothers, Sammy decided to continue with his education, attending the local technical college, eventually gaining a position as a trainee draughtsman in the local council planning department.

However, he soon became disillusioned, the monotony of preparing and drawing the same plans for different committees, compounded by the rejection of his work without any explanation. His ambitions to become a draughtsman gradually ebbed away. Many of his colleagues had worked at the same desks for over twenty-five years. By the time he had reached twenty, all his brothers were serving lengthy custodial sentences in prison, for violence, burglary and stealing fast cars.

Sammy occasionally visited them, quickly realising their pathway in life was predictable. No future; just more prison. Learning from their mistakes taught him several lessons. Be careful and keep ahead of the game. Trust no one and remember everything. These traits allowed him to develop a more successful career in crime than his siblings, realising the use of violence and theft was a fool's choice. Using caution and guile, he maximised his best natural skill: charm.

A chance encounter with an old friend he knew as a child called Max Campbell at one of the local 'blues'[2] introduced him to the night club entertainment world. Max had recently opened a seedy disco club called the Caribbean, near King's Cross railway station. He was recruiting for a supervisor to look after his bar staff and run the business in his absence.

Like Sammy, descendants of slaves, Max had immigrated as a child with his parents from the West Indies twenty years previously. But shortly after arriving, his father was killed whilst working on the railways, leaving his mother to bring him up alone.

Sammy's ancestral family's slave masters were English, whilst Max's were Scottish. Because they were considered as "merely possessions," slaves took on their master's surnames. Sammy Clarke and Max Campbell.

Max's mother had invested the compensation pay out from British Rail into his education and savings. But tragically, his childhood suffered another setback. Returning home from school one day, Max found his mother dead on the kitchen floor; a massive heart attack had robbed him now of his only remaining parent. He was sixteen years old. Apart from the savings, his only cherished possession from her was a fountain pen she'd given him the previous Christmas. Living alone, yet under the supervision of the Social Services, he continued with his education, rapidly excelling in most subjects. He was identified as a clever and intelligent pupil, likely to succeed in any career he undertook. Unfortunately, a career in crime was absent from the curriculum as his natural behaviour turned towards dishonesty, causing him eventually to be expelled. He left school at

---

[2] Blues were also referred to as shebeens by the West Indian community. Normally held in cellars of large terraced houses, where the illicit sale of alcohol and drugs accompanied loud reggae music. Prostitutes were encouraged to ply their trade for an entrance fee.

seventeen and found casual work in the local shops and business. But when he reached twenty-one, his prospects improved when he inherited his mother's savings of twenty-five thousand pounds.

He quickly invested most of this in a semi-derelict warehouse, converting it into the Caribbean Club, as he had identified a niche in the night club scene. Reggae.

Within twelve months he was attracting customers from all cultures and walks of life, extending from London and the West Midlands to Manchester. He soon became a wealthy businessman and moved into an exclusive town house in Clerkenwell. The brand-new BMW car simply cemented Max's reputation as the epitome of 'the boy did well'.

Sammy saw this and wanted it too.

Although Sammy admitted he had no experience in this line of work, Max remembered years ago when they had been caught by their local policeman for attempting to hide in a derelict factory whilst playing truancy from school. Sammy had convinced the officer he was taking his friend home because he was unwell, suffering from mumps. The policeman suddenly stepped backwards and quickly walked away. Once out of sight, Sammy told Max his brothers had used this before to evade capture, as apparently some male adults considered it to be a mild sort of plague. How they laughed. Max had never forgotten Sammy's quick wit and held him in high regard and affection. And now, he had grown into a young man with a beguiling manner and friendly disposition.

Within a week, Sammy had walked out of his job with the council and strolled through the front doors of the Caribbean Club.

The club was large single-storey building with an equally large cellar, originally built during the First World War as an engineering works, manufacturing components for the railways. For decades it had remained empty, close to dereliction, until Max bought it cheaply and spent almost all his inheritance on its refurbishment. Unfortunately, the club's clientele had little respect for his efforts and within twelve months its décor had suffered irreparably. Yet it became even more popular and its profits continued to increase. Max had considered further improvements but the main consensus of opinion with the customers was that any alterations would remove its authenticity. The salacious atmosphere reflected a genuine illegal shebeen. So, the club remained 'seedy with atmosphere'.

From the first night Sammy was fascinated by the dynamics of the Caribbean. He learnt about stock keeping, ordering and selling drinks, security and basic health and safety. He was given responsibility of paying particular attention to any staff suspected of skimming the profits.

His natural friendly manner was frequently tested, keeping disruptive troublemakers outside whilst making customers inside, feel safe and happy. Eventually, Max allowed him to hire the disc jockeys and additional weekend staff, banking the takings and paying wages. Within a month, Sammy was effectively in charge of running the club and all the staff. And he relished every minute of it. He had found his true vocation.

*

As the weeks progressed, Max regularly congratulated him on his efforts, rewarding him with a substantial pay rise.

Then one night, after closing time, Max invited him into his office for a drink, normal after busy weekends. But this night's meeting was very different. Max sat back in his ridiculously large leather reclining chair, with two glasses of rum set out on the desk in front of him. He suggested to Sammy that something more important than their normal business chat was on the agenda.

'Pull up a chair, Sammy, I want to talk some business with you.'

'Is everything OK, Max?' he asked nervously.

'Sure. I want to see if you're interested in something I'm going to propose.' He leant over and handed Sammy a generous measure of rum. Holding the glass tightly, pretending to drink, he curiously asked what it was.

Max took a drink. 'Sammy, I know I can trust you. I've known that since we were kids. What I'm about to tell you must not go out of this room. You understand?'

'Yes, of course.'

'OK. The Caribbean is doing well and that's mainly down to you, but you must realise it's not where I make most of my money. That comes from elsewhere. If I explain to you all about this, are you interested in becoming involved in my future plans? If you are, I want to make you a partner. What do you think?'

'Sure, Max. Tell me more.'

He sat forward and stared directly into Sammy's eyes. 'Where I make my real money is not exactly legal. What I'm offering you is the chance to make a shitload of money in a short time, but it isn't legal. You understand?'

'I'm still listening.'

'When you've been covering for me whilst I've been away, what do you think I've been doing?'

'I've no idea. It's your business, I've been happy keeping the club going.'

'That's another thing I like about you, Sammy. You're discreet. You never ask stupid questions. I need you to help me with a business deal that will make us both rich, but we've got to trust each other with our lives. It's a little dangerous but not life threatening. Still want in?'

'Yes, Max. Tell me more.'

'I know some people in Manchester who are connected with the importation of some valuable commodities. Coke, E, china white, ganga and acid. They want us to store some in the cellars here at the Caribbean. We're not involved with the distribution, just holding them here until they get their network set up.'

Sammy drank the rum in one, sat back and pondered on Max's proposal. Clearly, this was highly illegal and fraught with danger and he needed to know more about the enterprise before committing himself. 'Max, this is serious shit you're talking about. Just storing that stuff could bring the Babylon[3] down on us bad. What's the payback?'

'You're right, Sammy, it is serious. But the money is also big and we're not involved with the street traders. Of course, we don't want to be suspected of any involvement with drugs. In fact, we need to run this place differently and clean it up, so we can't turn a blind eye anymore to all the crap that gets swallowed, injected and smoked in this place. If the money is as much as they promise, we'll run the Caribbean at a loss, if we need to.'

'What sort of money are we talking about?'

'Five thousand pounds between us, every time they drop a shipment off.'

'You're shitting me!' exclaimed Sammy.

---

[3] The police.

'No. And once their network is up and running, we'll expect a delivery every week. All I want you to do is make sure we have adequate security here and no one finds out. Otherwise, we run the club as normal.'

Without hesitation, the men smiled at each other. Max stood up and poured two more drinks, offering another to Sammy. 'What about it, partner?'

Sammy took a long purposeful stare at him, paused and then shook his hand. 'Let's do it, Max, but if it gets too dangerous, I'm out. OK?'

'Agreed, partner.'

They slammed their glasses together and gulped back the rum, followed by several more.

6

Within three weeks Sammy's life changed so much. Working for more than fourteen hours every day without any sign of a day off, he was running the Caribbean alone.

Having not seen Max for five nights, he casually walked into the club and invited Sammy to join him in his office. 'After the club closes tonight, we'll be taking our first consignment. Is the cellar ready?'

'Yes, Max, I've had a false wall built at the far end that gives us the room you asked for. All the racks have been installed, together with the dead locks and overhead lighting. Everything is ready.'

'Good. Our friends from the north will be accompanying the goods. I want you to meet them. They'll be checking you out of course, so just say nothing unless they talk to you. Just use your discretion Sammy. This business is all about trust. Screw that up and we'll both end up in the Thames.'

'I understand, Max. I'll remain in the club until I hear otherwise.'

'Good man.'

It was past three in the morning before the last of the customers and staff finally left the club. The bar and tables were cleared, ready for the cleaners in the morning, and the main lights in the dance area switched off, leaving only the wall lights lit. Suddenly, a loud double knock came from the front doors, indicating their visitors had arrived.

As Max slowly opened one of them, three men entered and stood silently under the dim lights. For a moment there was an awkward chilling pause, making Max feel intimidated, but then one of them smiled and the atmosphere changed. All three were white, well built, two of them in their twenties, the third much older in his forties. They were all dressed in similar clothing, blue jeans and black leather jackets.

Max said, 'Come inside, gentlemen, and welcome to the Caribbean. Can I offer you a drink?' Standing next to him, Sammy remained silent.

The eldest said curtly, 'No. We don't have time. Show me where you're going to put the stuff.' Unlike the other two, his whole demeanour was menacing. The lower lobe of his left ear was missing and a scar to his right cheek suggested he was a man of violence.

'Come this way.' Max stepped forward, walked along the corridor past his office and down a flight of stairs to the cellar, leaving the two other men with Sammy.

After several minutes Max and the third man reappeared from the cellar who asked, 'Is this your partner, Max?'

'Yes, Bill. This is Sammy. Say hello to Bill, Sammy. You're going to be working with him.'

Sammy stepped forward, 'Hello, pleased to meet you.'

Bill studied him for several moments before extending his hand. 'Pleased to meet you, Sammy. So long as you do as I say, we'll be OK. Don't mess me about or you'll find me the biggest bastard you ever met. OK?'

Sammy paused, and decided it was his turn to stare defiantly. 'That seems fine with me, Bill.'

They smiled before shaking hands, but in that split second, both felt utter contempt for each other. Max and Sammy instinctively knew from that moment the stakes were going to be high and Bill was going to be pivotal in their enterprise. Crossing his path would be potentially dangerous and short lived.

Bill nodded to his two associates. 'Get the packages.'

They disappeared outside without a word and returned within the minute. Both carried several large brown paper parcels of various sizes. They followed Max downstairs. Now left alone, Bill continued to look at Sammy, attempting to make him feel more uncomfortable than he already was. Finally, he said, 'Sammy, do you know what you're getting into here?'

'Yes, I believe I do.'

'You're not very talkative.'

'No. I keep my mouth shut.'

'But your eyes wide open, eh?'

'Of course. I keep them open all the time.'

Bill smiled and placed a firm hand on Sammy's shoulder. 'Good man. Keep it that way.'

Max returned with the two men behind him. The handover was now complete. Bill turned to Max.

'OK, we're off now. Remember, you will be contacted tomorrow by someone called Jo-Jo. He'll tell you when his team will be coming here to move the merchandise. Depending on how quickly they can push it, will determine on when you get the next delivery. Make sure you keep if safe and sound, even if you have to sleep on top of it.'

Max replied, 'Will do, Bill. Have no worries, we'll look after it.'

'You better had, your lives depend on it.'

Bill forced a smile and took an envelope from his jacket pocket. 'Do the job properly and keep your side of the deal. See you later.' He walked towards the door, followed by the other two men, but as he was about to leave, he quickly glanced back at Sammy before disappearing from view.

Max sighed with relief when he heard the car drive away. He turned to Sammy. 'What was that about? Did you say anything to upset him?'

'No, of course not. He's just one of those bastards that tries to bully and intimidate anyone he meets. I'm used to all that crap; remember I've got four brothers that do all that and look where they are.'

Max shrugged and walked into the office where he opened the envelope. Inside, bundles of two hundred pounds were wrapped individually inside a £20 note. After stacking them into rough rows, they counted five thousand pounds. Max pushed half towards Sammy who picked it up and smiled. Never before had he held so much money. It would have taken him months to earn two and half grand down at the council offices. He was now on his way. Max poured two glasses of rum.

*

Unexpectedly, within two days Jo-Jo had collected the drugs. This was followed the next day by other assignment from the north, mercifully without the dour Bill. Once safely stashed away, a further five thousand pounds lay on Max's table.

The drugs began to move rapidly, with several new packages arriving almost weekly, culminating in both men receiving over £30,000 each within the first six weeks. Ironically, the Caribbean began to be more profitable too as their drug storage enterprise increased.

Sammy soon became a wealthy man. But he kept it quiet, especially from his family and close friends. He rented a small flat off the Holloway Road, close to the club and only used public transport. Knowing the venture would not last for ever, he secretly banked the bulk his 'drugs' income in an offshore Guernsey account.

However, Max did the opposite. He bought a brand-new Jaguar sports car. His overt spending appealed to women too and a regular to the Caribbean was an attractive young woman called Vicky Thompson, who openly flirted with him and showered him with compliments. He was flattered by her sexual advances.

Life was good.

7

———————◆⬡◆———————

Detective Sergeant George Morley, of the London Metropolitan Police, had over twenty-seven years' service. He was married with two teenage daughters, living in a modern semi-detached house near to Archway, on the Great North Road. He had lived there for many years but spent most of his life at work. He was the officer in charge of the King's Cross Vice Squad, supervising a staff of seven Detective Constables, but at the age of forty-eight he looked much older. His liking for beer, twenty cigarettes a day, a bad diet and working unsociable hours was now taking its toll. He was six feet tall, overweight and almost bald, apart from a strip of grey hair that ran between his ears above his neck. He had served in this post for over five years and successfully remained there for two reasons: no other Sergeant wanted the position and he loved his job.

Several years previously, at his last promotion to Inspector interview, he had failed abysmally and was advised never to apply again. He was not suitable for the next rank. This had made him very bitter and resentful, compounded further by officers with half his service being promoted above him. He frequently said to colleagues, 'They wouldn't know a criminal even if one sat on their face.' This unhealthy regard and his jealousy of senior officers frequently gave way to a state of insecurity, affecting his work and his private life too, where he often accused his wife and daughters of undermining him. They were always relieved when he stormed out and returned to work, even on his days off. Family holidays were a distant memory. For five years, Mrs Morley had taken her daughters to Cornwall every summer holiday to visit her sister. Without him, they were able to relax and enjoy themselves, always regretting their return journey. She was waiting for the girls to leave home and perhaps go to university, coinciding with George's retirement, before plucking up enough courage to leave him and build another life without him. No relationship was infinitely better than this loveless one.

However, he was a different person at work, friendly and approachable to his staff, always supportive of their operational commitments and personal needs. It was his Vice Squad, with all of them 'hand-picked' by him. In return, they gave him their absolute loyalty. As a team, they successfully investigated the increasing criminal activities of pimps operating near to King's Cross, without interference from other departments. Although prostitutes solicited in the streets and local budget hotels, it was the men controlling them who were significantly importance to the Vice Squad. These pimps were connected to organised crime in London and beyond, and their activities were of enormous benefit to the criminal intelligence gathering used by all the major crime departments. Such information was power and Morley recognised this, even for his personal gain.

The Squad knew all the pimps and prostitutes operating in their area and occasionally turned a blind eye when intruders or outsiders were forcibly driven away, never to return. Morley preferred to know the criminals operating in his area, not strangers from the outside. He referred to this as 'keeping a tight parish'.

However, several weeks previously there had been an enormous argument between him and one of his Constables, Barry Taylor. Although no one knew the nature of the rift, Taylor resigned from the Force and disappeared from the country. Other members of the squad were surprised, as they had been close friends. In fact, too close at times. It was common knowledge that they had travelled together abroad on several golfing jaunts, even on shooting and salmon fishing trips in Scotland. These were expensive trips and speculation as to who actually sponsored them became canteen gossip throughout the Met, never officially questioned by the senior management. With no evidence to support any wrongdoing, Morley denied any impropriety and screamed at those who dared to question his expensive activities. But always accompanying them was Alex Gilmour, a freelance journalist and long and close friend of Morley.

*

Today was like any other day. He arrived early at work, always the first in the office and usually the last out. Lighting a cigarette, he was thumbed through his diary and looked at his impending appointments. His spirits fell, and muttered 'Bollocks'. A meeting with the Superintendent had been scheduled for the afternoon. He hated sitting in front of the stupid man, listening to all his platitudes, every sentence starting with the words 'In my day'. All his meetings were tooth-achingly boring and completely needless. To avoid seeing him, he urgently required to arrest someone that morning. This presented little difficulty. The whole of the King's Cross area was a den of iniquity, with hundreds of wanted criminals flaunting themselves in public; it would only take minutes before he deprived someone of their liberty. He had several anecdotal phrases, his favourite, 'You can smell the crime' as soon as he stepped outside the police station.

Whilst considering his next move, the telephone rang. Before he could speak, a voice said, 'George. It's Gerry Simpson, Criminal Intelligence office. Remember me?'

'Yes of course, Gerry,' he lied, 'how can I help you?'

'We got a sighting a couple of months ago when a Mercedes car BBD 549Y was seen on the North Circular Road. The uniformed officers stopped it and checked it out. The occupants although not members of the club,[4] are suspected to be actively involved with the drugs scene in the Greater Manchester area. They said they were just visiting friends in town. Very vague. The officers searched the car. Nothing. Anyway, there's more. By coincidence this same Mercedes was seen by a passing beat patrol car, parked outside the rear of the Caribbean Club two nights ago. We've been trying to find out where these suspect dealers have been going to and now we think we know. It's probably more for the Drug Squad, but this club is bang inside your red-light area and you'll have better contacts than them. Can you keep an eye on it for me and let me know of any developments, before I pass it over to them? Then they can give it a good turn over.'

DS Morley wrote down the registration number and the registered keeper – Bill Wiggs.

'Got that, Gerry. Thanks for letting me know.'

'No problem. Any chance of another ticket to the strip show at the Adelphi next Christmas?'

---

[4] Having previous convictions.

'Yes, of course. Ask me a little nearer the time.'

He hung up, remaining ignorant as to who Gerry Simpson was. Nevertheless, this was good information. He was well aware the Caribbean Club was run by a guy called Max and another called Sammy Clarke, a member of the Clarke family, most of whom he had helped to put away in prison. If Sammy were to be locked up, that would make it a full house. He liked that.

He decided it was time to pay a visit to the Caribbean.

8

DS Morley parked his unmarked police car fifty yards away from the front doors to the Caribbean. It was just after two o'clock in the morning, as he watched the final customers leave. When all was quiet, he approached the doors. He had chosen this moment deliberately: no witnesses. Although he had little fear of being confronted, he knew he was in no physical condition to withstand even the mildest of assaults. His protective shield was the prolific knowledge he held of all the criminals operating on his patch. Tonight, he intentionally came alone. He was going to explore another opportunity of increasing his portfolio of 'easy to make money' for his imminent pension pot. Police protection.

As he climbed the two front steps and pushed the unlocked doors open, a voice shouted, 'We're shut.' He continued inside until he saw Sammy standing next to the office door. 'Didn't you hear me? We're shut.'

Ignoring his comments, Morley strode directly towards him. 'Not for me sonny boy, I'm Detective Sergeant Morley and I need to talk to you and Campbell now. Get this place closed and locked up first.'

Sammy immediately recognised him. How could he ever forget? He remembered him barging into his mother's house about a year ago and arresting his two brothers for robbing a pimp in Islington. He knew this policeman was a dangerous piece of shit. His mind began to race. Max was probably away up north, and he was alone in the building with a new shipment of merchandise that had arrived last night. There had been no collection, so the cellar was full; enough to send him to prison for twenty years.

As he began to lock and secure the front doors, he attempted to calm himself down. Morley was on his own and did not appear to hold a search warrant. Perhaps he just wanted a drink and a chat. Keep cool, he thought, use your charm.

He reminded himself it was normal to be visited by the local CID. He'd say to him, 'I'm surprised you hadn't been to see us before.'

He returned to the office to find Morley sitting in Max's large chair, already helping himself to the rum. He had poured himself a large measure and was swigging it back.

Sammy asked, 'How may I help you, Officer?'

'Where's Max Campbell?'

'He's away on business.'

'What sort of business?'

'I don't really know, I just run this place for him when he's away.'

'Do you know who I am?'

'To be honest, yes I do. You arrested two of my brothers last year.'

'Yes, that's right. Now, what are you up to, Sammy Clarke? I don't believe for a moment you're running a legitimate business here with Campbell. I want to know everything you're doing.'

'I'm sorry, I don't know what you mean.'

'Don't get clever with me Clarke.'

'You can check the books and takings, look around, if you don't believe me.'

Morley slowly lifted himself out of Max's chair and walked towards him. Sensing trouble, he instinctively stepped backwards. 'You listen to me, you little thieving black bastard. I know what you two are up to. I know you are dealing with Billy Wiggs from Manchester. You've probably got all his drugs downstairs in the cellar right now. I want to speak to you and Max together, here, tomorrow night. I may have a proposition for you. Meanwhile our meeting here tonight is secret. Top secret, Mr Clarke. Do you understand?'

Sammy tried to look unaffected, but his cool demeanour was betrayed by his heavy perspiration. He simply said, 'Yes, I'll arrange that, Mr Morley.'

'Good. Make sure you do.'

Morley moved quickly from the office to the front doors. He

unlocked them and walked out into the cold night, leaving them swinging on their hinges. Momentarily, Sammy remained stunned and anchored to the floor.

Quickly, his senses returned. He rushed to the doors to ensure Morley had left, catching sight of the police car as it turned left onto the main road some hundred yards away and disappear out of sight.

He locked and bolted the doors before descending into the cellar, checking the merchandise had not been disturbed. No, it was all there. But how did this Babylon Morley know they had dealings with Bill? If he suspected the drugs were here, why didn't he search for them? For the first time in a long while, he felt afraid.

He returned to the office and poured a large rum, sat down and began to consider what to do next. If Morley had wanted to bust him and turn the place over, he would have done it there and then tonight. What was this proposition all about? Was he to keep the drugs there, or hide them elsewhere?

Sammy needed to contact Max.

Another rum gave him some direction. Leave the drugs where they were. He knew where Max's woman, Vicky Thompson, lived. He would start there. Now.

*

Twenty minutes later, he knocked on the green front door of an Edwardian terraced house. Eventually a head appeared from the bedroom window. A woman's voice shouted, 'Who the hell is this?'

'Is that you, Vicky?'

'Who the bloody hell wants to know?'

'Vicky, it's Sammy from the club. I must speak to Max. Is he there?'

'Bloody hell, Sammy. Wait a second.'

A few moments later, the door opened. Instead of Vicky, Max stood there, dressed in only his pyjama bottoms, rubbing his eyes. 'What's the matter?'

Sammy entered without invitation. 'We need to talk now. In private.'

Max shouted upstairs 'Go back to bed, Vicky, it's only business.'

They walked into the back kitchen and sat down. 'Max, I've had a visit from the Babylon just now. It was Detective Sergeant Morley.

Believe me, he's a nasty piece of shit. He knows about the Manchester connection and that we keep the goods in the club. He wants to meet us both tomorrow night at the club, where he intends to make a proposal. What do you think it's all about?'

Max pondered before replying. 'Somehow he's managed to find out. But if he was going to seize the goods and lock us up, he would have done by now. I think he wants a cut. It'll depend on how much, that's all.'

'Should we move the merchandise from the cellar to somewhere else?'

'No point. He's got us anyway. No, we'll wait and see what he wants.'

'What about the Manchester lads. Have we to warn them?'

'Bloody hell Sammy. No! We'll both be dead men if they find out. Let's just wait. It looks like we may have another uninvited partner. Think about it Sammy, at least we wouldn't have to worry about the Babylon raiding the club if he's protecting us. No, he could be very useful.'

'Are you sure?'

'Yes, we could turn this to our advantage. You go home and let me deal with this.'

'OK, if you're certain. I'm just not used to all this Max. Sorry if I panicked but I had to let you know straight away.'

'No Sammy you did exactly right letting me know now. Don't worry anymore, I'll see you at the club tonight as usual.'

Sammy left and drove home, feeling a little easier. Max obviously had more experience with dealing with the Babylon. He would leave this to his judgement.

9

DS Morley was first to arrive in the office, even though he had remained on duty until 3.30 a.m. He had set in place an opportunity to make some more money before he retired. Once he was out of the Force, all his influence would disappear. What would he do then? It was a dilemma. He shuddered at the future prospect of spending more time with his wife. He had no hobbies and his only pleasure outside the job was travelling with his best friend Alex Gilmour, visiting unusual but expensive destinations. And that required serious money. Although Alex had been generous with him in the past, he had been obliged to make some extra money by taking a number of backhanders from several pimps concerned with their nefarious activities. He had found it surprisingly easy and very lucrative.

He was shrewd enough to hide his bribes in a separate bank account, located in the Isle of Man, where no record could be traced on the mainland. During the past eighteen months he had managed to accumulate over ten thousand pounds. Yet apart from his occasional jaunts, his personal lifestyle did not reflect his ill-gotten gains, nor did his downtrodden family enjoy any additional financial benefit. No, this was his retirement fund and he intended to swell its coffers further whilst he remained in charge of the King's Cross Vice Squad. He would make as much as he could in the limited time remaining. As he contemplated his impending visit to the Caribbean, his telephone rang.

'Morley. Vice.'

'George, it's Alex. Good morning, how are you?'

'That's funny, Alex, I was just thinking of you and our next trip.'

'Good idea, but I need to pick your brain. I'm going to be running a piece with the *Daily Chronicle* about an alleged link between a hooker and a prominent politician. Like you, George, I've got my snouts, but the only name I have is a girl called Vicky Thompson. Do you know her?'

'Let's have a look.'

He began to search through the paper filing system with details of men, women, boys and girls suspected of involvement in prostitution or cautioned or convicted for prostitution, including those living off the proceeds, over the previous ten years. Finally, he pulled a card out.

'Alex, this girl was cautioned, 'loitering for prostitution', over two years ago.'

'Not convicted?'

'No. Where a person is suspected of loitering or soliciting in a public place, they receive two separate cautions before they can be charged and appear before the magistrates. This is to deter them from a life of immorality. Well, apparently the legislators thought that, and normally I'd call them stupid buggers, but on this occasion she seems to have taken their advice by keeping off the streets, at least.'

'OK. Well, she seems to have been plying her services in some Mayfair hotels with the movers and shakers of the rich and famous. Gone upmarket from King's Cross. My information is that her pimp is a guy called Max Campbell, he owns a club somewhere near you. Do you know anything about him?'

'Well, what a coincidence. Yes, I do know this guy. In fact, I'll be seeing him tonight about another matter.'

'If you've got him lined up for something, can you hold back until I get my story? If the rumours are true, I may have a scoop. A vice girl and a politician is nearly as good as with a clergyman. Sex and politics sell papers by the lorry load. Could you tell me where he is? I'll make it worthwhile for you, George.'

'Are you attempting to bribe me, Mr Gilmour?'

'Of course, Sergeant Morley. I thought that was obvious.'

'Well, that's alright then.'

Both men giggled. They shared a sense of humour of complete disregard for the rule of order.

'OK, this Campbell owns the Caribbean Club, just down the road from here. As I've said, I'm still going to see him tonight but it's about something completely different. Do you want me find out where she's living?'

'Yes, please. Shall we meet up tomorrow night at my place after you've seen him?'

'No problems. I'll have the details for you then.'

'See you about nine.'

Morley sat back and lit another cigarette. His staff were now arriving and making far too much noise for him to concentrate. He decided to go for a drive and plan his day ahead. Within the past twenty-four hours he had received two independent sources of information about Max Campbell's criminal behaviour. Drugs and pimping. He instinctively knew that if Manchester's criminal underworld were connected with some of his local pimps, he was best placed to exploit their business ventures. Additionally, now a politician in London may have left himself exposed to a cleverly orchestrated 'honey trap' perpetrated by Campbell. And Campbell would have only one motive: money. Big money. If he played his cards right, some of that would come his way. After all, this was all in the Badger Game.

10

Max eventually lifted his head from the pillow, looked at his Rolex watch; just after noon. Since the visit from Sammy during the night, he had spent several hours examining his circumstances, knowing his present lifestyle was becoming too hectic: running the Caribbean Club, storing enough Class A drugs to put him in prison for life, not to mention pimping from his woman, Vicky. Now he had the Babylon to contend with.

He saw Vicky sitting at the dressing table, applying her makeup. He never really understood why she was devoted to him so deeply. When they first met several months ago, she had been vibrant, witty, attractive and clean. Now, she depended on him for her daily fix, entirely at his mercy. Whilst he had never physically ill-treated her, he possessed no emotional feeling for her now. In the past, he had always told his girlfriends when he no longer cared for them; most had taken the hint and left without any fuss. Some slapped him, often followed by the ceremonial cutting up of his expensive suits. But at least they had had the good grace to leave him alone.

But Vicky was different, refusing to accept it was over, unable to believe he had no feelings for her. Although she had now outstayed her welcome, Max decided she would serve a different, but useful purpose. To her delight, he falsely promised, a perpetual life of painless ecstasy, expensive clothes and jewellery. Believing every word, she became utterly subservient to his wishes, promising she would do anything for him.

This was put to the test when he asked her to perform sexual acts with a friend, who was owed a favour. Her reward was his apparent undying love and a long shoot of cocaine. Once again, she was in ecstasy.

His mind began to wander back to other recent events…

*

A little over a month ago, soon after the drugs had begun to flow into the Caribbean, Max had introduced Vicky to a friend of one of his many contacts. He didn't know it at the time but this man, Jason Moore, was a Member of Parliament from Gloucestershire, a divorced man in his late fifties, wishing to rekindle a loving female relationship. After becoming aware of his identity, Max had encouraged Vicky to meet him in the Belle Vue Hotel in Mayfair for dinner, followed by a night of unbridled passion and sex. To make it more palatable, he had taken her on a shopping spree. After all, he wanted her to look her very best and entice Moore into believing she was a professional woman, working in the City. Vicky had been initially hesitant about her role, but when he promised her an engagement ring the next time they went shopping, all her objections disappeared. She loved him unconditionally and he held the key to her addiction.

He had seen the familiar twitch and slight shuddering spread across her face and body. She needed her next fix, but this time it came with conditions. Again, flatly refusing his request at the start, her physical state quickly deteriorated until her needs became acute. Once the engagement ring was thrown into the deal, she acquiesced, agreeing reluctantly to his terms.

The following afternoon they had booked into the hotel and went directly to their suite.

Max remembered the porter was a little bewildered by the two large suitcases accompanying the couple, but no doubt had seen almost everything and nothing surprised him anymore. And his curiosity had soon vanished when Max gave him a generous tip for his efforts, leaving them alone to appreciate the room and the spectacular view outside. Vicky placed her arms lovingly around Max's neck, kissing him and longing for him to make love to her. But he moved them away and given her a smile. 'We have some work to do first. Why don't you go and fix us a drink from the little bar and have a shower?'

She shrugged. 'Sure, darling, but I don't want to really go through this with another man. I don't fancy the old man. It's not right.'

Max recollected their conversation. 'Listen, Vicky. We both know that we have to make a living. All I want you to do is go through this just once with this guy. I promise you'll never see him again and we'll go away to anywhere in the world. Think about it, Vicky, anywhere where you'd like to go. But you must show him you are keen, just this once. Like you are with me.'

'Why him, Max?'

'Cos he can offer us both an opportunity of making a great deal of money. He's a successful businessman and once you have convinced him you are a keen and willing lover, I can ask him for favours that will help to expand my business further and give us more money.'

'OK. But I'm only doing this for you, Max.'

'I know, babe, and I do really appreciate it. I promise I'll make it up to you. We can plan our future and think about where we're going to live.'

Vicky had looked at him with those puppy dog eyes, completely taken in by his deception. She began to feel the first cold shudder in her back, spreading throughout her body. She needed another fix soon.

Max had soon recognised her anxiety; he had seen it so many times before. He reached into his jacket pocket and found the package of powder. She pushed her hand out and he placed it gently into it. It was just enough. There was always a danger she would overdose if he became too generous with the level. She quickly grabbed her handbag and ran into the toilet.

Max shouted, 'Have a shower, Vicky, after you've seen to yourself. I've got some work to do out here for half an hour. Take your time.'

'OK, darling.'

And when Vicky was 'fixing' herself he knew she would be completely out of her head for over an hour. That had given him plenty of time to prepare.

Max opened both the cases. Inside, were several small surveillance video cameras, designed for covert filming, rented from a friend connected to a private investigation firm involved with wealthy divorce lawyers. The cameras were the size of a small matchbox, with silent movements and controlled remotely from a distance of up to thirty yards. Two were positioned inside separate bedside lamps, another fixed in a matching light shade, with a miniature stills camera above the curtain rail, hidden from view by the fabric pelmet. Unknown to Vicky, and certainly without her consent, these cameras would be running and operated by Max in the adjoining hotel room, of which she also had no knowledge.

Within fifteen minutes all the equipment was in place. Max slipped out of the door and entered the next room, where he set up the remainder of his equipment. When he tested it, the receiver showed that all the cameras were responding. Using five monitors he was now able to observe the bedroom, manually focussing each of the lenses, now connected to a master tape machine. This allowed all images to be copied individually and simultaneously. Everything was now set in place.

He returned to the room and found Vicky stretched out completely naked on the bed. She was dribbling from one side of her mouth and murmuring to herself. Her natural good looks and unblemished complexion were beginning to change, with her teeth became darker and her gums receding. She had lost nearly a stone in weight, leaving her face slightly gaunt. Although still an attractive woman, she was now prematurely ageing.

Max knew that she would eventually succumb to this severe abuse unless she received proper treatment, and he half promised himself that he would commend her to a drugs rehabilitation clinic after she had played her role in the honey trap to ensnare Jason Moore MP.

Max gently rubbed her shoulders. Slowly she awoke, slightly disorientated, and sat up on the edge of the bed. Rubbing her eyes, she faced Max and forced a smile. 'Sorry, Max, I must have just slipped off.'

'That's alright, babe, go and get sorted out in the bathroom. I want you looking your very best for our visitor this evening.'

Her expressionless face hid the disappointment; she wanted to spend this time with her man. She reluctantly stood up and went into the bathroom. Whilst showering she had an idea; she would make herself look so good, he would change his mind and send this old man away. Yes, that was what she would do.

After over an hour, when Max lay on the sofa looking at the television, she emerged from the bathroom wearing the red dress Max had just bought her, her hair and makeup styled in the way he liked. He looked up and whistled. 'Hey, babe, you look fantastic.'

She leant over him. 'Can't we just spend tonight here together, Max?'

He immediately sprang up from the sofa. 'For Christ's sake, babe, you know it's business tonight. How many times have I got to tell you? You will meet Jason Moore in the bar at seven thirty as we've arranged. I'll be sat at the next table reading a newspaper. He'll probably invite you for dinner in the restaurant, which you will accept, and afterwards bring him back here and do the business. Remember, I'll be outside this door just in case. You only have to do it once, but make sure you do it well. I want him to think he's the best lover you've ever had. It's really important, Vicky. Please do this for me. Just once, babe.'

'Just this once, you bastard. You'd better make it up to me later, Max.'

'I will, babe. I promise. Now let's go downstairs.'

As they stepped out of the lift, Max stood back, allowing Vicky to walk directly to the bar alone, just in case Moore had arrived earlier than planned. She walked to the table nearest the front window, sat down and ordered a dry white wine from the waiter. Max sat at the bar some twenty feet away, the closest place available without looking too suspicious.

Max remembered when Jason Moore had walked into the bar and immediately saw Vicky. A man in his mid-fifties, six feet tall and of muscular build, he regularly exercised and was in good physical condition for his age. He wore his hair combed forward to conceal a large forehead.

He had met Vicky once before in a Mayfair bar. She had been with one of Max's friends and had been required to provide her services to him; again, on Max's instructions.

Jason Moore entered the bar and walked over to her. 'How lovely to see you again, Vicky. May I order you another drink?'

'Yes please, Jason, may I have a Coca-Cola?'

He summoned the waiter over and ordered some drinks.

'Now, Vicky, you look absolutely wonderful. Have you eaten?'

'Thanks. No, I haven't.'

'Good, let's eat here. I believe the fish menu is excellent.'

When the waiter returned, he asked for a table to be reserved in the restaurant. They chatted for about ten minutes and then made their way to their table. Max watched them surreptitiously as they passed by. Vicky deliberately ignored him, which he found strangely appealing. Although ordering three courses, Vicky pushed the gourmet food around her plate with her fork, eating very little, then drank two brandies. After the meal, they walked back out towards the lift. Max gulped his rum down and strode quickly to the staircase, needing to be in the next-door room before Vicky began her seduction.

It was a close call. As he entered the adjacent room, the monitors were already flickering, showing clear images of her almost naked and him stripped to only his black socks.

During the next thirty minutes, Max filmed all of their love-making, surprised at her apparent willingness in her role. Puzzled, he again found this arousing, giving rise to some twinges of jealousy.

After he'd smoked a cigarette, Moore finally stood up and got dressed. He asked, 'When can I see you again?'

'I'll give you a ring, Jason, perhaps next week.'

'OK. You've got my number. I'll look forward to hearing from you soon. Goodbye'

Max saw Jason Moore leave the room without looking back. She disappeared from the screen and went into the bathroom. She came out a few minutes later to find Max standing near the window, looking out. She said, 'That's it. No one else.'

'I know, babe. Come on, get dressed and let's go home. I'll leave you alone for a few minutes whilst I get my cases in the car.'

'What's inside them, Max?'

'Some merchandise that's all. I had to do business, the same time as you.'

She looked at him blankly, not realising how despicably he had used her.

As he drove home, all the images of Vicky and Jason Moore kept spinning inside his head. The quality of them was better than he had anticipated. He would run several copies from the master tape and send Mr Moore one through the post, leaving no signs of evidence of his involvement. There would be no threatening letter at this stage. That would be sent later, following a disguised telephone call to his office in Whitehall. Max considered the sum of fifty thousand pounds was a fair price to put on Jason Moore's career. The Badger Game was now rolling. That was then.

*

...Max's mind now returned to the present time. Vicky was just finishing brushing her hair at the dressing table. The meeting tonight with DS Morley could prove difficult. He knew that Morley was Vice, not Drugs. Vicky could be a problem. After all, she was a prostitute and any suspicion of him living off her earnings could make him vulnerable and attract unnecessary attention. Vicky had served her purpose; she must now go away or disappear. Permanently.

11

Sammy arrived at the Caribbean as normal but was surprised to find Max already in his office. Unknown to him, Max had arrived very early. Two hours early.

Max knew DS Morley was going to offer some terms that would cost him dearly, so he needed some insurance, something to use as a counter lever against him. Morley was a bent Babylon on the take, and the courts would deem his crimes more serious than Max's.

The solution was simple. He rented some of the surveillance equipment used on Vicky and Jason Moore again, installing the video cameras in two table lamps on his desk facing towards where he knew Morley would sit. Three further microphones were placed discreetly around the office. Both sound and images were recorded onto machines set in the back of a white transit van parked outside the club, rented from the same company. Once Max had the evidence against him, Morley would no longer be in a position to dictate the conditions. This was his insurance.

Sammy walked into the office, Max was talking to someone on the telephone. He turned to Sammy. 'Can you give me five minutes, it's a little personal.'

A little surprised, Sammy replied, 'Sure, I'll be in the bar when you've finished.'

'Good man.'

Sammy walked out into the corridor but for some unaccountable reason stopped a few yards away. He heard Max continue his conversation. 'I need this woman to disappear. Can you arrange this for me?'

Sammy's jaw dropped. What did Max mean? Disappear?

Max continued, 'OK. You've got the details. Let me know when it's been done.'

Sammy heard him replace the receiver and sprinted quietly into the bar, out of sight.

Meanwhile, Max pondered and looked at the wall safe; it contained the master tape of Vicky and Jason Moore, to which there were only two keys. He held them both. This was to be his escape ticket if the Manchester connection became untenable. Several minutes later, Max joined Sammy in the bar.

'What time do you think this Sergeant Morley will get here?'

'He just said he'll see us tonight.'

'We've a large collection coming later. I don't want him turning up at the front doors at the same time.'

'Can we postpone it tonight?'

'No chance. If they suspect the Babylon are on to us, they'll cut us up into small pieces. No, we'll have to play it by ear. I've asked them to come early, telling them we have a large party from the Brixton. Let's hope they don't check us out. They seemed to be happy with that. I reckon they'll be here in about an hour, so we'd better get the cellar ready for them.'

'OK. I'll go and sort the racks out.'

Sammy descended into the cellar where he moved two large racks containing dozens of bottles of lager, empty drinking glasses and countless boxes of crisps. Fortunately, he had had the foresight to place the racks on heavy-duty castors, allowing improved mobility. On the wall behind them stood a small door with three padlocks. This opened into a concealed storeroom measuring three yards square, accessed only by Max and himself. No one else was allowed to venture down into the cellar. The collectors always remained upstairs in the office, where they would hand a note to either of them with the name and quantity of the drugs they required.

Shortly after ten o'clock, the Caribbean opened. Max unlocked the front doors and found the two regular collectors standing in the porch. Both were young black men in their early twenties, dressed in painter and decorator's overalls. Their small grubby van parked nearby was suitably connected with the painting trade, ladders secured on the roof rack with name 'Winston's Decorators' displayed along the side.

'Come in boys. What's your order tonight?' One of them gave him a note, together with a number of plastic shopping bags. 'Wait here, I'll get them.'

Max descended the cellar steps, giving the note to Sammy who quickly picked out the required items, placing them into the bags. Within five minutes Max went back upstairs, leaving Sammy to secure the storeroom door. The collectors grabbed the bags without speaking, placed them in the van, and drove away. As Max watched them, he knew although this was easy money, the impending visit tonight from Sergeant Morley could spoil everything. He must be ready.

Thank God, the only person he could really trust was Sammy.

12

Sammy was worried. He knew his friend and partner was ruthless, but could he be capable of killing Vicky? Although he had only met her a few times, he had grown to like her and failed to understand what she saw in Max. She was completely smitten with him, only wanting some affection in return. Why should she pay with her life for that? What else had she done to cause this? No, he simply could not allow that to happen. He would warn her she was in danger.

Standing in the cellar, collecting bottles from the store, he heard the loud reggae music start in the main dance area. Customers would soon be arriving. The bar had to be prepared, ready for service. He went upstairs and found Max talking to two young women near the office door. He walked past them into the bar and pushed open the vertical metal shutters. Four men rushed forward, all wanting to be served first. After the initial surge of customers, he saw Max appear at the bar door and nod his head, summoning him. 'Sammy, get one of the girls to cover the bar. That piece of shit is sat in my chair, drinking my rum. Go and join him but say nothing. I'm just going outside to get something from my car.'

Sammy walked into the office to find DS Morley sitting with his feet up on the desk. Meanwhile, Max opened the transit van doors and switched on the monitors and master tape recorder. The images of Morley were breathtakingly clear. He heard him ask Sammy, 'Where's he gone?'

He immediately locked the van doors, ran back into the club and entered his office where he said sarcastically, 'Help yourself to another drink, Mr Morley.'

'Just be careful, Max Campbell. You need to be shown some manners.'

'By you? What the hell do you want from us?'

Morley stood up slowly, turned his back deliberately and faced a wall cabinet in the corner of the office. 'Are the drugs from Manchester in there? No, of course not. Too obvious and too small. I'll bet they're somewhere in your cellar, hidden behind your stock.'

He turned back to face Max directly. 'Now let's all sit down. We have much to discuss.'

Sammy was about to speak but Max placed a finger on his own lips and shook his head. Sammy complied and remained quiet.

Morley continued, 'Don't let's get all shy. We all know what you're up to. The drugs arrive from Manchester, you store them here until they are collected and distributed to the street dealers here in London. Very nice. What I'm going to suggest is this. Carry on with what you're doing. I shall keep away, and more importantly, I can arrange for all my colleagues to do the same as well. I will protect you from any police raids, prosecution and ending up at the Old Bailey, where I can promise you, you'll both get life. What do you think?'

Max replied, 'I'm not admitting to anything to do with any drugs. I just run this club. But let's just suppose what you say is true. What would you want from all this?'

'Listen, Max. Do you think I'm bloody stupid? You're up to your thick black neck in all this. Not only that, but your girlfriend Vicky Thompson has been whoring herself in Mayfair and I know you've been living off her earnings. You're not only a major drugs distributor here in London, but also just a common pimp. So let's have a reality check. I'll allow you to continue with this venture but my cut is fifty percent. No negotiations.'

'Are you suggesting I pay you protection money, Sergeant Morley?'

'If you want to call it that. Yes.'

Max stood motionless for several seconds before replying, 'Sergeant Morley, thank you for coming tonight but I need to think about what you've just said. Can we meet here tomorrow lunchtime?' He leant forward and gave the officer the slightest of winks.

'OK. But you know the conditions. Don't mess me about.'

'No, I won't, Mr Morley.'

Morley looked at the glass of rum in his hand, drank it down in one gulp and walked towards the door. Slowing down, he turned back and said, 'We can make this work. There's no need to be enemies. I'll see you tomorrow.' He turned again and walked out through the front doors.

Sammy turned to Max and was about to speak but Max placed his own finger on Sammy's lips and shook his head.

Knowing he was out of camera shot he said, 'Listen, Sammy, I'm worried that Sergeant Morley thinks we're involved with drugs. I've no idea what he's talking about. Have you?' Max's shook his head with his finger still resting on Sammy's lips.

Sammy instinctively said, 'No.'

'I'm really worried about this. I don't know where he got this information from and I need to sort this out. I want you to take the rest of the night off. Hell, you deserve it. But get back here tomorrow at noon. I'm going to tell Sergeant Morley we have no idea what he's talking about.' Max winked and took his finger away and gave him a friendly dismissive wave.

'Thanks. I'll see you then.'

Sammy collected his coat and left the club through the rear door, confused. What was that all about? He decided to walk home. It was late spring but the night air was still biting cold. Recently he had become nocturnal, working nearly every night, taking no notice of the lengthening days as the seasons progressed. Breathing deeply the fresh night air enhanced his senses. His mind was racing with not only the events that night, but also how his life had changed. Two issues concerned him. The involvement of Morley with the drug storage at the club and Max's earlier conversation on the telephone about Vicky's disappearance. Max was certainly up something. But what? Suddenly he decided to act on the latter. He crossed the road to a waiting black cab and instructed the driver to take him to Max's home address in Clerkenwell.

Ten minutes later he stepped out of the taxi, asking the driver to hold the meter until he returned in ten minutes. He rang the front door bell. Soon, Vicky appeared at the door, both surprised and pleased to see him. 'Hello, Sammy. What are you doing here? Is Max at the club?'

'Yes, I've just left him. I need to talk to you urgently.'

She invited him into the kitchen and they sat down at the table.

'What's the matter, Sammy?'

'Listen, Vicky, I'm going to tell you something and you're not going to like it. First, how are things between you and Max?'

'All right. Why?'

'I know you won't believe me, but I'm certain Max intends you harm. I heard him tonight talking on the phone to someone about your disappearance. I don't know what's happened between you two but I think you should leave now. Tonight, before he gets home. I know I'm a criminal involved with drugs, but I don't like violence. I've seen enough of that with my brothers. Believe me, Max is a dangerous man, so you should leave while you can. But you must never tell anyone I've warned you, or we'll both be feeding the fishes in the Thames.'

She began to shake her head, not wanting to believe him, yet she knew deep inside that Max's affection for her was no longer there, especially after persuading her to have sex with Jason Moore and other men for his own benefit. Although he had never assaulted her, she knew he was more than capable of hiring someone else to do his dirty work. Yes, Sammy was right; she must leave before any harm befell her.

After reflecting for several moments, she said, 'I know what you say is right. Max no longer wants me in his life. I was foolish to believe he still loved me, but I need him for my medicine. What am I going to do?'

'There's a rehab clinic in Wembley, I've written it down on this piece of paper. Go and pack some clothes and ask the taxi driver outside to take you there. He'll know where it is. I'll go and tell him now. Just take this money for the time being and look after yourself.'

Sammy passed her the handwritten note together with five hundred pounds cash. It was all the money he had on him. She hesitated momentarily, but then accepted his gift. 'Bless you, Sammy. I wish I'd met you before Max.'

He quickly stood up and walked out through the front door towards the waiting taxi. After giving the driver instructions to take Vicky to Wembley, he raised his coat collar and began his long walk home in the spring night. Again, the fresh air seemed to clear his head. Hopefully, Vicky would be safely accommodated in the rehab clinic where she would have the opportunity to rid herself of her addiction and get her life back. Meanwhile, as he walked along the deserted streets, he was more than curious to know just how Max was going deal with DS Morley tomorrow.

13

Whilst Sammy was making his way home, Max had been busy editing the videos and the audio tapes of their meeting with DS Morley. He had good reason to smile, as he consumed another rum. He listened to them again. Perfect. Without either of them being incriminated, Morley had exposed himself as a dishonest police officer, unfit for public office. There was more than sufficient evidence to send him to prison for the rest of his life. Max had taken the initiative and now he had the authority to dictate terms. Morley had underestimated him by foolishly showing his hand.

*

Later that day, as noon approached, Sammy walked into the office and saw Max sitting on the leather sofa, drinking a cup of strong coffee. He looked tired and dishevelled.

'Bloody hell, man, you look rough. Have you been here all night?'

'Yes, Sammy. I've been busy protecting our future business. When Sergeant Morley arrives, you'll see exactly what I've been up to.'

Sammy's thoughts went immediately to Vicky. Obviously, Max had not missed her yet; too busy at the club all the night, and she was the last person he was concerned about. Sammy sat down next to him; both looking at the wall clock in silence, waiting for their visitor to arrive. They did not have to wait long.

DS Morley walked through the open front doors straight into the office. He went directly to Max's chair, sat down and put his feet up on the desk. 'Right, I'm not wasting anymore of my time. Do you accept my terms?'

Max leant forward. 'I think we may have a deal, Sergeant Morley.'

'Good, you know you have no choice, Max.'

'Well, it's not me that hasn't any choice. I rather think it's you.'

'What!'

Max walked over to the television set and video recorder on the side office cabinet, some three yards from where Morley was sat. He placed a video cassette inside and turned the screen on. 'Perhaps you would care to see this, Sergeant Morley, before we discuss matters any further.' He pressed the 'play' button and the scene from the previous night was played in full colour with crystal-clear audio. Every word he'd said had been recorded. Max had said nothing incriminating regarding any involvement with the drugs. No indication of him purposely preventing Sammy from speaking too.

Morley removed his feet from the desk. He was stunned. He had no inclination Max was clever enough to record their meeting in such a manner. The clarity of the images was too damning. The recording was of all the conversation and threats made by him against them both. It lasted for only five minutes but the content could change his life permanently. For the worse. The evidence against him was simply indefensible.

Max stepped forward and ejected the cassette. 'Please have this one. Of course, there are several others. And if you want to search this club for drugs, go ahead. I can promise you, there are none here and I know you can never prove there ever were either.'

Looking utterly dejected, Morley picked up the video cassette and stared at it in silence. Then he exploded. 'What the hell have you done? I'm going to kill you both for this. You don't mess with me.'

'Shut up. Other people have copies of these if anything untoward happens to either of us.'

Morley stood perfectly still, glaring at Max without blinking, gradually composing himself again. 'It seems we both have secrets on each other now. But if the courts believe this video was made under duress, this cassette is worthless.'

'Sergeant Morley, you're absolutely right. But do you really want to take that chance? I believe you have much more to lose than we do. Don't you think so?'

'I could break your black arses right now. Don't you dare talk to me like that.'

Sammy looked anxiously at Max. He knew Morley was a mean Babylon; he had witnessed him losing his temper before in his mother's kitchen, after one of his brothers had given him some cheek. But Max seemed to be calm and in complete control.

Suddenly, to Sammy's surprise, Max stood to his full height, arms folded behind his back, and grinned. Slowly, he shook his head. 'Now, you listen to me, you pile of white shit. It was you that came into my club threatening me. You have nothing on me, I've got this on you. There's a difference. And right now you're trespassing on my property. I also understand the law is very clear with trespassers, including police officers, who are on premises uninvited and not in the execution of their duties, and that I can use sufficient and reasonable force in ejecting you from here if I want to.'

Morley was shaking with rage. He was about to speak until he saw Max produce a baseball bat from behind his back. He slapped it menacingly into the palm of his other hand and took a step forward.

Morley placed both his hands into the air. 'OK. Do you think this is the end to all this?'

'No, I don't, Sergeant Morley. But you've made a big mistake. You've assumed we're all black thugs who don't have a brain. Well, you're wrong.

'Are you threatening me, Max?'

'No, but that is.' Max pointed towards the video cassette in hand.

'So what are we going to do now?'

'Just as you suggested last night. Providing you offer us protection, I'm prepared to give you a monthly bung. Under the circumstances, I think that's very generous, considering your position now.'

'How can I trust you not to send a copy of this to the Commissioner?'

'Think about it. It's in both of our interests if we work together. Why should we destroy each other? We've both played the Badger Game on each other. Except I've won. Haven't I?'

DS Morley looked at Sammy. 'What about him? He's got the dirt on both of us.'

'This man, I would trust with my life. Sammy is discreet. He never asks questions and after all, he's my partner. The deal includes him. And as you would say, Mr Morley, no negotiation. Now let's all sit down and discuss business.'

14

During the following three hours, Max freely explained to Morley the illicit operational arrangements in detail: the deliveries from Manchester, the storage at the Caribbean and collections by the main dealers in London. They agreed on a price of one thousand pounds per month in exchange for a guarantee of no police interference.

Max accepted the club would be run as a bona fide business. That would be Sammy's responsibility. Towards the end of their discussions, Morley said, 'Now we are partners, would you please let me know where your girlfriend Vicky Thompson lives. I've a friend who's a journalist and he's keen to speak to her.'

'What about?' asked Max.

'He's got a whisper that she has been involved in a sexual relationship with an MP. If he can speak to her and she's willing, there could be a chance she could make a lot of money. That sort of story sells a lot of papers and the national tabloids will pay top dollar for it.'

'How much?'

'I'm not sure, but it would probably be in excess of twenty thousand pounds. Naturally, he would make it worthwhile for you.'

'What happens if she doesn't agree to all this?'

'Without any supporting evidence, the story is just a story. The papers and my friend would be open to a serious libel action by the MP without the necessary sworn and signed affidavit from her.'

Max sat back in his chair. 'Sorry, I can't help you there. Sure, she was my girl, but I haven't seen her for several weeks. I don't know where she is now. Probably hustling in King's Cross or some cheap hotel nearby.' He looked directly at Sammy for a second, then looked away. 'No, Sergeant Morley, I've no idea where she is.'

Morley shrugged. The promise to his friend Alex Gilmour could wait, especially now he was on the threshold of earning thousands of pounds for doing absolutely nothing. His recording of Max and Sammy in the Divisional Crime Register as reliable 'snouts' would deter any of his colleagues from making inquiries into their activities without consulting him first. That was the protocol.

He stood up. 'Gentlemen, I hope we are all friends now and can do business. Providing we don't mess things up, you are free to carry on with your venture without any interference. We'll be the only three that know about this arrangement. Agreed?'

Max stood too. 'Agreed, Sergeant Morley.'

They looked at Sammy who remained sitting. He looked up. 'Yes, of course.'

'Good. You will not see me here again but I may phone you from time to time. If you need me urgently, here's my card. If I'm not on duty, try this number.' Morley wrote his home number on the reverse side and handed it to Max. All three men nodded to each other. The meeting was over. Sammy followed him through the front door, then Morley turned around. 'You're very quiet. I like that. If there are any problems between you and Max in the future, here's my card too.'

Sammy took it and placed it in his pocket as he watched Morley drive away. Returning inside, he closed and locked the doors behind him, still thinking of what Max was scheming. Telling Morley he had no idea where Vicky was seemed to confirm his suspicions he was planning her disappearance. What would he do when he got home and found she wasn't there? Sammy took a deep breath and entered the office. Max had poured two large glasses of rum. Looking at Sammy, he held one of the glasses high. 'Now we have insurance. Think about that: police protection. That's the best protection you can buy. You played your part well. Your face, when Morley realised how I'd set him up. Hell, man, you had no idea, did you?'

'No, Max, you're too clever for me.'

But Sammy did not share Max's enthusiasm. He felt the stakes had suddenly increased beyond his comfort level. He asked, 'What was all that about with Vicky?'

'OK, Sammy. I'm going to let you into a secret 'cos I knew you'll keep it to yourself. All that video filming I did on Morley, I also did it with Vicky and the MP. You know, the MP who Morley was talking about, in a hotel last month. She did a great job on him. Poor bastard had no idea he was being filmed.'

'Did Vicky know you were filming?'

'Not really.'

'What do you mean, Max, not really?'

'No, she didn't, but she agreed to go with this MP. I told her it was business. She'll be alright when I give her some more powder to shove up her nose and buy her some pretty clothes.'

'What are you going to do with this video of Vicky?'

'I'll send a copy to the MP first. No letter, just the film.'

'Who is this MP?'

'Don't want to say at the moment. But I think he'll be willing to give me more than the twenty thousand pounds this journalist would give to Vicky. Anyway, why should she get the money? She'd just blow it on drugs and be dead within three months. No, Morley isn't getting his hands on her.'

Sammy listened and remained quiet. Now he knew Max's intentions for Vicky's future were dire. With her disappearance, he was free to exploit her completely. Conversely, if she was on the scene, that could cause trouble. Like this MP, she would make a principal witness against him for blackmail. Soon his pimping and involvement with the major distribution of illegal drugs in London would be discovered. Morley was wrong. Max would go to prison not for twenty years, but potentially for the rest of his life. And he was connected to Max. With her disappearance, and his involvement in the Caribbean, he would join him. It was all a matter of association.

As he continued looking at Max, not listening to a word he was saying, he suddenly experienced for the first time a strong desire to turn his back on everything. Walk away and abandon his stake in the business. All the money he had recently acquired now seemed meaningless. But how could he do this? There was no exit strategy in this line of business. Rewards were high but short-lived. He would have to meticulously plan his escape, but meanwhile comply with Max's wishes to avoid him suspecting his intention to desert. But he knew that when Max finally returned home to find that Vicky had disappeared, he would waste no time in searching for her. Hopefully, she would remain hidden in the Wembley rehab centre. Normally, all contact with the outside world was difficult, especially if she had agreed to the full rehabilitation programme. If she signed the necessary consent forms, she would be protected until the treatment was completed.

He would have to leave Vicky to find her own luck. If Max discovered he had warned her and facilitated her recovery programme, he would pay dearly. Probably with his life.

So meanwhile he would play the game; run the Caribbean as normal but keep a close eye on Max and Morley.

15

The following day, DS Morley arrived at Alex Gilmour's place, a fashionable mews house in south Islington, near to the Underground. Built over three floors, with a small back garden, it was ideally located for work and recreation, perfect for a forty-six-year-old bachelor. Gilmour had lived there for many years and regarded his independence as sacrosanct. He'd been involved in a serious relationship many years previously, but he was jilted a week before the wedding and the pain and despair had been palpable. Following several months of wallowing in self-pity, he threw himself completely into his work, vowing never to allow himself to become emotionally attached to anyone again.

Since then, his relationships with women were always casual, usually lasting no more than three months. That was his safeguard. All physical with no emotional commitment.

He had been in the newspaper business from first leaving school, beginning with a small Lincolnshire town weekly gazette as a junior farming reporter. However, after only two years of reporting the monotony of rural and agricultural affairs, he'd progressed to the Leicester Mercury. There, in the rapidly expanding city, he became keenly interested in the police's initiative of fostering new relationships between themselves and the ever-increasing multi-cultural communities. From Leicester, he eventually migrated to London, where he became a political and criminal investigative journalist for several tabloid papers. However, five years ago, he had made the most significant change in his life; he'd abandoned his contracts and reporting to editors and became freelance. He found a lucrative opportunity investigating people, often in the public arena, who had fallen from the moral high ground and been caught up in the sex industry. The identities of these 'victims' were uncovered from the loose talk and gossip emanating from the extensive network he had nurtured in Whitehall and various local governments. His contact with the sex industry was exclusively through his old friend, DS Morley.

The friendship and trust between them had flourished during this time. Their successful collaboration was reflected in their healthy bank accounts. The system was simple. Morley supplied Gilmour with the information the police had collated against all the men who had used the services of prostitutes in the King's Cross area, including the seven brothels operating there. Witness statements were taken from these men to support a possible prosecution of the prostitutes, pimps or brothel keepers, but their details were leaked to Gilmour. Sometimes, details of the registered keepers of cars seen in the area, obtained using the direct link to the Driver and Vehicle Licensing Centre in Swansea through the Police National Computer, were passed over. These were a mixture of men seeking sexual services from the street workers, kerb crawlers, or others innocently driving in the vicinity or passing through. All were usually recorded by members of the Vice Squad. For most men, their mere presence in the red-light area was potentially too embarrassing to explain.

Once Gilmour had this information, he would usually contact them by telephone, inviting them to account for their behaviour, vaguely threatening to expose their movements inside the red-light area. Saying that he was a reporter and he was investigating the exploitation of young women trapped in the sex trade, he would subtly mention that their personal details could be omitted from the story if they contributed to a charity called Refuge for Sexually Exploited Women, which financed and supported sanctuaries for such desperate women trying to escape from their lives of abuse. A contribution of five hundred pounds would make the men's identities disappear and give the poor women an opportunity to improve their desperate circumstances and have the freedom of choice about their futures. Only a handful of men refused to cooperate with his request. All lived to bitterly regret that, later suffering from scandalous exposure in the national press.

However, over four hundred and fifty men he had contacted

during the past eighteen months had willingly agreed to donate to this worthwhile cause. Most felt an enormous sense of relief, firstly at avoiding the publicity and the consequences of a ruined personal and professional life, and secondly at donating to a charity that saved the poor souls from a life of abuse and poverty. This was a moral bonus.

All very commendable on the surface. But it was a complete scam. The Refuge for Sexually Exploited Women was in fact a secret offshore bank account, the single signatory being Alex Gilmour from which he had received over two hundred thousand pounds during this time. He felt particularly smug as he was protected by his friend DS Morley, who dealt with any complaints made against him and the donations. Presently, none had been made.

He knew that Morley was unaware of the exact amount of money he had duped from these men, although he probably suspected it was substantial. Nevertheless, together they had enjoyed an unequal amount of proceeds from the scam. But he knew time was running out. With his imminent retirement after thirty years' police service, Morley would be unable to supply information to him for much longer. The gravy train had only a limited time to run.

*

The intercom sounded. 'Come in, George,' Gilmour said, 'I've been expecting you.'

The buzzer sounded loudly as the front door opened. Morley entered and ascended a short flight of stairs into a large open-plan living room, facing directly onto a small private patio. Gilmour stood next to the drinks cabinet. 'Usual?'

'Yes, please, Alex.'

Gilmour handed him a Scotch and they sat down on the luxurious cream leather sofas, facing each other. 'What have you got for me, George?'

'Unfortunately, not a great deal at the moment, but I'm working hard to change all that. This girl Vicky Thompson is apparently no longer Max Campbell's girl. I'm not too sure that's right but I'll be visiting Max's home when he's out at work and checking to see if she's still there.'

'Won't you need a warrant?'

'No, he's a pimp. I can think of several reasons why I need to enter without bothering a magistrate. For instance, I may receive an anonymous phone call from a member of the public to the effect that screams have been heard from inside Max's home. In that case, knowing he's a pimp, I'll have to enter, by force if necessary, to save life, even if it's a false alarm. It's a power under Common Law that all Constables have, and I must say it's bloody useful at times.'

'OK. Let me know when you've found her. There's a grand in it for you.'

'Should trace her in the next twenty-four hours.'

'Great. What else has been happening in your sordid world?'

'Got a bit of a deal going off with these guys down at the Caribbean Club. It's in the early stages but I'm hoping it will develop into something interesting.'

'You're being a bit shy with the details, George. Are you going to tell me more?'

'Sure. These two guys, Max and another called Sammy, have got themselves involved with the Manchester drug scene. There are some serious bad bastards up there. Anyway, they have agreed to store significant quantities of drugs at the club, where they can be collected later and distributed around London. I think they are making serious money, so I've put a proposition to them. They're going to give me a flat monthly rate for allowing them to continue operating. Naturally, I'll be keeping a watchful eye to ensure none of my colleagues get too interested in them as well.'

'Sounds good. Make sure the Manchester lads don't find out. Otherwise you'll be in deep shit.'

'I know, Alex. But these boys won't say anything either. It's probably worse for them. They realise that if the Manchester mob know I'm aware of all this, they're as good as dead.'

'Just take care. Don't let's get too greedy. We've got a good system going with your punters.'

Morley knew that his friend was making a stack of money from these men. They never made any complaints about how their money was being purportedly spent with the charity, and although he had benefitted from expensive holidays, the bulk of the money was kept by Alex. He looked around the home, knowing that expensive furniture and fittings were continually being added or upgraded. Alex's growing collection of original oil paintings adorned every wall. His suits were tailored in Savile Row and the brand-new Mercedes sports car parked idle in his garage bore witness to his considerable income. He was flattered Alex had warned him to be careful, but he wanted to make more money, just like him. A great deal more.

16

A month after the meeting with DS Morley, Max was sitting at his desk contemplating the next delivery schedule. Business was booming. The weekly drops from the north were now twice a week and the next consignment would be the third in eight days. Thousands of pounds were injected weekly into both of their bank accounts. Max was happy, except for one niggling matter. Vicky. Where had she disappeared to? He had repeatedly asked Sammy if he knew where she was. His answer was always the same: 'No Max. No idea.'

He had engaged several private investigators to trace her whereabouts without success. If she remained absent from his life, he was never sure she might reappear from nowhere. Such an uncertainty would jeopardise the plans he had for the Jason Moore enterprise. Meanwhile, because of the investment he had made, he continued to pay for these enquiries to be made. Confident she would turn up sometime in the future, he was completely unprepared for how soon his prediction would come true.

The telephone rang. That was unusual. No one telephoned him at midnight. He answered, 'Max. Can I help you?'

There was a strange silence, just the sound of faint breathing.

Again, he said, 'Hello, this is Max. Can I help you?'

'Max, do you still love me?'

Max sat bolt upright. 'Is that you, babe?'

'Yes.'

'Where are you? I've been so worried about you.'

'Have you really?'

'Of course I have, babe. I love you and missed you so much. I need you back in my life. Have you forgotten about the plans we made? Please come home.'

'Do you promise not to make me go with other men?'

'Of course, babe. Never again. You're my woman. I'm not going to share you with anyone else, especially if you promise never to leave me again.'

'Are you sure you still want me?'

'Yes, babe, and I promise to get you that ring.'

'Do you mean that Max?'

'Yes. You bet I do. Just come home now, babe.'

'OK. I'll be home in an hour. I've still got the key.'

'I'll see you at home in a couple of hours, I've got some jobs to do here first. Sammy's taken the night off.'

'OK. You know I love you, Max.'

'Of course I do, babe. I love you too. See you soon.'

He hung up and sat back in his chair. After several minutes of quietly planning, he shouted, 'Sammy, can you come here please.'

Sammy put his head round the door. 'What is it Max? I'm busy behind the bar.'

'Sorry about this, I've got to dash out. Some important business has to be done. Will you be alright locking up tonight?'

'Yes, I suppose so. Will I see you here tomorrow?'

'Of course, we have another delivery.'

'OK, Max. See you later.'

Sammy disappeared back into the bar, leaving Max alone. After closing the office door firmly, Max made a telephone call. It was answered on the second ring. 'Your target will be at my place in an hour. You'll find the front door key next to an iron boot scraper on the left. I don't want any signs she was there. Do you understand?'

A soft voice replied, 'Understood. But the fee is another two thousand pounds for doing the house cleaning.'

'OK. Come here to the club tomorrow night at this time. I'll settle up with you then.'

'Cash.'

'Yes. Just make her disappear.'

A small part of his conscience whispered, 'But she still loves you.' He immediately dismissed it and suppressed all his feelings. Vicky was a liability. As a material witness, she could send him to prison for a long stretch, not only for his pimping activities but also his proposed blackmail bid against Jason Moore. Once she discovered he had filmed her performing sex without her knowledge, he was vulnerable to a life of incarceration. There was only one solution.

*

Within the hour a black cab pulled up outside Max's house. Vicky stepped out and paid the driver. She was now clean of drugs, and following her short but painful rehabilitation programme, she was determined to look after her health. The medical staff had been very supportive, convincing her that she must take control of her own life and seek fulfilment in a better future. A new beginning was their prophecy. Start up with new relationships and challenges and leave the past firmly behind, had been advised. She had been a model patient during the therapy, wholeheartedly accepting all their counselling and guidance, except for one thing.

Her love for Max was indelible. Perhaps she could try just once more to live a normal life with him, with no drugs or sex with other men. Just one more chance.

As she entered the house, knowing Max had now proposed a stable future, if not marriage, her spirits soared. For the first time in a long time, she was truly happy, felt vibrant and alive. She would go and make herself look fantastic for him and hopefully he'd be proud of her for kicking the addiction. She looked at her watch; there was not much time before he would return.

She sat in front of the dressing table in the main bedroom, brushing her hair then applying Max's favourite lipstick. As she pressed her lips together, a sudden pain shot across her neck. She quickly glanced in the mirror and saw the image of a person dressed completely dressed in black. Her eyes fixed on the face but it was hidden by a full-length balaclava completely pulled down over the neck. Unable to breathe, speak or scream, she pleaded inside for mercy. She attempted to place her hands on the offending arms but her strength simply ebbed away; she was unable to protect herself. A state of complete desperation filled her body until a cold numbing sensation followed, causing her to lose consciousness. As she closed her eyes, the last image she saw was her twisted lipstick-smudged face. She relaxed and the pain disappeared. The hurt was over.

Her executioner was a professional. Utterly ruthless and without pity, he caught her as she fell to the floor and carried her to the kitchen, where a large plastic sheet had been laid out. He placed her gently upon it and rolled the sheet tightly around her. Through the transparent plastic, her eyes remained open. Her facial expression still showed surprise and bewilderment. This was not how it should have been. She was going to marry Max, but now she was dead.

He returned to the bedroom and collected her handbag and the small suitcase she had brought from the clinic. He checked and double-checked, ensuring nothing else was there that might show her presence there. Nothing. However, he failed to look in the top drawer of the dressing table, where Vicky had left her leather purse. It was the only tangible trace of her existence in the house.

Outside, a large Volvo estate car was waiting near to the front door. Switching off the porch light was the sign to the driver to raise the tailgate and to assist his friend with the large roll of plastic sheeting. Together, they bundled it into the rear of the car and quietly closed the door. Within two minutes the car had driven away, leaving only silence in the cool still air.

Less than an hour later, Max returned home. He entered the house and immediately searched for any trace of Vicky. Although he could vaguely detect her perfume, he could find no signs she had ever returned. He poured another rum and cynically lifted his glass. 'Here's to you, babe.' He gulped the spirit down in one and retired to bed, where he slept soundly until lunchtime.

17

The district surrounding King's Cross had several guises. By day, it was a busy hub for commuters dashing to and from work or other appointments. By night, the streets changed into a world of vice. Sex was openly and unashamedly sold to anyone willing to pay. Street working prostitutes were normally very territorial with their patch. Rivalry between 'pick ups' often spilt over into violent brawls, usually broken up by their respective pimps. Ironically, although physical assaults were commonplace between the women, there was an unwritten code of sharing information regarding those punters who displayed any violent tendencies towards them. After all, these women never truly conspired to become prostitutes. Circumstances did that.

Most of the young women plying their services had a drug addiction, or a dependency at best. The opportunity of earning over five hundred pounds per night, even after surrendering their pimp's share, was far too tempting. The remainder going to the drugs dealers supplying their addiction. It was a vicious circle from which there was little or no escape. Eventually, the women often became expendable, discarded and replaced by younger victims, who in turn enjoyed the endless supply of recreational drugs and promises of a better life. The shelf life for many of these unfortunate vulnerable women was often less than eighteen months.

18

Alex Gilmour moved easily and unimpeded in both the political and commercial circles of Westminster and the City. His extensive networking and knowledge of the current movers and shakers commanded much influence, but at a cost. He was reviled by most, quickly attracting a reputation as 'a man to avoid where possible yet ignored at your peril'. He thrived on gossip, generously rewarding those who informed him of any potential scandal. The victims were normally all men of considerable wealth or well known in the public arena. His motive for discovering and exposing embarrassing liaisons was simple. Money.

He usually approached a victim and offered them the opportunity of buying his story. A gagging contract of sorts. If they ignored him, he would sell the story to the highest tabloid bidder. But normally, the victim bought the story in a hurry at an extortionate price. Either way, Alex enjoyed another highly lucrative tax-free payment. After all, he was a master player of the Badger Game.

Although his close friend George Morley was very useful in providing him with information, allowing him to generate enormous sums of money with the minimum of effort, he knew this relationship had only three years to run before George's retirement. Furthermore, he considered George's venture into the protection racket, involving substantial quantities of illegal drugs shipped into London, without the knowledge of the Manchester suppliers, was potentially fraught with danger. He was aware of the vicious manner in which these gangs operated in that city. Killing was merely a side-line activity to their extensive criminal narcotics empire. George had overstepped the mark.

He then considered Max Campbell. Now he appeared to be a shrewd operator who moved comfortably amidst the criminal underworld, nerves of steel and ruthless in the extreme. George however, was simply out of his league, and his recent exploits had made him a liability. He realised there was little choice but to gradually distance his relationship from his friend. But how would he react?

His mind turned to the Jason Moore affair with Vicky Thompson. Although he had asked George for help in tracing her, without avail, he would make his own enquiries too. Visiting the red-light area that night, asking a few girls working on the streets and in the bars if they knew anything about her, would probably be more successful. He knew money made anyone talk, it was just the amount that varied. Pressing twenty-pound notes into their hands would do the trick for such information. George, on the other hand, was less sophisticated; he simply threatened them.

It was just after 9 p.m. when Alex walked through King's Cross railway station, having taken the Tube from Islington. He turned towards St Pancras and disappeared behind a row of closed shops. Within ten minutes he had spoken to three women, spent two hundred pounds and established Vicky had been recently discharged from a Wembley rehab and had returned to her boyfriend's place. All the women confirmed he was Max Campbell, who ran the Caribbean Club.

Alex went into a nearby hotel and ordered a drink. He must think of his next move. There was little purpose informing George of her whereabouts now; yet approaching her could be risky. The safer and wiser option was to approach Max Campbell directly and explore another opportunity to expose the Jason Moore scandal. There was little doubt Max would influence her possible decision to play her role.

With his decision made, he walked out of the hotel and hailed a cab. Opening a rear door, he looked at the driver and said, 'The Caribbean Club please.'

19

Max awoke to the sun streaming through the large bedroom window. After showering, he dressed then looked into the wall mirror, planning his next move. He looked around for his hair brush and opened the top drawer where he normally kept it. He saw the familiar brown handle and grabbed it with his right hand. Then he froze. Tucked between his belts and socks he saw Vicky's purse. He gently picked it up. He could smell her perfume and remembered her long, delicate fingers opening the metal clasp. He shook his head violently, muttering 'Get a grip, Max.'

He threw the purse against the wall and its contents flew out onto the carpet below. He went downstairs into the kitchen and picked up a small plastic bin liner. Returning to the bedroom, he stooped down and picked up the assorted tickets, cards and papers. Even the bank notes were thrown into the bag. He wanted nothing of hers to remind him of what he had done. As he stood up, he noticed a piece of writing paper, folded into four, under the bed. He opened it and read 'St Agnes Drug and Alcohol Rehabilitation Clinic in Wembley.' Then he immediately recognised the handwriting. All in block capitals, slanting slightly forward. It belonged to Sammy, his partner, the man he would trust with his business and life. His best friend who had repeatedly denied knowing where she was.

He sat down on the corner of the bed, wondering how he might challenge Sammy about this note. He reached over to the bedside telephone and called directory enquiries for the number of the clinic. He made a second call. 'Good afternoon. My name is Dr Anderson and I'm ringing about one of my patients, Victoria Thompson. She's here with me now at the surgery. May I ask you how long her treatment lasted with yourselves as she is a little confused?'

A woman replied, speaking with a strong Eastern European accent. 'Let me just check for you, Doctor. Can you confirm her date of birth, please?'

Max was alarmed. He was unprepared for the question. Turning aside he said loudly, 'What's your date of birth, Miss Thompson.'

Unable to remember her exact birthday, he spoke again to the woman. 'She's shaking her head. Our records show her date of birth as 9th September 1960.'

'We've got it as 9th September 1962. Never mind. Yes, I can confirm she arrived four weeks ago on Wednesday 23rd May. She was discharged yesterday, having made an excellent recovery.'

'Does it give a forwarding address?'

'No, sorry. Would you like to speak with the senior consultant about her?'

'No, thank you. That won't be necessary. You've been very helpful. Good afternoon.'

Max hung up and lay back on the bed. That changed everything. Could he trust Sammy? How would he react if he found out Vicky had returned and immediately disappeared? He must put him to the test tonight. But how?

20

Max arrived at the club before Sammy. He sat in his office preparing his questions, upset to even suspect Sammy had lied to him, but the note was real. It remained folded in his jacket pocket. He had decided not to reveal it for the time being. The presence of the note meant he had had some contact with Vicky and that was too risky. She would remain missing as before.

Half an hour later, Max heard the front doors unlock. Sammy walked along the hallway but as he passed the office door he was startled when he saw Max sat at his desk. 'Bloody hell, you gave me a scare then. What are you doing here so early?'

'Had some business to catch up on. They've got the road dug up outside my house, so I came in. It's quieter and I've had to make a few calls.'

'OK.' Sammy was about to leave when Max asked, 'Have you seen or heard anything about Vicky?'

'No. Nothing. Why, are you missing her?'

'Not really. I just wondered if you know where she might have been.'

'No. Haven't seen her in weeks. Do you want me to ask about?'

'No. Forget it. We've got other things to worry about. We'll be getting another shipment tomorrow night. What's it like down there?'

'To be honest, it's getting a bit crowded. We'll need to find somewhere else before long, but not just yet.'

'Yes, I know. We'll talk about that later.'

Sammy nodded and left. But as he entered the bar he stopped and reflected on Max's question. Had he found out about the rehab? Where was Vicky? Had something happened to her? He must tread very carefully. Perhaps his days at the Caribbean with Max were now numbered. He must make plans. Soon.

Suddenly he heard a loud knock on the front door. He looked at his watch. There was another ten minutes before the club opened. He shouted, 'We're not open yet.'

A voice replied, 'I know that. Will you let me in, please, I would like to see Mr Max Campbell.'

'Who is it?'

'Please let me in. I wish to talk to Mr Campbell. It's urgent.'

Max had been attracted by the noise from outside. 'Let him in, Sammy, but hang about. Just in case.'

Sammy unlocked the front door and opened it wide. The man entered without speaking and then saw both men. 'Is one of you Max Campbell?'

'Yes, I am. What do you want?'

'My name is Alex Gilmour. I'm a freelance journalist. May I speak with you in private please?'

Max gestured him to come into his office, giving Sammy the slightest nod. 'Please sit down, Mr Gilmour.'

'May I speak to you in private?'

'Of course.' Max indicated for Sammy to leave, giving him a reassuring wink.

Once the door was shut Max asked, 'Now, what's all this about?'

'OK. Please listen to what I have to say first, then we'll talk more in detail.'

'Go ahead. I'm listening.'

Alex leant slightly forward. 'Max, I know all about the arrangement you have with Sergeant Morley. The drugs you store here in the club that come from Manchester, how they are collected from here and distributed onto the streets of London. Don't worry, DS Morley and myself are partners in numerous enterprises and I've no intention of muscling in on yours. That's not what I'm interested in. I'm an investigative reporter, working for myself, finding out about the sordid lives of the rich and powerful. One story that interests me is the relationship an MP has had with a woman called

Vicky Thompson. Your woman, I understand?'

'Very interesting. Unfortunately, she used to be my woman, but I've no idea where she is now. Why do you want to find her?'

'That's a good question. Once I've tracked her down, I want to offer a substantial amount of money, if she agrees, to give me permission to print a story of their relationship. She is a prostitute and he's an MP and a member of Her Majesty's Government. That's a good story. Several national tabloid editors would pay good money for that. But we would need her signature on a contract to support this.'

'So, without her you have no story?'

'That's about right.'

Max sat back in his chair and stared at his guest. After several moments, he said, 'Let's talk hypothetically. Let's imagine that some film and photographs of the encounter existed. Would you still require the woman's consent?'

'If there are any clear images of both parties performing sexual acts, then that would be a completely different matter.'

'How different?'

'I would suggest the sum of twenty-five thousand pounds would be a reasonable payment, provided the images were to a high standard.'

Max stood up. 'Just hold on to what you've just said.' He walked over to the wall safe, unlocked the door and brought a folder back to his desk. 'Have a look at these photographs. Are they clear enough or would you like a brighter light?'

Alex picked up the bundle of all six by four inches colour photographs. He studied each one thoroughly. 'Hell, Max, a blind man on a galloping horse could see these little beauties; they're bloody perfect. You're sitting on a potentially big pile of money. How did you get these?'

'Really, Alex. Call yourself a reporter. Never divulge your sources. Isn't that true?'

'Yes, you're right.'

'There is a video of all this and more.'

'Is the woman in these Vicky Thompson?'

'Yes.'

'Did she consent to these images being taken?'

'Yes, but she's disappeared now.'

'Well, that's between you and her. Max, I'm speechless.'

'Yes, and so was Sergeant Morley when I videoed him attempting to threaten me with extortion. So now, I want you tell me all about Sergeant Morley and yourself.'

'That's fair enough. We have known each other since childhood and in recent years he has supplied me with useful information regarding men pursuing the services of prostitutes. Once I've given them the opportunity of buying this information, they are very happy to see any embarrassment disappear with their payment.'

'You mean blackmail.'

'You might say that. I prefer playing the Badger Game.'

The men looked at each other. Max was the first to smile. 'Tell me, Alex, what would Sergeant Morley say if he knew of this meeting?'

'Max, we both have our own ways of making money. The only person that connects us is Sergeant Morley. He's a bent cop, yes. But I can vouch for him to be trustworthy and not to spoil things. I'm not sure what he would say about this meeting, but frankly I'm not too bothered about it either. What I'm discussing with you has nothing to with your joint business. To be honest, I'd rather not be involved with the drugs scene. Too risky for me, Max. I'm only interested in squeezing this MP punter for as much money as I can. Naturally, I'm prepared to cut you in fifty-fifty. But you might not want to do that.'

'You're right. But not at this stage. However, I'm prepared to sell you all this package, including the videos, for twenty-five thousand pounds now.

'Before I answer that, what is your relationship like with the Manchester syndicate?'

'Why? I thought you weren't interested in all that.'

'Well, here's a thought. The MP we're talking about is called Jason Moore. You know that, don't you?'

'Of course.'

'Apparently he works in the Department for Trade and Industry.'

'So?'

'That Department has the authority to issue special importers' permits, allowing pretty much anything to enter this country without a border control. A little similar to a diplomat's pouch, but on a bigger scale. Let's imagine, if Mr Moore could obtain such a permit. Think of what opportunities there are. For example, a permit issued for scientifically modified crops from Pakistan would allow them to enter the UK unhindered. But what other crop do they grow in that part of the world?'

'Heroin.'

'Exactly. Now, if you speak to your contacts in Manchester, I bet they would give you ten times what you want to sell to me. Think about it.'

Max poured a rum and swallowed it in one. His eyes fixed on Alex. He was thinking. This man was right. If he could convince the Manchester mob there was a chance to import a shitload of heroin, they'd be talking about millions of pounds. This had the potential to make everyone a fortune. Perhaps he should contact them the next day and discuss it with them.

'Alex, if I were to go down that route, what's in it for you?'

'Well, that's a good question too. We can discuss that later. Obviously, we're talking about a great deal of money but remember, I have contacts in Whitehall and the Government. I can arrange a meeting with Jason Moore without attracting any suspicion. I would point out to him he need only obtain a permit in exchange for that folder you have. No money. Just a favour. No one gets hurt.'

'Alex, you're one clever bastard.'

'Think about it, Max. Make some enquiries with the Manchester lot but I must ask you for one condition. This is a deal breaker.'

'What is it?'

'My identity must only be known to yourself.'

'That's fine with me. I only hope the Manchester mob don't insist on knowing who you are.'

'You must explain that's my only condition. If they agree, I'll arrange for Jason Moore to apply for the import permit. Obviously, the Mancunians must organise the shipment. I suspect they'll have an extensive network stretching all the way over to Pakistan.'

'Leave that with me.'

Alex stood up and stretched his hand over the desk. They shook hands. Max said, 'I'm glad you called in. You must give me a week or so to make the necessary enquiries. How can I contact you?'

'Here's my card. I'll look forward to hearing from you, Max.'

Alex walked out of the club as the customers were coming in. Max sat back and reflected on their conversation. The only contact he had was with Bill. He would ring him the next day and organise a meeting urgently.

Meanwhile, he had Sammy to consider.

21

But Sammy was one step ahead. He had been listening to Max's conversation with the visitor from the small storeroom next to the office. Unable to hear every word, he understood enough to realise Max was going to use the video of Vicky performing sex with an MP, to impress the mob in Manchester.

Ten minutes after the visitor had left, and with Max still in his office, he placed a call to the Wembley rehab centre from behind the bar. The receptionist was vague about Vicky's details but eventually informed him she had been discharged the previous day. That was all he needed to know. Now he feared she had disappeared permanently. And so must he.

Shortly after 2 a.m., as the club was closing, Max called out, 'Sammy, in here please.'

Sammy joined him in the office.

'Sammy, I've got to go up to Manchester tomorrow to sort some business out. Will you look after the club for a couple of days? I should be back by the end of the week. Don't forget, there's another shipment coming tomorrow night.'

'No problem.'

The men looked at each other for a split second. Something had changed, and Sammy realised their partnership had ended abruptly.

Max smiled. 'Thanks, Sammy. Can you close the door; I've got some more calls to make?'

'Sure.'

Thirty minutes later, the Caribbean closed. It had been a relatively quiet night, with just a handful of the regulars trying to hang on for late drinks. Sammy mentioned stock-taking, but no one listened. They just grunted their disapproval before finally leaving. He locked the front doors behind them and returned to the bar to clean up. Max had remained in his office all night, making his telephone calls.

The club had been cleared, ready for the next day. Sammy knocked on the office door. 'Come in, Sammy. Something's come up. Is there any chance you can come in at six tonight? There's a special delivery and I'll be up north.'

'OK. Is it the usual delivery?'

'Kind of. You'll see when it arrives.'

'Do you want me to contact you when it's been delivered?'

'No. I'll call here at ten, just before you open up.'

'OK. I'll speak to you then. Bye.'

'See you later, Sammy. Thanks.'

Sammy left the club. He sensed there was something final in Max's eyes. He knew he was a marked man with an expiry date. A special delivery? He was not going to hang around to find out and disappear like Vicky. Fortunately, he had already made some plans.

He caught a taxi to his flat off the Holloway Road. Checking to make sure he was not being followed, he entered his flat through the front door, walked along the ground floor hallway and out into the back yard, where a small outhouse stood. Unlocking the old badly fitting door, he reached inside and picked up a leather holdall, hidden from view behind a number of cardboard boxes.

Although his plan had not been exactly finalised, at least he had prepared for this moment. His immediate disappearance. Unlike Vicky's, he had full control over his.

He left the back yard, now dressed in scruffy jeans, half-length reefer jacket and a floppy woollen multi-coloured Rasta hat. Nothing unusual. Most West Indian young men walking the streets at that time were similarly dressed. Inside his bag were clothes, a newly issued passport and several bank cards for overseas accounts, where he had placed most of his money.

Within three hours he had changed into a smart suit, walked through the departure lounge at Heathrow and boarded a British Airways plane bound for JFK airport, New York.

By the time Max finally got home, Sammy was mid-Atlantic, in first class.

22

Later that day, Max received a telephone call. 'He's not here.'

'Are you sure?'

'Yes, we've been waiting here since five. I'm telling you, he didn't show up.'

'Stay there until he does, I'll be there just after nine. Wait until I get there.'

Max hung up. Where was Sammy? Asking him about Vicky last night was a mistake; he must have suspected something. Could he have found out that she had been discharged from rehab? Of course. He had rung, purporting to be her doctor, so Sammy could have done the same. A wry smile spread across his face. 'Sammy, you're a clever bastard too.'

His telephone calls to Manchester had been met with a positive curiosity. The contact with Bill had created great interest with his boss. Max had no knowledge of the hierarchy running the Manchester mob, but he had been told to prepare for the main 'Godfather' to travel down in person to the club at midnight that night, along with the next consignment. They would be arriving in separate vehicles.

Meanwhile, he had Sammy to deal with. The decision to waste Sammy from his life was more difficult than with Vicky. He had grown to respect him and rely on his discretion and hard work. He would be difficult to replace. Reluctantly, he would have to work extra hours to keep the Caribbean running, even though it was only a front for the drug business. Yet there was a part of him that rejoiced in Sammy's desertion. He could avoid responsibility for killing him. For the time being anyway. But where had he gone? He knew too much. Sammy was a cunning operator and he would have planned his disappearance, covering his tracks well. The search for him would not be easy.

Two hours later, Max arrived at the Caribbean. He unlocked the front door, walked into his office and shouted, 'It's Max here.' A few seconds later two men dressed completely in black, including balaclavas, appeared in the doorway. Both were carrying Glock 19 pistols, pointing them at his head. 'Thank you for your time, gentleman, I assume the price remains the same, even though he's still at large?'

They lowered their firearms. The smaller of them spoke, in a harsh Ulster accent. 'Aye, but you'll be in credit a bit. Call again when you need us next.'

'I certainly will. Incidentally, has the last target been disposed of?'

'Yes, pumped full of shit and at the bottom of the Thames.'

'Excellent. Thank you. Good night.'

The men left the club. Their identities were a secret, even from those who hired their deadly services. Paradoxically, these assassins were well known in the criminal underworld, yet no one knew who exactly they were. Rumours suggested they were members of one of the paramilitary organisations from Northern Ireland. They were ruthless, reasonably inexpensive and, above all else, discreet.

Shortly afterwards, a knock on the front door announced the arrival of the next consignment and the boss from Manchester. Max opened the door to see the usual three men with their packages. He instructed them to put them by the cellar door and watched them leave without another word.

Seconds later, the enigmatic Bill entered. 'Are we alone?'

'Yes, just me.'

'Where's your partner, Sammy, tonight?'

'It's his night off.'

'Good. Stay there, I'm going to fetch the boss.'

Max felt apprehensive. Bill had an intimidating presence so what was his boss like? What would happen if they wanted to see Sammy? Perhaps they knew of DS Morley or Alex Gilmour?

His sense of impending doom suddenly vanished. A small gasp of astonishment escaped his lips and his eyes widened. Standing before him was a slender attractive woman in her mid-thirties, about five and half feet tall, with shoulder length blonde hair and piercing blue eyes. Dressed in an immaculate trouser suit, she wore expensive perfume, perfect makeup, with finely manicured nails. She was the most beautiful woman Max had ever seen. He failed to disguise his shock. He was completely captivated.

She slowly walked in and approached his desk. 'Good evening, Mr Campbell. My name is Gemma Baldwin. I'm very pleased to meet you.'

Max was utterly confused. His expectation of the 'boss' was the exact opposite of who he was now looking at. Instinctively he sprang to his feet. 'Thank you for coming to see me at such a short notice. Please take a seat. May I offer you some refreshments?'

'No, thank you. I wish to get straight down to business. I understand you may have a proposition for me that I might be interested in. And I would like to discuss this immediately, before I return to Manchester tonight.'

Max opened his desk drawer and slightly hesitated before placing in front of her the folder containing the images of Vicky and Jason Moore. He put the VHS video next to it.

He then explained in great detail the events leading up to the secret filming and the identity of Jason Moore, especially his current role in the Department for Trade and Industry Ministry. He conceded his initial motive for filming him in such a compromising situation was to chance his arm with a simple Badger Game, hoping to receive a respectable amount of money for the damaging material, guaranteeing his discretion and silence. However, since he had discussed this with a third party, who freely circulated in the political corridors of Westminster, he was come to appreciate these images had the potential for a far more lucrative reward. He told Gemma about Jason Moore's role in his department and of the opportunity of obtaining a special import permit that bypassed border controls into the UK from anywhere in the world, even Pakistan.

After he had explained the significance and potential opportunity of such a permit, he sat back and allowed her to digest the details in silence. She looked at Max, followed by another glance at the photographs. 'Are these images all on this video?'

'Yes, but much better. The film is dynamite; it clearly shows Jason Moore's disfigurement around his neck. There can be no doubt as to his identity.'

'Who's the girl?'

'She's called Vicky. A small-time hooker from Soho. She agreed to perform the show at a price. She's wasn't cheap but I think you'll agree she earnt every penny. Apparently, she's gone abroad to Spain for a while. Malaga, I think.'

'Did she know who the guy was?'

'No, just a punter. A wealthy businessman working in the City.'

'And who's the contact you have in Westminster?'

'That's where it gets a little awkward. He has specifically asked for his identity to remain secret. Of course, if you threatened me with fear for my life, I would have to tell you straight away.' Max looked at Bill standing in the corner. He liked that and smiled.

'No, there's no need at this stage. I respect discretion and honesty. But remember, Mr Campbell, behind this lipstick lies a predator. I wouldn't think twice about unleashing my boys on anyone who crosses my path. You do understand that?'

'I do, clearly.'

'Good. I'll take these pictures and video with me and think about your proposal. I must be honest, this is not my usual line of business but I can see there is potential for me to increase my hold on the home market. I can assure you, I will not use these myself, they belong to you, and if I decline to go ahead with this, Bill here will personally return them. Now, what are your fees, Mr Campbell?'

'If my information is correct, a special permit of this nature would allow up to a thirty-two-foot container to enter the UK unimpeded. I would suggest that with the appropriate disguised packaging and documentation, you would have the opportunity of importing many tons of high-grade heroin from Pakistan, with a present street value of tens of millions of pounds.'

'Yes, Mr Campbell, I've already thought of that. How much are you wanting?'

'If I can arrange this permit, may I suggest half a million pounds would be suitable?'

'It could be. But I need a few days to explore the feasibility of buying such large quantities of the merchandise. If you think the girl in this film was expensive, I can assure you I will have to invest millions. I'll be sending two of my boys to Pakistan tomorrow. I shall wait until I hear from them. Let's say in three days, at this time. I'll ring you here.'

'I understand, Miss Baldwin.'

'It's Mrs Baldwin. I'm a widow. My husband died unexpectedly last year.'

Max looked into her cold blue eyes and inwardly shuddered. Clearly, she was not grieving for him. Suddenly, his betrayal and treatment of Vicky became acutely poignant. She stood and extended her hand towards Max. He jumped to his feet and gently shook it. 'Thank you for coming to see me, Mrs Baldwin.'

She looked away without saying a word but as she reached the doorway, she half turned and glanced back towards him. He smiled, but her face remained expressionless, then she disappeared towards the front door. He followed her and Bill, and he saw two men of giant stature open the rear doors to a large Mercedes saloon. Max knew they were both carrying firearms.

Sitting inside, she was completely hidden by the tinted windows as the large car quietly accelerated away, with only the sound of the large tyres on the gritty road surface. Max gestured with an awkward wave, unnoticed by the occupants.

He sighed loudly and re-entered the club. It had been a busy and eventful day. He had lost a partner, yet perhaps gained two more: Alex Gilmour and the beautiful Mrs Gemma Baldwin. Both shrewd, cunning and self-assured. But she was frightening and dangerous. He had the chance to make more money than he could ever have imagined. But would he live to reap the benefits? Gradually, he began to recognise the significance of why Sammy had not just deserted him, but also this way of life. He had, in effect, taken early retirement. He was never coming back. Was he?

23

The Caribbean remained closed that night. Max placed a notice on the front door.

Closed until further notice. Undergoing emergency electrical improvements. Sorry for any inconvenience.

He decided to take a couple of days off. His life had become a whirlwind of change and he needed time to organise and plan his future, try and find a reliable replacement for Sammy. He called around to Sammy's flat, off the Holloway Road, and discovered his landlord had no knowledge of him disappearing. The rent had been paid, three months in advance, but after Max had pressed a hundred pounds into his hand, the landlord allowed him to go inside and have a look around. Everything was just as if he was returning at any time. His wardrobe was full of his clothes, food in the fridge, even his toothbrush and toiletries remained untouched in the bathroom. Max concluded Sammy had left in a hurry.

Two days later, he returned to the Caribbean to receive another consignment from the north. The usual three couriers placed the packages outside the cellar door and left, in silence. He stored the packages in the stock room and returned to his office, intending to return home. His telephone rang. 'Caribbean.'

'Max?'

'Yes, who's this?'

'Max, it's Alex. Can I come and see you? I've got some more

business to discuss that would require your expertise. Believe me, it would be of financial interest to you.'

'Sure. What time?'

'I'll grab a cab. Be there in twenty minutes.'

'OK. See you then.'

Within twenty-five minutes the men were facing each other over Max's desk.

'Max, I've heard through the grapevine that a prominent High Court Circuit judge has been paying for sex with a girl from Islington. According to our friend Sergeant Morley, she's a convicted prostitute called Julie Brecon. Do you know her?'

'Julie Brecon? No, I don't think so.'

'Never mind. It appears she only operates in the highest of circles, usually from classy hotels in Mayfair. If we can tempt her into performing another honey trap like you arranged before with our MP, but this time with the judge, we may have an opportunity of making a lot of money. What do you say?'

'Sure. I need to find out where this girl is.'

'No problem there. I've got all her details here, recent photographs and where she lives, compliments of Sergeant Morley.'

'Does she have a pimp? If so I need to buy him off.'

'No need for that either, she now operates alone. The guy she did pay to look after her when she was working was locked up yesterday by Sergeant Morley's team for "living off her immoral earnings". Apparently, he's already on a bender[5] from a previous conviction. He's out of the picture for years now. She'll be needing someone to look after her. According to our friendly Vice Squad, she hangs around in the Majestic Hotel about six in the evening, hoping to attract businessmen staying there overnight. She probably gets a free dinner too. As you can see from the photos, she's a real looker, intelligent too, and above all else, looks after herself. She's clean from drugs and doesn't mix with the other toms.[6] Will you meet up with her tomorrow and work your charm on her?'

Max looked at her photograph and was pleasantly surprised. 'OK, no problem. Who's the judge?'

---

[5] Suspended prison sentence.

[6] Prostitutes.

'His name is Gordon Black. He's a widower who dispenses justice at the Crown Courts in the Greater London area. According to my contacts, he's well known in his field, yet a secretive and private man in his personal life. Evidence of any relationship with a prostitute would be scandalous and ruin his illustrious career. Unless, of course, he wanted to buy my story. Do you know how much money these buggers earn from the public purse? Over eighty thousand pounds a year, the dirty old man. Still, there's no accounting for stupidity, eh, Max?'

'Do you think she'd be willing to talk to me about her punters?'

'To be honest, I don't know, Max. You'll have a better idea when you see her tomorrow.'

'Yes, you're right. Anyway, to change the subject, I've got something else to tell you. I had a visit from a Mrs Gemma Baldwin from Manchester. She's the real boss lady up there and we discussed your idea about the special import permit. She's the original she-devil, looks absolutely stunning but dangerous as a rattle snake. You wouldn't want to mess with her. Her boys are real dangerous bastards, they'd kill you just for the fun of it. But she's interested in our proposal and is sending two of her thugs over to Pakistan to enquire into how much heroin there is available for a one-off massive shipment. If the signs are promising, she'll agree to our terms of five hundred thousand pounds once she has the permit in her hands.'

'Bloody hell, Max. That could change everything. Your fifty thousand has potentially become two hundred and fifty thousand, once we've split the half million. Of course, obtaining the permit is going to be a bit tricky. But think of the pay-out! We must lean heavily on Jason Moore for him to cooperate.'

'Yes, that's exactly what I thought. Incidentally, she's not interested in who you are, but you might want to make some enquiries into her background. Could be useful.'

'You're right, I'll do that later. Meanwhile, may I suggest you concentrate on your meeting with Miss Brecon tomorrow night. Perhaps I can ring you after, to see how you went on?'

'Sure.'

24

At six o'clock the following evening, Max strolled into the lobby of the Majestic Hotel, Mayfair, wearing his best suit, shirt and tie. He entered the main bar and ordered a rum and coke. He was the epitome of a suave gentleman conducting business in the capital. A picture of sartorial elegance.

Within five minutes a woman walked in and sat at a table near the front window, where she was shortly joined by a waiter. She looked about the room and saw four other men drinking at a nearby table. They were obviously too interested in sharing a joke and drinking freely on their companies' expense accounts to notice her. Her eyes continued around the bar until they rested on Max. He was reading a newspaper but sensed her stare and casually looked up. They looked at each other before she smiled. He returned her smile and he gently nodded his head in acknowledgement.

She was Julie Brecon, a white woman in her early twenties, slim built with long blonde hair sweeping over her shoulders. She was wearing a cream jacket with a navy-blue skirt and high heels. She looked up again, then modestly looked away. That was his cue.

Max stood and walked over to her. 'Please excuse the intrusion, but I wondered if you would join me in drinking some champagne? You see, I've closed on an important deal this afternoon and I want to celebrate my good fortune. But not on my own. Of course, if you are busy or meeting someone else, please forgive me.'

He knew instantly she was keen. She smiled again. 'It would be my pleasure in sharing your good fortune. No, I'm not meeting anyone else. I'm here on business, like you.'

Max knew exactly what her business was. So far, so good. The waiter returned and he ordered a bottle of their best champagne. He needed to impress. Once they finished the champagne, she agreed to accompany him to the restaurant, for dinner. Over the meal Max explained he was a single man, living near the Thames, and owned a night club. And that day he had successfully closed a deal to buy a club in Brighton next year. She was completely taken in by his charm and began to relish mixing business with pleasure. After settling the bill, he then played his best card. 'Julie, I'm sorry to have kept you talking all this time but it's been a long time since I've spent such a lovely evening with someone like you. You must be tired. If you wish, I'll leave you in peace but I would really like to see you again.'

Her answer was both swift and predictable. She stood and offered him her hand and led him towards the hotel lift. Max pretended to look puzzled but she placed her finger gently on her lips and whispered, 'Follow me.'

Once inside the room that she regularly rented, Julie closed the door behind them and began to remove his jacket. She kissed him lightly on his cheek before saying, 'Honey, although I've had a fantastic night too, you must realise I'm a working girl who has to pay the bills. You do understand, don't you?'

Max pretended to be surprised, sighed and asked, 'How much will it be, Julie?'

'Two hundred pounds for the night, honey.'

He held her hands. 'What about if I give you five hundred, how long would you stay for that?'

'Hell, Max, all night, including breakfast.'

'Good. Leave my jacket on, I'll take you to my place.'

She drew back. Going somewhere unknown with an unfamiliar man was a definite no-no. It made no difference how tempting the money was, this presented an unnecessary risk. 'I'm sorry, Max, but you must realise I can't do that on our first meeting. Whilst I'm here, I feel safe. The hotel duty manager knows why I'm here because I pay him for my security. I don't wish to offend you, but I don't know you. You could be a serial killer for all I know.'

The irony was not wasted on his cynical sense of humour. He moved forward, whispering, 'Julie. You're absolutely right. Please forgive me. I would love to spend some time here with you, and perhaps, when you get to know me better, you'll come and visit my place then. Instead, please take this as a token of my impatience.'

Max handed Julie five hundred pounds and dropped his jacket onto the carpet. She smiled again and placed her arms around his neck 'Come here, my rich handsome black man.'

This last remark sent a bolt through his spine. He wanted to kill her there and then, yet realised she was an important commodity, similar to the drugs in his cellar; an opportunity to make a great deal of money. He closed his eyes, murmuring to himself, not about any sexual gratification, but the manner she was going to pay. Her flippant remark would come to cost her significantly more than the five hundred pounds she had now stuffed firmly inside her expensive designer leather handbag.

25

During the following weeks, Max saw Julie as much as he could. Re-opening and running the club without Sammy was difficult. He had been unable to recruit anyone suitable and the deliveries and collections were now almost daily. With little free time to himself, keeping everything going was manic. However, he was virtually printing his own money.

Occasionally, he hesitated in his pursuit of Julie. This venture with her and the judge was an opportunity to make a relatively small amount of money compared to the fortune he was accumulating every week. Yet it was too irresistible; it was the Badger Game and perversely, he enjoyed the power he held of his victims.

Meanwhile, Bill had arrived with a package and a message from his boss. He attempted to recite her reply verbatim: 'I'm happy to progress with your proposal to the next stage. Inform me when the permit has been issued. I require twenty-eight days to organise the shipment. Please advise me by the end of each month of your progress.'

That same night, after the club closed, he collapsed into his office chair. The chaos of his life would be too stressful for many, but he relished it. Amongst this turbulence, he saw Julie three to four times a week. He had taken her to the Caribbean and introduced her to the staff. She enjoyed listening and dancing to the loud reggae music.

*

A little over a month later, she agreed to return with him to his house. As he predicted, she was impressed further with his house and valuable contents. His motive for establishing a relationship in which she could trust him remained undiminished. Their conversations were lengthy and varied. But that night, after dinner, she was different, openly confiding in him about her regular clients.

Max made his move. 'Julie, I want you to know that I'm very fond of you and although I realise you value your independence very much, I'm hoping that maybe we might have some kind of a future together.'

'I feel the same way too, Max, but I need a little more time. If you want me to move in with you, I'd love to, but not just now. For the time being, I've got my clients and I want to save enough money to fall back on, just in case. I've been penniless once; it'll never happen to me again. Please understand.'

'Of course I do. You know I'll never ask about your customers. Only this. How many do you have?'

'Three, that's all.'

'Are they proper gentlemen? Do they treat you well?'

'Of course. Two of them are married businessmen who I see occasionally. However, my favourite is called Gordon. He's really quite adorable, an old man and only wants me to lie in bed with him. There's hardly any physical contact and definitely no sex. He's a proper gentleman and pays me well. He talks about his wife who died many years ago. Apparently, I remind him of her when she was young. I don't know much else about him.'

Max stayed expressionless, nodding his head slightly. But inside he was jumping for joy. Jackpot. He asked casually, 'How often do you see Gordon?'

'Every Thursday evening at seven. We always have dinner then go to his room where I stay for a couple of hours. To be honest, I just cuddle him and gently stroke his shoulders before he falls asleep and then I leave. He always pays before we go to the room. It's all very civilised. I'm lucky to have a client like him; it's easy money without any hassle or danger.'

'Sounds like the perfect business arrangement.'

'Yes. I believe it is.'

'Have you ever been to his place?'

'Hell, no. I don't know anything about him. He might not be even called Gordon. But I've been seeing him at the Majestic on Thursday nights for over twelve months now. That's where you met me.

Remember?'

'Yes, of course.'

'After dinner we go to his room. It's always the same one. He rings me when he's out of town working. So, you see, it's a perfect arrangement.'

'Are you seeing him this Thursday?'

'Oh yes. I always make sure I don't eat during the day. As you know from when we first met, the food is delicious.'

Max smiled. 'It certainly is. Hope I can see you at the weekend?'

'Of course, I'll come down to the Caribbean and meet you after work.'

'Good idea.'

Later, he drove Julie home. She lived in a spacious yet modestly furnished first-floor flat above a ladies' hairdressing salon, close to the main shopping area of Islington. She saved most of her earnings, never bringing her work home, and her business and private life were completely separate.

Once Max had left, she considered his earlier comments but decided not to move too quickly. She had been devastated when deserted by the man she had truly loved three years ago and vowed it would never happen to her again. She liked Max, but he was not the man she wanted to eventually settle down with. But for the time being he was fun to be around. Her bank balance was becoming increasingly healthy and she calculated another six months would be sufficient time for her to retire and move back to Harlow and buy a small fashionable women's dress shop. She would reinvent herself as young and ambitious entrepreneur.

*

Meanwhile, as Max was driving home, he was also making plans. Julie had told him her next appointment with Gordon was in three days' time. There was much to prepare.

The following day, he contacted the Majestic Hotel and spoke with the receptionist. After convincing her that a good friend of his called Gordon Black had recommended a particular room he used, she reserved the same room for two days: the days prior to and following his visit. It was room 205 on the second floor.

Several hours later he rang the hotel again and spoke to another receptionist. He booked another room on the same floor as close to 205 as possible, on the same day Gordon and Julie would be together. From this room, he would be able to record events unfolding nearby.

*

Once again, he arranged to hire the snooping equipment. As a repeat customer, it was immediately delivered to the club. This time the latest version of improved cameras came inside the custom-made suitcases. The lens zooms had more range and was considerably smaller than those he had previously used to film Vicky; each fitted with poor lighting condition enhancers, similar to night infra-red, just in case any artificial lights were turned off. Six microphones, no larger than a match head, were also attached. All controlled remotely. The miniature cameras, now the size of a thumbnail, were the state of the art in the surveillance industry. Only the military and security services had access to such sophisticated equipment. But it did not come cheap. Max fully understood that concealment from the judge, Julie and the hotel staff was paramount. If these were discovered, all his efforts at wooing Julie and the hundreds of pounds he'd spent would be wasted. Not including the phenomenal cost of the equipment.

He immediately dismissed the doubt. It would work. It must work.

26

Max booked into the Majestic Hotel, Room 205, the following
Wednesday night, using the name Sammy Clarke. This amused him as
he approached the lift with his two custom-made leather suitcases.
Within two hours he had concealed tiny cameras inside the central
light shade, on a heavy velvet curtain pelmet, adjacent to the bed, and
behind an air conditioning grille directly opposite the headboard.
Everything had been securely attached with special plastic tape and
programmed to remain on standby mode. He tested and re-tested the
standby switches and examined the clarity of the recorded images.
Once he was satisfied, he ruffled the bed and collected his empty
suitcases, returned to the reception desk and explained there had
been an emergency, necessitating his return home. He would,
however, be returning for his second night's stay in two days' time.
He settled the bill and left soon afterwards.

*

Shortly before six the next night, he again booked into the
Majestic using the name Leo Downing. He had changed his
appearance. Now casually dressed and sporting thick-rimmed tinted
spectacles, he carried his two suitcases containing the recording
equipment. He took the lift to the second floor and walked past
room 205 without a glance, continuing to the door showing 209, just
two rooms away. He opened the door and went in, placing the cases
on the bed.

Within ten minutes he had set up the main receiver and recorder.
Nervously, he tested the cameras; they immediately switched from
standby to filming mode. He checked their mobility, zoom and

clarity. Perfect. He opened the door to the corridor, leaving it slightly ajar, enough to hear anyone approaching from the stairwell or lift. He sat down on the floor with his back to the wall, peering through the gap of the open door. Glancing occasionally at his watch, he waited in silence. The time passed slowly.

As it approached 8 p.m. he stretched, rubbing his lower back and moving his legs. Then he heard a woman's voice. 'Come on, Gordon. Let's have you to bed. You need a good night's sleep.' It was the unmistakable voice of Julie. He looked through the gap and saw her approaching room 205, with a portly grey-haired man in his sixties following in a sheepish manner. This was His Honour, Judge Gordon Black.

As Julie opened the door to room 205, Max simultaneously closed his, switching the lights on and rushing over to the camera activation button. He pressed it firmly down and the monitors immediately sprang into life. The initial flickering images soon gave way to well-defined clarity. The microphones immediately began to record the sound. He double-checked. Both images and audio were of excellent quality.

During the following fifty-five minutes Max recorded the couple undressing and lying on top of the bed, naked. Just as she had described to him, Julie caressed the old man before he fell fast asleep. Max's concern with poor lighting in the room were unfounded. They had kept the bedside lamps on all the time. Cynically, he whispered, 'How thoughtful, Julie.'

Once the judge had fallen asleep, Julie slipped off the bed and dressed. As she faced one of the cameras she stopped and appeared to look directly into Max's eyes. He stared back and felt a chill running down his back. She was looking straight inside him. Had she discovered him snooping? They both seemed to be locked into each other's gaze, before she moved away to collect her top and skirt from the bed. As she stretched her arms to put on her blouse, Max saw something he had never noticed before. A small tattoo of a bird above her left breast. It was a swallow. How had she missed that?

She quickly finished dressing and left the room. Max walked over to his door and placed an ear to it. He heard her walking back along the corridor towards the lift, then returned to the monitors and connected them individually to the master copier. He shut down all the cameras and microphones and began to edit the recorded pictures.

By midnight, he had completed the job. Sufficient video film and over fifty photographs of Gordon Black lying in the arms of a naked young woman. Young enough to be his granddaughter. Max knew he held the jackpot. The judge would give generously to avoid any scandal on the strength of these pictures. Another Badger Game victim had inadvertently fallen into his sordid world.

His next move was dealing with Julie. Unknown to her, two strangers would enter her life very soon. As with Vicky, she was worth far more dead than alive.

27

Max arranged the meeting at the Caribbean for midday. Only Alex Gilmour was invited.

Max spoke first. 'Alex, we've much to discuss. First, I've had the thumbs up from the "Manchurian she-devil". She wants us to start working on Jason Moore, with weekly updates on our progress. She needs twenty-eight days' notice to get things sorted out, once the permit is issued. Secondly, I've got another catch. Judge Gordon Black. Another video, together with a handful of very compromising pictures with our lovely Julie. I'll show them to you in a minute, but I tell you, they're bloody good. What I'm going to do is send both men copies of their exploits and nothing else. It's the classic first rule of the Badger Game. About a week later, they'll receive a typewritten letter explaining that their activities will not be published or exposed whatsoever provided they show some cooperation. Once they have had time to reflect on this, you will contact them and ask them if these images are simply rumours. As a journalist, you listen to much gossip.'

Alex sat forward. 'Max, you're a right clever mean bastard and I love it. Once you've got the first two stages in place, I'll take over. It's imperative you and I are never connected with each other. I can show my face in public because they know my job is sniffing out the improprieties of human nature. Once they realise rumours are beginning to fester, I expect they will want to quash them immediately and pay up.'

'I agree. I'll send the pictures to both of them tomorrow.'

'Do you know where to send them?'

'Not too sure. Have you any ideas?'

'Yes. Send Jason Moore's to his constituency office in Gloucester and Gordon Black's to the Lord Chancellor's Office in Whitehall. Obviously marked "Personal and confidential" in an official Post Office envelope. Remember, since the Northern Ireland problems started, some mail is intercepted. We can't afford to have them opened by someone else.'

'You're right. Thanks.'

Both men nodded. They clearly understood their partnership was at a point of no return; their actions would either reap huge financial rewards, irrespective of the catastrophic impact they would have on these two men, or they would bring the whole Establishment falling down on their heads.

Alex, completely unaware of the fate already bestowed on Vicky Thompson or awaiting Julie Brecon, was playing two hands: one with his old friend George Morley, the other with his new one; Max Campbell. But could it last?

28

Within the week, Max had posted the uncompromising images to both Judge Gordon Black and Jason Moore. Their respective packages included photographs only. No correspondence or note indicating where they had originated from. It was a game of psychology. Making the victim aware of their indiscretions was the first stage.

Gordon Black simply made the decision to destroy the evidence and take his own life.

Following the police investigation and the subsequent inquest, a sense of utter bewilderment into why Justice Black's killed himself was widely reported in the national press. But Alex, unaware the photographs had all but been destroyed, became increasingly anxious he might be connected with his death.

He now made the decision to have no contact with Max, withdrawing any interest in their future involvement. Although the full offence of blackmail had not been committed, due to the absence of unlawful demands accompanying the photographs, there were elements of passive menacing present. He decided to keep his counsel and temporarily suspended all his nefarious activities with Max and George.

Jason Moore, however, took the more predictable route. He waited until he received his second package several weeks later from Max. This contained new images and a typed note simply stating, 'There are other photographs and a video too.' There were no threats or demands, just a statement indicating additional material existed. This was the second stage.

*

A month later, Alex received a call at home from Max. 'Alex, I need to meet you to discuss some outstanding business. Perhaps we can meet in a bar called Ben's opposite Borough Market, tomorrow at noon.'

'I'm not sure that's a good idea, bearing in mind what happened to our first intended customer.'

'I know. That was unfortunate. But our second looks more promising.'

'OK. But I'm not happy, Max. I'm walking away if this starts getting out of hand. I didn't expect the material would cause the judge to act like he did.'

'Yes, it proves how powerful these images are. There's no hiding away from them.'

'Exactly. I'm still a bit concerned about all this. I don't want it to happen again.'

'It won't. Let's talk before you make your decision. Remember, this could be the business opportunity of a lifetime. I'll see you tomorrow.'

Alex replaced the receiver and stared out of the window. Although he would agree in principle to carry on, he decided the next time he met with Max he would take some precautions. He would wear a wire beneath his shirt and listen to what Max had to say before committing himself further, ensuring he made no incriminating remarks himself.

*

The following day, shortly after noon, both men sat in a small cubicle, tucked away out of sight in Ben's bar. With seating for only four, it was private and hidden from the main bar area, where they ordered coffee.

Max asked, 'How are things with you, Alex. Not seen you for a couple of weeks?'

'I'm fine, Max. Let's get straight down to it. What have you got to say?'

'Our friend from the big house by the river has received the first two packages. I think perhaps it's time you make some of your own enquiries and challenge him about some whispers you've heard about his liaisons with a young hooker. He'll obviously deny it, but once he believes the story can be exposed, then I'll step in and tell him what I want. That's all. You'll have no other involvement until he agrees to the terms. Then you'll be the go-between, as we've discussed. Think about it, Alex. A quarter of a million pounds for brokering a deal, without any risk.'

Alex thought carefully about what he was going to say. The wire was recording every word. 'I'll speak to this person. But if he flatly refuses to admit this and intends to report the matter to the authorities, then I won't be able to stop him.'

Max scrutinised Alex's reply and body language. He was hiding something. Speaking in a different manner, not confirming their previous agreement; he was behaving differently. Suddenly he realised. The bastard was wired, and the conversation was being recorded. He reached into his inside jacket pocket, took out his pen and wrote on a drinks coaster, handing it to Alex. 'Are you wired?'

Alex read the question and realised he had to make a quick judgement. He slowly opened a button on his shirt to reveal the small microphone. Max leant forward and tore it away, throwing it onto the table.

Looking at him, Alex whimpered, 'I can't take any chances, Max. That judge topped himself because of what we are trying to do. How do I know you're not turning Queen's Evidence and trying to trap me into some admission?'

'Bloody hell, Alex. Don't you think I'm in this far more deeper than you? With my involvement with the Manchester mob, what I'm doing at the Caribbean and this with you. Hell, if I get locked up I'm going down for life. And when I'm inside they'll finish me off. No, I want to carry this matter through and get a permit off this man, Jason Moore. Once we've got that and our money from the pretty Gemma Baldwin, I'm out of here for ever.'

'I'm sorry, Max. I'm just concerned with it all. You're right, we must trust each other. Otherwise we're doomed. It won't happen again.'

Max stared at Alex, wanting to seriously hurt him but instead he regained his composure. 'OK. I know you're frightened but if you do anything like this again, I'll kill you. You know I will, don't you?'

Shaking with fear, Alex replied, 'I do.'

'Right. Let's start again. Will you go and speak to Jason Moore and ask him about these rumours?'

'Yes, of course.'

'Good. Now we're partners and friends again. Let's stick to the script. Let me know when you have spoken to him. Then I'll implement the final stage. Agreed?'

'Agreed.'

They stood to leave, but for a few moments stopped and looked at each other. Alex shook his hand, 'Sorry, Max. I just don't have your courage, I'll be more trusting from now on. And don't worry, I'll arrange to meet Jason Moore and see how he reacts. Give me a couple of days. Shall I ring you at the club next Friday night?'

'Yes. Let's just forget what's happened here today and stick to the original plan. I'll look forward to hearing from you.'

They walked out of the bar and left in different directions, both reflecting on their meeting.

During his journey home, Alex remained unsure whether Max had really forgiven his behaviour but decided nevertheless to chronicle details of his involvement with Max, including the activities with Gemma Baldwin, Jason Moore and Judge Gordon Black. The moment he arrived home he immediately typed a five-page document containing these details which he signed and sealed. The following day he delivered it to his solicitor, with strict instructions written on the envelope: 'Only to be opened on my death or unexplained disappearance.'

Max took a different approach. He was furious with Alex's intention to deceive him and he would suffer the consequences. His trust had been betrayed again: first Sammy, now Alex. Sammy had had the good grace to leave without trace. By contrast, Alex stood to make a quarter of a million pounds for simply setting up a meeting with Jason Moore and discussing the terms of the special importation permit. No, he was going to dramatically trim down his contribution to zero. For him, a watery or hidden grave would be his reward and destiny.

29

Two days after the meeting, a black cab stopped outside a large building close to the Foreign and Commonwealth Office in Whitehall. A smartly dressed man in a pinstripe suit paid the driver, opened the rear door, unfurled a black umbrella and dashed through the pouring rain towards the imposing front porch. As he reached its shelter, another man stepped forward. 'Jason Moore, may I have a word please?'

Moore stopped and looked at him. 'Who are you?'

'My name is Alex Gilmour, I'm an investigative journalist. May I speak to you in private? It is important, Mr Moore.'

'What about?'

'It's rather delicate. I don't want to discuss it here. Can we go somewhere less public?'

'Not until you tell me what it's about.'

'Mr Moore, have you been sleeping with a young woman called Vicky Thompson?'

'What the hell are you talking about? Out of my way before I call the police.'

Alex reached into his coat pocket and held out a photograph of Moore with Vicky. 'That's what I'm talking about.'

He stared at the picture. He had seen it so many times before, it was seared into his mind. Since receiving the first package three weeks ago, he had not slept properly. The images of his affair with Vicky had now become a regular nightmare. The blood drained from his face. He was like a wounded animal, waiting for the fatal blow to put him out of his misery.

He looked at Alex. 'Are you blackmailing me?'

'Hell, no. If you want to report this matter to the police, go ahead. I'm here to tell you that someone has evidence to suggest you have had a sexual relationship with a woman called Vicky Thompson, a prostitute and heroin addict. Apparently, they don't want any money, just a favour.'

'What favour?'

'I can't discuss it here. Let's go somewhere private so we can try and sort this out. Just remember, I think you are the victim here. I'm just the go-between.'

'Come with me.'

Jason entered the building through the swing doors, followed by Alex. The large hallway was a grand example of late Victorian Gothic design. Marble columns soared up to the high ceiling. A large stained-glass roof lantern allowed some sunlight to shine through. Jason walked directly towards a room next to the security reception area. On the door was an 'Interview Room' sign. He spoke to the woman behind the counter. 'Doris, I'm just going to speak to this gentleman for a few minutes. No need to book him in. He won't be going upstairs.'

'Very well, Mr Moore.'

They entered the austere windowless room, as the central florescent light tube flickered into life. As they sat facing each other, Jason said, 'Now tell me exactly what is this all about.'

'OK, Mr Moore. As I said, I'm an investigative journalist and I've spent many years looking into the conduct and behaviour of people who are powerful and/or famous. I'm not particularly proud of what I do but these stories sell very well to the tabloids.'

'Sounds like a parasite, living off the weaknesses of others unable to defend themselves.'

'Yes. I cannot disagree with you. However, I have been approached by an anonymous source that has divulged to me evidence of your recent affair with this young woman. I appreciate you may have been completely unaware she was a prostitute, but the fact remains, such a relationship when you're in high public office is considered inappropriate by the Establishment and the public. Apparently, there are some terms and conditions, and if you agreed, that would guarantee to make this affair go away permanently.'

'Now this is blackmail. These are demands with menaces.'

'You're right. It is blackmail. But perhaps you want to hear what they want before you consider the ramifications of such a scandal?'

Jason sat back in his chair and thought of the consequences of his stupid indiscretion. Could his political career survive a tabloid onslaught? The mere suspicion of such behaviour was serious, but there were damaging photographs, clearly showing the scars on his neck and shoulders. There was no mistake; it was him. He would be ruined, losing his seat in Gloucester, no prospect of returning to the financial sector, where he had originally qualified. He had worked all his political life, spanning over twenty years, to accomplish his position in the Ministry. His next promotion would place him inside the Government Cabinet itself. Ambition was all encompassing. Reluctantly he asked, 'What are these terms and conditions?'

30

Back to the present

John Evans awoke early. The previous night's visit from Yvonne had left him in a quandary; should he agree to, or decline her invitation to help with the investigation? He finally asked Charlie for her opinion. As usual, she poignantly pointed out to him that although he enjoyed his role as an investigative journalist, he had never been happier than when he worked with Phil and Yvonne investigating her mother's death of all those years ago. Not only was it another opportunity to work with his old friends again but the case had all the ingredients that appealed to him, criminal corruptive practices of people in public office. A perfect combination. Finally, she had concluded, 'After all, you're only being contracted to gather available intelligence. How dangerous could that be?

So, with some reservations, he agreed to help Yvonne. He contacted the sponsors of the two investigations he had previously committed to undertake and was pleasantly surprised to find they were sympathetic in allowing him three month's grace. He considered that would be sufficient time to progress adequately with Yvonne's investigation.

At noon he contacted Yvonne, informing her of his decision.

'Fantastic, John. Can you come down to my office, it's a short walk from the main Home Office building? I need to give you all the main files we have and, of course, to sign the Official Secrets Act forms.'

*

Two hours later John walked into a modern building called Glebe House. The frontage was all glass. The main entrance had an atmosphere like an art gallery, with a large display of original paintings. The central feature consisted of five pictures creating one image. An oak tree in a sunset. Following Yvonne's instructions, he caught the lift to the third floor and knocked on the door simply marked 3:5. Immediately the door swung open. 'Come in, John, and sit down. Coffee?'

'No thanks.'

'OK. Here's the file for you to take away. Obviously, I have copies too. Inside you will see everything we talked about last night. Here are the forms you must sign and the terms of the contract. I have your temporary police warrant card and authority signed by the Deputy Commissioner, allowing you full access to all police premises other than custody suites, private offices and other sensitive areas. In theory, you're a Special Constable with an administrative rank of Inspector. In addition, you have copies of the personal files of all the officers in the King's Cross Vice Squad. If you require any others, you must contact me. That's about it. Anything I might have missed out?'

'Not that I can think of. If I do, I'll let you know.'

'Good. Would you let me know on a weekly basis of your progress? It's only because the Deputy will be asking me.'

'Sure, I'll ring you as soon as I get a lead or in any case next week.'

'OK, John. Before we end, I must tell you something that must never be repeated again to anyone. As you know, all the evidence you uncover and seize must be legally binding. Nothing made under duress, tricked or unlawfully taken. We, the police, and that includes yourself, must be prepared to withstand cross-examination at Crown Court. However, if you were to employ the services of someone I'm unaware of, then I could swear an oath I had no knowledge of how such evidence was obtained. So far as I'm concerned, it was anonymously given by a member of the public. Do you understand what I'm saying?'

'I certainly do. You will have no idea who might be assisting us in this inquiry.'

'I rather think I can guess who. But you mustn't tell me until this is all over. To accommodate this additional cost, you must set up a separate account titled 'intelligence gathering expenses'. Because this is public money, all expenditures must always be accounted for. OK?'

'I fully understand where you're coming from. We're going to be dealing with people who know the rules as well as we do. Enough said.'

Yvonne simply nodded and gave him a wink. That was her sign of approval. John sensed the meeting was now over. After all, Yvonne was a high-ranking police officer whose workload was enormous. 'OK, Yvonne, I've got enough to start with.'

'Great. If it's urgent and you can't get me here, try me at home.'

'Will do.'

They stood together and smiled. As he left, she said, 'Welcome back on board, Inspector Evans.'

*

John left the building and returned home. He needed to make a call.

'Hello,' came the reply.

'Is that the best investigator that ever lived?'

'Bloody right it is. Hell, it's good to hear from you, John. What are you doing?'

'Well, that's a very good question. More to the point, what are you doing for the next few months?'

'I was going to see my daughter and the grandkids in France but if you are going to tempt me with a bit more excitement, I can go later.'

'I might be able to do that. What's more, there's some money in it too. Not too much of course.'

'We need to meet up. Are you still living in North London?'

'Yes, same place. Come and see us tomorrow if you can. Charlie will be thrilled at seeing you again. Just watch your language.'

'Bugger off. I'll be there at two in the afternoon.'

John hung up. His thoughts went back to eight years ago when he, along with Phil, and Yvonne, had assisted him in uncovering a web of corruption amongst senior police officers. Like himself, Phil had been wrongly suspended from duty and threatened with imprisonment unless he bore false witness against John. But his forthright and unwavering character had endured.

Since retiring from the Force, Phil had successfully run his own private investigation and surveillance company. Even as a serving police officer he was not a conventional investigator, often bending the rules to establish the truth. Now, free from the shackles of legal accountability, his methods had become even more questionable, especially trespassing. As a private citizen, he worked in the shadows; any Magistrate's search warrant was unnecessary. Yet somehow, he always managed to get results. John suspected he would require Phil to go places where he was be unable to explore.

He looked forward to seeing him again the next day, but meanwhile, he had to carefully examine all the documents in the police folder and prepare a list of things to do.

His first query was ex-DC Barry Taylor, apparently no longer living at his last known address. John wanted to establish why he had resigned from the Force so abruptly. Yvonne had included his personal details in the main file. According to an entry several years previously, he had applied for compassionate leave to attend his thirteen-year old niece's funeral. She had been the victim of a road traffic accident when crossing the road near to her school. There was an address of Taylor's sister, 87 Claremont View, Highbury, North London. Perhaps she was the girl's mother and may know of her brother's whereabouts.

He then turned his attention to DS George Morley's file and discovered he had been a serving police officer with the Met for over twenty-seven years, promoted to Sergeant after only twelve. Although qualified on paper for promotion to the next rank, clearly something had occurred, preventing him from accomplishing the next rank. His personal record revealed he had been in charge of the King's Cross Vice Squad for five years, achieving high detection rates of pimps living off the immoral earnings of prostitutes, trafficking young women into street prostitution or local brothels. Recorded offences of street disorder and soliciting were the lowest for decades. The last King's Cross divisional annual report submitted to the Commissioner stated the red-light area was under control, with the visible public presence of prostitutes at a minimum.

John concluded, DS Morley was apparently the right officer in the right job. There were no adverse comments relating to his conduct or performance. He appeared to be hard working, conscientious, popular with his colleagues and trusted by his managers. A model supervisor. The file contained only scant detail of his personal life.

Married with two teenage children. No mention of friends or associates outside the Service.

DS Morley had a dull file, squeaky clean, nothing remotely controversial or suspicious. John read his file again; it was too good to be true.

31

John opened his front door. Before him stood his old friend Phil Smith. They had known each other for over twenty years, since their formative years serving with the Leeds City Police, when for a time he was a Detective Constable and Phil his Sergeant. They had a close bond, and although long periods of absence separated them, they were able to pick up their friendship instantly.

Now in his late fifties, Phil was in excellent physical health, exercising daily, and stubbornly refusing to accept the inevitable ageing process. Standing slightly over six feet tall, he appeared to have changed little in the eight years since they last met. He had been widowed for many years and brought up two teenage daughters whilst still serving, balancing the demands of a single parent with those of his police duties. He was a specialist in police convert surveillance and utilised these skills when he retired, establishing a successful business, sub-contracted by government agencies throughout the world. He was particularly sought after in the wider private sector, investigating commercial sabotage and/or the conduct of dishonest employees. He invested a great deal of money in the latest state of the art 'snooping' technology devices. However, he had decided recently to scale down his activities and spend more time with his growing family. He now enjoyed his six grandchildren and looked forward to a long and happy retirement.

Then John contacted him and it all changed. He was unable to resist his request. Was this going to be his last case? As investigators, they were like chalk and cheese, hardly ever agreeing on their respective methods, yet the closest of friends. Their relationship was based on trust, honesty and reliability.

'Bloody hell, John, you're getting a little broad around the waist. Charlie must be ironing your shirts on a wok.'

John shook his hand. 'Thanks for the compliments, Phil. I've really missed your wit. Not.'

They hugged each other with affection, their banter mandatory before any serious conversation; it was the custom. These old habits often confused others; too offensive and uncomfortable.

'Unfortunately, Charlie's not here, she's had to dash to the office. Sends her love though.'

'You've got me here under false pretences. You don't think I've just come to see you, do you?'

'Sit down, you old bugger, I've much to tell you. I believe we have a very tasty inquiry that requires all our wit and guile. It's potentially dangerous, involving a corrupt cop, dead prostitutes and a shady journalist. I've absolutely no doubt other unsavoury characters will appear as we progress with our investigations. Secrecy and stealth are the game here, Phil.'

'Bloody hell, John. Tell me more.'

Over the following two hours John explained how Yvonne had invited him to examine the background of the known events to date, together with the broad outline of their evidence gathering venture. Under no circumstances were they to intervene directly with the investigation, especially interviewing suspects. Seizing evidence, verbal accounts from witnesses and collecting intelligence were their objectives. Phil had known Yvonne briefly towards the end of his police career when she had barely started hers. He had been very impressed with her on so many levels. She had a naturally enquiring mind, attention to detail and an ability of challenging traditional police methods, frequently turning problems into opportunities.

'How's my young girl doing?' asked Phil.

'You mean DCI Hall? Very well. Just remember she's not your girl, nor anyone else's. Definitely going to the top of the tree, very capable and ambitious. Perhaps we can all meet later. Be like old times.'

'Hell, John, she's a proper flyer. I'm pleased, the Service needs officers like her, not old farts like us.'

'Speak for yourself. Anyway, let's get down to business.'

John suggested their first call was to speak to ex-DC Barry Taylor's sister in Archway.

'I'll go and see her,' said Phil.

'Unfortunately, we don't know her name as she is probably married. But we can check with the council rates office to find that out.'

'No problem there. I'll do that. Incidentally, how old is this Barry Taylor?'

'Let me have a look.' John thumbed through his personal file. 'Forty-seven. He spent most his service north of the river, mainly in CID. There's a note here from DS Morley requesting him to join his team. Wait a minute, there's another. It seems like he's followed his old skipper from one department to another. There's no indication in the file as to why he resigned, just his original report to the Commissioner of him quitting with twenty-eight days' notice.'

'I'll tell her I'm from the Police Pensions Department and I need to know his whereabouts. We've miscalculated his future pension. He'll qualify for a higher level, but we need him to sign the necessary forms personally, to safeguard anyone impersonating him.'

'Will it work?'

'Should do. I've done it before.'

'OK. If we can get hold of him, I think we've a chance of opening a big can of worms. Apparently, his friendship with DS Morley ended abruptly. We need to explore that. It would appear he's gone abroad, possibly Spain, so the Met will have to pay for a plane ticket, provided it's somewhere reasonably accessible, to speak to him. Meanwhile, if you go and see her, I'll make some enquiries with Alex Gilmour.'

'OK, John. Shall we meet up tomorrow?'

'Yes, there's a pub in Highgate main street called the George. We'll start meeting there, not here.'

'Good idea, we don't want to mix business with pleasure. I'll be staying with a cousin of mine, she lives in Camden but works abroad most of the time. I'll give you her number if you need to get in touch urgently.'

'OK. We'll meet up at six tomorrow and compare notes.'

Phil smiled and walked towards the front door. 'It's good to see you again, give my love to Charlie. Let's nail these bastards before I retire for good.'

They shook hands before Phil drove away in an old rusty white Ford Transit van. John suspected although the vehicle appeared scruffy, in need of maintenance, that was just a ruse; it was probably powered by a powerful V6 engine and sped like a thoroughbred horse. No doubt it would also be fitted with expensive sophisticated electrical snooping and tracking equipment, ideal for their tasks ahead. Most people would assume it was just road legal, a good runner and nothing more. Phil was a professional, leaving nothing to chance.

32

Following his visit to the Central Library, census and public records, Phil established the identity of Barry Taylor's sister and all the occupants at 87 Claremont View, Highbury. She was called Sandra Browning and appeared to live with her two adult sons, Robert and Richard, with no record of any other occupants at the address.

He caught the Tube to Highbury and walked directly to the house. He was dressed in a faded Harris tweed jacket with leather elbow patches and a pair of old brown corduroy trousers. Wearing dark-rimmed spectacles, his dark grey hair sported a side parting, heavily stuck down with an abundance of gel. He carried a worn-out leather briefcase containing the bogus paperwork and identity card he had worked all night on.

As he approached the front door, he mentally rehearsed his script. He was cold calling, expecting the unexpected.

After he'd knocked several times on the modern frosted-glass door, the silhouette of a figure appeared. The door opened halfway. He saw a woman in her early fifties, wearing a hair net with rollers tightly fitted to her scalp, smoking a cigarette. The view over her shoulders into the room behind told a story. The missing wallpaper, a threadbare stair carpet, and her shabbily stained jumper with loosely fitting trousers, suggested she was a woman of little means.

She stared at him. 'Who are you?'

'Good morning. Are you Sandra Browning?'

'Yes I am. Who wants to know?'

I'm really sorry to bother you, but my name is James Miller. I work for the Pensions Department of the Metropolitan Police.

Here's my identity card.' Phil waved the card in front of her. She gave it a quick glance before he replaced it in his wallet.

'What do you want from me?'

'May I talk to you in private?'

She hesitated slightly before inviting him inside. He looked a harmless insignificant old man. The disguise had worked so far. She took him into the front living room and gestured for him to sit on the sofa. It was completely hidden underneath several piles of damp clothing awaiting ironing. The whole room smelt fusty, devoid of any loving care. The furniture was old and worn out, with the two sofas' upholstery badly damaged. A smell of sour milk and stale cigarettes permeated throughout.

Phil sat awkwardly on the edge of the sofa. 'May I call you Sandra?'

'Yes, if you want.'

'Thank you. Sandra, do you have a brother called Barry Taylor who used to work for us?'

'Yes. But he chucked it in with you lot last month, didn't he?'

'Yes, that's right. The reason why I've come to see you is because we are anxious to get in touch with him, as there are several documents he needs to sign for his pension when he reaches sixty. He served with us for many years and so he's entitled to receive a pension then. If fact, if he was working for any other Government agency, he could transfer the pension over. Unfortunately, we don't know where he is. He appears to have moved from the last known address we have. Can you help?'

'How did you find me then?'

'Good question, Sandra. We noticed he applied for some compassionate leave several years ago to attend his niece's funeral. Please forgive me for asking, but were you the girl's mother?'

She looked at him without any expression, simply nodded her head. 'Yes, that's right. She was my little girl Jane. Only thirteen years old and ran over by some drunken bastard who left her in the gutter without stopping.'

Phil felt more than a twinge of guilt, yet persevered. 'I'm very sorry to bring this up, but these details are recorded on Barry's personal file which I have here.' He opened his case and took out an official file with the Metropolitan Police logo on it. He thumbed through the false papers until he stopped in the middle. 'Yes, here it is. Sandra, I apologise again for all of this, but do you know where I can get in touch with Barry? As I've just said, he no longer lives at the address we have.'

She sat down on a pile of damp washing opposite him and wiped a tear away from her cheek. 'Me and Barry have never been that close. In fact, I haven't seen him for nearly two years. But I got a postcard from him last week out of the blue. Just a minute, I think it's stuck on the side of the fridge.'

She disappeared for a few moments. 'Here it is. Looks like he's living in Spain.'

Phil studied the postcard carefully. The picture showed a traditional Spanish town with the text 'Torrox in the province of Malaga'. The message simply read, 'Hi Sandra, hope you are keeping well. Having a great life out here. Come and join me sometime. Contact the Olympia Bar, Torrox, anytime.'

He looked at her. 'Will you go and see him?'

'No. I've no money, can't afford the airfare. Still, it looks lovely, better than this dump.'

'Very good, Sandra, that's been a great help. I'll write to him there and send all the forms for his signature.'

'Can you mention in your letter, I'd like to come if he can pay for my ticket? My two boys are in and out of trouble with you lot. Just like their Dad. I've had enough, they're old enough to look after themselves now. Spain looks lovely, but it looks like I'm stuck here for the rest of my days.'

'Leave that with me, Sandra, I'll give him the message.'

Phil stood and walked to the door, then turned. 'Sandra, I'm really sorry for your loss. I do hope you can get out to Spain soon.'

He left the house and walked down the street towards the Underground station, silently promising himself that no matter what the outcome of the investigation, Barry Taylor would be told of his sister's plight.

33

Since his meeting with Phil, John had made several telephone calls to his trusted circle of good friends and investigative reporters regarding Alex Gilmour. A picture of murky deals, connections to the London underworld and an unbelievable ability to expose the indiscretions of the powerful and famous began to emerge. He always appeared to find scandalous behaviour in the unlikeliest of places. Though it was widely accepted by his fellow journalists that he did occasionally scoop genuine newsworthy reports, these were few and far between, and his sources were always considered dubious.

As a freelancer, his stories were normally sold to the highest bidder, and later published in various popular scandal-exposing tabloids. His nickname amongst the Fleet Street editors and reporters was 'the leech'. Yet he lived a grand and lavish lifestyle, far better than any of his contemporaries.

Gilmour's unhealthy relationship with the police was common knowledge. Information about individual corrupt detectives was always shrouded in mystery but fortunately, John had the information connecting Gilmour to DS Morley. That was where he would concentrate his efforts.

Utilising his press pass he visited the various tabloid newspaper archives, including those held at the Central Library. For hours he trawled through the thousands of scandal cases contained in their microfiche files, specifically focussing on those stories reported by Gilmour.

After five hours, he had uncovered seven articles reported by him, spanning the past five years. All had a similar theme. Men in public office who were allegedly sexually involved with prostitutes in the London area. A closer examination revealed all these incidents had originally occurred north of the river, in the red-light area and the jurisdiction of the King's Cross Vice Squad.

They included a vicar, local councillor, head teacher, dentist and an eminent research scientist, all in their fifties and sixties, their respective careers in tatters. John sighed heavily. He considered the permanent damage inflicted on these men's reputations. And for what? Gilmour had collected his 'pieces of silver' and moved on, leaving in his wake destroyed men.

He concentrated on the head teacher, Albert Jones. According to the initial press report, he had been found in the King's Cross red-light area, in his car with a prostitute. A report in the *Evening Standard* revealed both were partially naked with Mr Jones being unable to account for his behaviour. Several months later, another article written by Gilmour revealed the details at his subsequent employment disciplinary hearing. Although Mr Jones vehemently denied any involvement with the prostitute stating he was simply in the area to collect a friend from the railway station, the circumstantial evidence against him was overwhelming. The local education authority dismissed his pleas and terminated his employment, after thirty-three years of loyal and exemplary service. There was no right of appeal. According to the report, he resided in Kilburn, North London, close to the boys' grammar school where he had served throughout his career.

John reached for the telephone book and soon found his number. He walked over to the line of public telephone boxes in the main entrance of the Central Library and made the call. A man's voice said 'Hello.'

'Is that Mr Albert Jones?' asked John.

'Yes.'

'Good afternoon, Mr Jones. I'm sorry for bothering you but my name is John Evans. I'm an Inspector with the Metropolitan Police and I'm investigating past cases involving possible unlawful collusion between police officers and the press.'

'What is it you want?'

'I understand you became embroiled in a scandal last year that ultimately cost you your career. I'm investigating similar incidents that involved men like yourself and the possible criminal conduct of some members of the Metropolitan Police. You must realise, Mr Jones, I cannot discuss it any more over the phone but is it possible we could meet up somewhere?'

'Will it help me clear my name and restore my reputation?'

'I can't promise anything, sir, but if you can give me your side of the story, I may be able to establish the truth if any wrongdoing has occurred.'

'Very well. You can come here, provided you're not in uniform. Don't want to give the neighbours any more ideas about me.'

'Thank you, Mr Jones. Are you in this afternoon?'

'Yes. Let's say about four. Do you have my address?'

'Is it the same as in the phone book?'

'Yes.'

'I'll see you then.'

*

As the local church clock struck four, John walked along a tree-lined avenue until he came to the semi-detached house with the neatest lawn and herbaceous borders in the street. He opened the garden gate and approached a keyhole porch along a recently swept path. Before he reached the door, it opened. Standing there was a man in his late fifties but looked considerably older, dressed in a brown woollen cardigan and dark loosely fitting trousers, smoking a pipe. He leant forward and asked, 'Mr Evans?'

'Yes, and you're Mr Jones?'

'Of course. Please come in.'

John was invited into a study facing a back garden which was as immaculate as the front. Clearly Mr Jones had plenty of spare time. Once they were sitting down, John said, 'Before we discuss your case any further, I must ask you to keep our meeting confidential for the time being. As you will appreciate, I'm investigating the conduct and behaviour of some serving police officers who may have committed serious disciplinary breaches or even criminal offences. Of course, they may not have done so, in which case their position in the Force remains unchanged. But before the Commissioner can make any decision, I must explore and examine all the events and circumstances that come to my attention. One of these is your case. If you have no objection, I would like you first to give me a brief verbal statement surrounding the evening you were seen and spoken to by the police. Are you willing to share that with me?'

'Yes, I am.'

'Thank you. Please continue.'

Well, on this particular evening, I had driven into town to collect an old friend who was arriving at King's Cross railway station at about nine-fifteen. Unfortunately, I was running late and couldn't find anywhere to park my car close to the entrance. So, I continued driving in the area for about fifteen minutes. Eventually, I found a space, but it was a considerable distance away and by the time I'd reached the station, it was too late. My friend had continued on his journey and caught the Tube. When I returned to my car, I noticed there were several women hanging around on the street corners where some of them spoke to me, asking 'Are you doing business?' but I ignored them. I know I'm a school teacher and spent too much of my life with my head inside my books. And I'm not as streetwise as some of my pupils, but I knew what they were asking of me. I got into the car and the next thing I remember was being woken up by the police with a woman lying next to me in the back seat. My trousers had been removed to around my ankles and shirt ripped down the front. The woman was topless. That's about all I can remember before I lost consciousness again and waking up in King's Cross Police Station the following morning. That's all I can tell you, Mr Evans.'

John had been busy taking notes and thought about his next question. 'Mr Jones, can you recollect anything about the moments immediately after you got back inside your car?'

'No. I didn't even have the opportunity to fasten my seat belt. I may have felt something cover my face from behind, but I can't be sure. I just passed out.'

'Did you tell the police this?'

'Yes, but they just laughed at me.'

'What about the woman in the car with you. Can you remember anything about her?'

'Not really. She had orange frizzy hair and bright lipstick to match.

That's all.'

'Did the police say anything to her?'

'Yes, but it was all done outside the car. I don't know what they were talking about. Remember, I was completely out of it. I could hardly keep my eyes open. I've never taken any drugs in my life, so I can't be sure, but I think someone did administer something to me on that night.'

'When you were taken to the police station, were you seen by a doctor?'

'I don't think so. They just got me out of a cell first thing in the morning and told me I was being released without charge. I asked them why I had been arrested; they just said on suspicion of being in charge of a motor vehicle whilst being unfit through drugs. That was it.'

'Were you given any documentation by the police when released from custody?'

'No. Nothing.'

'OK. Do you remember which police officer dealt with you at the scene of your arrest?'

'No. I've tried to find that out. I even called at the police station for those details. They told me there was no record of my detention.'

'What happened after you were released?'

'Nothing. I thought it was a little strange but was glad in a way it was all over. Then about three weeks later, a journalist called Gilmour contacted me at work and told me he had heard I had been with a prostitute and wanted to know if it was true. I told him it was all a pack of lies. He seemed to threaten me with some kind of ultimatum; if I was willing to make a donation to some charity that dealt with the trafficking of child prostitution, he would ensure the story would never see the light of day. I told him to get lost. Three days later, the whole sordid and fabricated affair was published. By lunchtime I'd been suspended and so my nightmare from hell began.'

'Did this journalist, Mr Gilmour, give you any further details regarding this charity?'

'No. I only spoke to him once. I did try to contact him through the papers covering the story by leaving a message with their switchboards for him to get in touch. But I heard nothing.'

'What happened after that, Mr Jones?'

'About three months later, I was summoned to appear before a disciplinary hearing with my education authority. I told them the whole story was pure fiction and of my reasons for being the area. I even brought my friend who I had missed at the railway station, to corroborate my account. After an hour, will little deliberation, they instantly dismissed me, saying that they no longer had confidence in my ability to continue as head teacher or of any other position in the school. They told me I'd lost the moral high ground expected of a man in my position. They paid my salary for the next three months and that was it. No job, no reference and no prospects. Since then I've been living off my savings and frankly, they're running out. Before long I'll have to sell this house.'

John attempted to reassure him. 'I'm sure it won't come to that.'

'Mr Evans, whether you establish the truth of all this or not, I want to assure you I'm innocent. I didn't do any of the things that were reported in the newspapers. I was set up. I'm certain someone purposely drugged me and because I refused to pay any donation to a charity I considered to be dubious, I paid the ultimate price for something I didn't do. I was simply in the wrong place at the wrong time.'

'I'm really sorry to hear this. Mr Jones, I cannot make any promises or give you false hope, but I can assure you, if my investigations reveals you have been wrongly treated by the police and prove that what happened to you was untrue, I shall give you every support in restoring your reputation. What I would like you to do is write all this down now, so I have a written statement of your account. I can assure you, this inquiry is very secret, with only the Deputy Commissioner aware of it. Therefore, I must ask you keep our meeting and this conversation in the strictest of confidence.'

'I will, Mr Evans, and thank you. I now feel someone is finally believing me; nearly all my family and friends have disappeared. There's one other thing. I've been diagnosed with terminal cancer with only about six months to live. If I'm not here, after you've established the truth, will you make it publically known I was completely innocent of all these wicked and pernicious accusations?'

As they stood up, John reached out and gently shook his hand. 'Mr Jones, I promise you, if I discover you have been maliciously targeted by unscrupulous police officers, you will receive a public apology from the Commissioner and those responsible will face the full rigour of legal process. Your reputation will be fully restored.'

'Thank you, Mr Evans.'

John saw a tear welling up in the man's eyes and instinctively knew he had been telling the truth. He was witnessing the true human cost, the consequences of unlawful police practices and press intrusions; the complete ruination of a man's reputation for the sake of sensationalism and personal gain. And Gilmour had made a few thousand pounds out of the misery inflicted on this hardworking and honourable man. By contrast, Mr Jones had lost most of his self-esteem and the savings accumulated throughout his working life. How many others had suffered from the same indignity inflicted by Gilmour? How was he obtaining this information? It could only be from one source. Detective Sergeant Morley.

As John was leaving, he opened the garden gate, turned around and saw Albert Jones standing by the front door. His sloping shoulders and gaunt face portrayed a sorry state. John decided he would do everything within his power to help him and others, who had been caught up in the web of deceit spun by Gilmour and Morley.

Something snapped inside him. It was a seismic shift in his sense of integrity. He had always followed the rules, never venturing outside them. Even at the cost of seeing guilty criminals walk free from justice, he would never jeopardise his impartiality in collecting and presenting evidence. Albert Jones had fallen dreadfully from grace into penniless obscurity through no fault of his own. John was determined to stop this, at all costs.

He looked at his watch and made his way to the George to meet up with Phil.

34

The George was part of a larger building, once named the Grange, that had belonged to a prosperous merchant called George Stepson. Built in the early nineteenth century, it was a fine stone residence with ten bedrooms, set in its own grounds in the centre of Highgate, tucked away from the filth and industrial fallout of London several miles away. It had long since merged into the metropolis, yet remained a desirable residential area, with property values to match. Over the past seventy years, most of the grounds of the house had been purchased by private developers who built large terraced houses with modest gardens. The pub itself was set on the side of the main building and boasted an excellent restaurant and three separate bars. It was a regular haunt for many of the local residents, including John.

As he walked into the lounge he saw Phil already enjoying a pint of beer. Within a few minutes they were discussing the day's exploits. Another beer followed.

John was pleased with their progress. 'Good work, Phil. Now we've discovered where Barry Taylor lives, we must try and speak to him. Not that I want to spoil your anticipation, but I think I should fly out to Spain and find out from him personally why he resigned in such a hurry. In the meantime, I'd like you do something that's more clandestine and more fitting with your line of work.'

'Sounds interesting. What is it?'

'After speaking with Albert Jones today, I believe there is a direct connection between Alex Gilmour and DS Morley, but we must try to determine that as a fact. We already know the late Gordon Black and Jason Moore were found in similar circumstances and on both of those occasions there were photographs and possibly video footage present. But this was not the case with Mr Jones. I'm wondering whether someone else is now involved, because I think this is far too sophisticated for Morley. Does Gilmour have other connections?'

'Yes, I think you're right. Such covert equipment costs a fortune, even to hire.'

'Exactly. That's why I'm going to ask you if you would perhaps pay Gilmour a visit and place some of your equipment in his home. Preferably when he's not in. Let's start turning the tables on the predator.'

'OK. Do you know where he lives and what his routines are?'

'I know he lives somewhere in Islington. It won't be hard for to find out where. He often attends the parliamentary hospitality lounge on Friday lunchtimes. Apparently, it's a good time to see if there are any whispers amongst the senior civil servants. Remember, he thrives on gossip, so I'm going to start a rumour of my own tonight. I just need to speak to someone I know in Whitehall.'

'Why Fridays?'

'Because most MPs have started their journey back home for the weekend.'

'That's in two days' time.'

'Yes. If you see him leave with his attaché case, you'll know he'll be out for a few hours, usually until the bars have closed after three. With a bit of luck, you should have his place to yourself for at least four hours.'

'More than enough. What exactly do you want me to do?'

'I'll leave that to you Phil, but certainly his phone needs tapping and perhaps a couple of cameras inside. Let's see what company he's keeping. You do realise this is highly illegal.'

'Not if I do it.'

'Exactly. And that's why you're working on your own. I've no idea what you're getting up to. If necessary, I'll deny having ever seen you before in my life.'

They grinned at each other.

'Hell, John, you've changed. I never thought I'd ever hear you say that.'

'Phil, after today, it's all changed. These bastards are making a fat living out of the misery and ruination of innocent men who have committed no offence other than at worst a stupid indiscretion. Some, like Albert Jones, didn't even do that.'

'I'll go and sort that out. When shall meet up again?'

'What about here, next Saturday lunchtime. By that time, I'll have been to see Barry Taylor and hopefully your little 'snoopers' will be in situ.'

'Agreed.'

35

When John arrived home, Charlie was busy preparing dinner. He went directly to his office and called another journalist, Ben Child, who had a particular dislike of Alex Gilmour. Without explaining his motive in detail, John created a rumour that a member of the Government Cabinet had been caught by the security services cavorting with a young woman from the Italian trade delegation at the last Party Conference in Blackpool. John asked Ben if he could ring Gilmour and arrange to meet him that Friday lunchtime, at the Westminster Members' Bar, where the rumour would begin to ferment.

'Where did you hear this?' he asked.

'You know, Ben, just a rumour. But I know he'll take the bait, it has all the ingredients for a scandal. There's a good reason why I want Gilmour to know, but I can't tell you now. Later, Ben, I promise.'

'Is it likely he will profit from this meeting with me?'

'No. Not at all. In fact, it could cost him dearly.'

'Then I'll do it. I owe that bastard after he stole a perfectly good story from me, gave it his usual spin, then blamed me as the source in front of the libel judge.'

'I remember. You were found not guilty though.'

'Yes. But it cost me a fortune in legal costs.'

'If you can do this for me, I assure you, if it's successful he'll not be stealing any more stories from anyone again. Just make sure there are no witnesses when you tell him.'

'Leave that with me, John.'

John replaced the receiver then picked it up again and rang Yvonne at her office. He informed her of the enquiries so far. Initially, she was a little hesitant when he mentioned flying to Spain to see Barry Taylor, but he reminded her it was the best lead so far. He failed to mention Phil's imminent trespassing into Gilmour's home, where they hoped to prove the link between him with Morley.

'John, I know you'll find the evidence we require, but please take care. Do you want me arrange for another officer to accompany you to Spain?'

'No thanks, Yvonne. Best working on my own.'

'Thought so. Incidentally, I'm arranging for DS Morley's phone to be monitored too. If he's using our phones for his ill-gotten gains, we'll know who he's talking to.'

'Good idea.'

'Ring me when you get back.'

John had set the trap. Gilmour should be absent from his house for several hours, allowing Phil sufficient time to do his business. Meanwhile, he would fly out to Malaga the next day and go and see Barry Taylor. Not bad for one day's work, but now it was time for dinner.

36

It was six o'clock in the evening when the British Airways plane touched down on the runway in Malaga. The sky was clear blue as John walked across the concrete runway towards the terminal. He immediately felt the warm Mediterranean sun on his face. Once through passport control, he went directly to the car hire desks on the lower floor. Carrying just an overnight case, he only required a small car for one day to travel the short distance to Torrox, thirty miles east of Malaga along the coast.

Thirty minutes later, he was driving a Renault saloon on a newly constructed highway, leaving the city behind him. To his left stretched the high coastal mountains and to his right, the shimmering azure blue sea. The warm wind blew through the open window, slightly ruffling his greying hair. Momentarily, he completely forgot the purpose of his visit.

Eventually he turned off the highway and climbed a steep road signposted Torrox Centre. The spread of large cheap tourist developments, scattered haphazardly along the coast, had not reached the small town yet. Jutting out from the mountainside facing the sea, it was virtually untouched, retaining most its original Spanish charm. It was serviced by only two roads: the one John had driven up and another that disappeared towards the Sierra Nevada Mountains. He turned into the central square and saw an old white-painted church at the far side, with shops and small restaurants encroaching onto the marble-paved piazza. Most were still trading.

He parked the car and started walking along the edge of the square, where to his surprise he immediately saw what he was looking for; the Olympia Bar. It was a simple tiny makeshift lean-to, temporarily built onto the side of a bustling restaurant, holding only eight tables with mismatched chairs. John sat near the bar.

A young woman appeared from behind him. '¿Si?'

'Una cerveza, por favor.'

She nodded her head and disappeared. He had taken the time to memorise some handy Spanish phrases. Asking for a beer seemed important enough.

After two more drinks, he took out the small black and white photograph of Barry Taylor he had previously removed from his police personal file and studied it again. According to Yvonne, it was only taken last year when his warrant card had been renewed. He continued to look around, noticing the shops were beginning to close and the restaurants empty. Still no sign of him. Phil was certain this was the correct bar. He would have to be patient. He looked at his watch; it was now ten thirty and he was the only customer remaining, and still no sign of him.

He began to consider driving back to Malaga to find a hotel and returning back in the morning. Most places would close their doors after midnight. He glanced at his watch again. Eleven o'clock.

As he stood up to leave the table, he heard a voice. 'Hey. Where have you been all my life?'

John was taken off guard. He spun round and saw a middle-aged man trying to talk to a young woman walking in the opposite direction, away from him. She ignored his advances and continued on her way. He shrugged his shoulders and walked towards John, saying, 'Can't win them all mate, can you?'

John simply replied 'No.'

The man was stocky, tanned, over six feet tall with short dark brown hair, wearing a T-shirt and shorts. John glanced at the photograph again. This was his man.

As he walked past, John asked, 'Are you Barry Taylor?'

The man stopped dead in his tracks and turned, 'Who wants to know?'

'My name is John Evans. I've come from London to speak to you.'

'And how did you find me here?'

'I'll explain that later. Can we talk, please?'

'What about?'

'Somewhere private, please?'

'Do I need a lawyer?'

'No, of course not. I'll soon explain why I'm here.'

He invited John into the back area of the bar, lit only by a small gas lamp and with the smell from the cooling grills in the restaurant kitchen next door. 'Now before we go any further, tell me how you found me and why you're here.'

'Mr Taylor, like yourself, I resigned from the Police Service some years ago. However, I've been invited by the Metropolitan Police Commissioner to investigate some suspicious deaths involving prostitutes that operated out of the King's Cross area. I know you served in the Vice Squad covering there before you resigned and I'm not here to make any accusations against you. As for finding you here, I must confess we were a little underhand about that. We went to see your sister Sandra and she showed us the postcard you sent her.'

'How did you find her?'

'Your personal record showed you attending your niece's funeral some years ago and her details were there.'

'But she wouldn't have just told you where I was. What did you say to her?'

'I'm going to be perfectly honest with you. We told her we were from the Police Pensions Department and needed to contact you urgently. There were some important forms for you to sign. I'm sorry for the deception but it was vital for us to speak to you.'

'Bloody hell. I should punch you on your nose right now.'

'Frankly, I wouldn't blame you if you did. But before you do that, would you please hear me out?'

'It'd better be good.'

'OK. Whether you talk to me or not, I have a message from Sandra anyway. She'd love to come out here to see you but she's unable to do so at the moment. When my colleague went to see her, it was clear she's fallen on hard times. It seems her sons are in and out of trouble and her husband is doing a ten-year stretch in Strangeways.'

'Sandra is all the family I've got now. She's a good sort, my sis.'

'Perhaps I shouldn't say this, but I think she has no money to come out here and is too proud to ask you for the airfare. She doesn't seem to have much joy in her life. Anyway, I've passed the message on. That's up to you.'

'Life's dealt her a bad hand. Since losing her poor little girl, the bastard she was with, went out and blagged some old ladies in their home, leaving her with two feral teenagers. Poor sis. I'll send her some money and tell her to get over here.'

'So even if you don't want to talk to me, at least some good has come out of my visit. But may I carry on?'

'Go on, I won't hit just now'

'OK. Can I please confirm with you that you were you a member of the Kings Cross Vice Squad until last month, when you resigned from the Force?'

'Yes.'

'I must stress at this stage, no suspicion has fallen on you, but we believe you may hold some vital information that can help us.'

'Go on. I'm listening.'

'As you know, there's no extradition treaty between Spain and the UK at the moment. Whether that will change in the future is anybody's guess. The reason why I'm mentioning this is to assure you that you don't have to cooperate with our investigation, but obviously we would appreciate any information you could give me.'

'It depends on what you're asking.'

'It's my understanding you were very close friends with George Morley. Is that right?'

'Yes, I knew him for many years, both in and out of the job. You could say at one time we were good mates.'

'What happened?'

'We just had a disagreement, that's all.'

'Forgive me for probing you on this, but I believe you had more than a disagreement with him. After all, it caused you to resign didn't it?'

'Who's told you that?'

'To be perfectly honest, no one. Apparently, it was just a rumour going around. Are you willing to tell me the reason why you quit?'

'Does anyone else know where I am?'

'No, only Sandra, and when I return to London tomorrow, I can tell her to be very quiet about that.'

'OK. You've been fair to me and if you can pass a note to Sandra with some money for her to get over here, I'll tell you what I think you want to know. Mind you, I'm not giving you any written statement and I'll deny we're having this conversation. So don't bother recalling me to Blighty to give evidence for any prosecution. I'll tell you, but you'll have to prove it without me. Agreed?'

'Agreed.'

Barry Taylor then looked hard at John. 'Let me see some identification first. You could be anyone.'

'Here, this is my warrant card, signed by the Commissioner himself, and my passport.'

He examined them closely and smiled. 'You're getting too old to do this, Mr Evans.'

'Thanks, but I think you're right.'

'Go on, ask away.'

'We believe DS Morley is involved in some unscrupulous scam involving someone else outside the Force. Perhaps you could tell me what you know? It's all off the record of course.'

Taylor smiled again. John sensed he was in for a long night and took his notepad out. He paused, then said, 'I'm ready. Please tell me what caused you to resign from the Force and spoil your relationship with DS Morley.'

'Me and George go back a long way. We joined up about the same time and seemed to follow each other as we were transferred from one department to another. Our wives were good friends too and we often got together at weekends and even went on holiday a couple of times. About five years ago he was transferred to the King's Cross Vice Squad and invited me to join him a couple of months later. In the beginning, everything was great. Then one night, he asked me to go with him to visit a pimp called Johnny at some shebeen. When we arrived, Johnny got in the back of the car and George held his hand out to him. The guy placed a wad of pound notes into it, saying, "I can only give you a ton this week. My girls have been very quiet." George told him he wanted two hundred next week or he'd bust him for "living off immoral earnings". After this Johnny walked away, George looked at me, smiled and said, "Let's go for a drink." Although I knew exactly what had happened, I just agreed with him.'

'So you knew he was taking a bribe off this Johnny?'

'Of course. We went for a drink and he told me he had a number of "nice earners" off Johnny and three other pimps. Since being overlooked for any promotion, he seemed to change. He became bitter and decided he would take every opportunity of creaming the pimps for as much money as he could whilst he was still in the job. Once retired, he would be a nobody. He handed me fifty quid and told me to keep it strictly "mum", promising to include me in with his dealings. I was a little reluctant at first, but he convinced me that no one was getting hurt and the pimps wouldn't grass us up as they were being protected from getting locked up. As George said, "Everyone's a winner."'

'So you agreed to taking money from the pimps, along with DS Morley?'

'Yes. But remember, I'll never admit to it.'

'Fair enough. Can you remember the names of these pimps?'

'No, apart from Johnny. George dealt with all that.'

'What about the women?'

'Yes, I remember some of them.'

'Can you remember two young women called Vicky Thompson and Julie Brecon?'

'Only Vicky Thompson. She's a pretty girl. I saw her once in a pub with George. I later caught her hustling near the railway station. If I remember rightly, she got a caution. I know we never saw her again on the streets. She either went straight or operated in the hotels.'

'Would you have submitted any paperwork about that?'

'Hell, yes. The first time they get done, they receive a caution. It's quite a detailed report, so it must be somewhere.'

'Would there be a copy somewhere else?'

'Yes. Social Services would have one.'

'OK. I'll chase that up later. Going back to you and George. What happened next?'

'He got greedy. His old mate Alex Gilmour spoilt everything. All of us in the Squad had to submit sightings of cars driven by punters cruising around the red-light area looking for business.'

'Why did you do this?'

'Some of the toms got badly assaulted by the punters, so if we had some details of their cars, we had a starting chance of finding out who they were.'

'What happened to these details?'

'They'd be submitted on a crime intelligence form and placed inside the office register.'

'What do you think DS Morley did with them then?'

'It seems all the details of these cars were later checked out by George and passed on to Gilmour.'

'Are you sure of this?'

'Yes. He told me. There was more money in it and he wanted me to get involved too.'

'Do you know what Gilmour was doing with these details?'

'Of course. He was contacting the men and threatening to expose their presence inside the red-light area unless they contributed to some bloody fake charity.'

'So, what happened between DS Morley and yourself?'

'I told him I didn't mind squeezing some cash out of the pimps, but this was different. This was cold-blooded blackmail and those men didn't deserve that. Some of them were driving through quite innocently, not even looking for a girl. But the final straw was when he got in with the owner of the Caribbean Club, a black guy called Max Campbell. George was hustling him with some extortion, promising him protection from police raids. I'm not sure why, but he certainly had some dirt on this guy Campbell. Following all that, we had a massive row in the office after everyone had gone home. He threatened me that I was in it far too deep already. I lost my temper and smacked him in the face and told him he was a piece of shit.'

'Did you have any dealings with this Max Campbell?'

'No, I never met him. He seemed to have kept his nose clean.'

'What did you do then?'

'I stormed out, went home and got drunk. I live on my own since my missus walked out last year for a younger version. Kids have grown up and flown the nest. So there's just me. After a few drinks, strangely things started to clear in my head. I decided to quit the Force. George would get caught before long and I wanted to be well clear when he did. I've no one to answer to, so I came straight out here. I'd been to Torrox many times on holiday before and knew it wouldn't cost much to set up a bar here. So I jumped ship and packed my bags the same day.'

'But you had over twenty-three years' service. You had less than seven to go before you qualified for a full police pension.'

'You're right. But if I got dragged down with George, I'd have probably been lucky getting away with my liberty. My pension would have disappeared. Wouldn't it?'

'Yes. You're right. I don't condone your actions for a moment. In fact, Mr Taylor, if we were in the UK, I'd probably have you arrested. But we aren't. So, under the circumstances, I can see why you did quit and come out here. At least you've got your freedom and will eventually collect some of your pension when you're sixty.'

'So, what are you going to do with all this information now?'

'To be frank, we knew most of this already. But it's helpful to have it confirmed by yourself, even if we can't use it in a court of law. This Max Campbell is new to our investigation, so we'll be taking a closer look at him. Finally, do you know if there was anyone else DS Morley may have been squeezing for protection money?'

'Let me think. I don't think so, just this Max Campbell. I heard him talk about his monthly fee but nothing else. It was obviously top secret. That's all I can remember.'

'OK, Mr Taylor, that's been very helpful. Thanks for your time.'

'Don't go just yet. Can you give me a minute?'

John returned outside to where he had been sitting earlier. After a few minutes Barry Taylor came out with a letter and two glasses of ice-cold beer. 'Will you give this to Sandra for me? And this is for you. It's probably the only time you've drunk a beer with a bent cop.'

John took the envelope and replied, with a wink, 'I wouldn't be so sure about that.' They both smiled and raised their glasses. Then they shook hands before John returned to his car and drove out of the Torrox, back towards Malaga, in search of a hotel still open for business.

John thought about his meeting with Barry Taylor. He'd been an ex-cop on the take who had finally shown some moral judgement. Whether he would ever be punished in a court of law or not, he now had little to show for his exploits, scraping out a living from a shack.

Yet he wished him and his sister a better future. They both deserved that.

37

Whilst John was waiting in the departure lounge at Malaga airport for his return flight to Heathrow, Phil was parked in his van about fifty yards away from Alex Gilmour's house in south Islington. It was Friday morning and he hoped John's contact had convinced Gilmour enough for him to leave home for a couple of hours. Today, Phil was dressed as an electrical engineer with the logo Home Counties Electrics on his blue overall breast pocket and across his back. A large electronics case contained all his covert surveillance equipment. Sitting in the rear of the van in a large comfortable chair, he peered towards the house through the rear silvered back windows, intentionally kept dirty. In reality, they were one-way mirrored and specially adapted for the van.

Running down the interior length of the van were a variety of wireless imaging receiving units, all serviced by their own monitors. These were supported by high intensity listening devices, capable of receiving live audio transmissions nearly a mile away. Everything was in place and ready for him to enter the house and install his miniature cameras and microphones.

He had previously applied for a business parking permit from the local Highways Department, lasting twenty-eight days, allowing him a continuous stay. The nature of his business was rewiring a number of properties that required immediate access in case of emergencies. The fee was a hundred pounds. John would look after that.

He checked his watch: eleven thirty. He glanced back towards the front door and noticed it move. Out stepped Alex Gilmour, dressed in a smart dark grey suit, carrying a briefcase and an umbrella. He closed the door behind him and walked towards the Underground station. Phil waited until he had disappeared from sight and then waited another five minutes, just in case he returned unexpectedly.

Leaving his van through the rear door, carrying the silver-coloured metal electronics case, Phil walked directly towards the house. He carefully watched for any movement from the adjoining houses. The street was deserted as he approached the door, where he discreetly inserted and gently twisted the finely fabricated skeleton key concealed in the palm of his hand. Phil was good at opening locks, especially Yale types.

During his many years as a member of the Burglary Squad in the West Yorkshire Police, he had learnt these skills from some of the best house breakers in the country. He remembered criminals were vain creatures. By complementing them for their professional MO after they had been arrested, he would ask them the secrets of their trade. Most declined, but some openly volunteered, especially when they were requesting bail whilst on remand. Legitimate locksmiths were another source of his extensive knowledge. He knew that using skeleton keys was principally about listening, accompanied by a delicate touch. The tumblers inside the lock had their own characteristics that surrendered individually according to their condition and age. This lock was old, but sufficiently lubricated to yield without difficulty.

Within twenty seconds he opened the front door slightly. He waited silently and without movement. Then he heard what he was expecting: the intermittent sound of the activated internal intruder alarm. The initial part of the intrusion was the biggest risk, as he had only twenty to thirty seconds to locate the control box before isolating it from the mains. Otherwise the external bell would activate, and his visit aborted. Fortunately, during the previous day, he had walked past the house and noted the model and manufacturer's name on the bell housing fixed to the front of the house. He also knew that the internal control box, once located, could be deactivated by drilling directly through the bottom circle of the letter B on the case front with a 10mm drill bit, into the mother board set immediately behind it. Apparently, this crude intrusion forced the unit to close down as long as the drill bit remained in place. Apart from a small hole, there were no visible signs of tampering, and the system would sound normally when re-activated or switched to standby once the drill had been removed. Gilmour would be unaware it had been interfered with.

Phil moved quickly to the cupboard under the stairs and immediately located the control box next to the door. His electric drill was spinning as he stepped forward and it bored straight through the front plate, exactly where he had anticipated. The drill penetrated easily into the box and struck the relay behind, quelling the intermittent sound straightaway. It was now unarmed.

Moving quickly, he inserted a miniature camera into the shade of the hall light, then passed into the living room and placed another between two large books resting in well stocked bookcase. Microphones, disguised to look like insects, smaller than the size of a pea, were placed in various locations throughout the room. They all had a battery life of four weeks. The telephones in the kitchen, office and bedroom were altered to another shadow extension line, serving a receiver and recorder in Phil's van.

It took him less than twenty minutes to complete. As he left the building, Phil calmly walked past the hallway cupboard, reached inside and withdrew his drill. The intermittent sound returned, leaving him enough time to leave and secure the front door. By the time the system fell back into standby mode, he was approaching his van. Before opening the van door, he stopped to hear if the exterior bell box had activated. No, just the sound of the traffic passing by.

He unlocked the van, got into the driver's seat, swung around and disappeared into the back, switching all his monitors on. Apart from the camera in the living room that must have moved slightly, all the other equipment appeared correctly positioned. Once he was satisfied everything was in order, he stepped back outside and locked the doors. As the van appeared to be in an unroadworthy condition, it deterred most opportunist thieves from taking any notice of it. But beneath its rough and uncherished exterior, lay a vehicle in perfect mechanical order, secured by a specially designed electric iron bar bolting system fixed to all the doors, with shatter-proof windows. If anyone attempted to move it, the tyres would automatically deflate, activating an audible screech so loud and piecing it would put off the most committed of thieves.

Carrying a different case, Phil strode down the street, past Gilmour's house, towards the Islington shopping centre and entered the nearby public library. He went directly to the gentlemen's toilet, only to emerge five minutes later wearing a sports jacket and grey trousers.

He made his way to the Underground station and caught the Tube to King's Cross. He was on another mission. It was lunchtime and some of the street workers would already be loitering in the surrounding street waiting for punters driving past. He felt in his jacket pocket and took out the poor-quality photographs of Vicky Thompson and Julie Brecon, together with a clutch of ten pound notes.

Initially, none of the women had any knowledge of Vicky or Julie but as he crossed the busy street one approached him and asked, 'Do you want business, Granddad?'

'Cheeky bugger. Not really, but if you can recognise either of these women, I'll pay you.'

She looked closely at the photographs. 'Are you a cop?'

'Do I bloody look like one?'

'Not really, you're too old.'

'Well do you recognise any of them?'

Pointing to one of them she replied, 'Yes, that's Vicky. I don't know the other girl.'

'Good start. Tell me all you know about Vicky and then I'll start handing some of these over to you.'

She looked at the money spread out in Phil's hand and didn't hesitate. 'I haven't seen Vicky for ages. Rumour is that she's out of town, probably at some rehab clinic again.'

'I need more than that.'

'She's Max's girl. Got really keen on him. You know, Max from the Caribbean Club, down the road.'

'When did you last see her?'

'It must be about five months ago. Heard she went to some clinic place in Wembley. Snorted too much shit. It happens. That's all I can tell you, sweetheart.'

Phil put sixty pounds into her hands and she blew him a kiss. 'If you want, I'll give you a good time for another forty. Call it a straight ton.'

'No, thanks darling.'

She shrugged, stuffed the notes inside her boots and walked to the street corner, peering intently at the passing motor cars. Phil made a note of Max and the Caribbean Club and approached the nearby public telephone box. Surprisingly, the telephone book was mainly intact, but inside it stank. He shuddered to think what had happened in such a confined space and held his breath until he found the Caribbean Club listed, together with its address. Referring to his *London A-Z*, he soon located the road. Not too far to walk.

*

Twenty minutes later he stood outside an old single-storey brick building with slightly sagging red corrugated metal roof panels. Shabby and in disrepair, it was located at the end of a short cobbled cul-de-sac, wedged in between two large warehouses. It was a desolate place. Although only fifty yards from the main road, there were no signs of life, not even parked vehicles, apart from the burnt-out shell of an old Morris 1000, torched many years previously. Drainpipes hung precariously to the walls, with most of the original windows permanently bricked in or boarded up. Running alongside the back wall was a passageway, where several refuse bins were stacked awkwardly. Years of accumulated rubbish were scattered all around. The air stank of rotting food, urine and rats.

To the unfamiliar eye, the building was derelict, apart from the hand painted sign 'Caribbean' above the entrance. This was serviced by two old wooden doors, devoid of any paint, with two large metal handles fastened together by a heavy chain and a single five-levered padlock. The porch was littered with thousands of cigarette butts and empty beer bottles and cans. A quick glance revealed a dilapidated burglar alarm box hanging at an angle in the apex of the gable end above the doors. It was a very old model with the hammer and bell visible under the bottom edge of the outer casing. The system was probably controlled by a simple zone activated system. No delays, no touch pads or closed-circuit television. To a professional burglar, it was perfect; unfit for purpose. This caused Phil to smile.

However, he shuddered again to imagine what the interior was like, probably just like the telephone box. The thought of the filthy floors, furniture and toilets, mixed with the stench of stale drink, smoke and dubious food on offer, filled him with dread. He breathed deeply in the fresh afternoon air, glad to be spared a visit inside for the time being. But he suspected he would find out exactly what joys from hell were inside before long. Fortunately, not today.

He took several photographs with his watch camera before walking back to the main road. He remembered the library was still open. There, he would be able to find out more about who this 'Max' was, the licence holder and owner of a dump that dared to have such an exotic name.

38

Saturday lunchtimes at the George were normally busy. But today it was raining heavily, causing many of the regulars to stay away. This gave John and Phil the opportunity to catch up with developments in relative peace. John began by describing his trip to Spain. Speaking to Barry Taylor had confirmed their suspicions of the connection between DS Morley and Alex Gilmour. Morley had supplied the identities of men visiting the red-light area in their cars to Gilmour, who in turn contacted the drivers and threatened them with public exposure unless they contributed to a bogus charity. This was Gilmour's moneybox.

Phil, in turn, told of his adventures into Gilmour's house where he had installed the cameras and microphones and tapped into his telephones. He intended to return to his van later to check for any information. He described how he had spoken to one of the street workers who had recognised Vicky Thompson from the police photograph. She had told him of her admission into rehab somewhere in London, possible Wembley, and perhaps most importantly, her boyfriend was called Max who owned the dreadful Caribbean Club. He had established at the Public Records Office in the local library that he was called Max Campbell and lived in an exclusive house in Clerkenwell.

'Bloody hell Phil, good work, things are progressing nicely. Barry Taylor mentioned this guy Campbell too. Apparently, Morley is leaning on Campbell for 'police protection' so he's obviously up to no good as well. I think Campbell will be pivotal in our investigation. I'll get Yvonne to run a full intelligence check on him. Incidentally, she's having Morley's phone monitored too. We need to establish what's exactly happening between these three men.'

'I think the best thing to do now, John, is to wait until we find out more information when our friend Gilmour starts talking. If I find something that you need to know urgently, I'll have to ring you at home.'

'Agreed. It's not that I don't want you to visit me, I don't want to get Charlie mixed up in all this, and besides, I never talk about my work with her cos she lives her own busy life, so I'm not going to start now.'

'Don't worry. I understand. It's easy for me, I don't have much of a social life, until I see my kids. I've figured this case will only take a few weeks and then I'm hanging everything up. Disappearing into the sunset and all that crap.'

39

Shortly after dusk, Phil returned to his van. He entered through the driver's door and slipped into the rear, switching on the monitors, sound speakers and recorders. The sound of Gilmour's voice immediately became clear. He was talking on the telephone. Phil picked up the receiver of the shadow line: '…no, that's right, George. Leave it with me. Bye.'

The monitors flickered into view, one showing Gilmour sitting on the lounge sofa looking out of the window. He appeared to be drinking a glass of white wine. He reached over to the telephone and dialled out. Still listening, Phil heard him say, 'Max. What time are you opening tonight?'

'Usual time, nine thirty. Why?'

'George is asking some awkward questions that involve you. Can't talk over the phone about it. See you then.'

'OK.'

Phil looked at his watch. Two minutes past eight. Without any hesitation, he grabbed his ignition keys, squeezed back into the driver's seat and started the engine. Instantly the quiet burble of the V8 engine sprang into life. He drove towards the Caribbean Club, some two miles away. He was unprepared for this entry, having no prior knowledge of the burglar alarm, only the crude padlock and chain around the front door handles. He would have to 'wing' this and take his chances. The opportunity of unearthing new information about the connection between Gilmour, Morley and Campbell was too tempting. With the adrenalin coursing through his veins he drove within the speed limits, making mental preparations.

As he approached the cobbled street to his right, Phil pulled up on the main road just past the junction and left the van, carrying a leather case. Continually looking around for any signs of life, he approached the club building. Nothing; quiet as the grave. Even the street lamps were unlit, smashed beyond repair. The Caribbean stood alone in the dark shadows of the surrounding taller buildings.

He walked towards the front doors and quickly looked through the eye-level letterbox. No internal lights, just blackness. He turned his attention to the padlock. With a small torch held between his teeth he inserted his small wire skeleton key and felt the tumblers softly fall and quietly click on release. The lock opened easily. He used another crude wire key on the original door lock and that opened in seconds. He paused before opening the door, anticipating an exterior alarm bell to activate.

Opening the case, Phil took out several sections of black metal rods that connected to each other. The rod now measured over twelve feet long. To the top end, he fixed a small can of self-expanding foam, its trigger fitted with a length of cord. He lifted the rod until it gently touched the bottom edge of the rusty yellow alarm box, fitted close to the apex of the roof. Once the nozzle of can touched the gap between the hammer and the bell, he pulled the cord for only a second, allowing a white liquid to spill out. Letting go of the cord, he lowered the rod to the ground, quickly dismantling it and replacing it inside the case. The foam had expanded sufficiently to fill the gap, preventing any contact with the bell. Although the alarm would activate once he entered the club, it had now been rendered silent. To make matters better, no obvious visible signs of interference were apparent.

He returned to the porch, pushed open the front doors and entered the building. Holding his torch in front, his earlier fears were confirmed; it stank. Undeterred, he walked along the corridor, into the office, where he found the telephone on the desk. He quickly unscrewed the mouthpiece, placed a tap inside, before resealing it and placing it back in its original position. With no time to place any cameras, he positioned two microphones, one under the desk and another above the central ceiling light, obstructed slightly by the overhanging torn lampshade.

Glancing at his watch, he knew there was no time left. He ran back to the front doors, closed and locked them before resetting the padlock on the chain. He double-checked to see if everything was in its original place before returning to the main road where the van was parked.

Once inside the sanctuary of his van, he sighed with relief and looked at his watch. Nine o'clock exactly.

He drove some distance away, until he was out of sight yet within range of the newly installed equipment. He parked up and moved to the rear. Sitting in his comfortable chair, he realised just how much he was sweating. His heart rate was still racing, but he felt invigorated. This was life on the edge. Leaning forward he switched on the sound recorders and plugged the telephone to loudspeaker mode, settled down and waited.

Ten minutes later, he heard the noise of doors opening. He knew the keyboard for the burglar alarm would show movement in several zones of the club where he had tripped it, but with the lack of the exterior bell, the operator would assume there was a fault on the system, possibly caused by rodents.

He heard footsteps become louder followed by the sound of touch keys being pressed on the alarm system's board. A man's voice muttered 'Bloody thing.' The footsteps continued. Fainter, then louder.

Eventually the sound became clearer. The man had walked into the office where the microphones were. A drink was poured, followed by the sound of someone sitting in a soft chair. Seconds later, a soft knock on a door in the distance. More footsteps, this time two sets. Phil checked to ensure the recording was working. It was.

'Hello, Max. Sorry to bother you before you open but it's important. George spoke to me earlier this afternoon and told me about Vicky Thompson and another girl called Julie something. Apparently, the Met have circulated reports of two women fitting their descriptions being found in the Thames recently. He wanted to know what you and another man called Sammy, knew about them. I've no idea how he got to know about you and me. But we can't underestimate him. He was obviously worried about the business arrangement he has with you and how it could affect his position.'

Max shouted, 'The little bastard. He's only supposed to be watching my back, not getting scared. Sergeant Morley is a spineless little shit. What's your relationship like with him?'

'It used to be close, but frankly he's now out of his league. If he gets any wind of the Manchester mob and our hapless MP operation, we're both done for.'

'I'm already ahead of you, Alex. With the planning for our export goods in an advanced state, we could lose it all. Probably join those girls in the Thames.'

'What happened to those girls anyway, Max?'

'I've no idea. I know it looks a little suspicious, them being my ex-girlfriends and all that, but that's just a coincidence. They were both operators in a dangerous world. They knew the risks.'

'What are we going to do with George now? Do you want me speak to him?'

'No. I don't want you anywhere near him from now on. I shall deal with him in my own way. He's become a liability to both of us. No doubt you've had a business going on with him as well?'

'Yes, a little one. But that's now run its course. It was fine whilst it lasted but George will be retiring in the next few years, and frankly, he'll have nothing to offer then.'

OK. Just keep quiet about everything. How's the special permit coming on?'

'Slowly. Our friendly MP is working on it. Haven't heard from him in nearly a week. Might ring his office next week to get an update. Remember, Max, we knew this would take some time to set up. We'll have to be patient.'

'Let's hope the Manchester lot feel the same way. They've more invested than us.'

'I know Max. I'll contact you after I've spoken to him.'

Phil heard the shuffle of chairs and footsteps becoming fainter, followed by the closing of the front doors. Suddenly he heard the dialling sound of the telephone. Max must have returned quietly to his office. His voice said, 'There's another job. It's the Babylon on your list. I know it's going to be expensive. No concealment this time. Just an unfortunate piece of bad luck. I'll know when it's been done when I read it in the newspapers.' The line went dead.

Phil stared at the recording machine. It was all there. The connection between Gilmour, Morley and Max had been identified.

Additionally, the involvement with some Manchester criminals and the special permit through Jason Moore had surfaced. And now the imminent murder of a Metropolitan Police officer, bent or otherwise. He needed to contact John urgently.

40

John had settled into his nightly routine, shower followed by a cup of tea before retiring to bed. Charlie had already gone upstairs and as he walked through the hallway towards the stairs, the telephone rang. He looked at the clock: ten thirty. It was late.

He picked the receiver up. 'Hello.'

'John, sorry to call so late, but there have been some important developments. I need to speak with you now.'

'Now Phil?'

'Yes. It could be a matter of life or death.'

'Come over here now.'

'Hoped you would say that. I'm parked at the end of your street next to the telephone box.'

'See you in a couple of minutes then.'

John went upstairs and saw Charlie sitting upright in bed, reading a magazine. 'What is it?'

'I'm really sorry about this but that was Phil on the phone. It seems something has turned up and he needs to speak to me now. He'll be here in a minute. Sorry.'

'Don't be silly, John. You know I'd love to see Phil again, it's been ages. I'll come down with you and make some coffee.'

Descending the stairs, they saw the silhouette of a man through the front door opaque glass. As John opened the door, Charlie rushed forward. 'Phil it's lovely to see you again.' They kissed each other on the cheek. 'Sorry, I'm in my pyjamas. I'll go and put the coffee on.'

'Thanks, Charlie. It's been a long time and I apologise for the lateness of my visit.'

They went through into the kitchen. With Charlie pretending not hear their conversation, Phil sat down and opened the large aluminium case he'd been carrying. As he set it up on the table he said, 'Have you got a socket for this?'

'Sure, give me the plug,' said Charlie, still not listening.

'John, we've got some serious developments tonight. I've been listening into a conversation between Gilmour and this fellow Max who runs the Caribbean Club. Cutting to the chase, I was obliged to go inside this filthy cesspit and set up a couple of microphones in his office. I want you to listen to their conversation and the phone call Max made after Gilmour had left.'

All three sat with their cups of coffee listening to the audio tape. For a few seconds, there was just a continuous hum before the recording picked up the sounds and eventually the conversation. Once Phil had played both recordings he looked at John, but it was Charlie who spoke first. 'Bloody hell. That's dynamite. What are you going to do with that?'

John frowned. 'I need a few moments to take all that in. Play it again, Phil.'

They listened to the recording three times before John gave his decision. 'We need to speak to Yvonne tonight. I'll go and phone her now. Let's have another drink. Make it a whisky, Charlie.'

'Doubles,' added Phil.

John returned ten minutes later. 'You're stopping here tonight, Phil, don't trust you with my whisky and your driving licence. Anyway, Yvonne will be here at nine thirty in the morning. Let's catch up on old times.'

Charlie stood up. 'Well, if that's your game, I'll go and prepare your room Phil, and I'll bid you both good night.'

41

Next morning, with slightly thick heads, both men sat quietly at the kitchen table whilst Charlie served them omelettes with toast and strong coffee.

'You two are getting far too old for all this. You'd better get yourselves sorted out, Yvonne will be here soon. Shame I'm going to miss her but I've got the Tube to catch.'

Phil smiled at her. 'Thanks, Charlie, it was lovely to see you again last night, especially in your pyjamas'

'Sod off, you dirty old man.' She leant over and kissed him on his forehead. 'Don't make it so long next time. I'll see you later this afternoon, John. Give Yvonne my love.' Then she was gone, leaving them both discussing the previous night's events.

Fifteen minutes later, Yvonne arrived. It was eight years since she'd seen Phil. After quickly embracing him she said, 'Phil, what a pleasure to see you and John again. I hope you're behaving yourself and not contaminating him with your shady habits.'

'Lovely to see you again too,' he said, not committing himself.

John invited them all to sit down 'Yvonne, thanks to Phil's interventions we've unearthed a number of disturbing matters. Before we do, remember they'll not stand the rigours of cross-examination at the Crown Court, so let's call it compelling intelligence rather than evidence at this stage.'

'My God. You've been trespassing again, Phil, haven't you?'

He looked at her. 'Shut up, Yvonne. I remember you when you were only too willing to take chances. Have you forgotten?'

'No, I've just got a lot wiser.'

'Just listen at what I've uncovered first, then you can do with it as you wish. I've got some results here that you wouldn't have managed through your rule-ridden procedures.'

'Shut up, you two' interjected John. 'Let's leave that till last. First, let me tell you about my visit to Spain and the distraught Mr Albert Jones I met a few days ago, who I honestly believe was framed for some indiscretion he never committed.'

John outlined the conversation he had had with Barry Taylor where he suspected Max Campbell was paying Morley protection money. He also mentioned the connection between them, Alex Gilmour and the Manchester mob, 'Taylor didn't know what this was really about. That's something we'll have to work on.'

After John had finished, Phil spoke vaguely about the surveillance equipment he had placed in Gilmour's house. But just as Yvonne was about to interrupt, Phil said 'Listen to this first before you say anything.' He started to play the audio tapes between Gilmour and Campbell, replaying the part mentioning the ominous threat made against DS Morley's life.

She stared at them in silence, stood up and walked to the patio doors, peering outside into the back garden. John and Phil glanced at each other and shrugged their shoulders. Eventually, she turned around.

'Boys, you've done well. I need to sanitise all this information before I take it upstairs to the Deputy Commissioner. I believe you have uncovered a wider corruption circle than we anticipated. Morley will be dealt with today. He'll be airlifted out of all this and taken into immediate custody. Max Campbell was registered on his informants' schedule, preventing any other police officer approaching him without clearing it with Morley personally. It's the perfect protection for any criminal. I've got something else to tell you. Late last night I received a message. Jason Moore, the MP has apparently regained consciousness and he's asking a lot of questions. When I get over there, he'll be answering some of mine. We may have to offer him the choice of turning Queen's Evidence or of spending the rest of his life behind bars. Meanwhile, I shall require a copy of this tape and a full written statement of all your investigations so far. Phil, don't worry about any of your unlawful activities; I'll speak to the DPP's[7] office this morning in an attempt to grant you some type of immunity. For the time being, continue to monitor Max Campbell's and Alex Gilmour's phones and let me know of any further developments. John, once I've made some calls, I'll get back to you with all the details. When I do, I'll want you to place the advert in *The Times* saying 'Pakistani grains and pulses ready for research', together with a Post Office box number. It looks like I'm going to have a busy morning, planning a future operation. I'm sure this will now be going to the very top; we're looking at suspected murders, blackmail and conspiracy for the wholesale importation of tons of heroin. Not to mention the real threat to the life of a serving member of the Met, whether he's bent bastard or not. Anyway, well done, again. I'm proud of you.'

'Thanks, Yvonne. Are we still friends then?' asked Phil.

'You can shut up this time, you old bugger.'

'I'll take that as a yes.'

John asked, 'Yvonne, can you see if you can get some photographs of this Max Campbell? I wouldn't know him if I walked past him in the street.'

'Sure. Leave that with me.'

---

[7] Director of Public Prosecutions.

42

Yvonne returned to her office and placed a call immediately to the Deputy Commissioner, Sir John Simpson.

'Good morning, Sir John. This is DCI Hall. I'm sorry for the intrusion, but I must have a meeting with you as soon as possible. The inquiry you asked me to look into several weeks ago has uncovered some disturbing developments that, in my opinion, have the potential to cause a catastrophic saturation of heroin into the UK.'

'Are you requesting a golden interview?'[8]

'Yes, sir.'

'Get around here now and bring all the information with you. I'll summon Commander Higgins to attend as well.'

'Thank you, sir. Traffic permitting, I'll be there in twenty minutes.'

The Deputy Commissioner's office suite was on the first floor of the New Scotland Yard building, in a corner location with large windows on two sides. Modestly furnished, but with a large conference room with seating for thirty, it was the engine room for the day-to-day running of the largest police force in the UK. As the Deputy, he was responsible for the strategic and tactical performances of the Met, whilst the Commissioner was the public and political figurehead, briefed only with a summary of ongoing events and leaving the details to Sir John and his Command Team.

When Yvonne finally arrived, she was ushered inside by Sir John's

---

[8] Clearing the diary of immediate appointments.

secretary. Two men were waiting: Sir John and Commander Jim Higgins, Head of the Metropolitan Police Crime Division.

Feeling a little apprehensive, Yvonne took a deep breath. 'Good morning, gentlemen, please allow me a few moments to set up this equipment.' Once the equipment was ready, her briefing took over an hour, with both men frequently asking questions and taking notes.

Afterwards, they studied the information again and discussed their future actions. Sir John made his recommendations. 'Firstly, Yvonne I want you to take immediate control of the investigation into the suspected murders of these two women and the criminal conduct of Morley, Gilmour and especially Campbell. Also, I want Jason Moore sorted out. But your first task is to deal with DS Morley. He must be arrested and kept incognito, if only to keep him out of harm's way. He may be of value to us before we throw the book at him. Your assistants, John Evans and Phil Smith are 'old school', they've operated outside the rules of evidence gathering and much of their findings will never stand the scrutiny of legal challenge. Nevertheless, they should be commended for their tenacity. We must build our case from their intelligence. In view of the fact we are dealing with an MP who has been seriously compromised in his official ministerial role and the possible involvement with criminals in London and Manchester intending to import enormous quantities of heroin from Pakistan, I'm proposing to hold a top-level security meeting. I shall be inviting representatives from the Security Services, Border Control, the Foreign and Commonwealth Office, together with the National Coordinator of the Drug Enforcement Authority. I'll also speak to the Chief Constable of the Greater Manchester Police. Mr Higgins, I want you to start enquiries about the possible connection between these men and the Manchester criminal underworld.'

Turning to Yvonne, he continued, 'I shall ask your father to come to this meeting too. If we can all work together, perhaps we might have an opportunity of bagging all these criminals in one swoop. Perhaps. Unfortunately, I'm not inviting you. With your father there, it's not the right protocol.'

'I understand. Sir John, what about Jason Moore now he's regained consciousness?'

'I want you to go and speak to him too. His role in the Government and as a Member of Parliament is now untenable. However, you could suggest to him that he could save some of his reputation if he were to cooperate with us in this matter.'

'What should I say if he wants to apply to turn Queen's Evidence and go on the Witness Protection Scheme?'

'Don't let's be too hasty about that to begin with. We'll see what he has to say first.'

'I understand, sir.'

'Meanwhile, get your man to place the advert in The Times.'

'Before you've had the meeting?'

'Yes. I'm going to sanction that now.'

Commander Higgins spoke. 'Yvonne, it looks like we have two unsolved murders, Vicky Thompson and Julie Brecon. And this Max Campbell is our prime suspect. He appears to have been playing the Badger Game for some time.'

Sir John interrupted him. 'I don't like this phrase Badger Game. So far as I'm concerned, it's just bloody plain extortion, or to call it by its proper name, blackmail, and contrary to section 21 of the Theft Act.'

'Yes, sir,' Higgins replied with a wry smile, before continuing with his instructions. 'Yvonne, you have done well so far but there's a great deal of work yet to do. Leave the wider scope of the investigation with Sir John and myself; you concentrate on Campbell and Gilmour when our DS Morley is in custody. I shall be authorising all of Mr Smith's covert surveillance equipment from today. So, from this moment, all the audio, imagery and telephone conversations will be legally admissible.'

'Thank you, sir. That makes me feel more comfortable.'

'Me too. I'll sign the forms now.'

Sir John leant forward. 'We now have a plan of action. I'll leave you two to sort the finer details for your operations. I need to organise the wider implications. There is the potential for some heavy political fallout if this goes pear-shaped. I want to be kept up to date on a daily basis. Yvonne, you will report directly to Mr Higgins only. We must be vigilant with all of this. There's a great risk we may lose the main players from Manchester. Keep it tight.'

Commander Higgins and Yvonne stood and walked towards the door. Before they left Sir John said, 'Good luck.'

As they descended the rear staircase, Commander Higgins said,

'Yvonne. I'm going to give you a great deal of discretion with this inquiry. Sir John is good at what he does but he's never been a streetwise detective. We are dealing with a couple of savvy crooks who will stop at nothing to feed their greed and filthy habits. I like the look of your old chums, they know how to handle themselves, but remember, our role is to make sure we all stay within the constraints of the law. Make sure you keep them out of harm's way. Do you understand?'

'I do, sir. We go back a long time.'

'Yes, I know. I've done my homework on both of them. John Evans is a man of principle, prepared to sacrifice everything and challenge everyone in the name of integrity. Phil Smith, I like. He reminds me of my old boss. He gets results, but through the old ways. These are no longer acceptable, and we must be guarded against this marvellous old maverick.'

She smiled. 'Thank you, sir. I know exactly what you're referring to. I'll take full responsibility for them.'

'That's what I wanted to hear. You concentrate on these three men and Jason Moore. Once this special permit appears to be a goer, I'll deal with the heroin and the Manchester connection. Yvonne, I'm looking forward to working with you.'

They walked to the front reception, shook hands and left the building, going in different directions. Once she arrived back in her office, Yvonne reflected on his comments. Both John and Phil were not just colleagues, but dear old friends. Unfortunately, times had moved on; policing had changed, and it was now more accountable and under closer public scrutiny. There was no longer the onus on the police to prove guilt; it was simply a case of gathering the evidence. A High Court judge had recently commented, 'The prime purpose of the police is to gather all the available evidence. The courts do not deal with the truth, only the evidence presented before them. The truth is a matter for the jury to decide.'

She knew Phil did not agree with that ruling and it was futile to try to convince him otherwise. She also knew he would have to be 'reined in' when he stepped out of line. Otherwise all the evidence submitted to the prosecution could be jeopardised and allow the guilty to walk free.

43

Within two hours of the meeting, Sir John Simpson had spoken to the Police Commissioner and the Home Secretary. Arrangements were provisionally made for Executive members of the Security Services, UK Border Control, and the National Coordinator of the Drug Enforcement Authority, together with the Chief Constable of Greater Manchester Police and Sir Graham Hall from the Department of Trade and Industry (DTI), to link up on a conference telephone facility. Decisions at the highest level were necessary to prepare a strategy to identify and arrest the most influential criminals concerned in organised crime within the UK. The issue of a bogus importation permit would serve that purpose, but the political and social effects of it failing could be catastrophic. Running a meticulous surveillance operation both within the country and perhaps abroad would be logistically challenging and expensive.

The intervention of the Home Secretary gave immediate direction. The special permit would be issued with strict transit conditions and the operation would be financed by Whitehall. Sir John would be appointed Gold Commander with overall responsibility, supported by the Home Office, Foreign and Commonwealth Office, Sir Graham Hall (of the DTI) and the Department for Border Control. Silver Commanders were also appointed from the National Drug Enforcement Authority and the Greater Manchester Police.

By noon, an action plan had been formulated. All parties began to appoint their teams, with special liaison officers trained in cross-departmental protocols, thus allowing a web of transparency to emerge between the various agencies.

By one o'clock, Yvonne received her instructions from Commander Higgins.

44

A hundred miles away in a private ward of the Gloucester Royal Hospital, Jason Moore began emerging from his coma, mumbling incoherently as he gradually regained consciousness. At first, his lucidity was intermittent; for moments he clearly saw the ceiling above him but soon slipped back into a heavy sleep. When he finally awoke he was in severe pain, his temples throbbing with the heavy pumping of blood to his head. Gradually, he became aware of something mentally disturbing. What had happened?

Confused, he screwed up his eyes and looked at his immediate surroundings. Tubes from his arm seemed to be connected to a machine behind him that was making a distinct beeping sound. Looking down towards his feet he saw he was wearing a white gown and lying on top of a bed. It was at that moment he realised he was in hospital and remembered the dreadful events leading up to his present circumstances. He tried to raise his head and caught a glimpse of someone sitting near the doorway. He re-focussed his eyes and to his disappointment vaguely saw a uniformed police officer sitting on a wooden chair, reading a newspaper. He lay quietly back again and drifted off again into his own world.

A little later, he made another involuntary sound and opened his eyes. He stared directly into the eyes of a young woman, dressed in a light blue smock.

'Good morning, Mr Moore. Welcome back. I'm your nurse and I'll go and fetch the doctor.'

He was unable to speak, just make another gurgling sound in his throat. He noticed the policeman approach him and smile.

'Good morning, Mr Moore, we thought we'd lost you. My boss wants to talk to you urgently.' With that, he disappeared from his sight.

Again, he was confused. His recent lucid period was lost. Where am I? Why am I here? Why are the police here? His thoughts were interrupted.

'Hello, Mr Moore. My name is Dr Hewitt and I'm delighted you have regained consciousness. You have been here in the Gloucester Royal Hospital for ten days. Can you remember anything that may have happened to you before you came here?'

'No.'

'Do you know your full name?'

'Yes. My name is Jason Moore. I'm an MP, aren't I?'

'Yes, you are. Can you remember what happened?'

Moore looked towards the window. Dr Hewitt was experienced at questioning patients who were returning to reality. Interrupting this important question often prevented the patient from searching back through their mind. This search usually took several minutes and stimulated the part of the brain that was temporarily blocked, allowing the 'log jam' effect to eventually loosen. This, in turn, liberated the snagged impulses coming from the memory bank.

Jason Moore continued to stare in silence. After nearly ten minutes he muttered, 'Oh God. I know why I'm here. What am I going to do?'

'Whatever happened before you were admitted into this hospital, Mr Moore, you have come back to us and you can now get on with the rest of your life.'

'I know what I did. I wish I was dead.'

'Mr Moore, you may have your reasons why you did this. I'm not going to ask you. I'm just concerned with your physical and psychological wellbeing. There are medically qualified staff here in the hospital who will deal with your development and offer you their excellent services. Once you are on the road to recovery, you'll be stronger and more able to meet these challenges ahead.'

'Why are the police here?'

'That I don't know. But you mustn't worry too much about them for the time being. You're my patient and until I consider you are fit and well, they can't interview you or take you away from here. Do you understand, Mr Moore?'

'Yes. Thank you, Doctor.'

Gradually, Jason Moore's condition began to improve. He noticed the uniformed police constable had been replaced by a plain clothes officer. Clearly, they had every intention of interviewing him before he left hospital. His mind started to wander back to the photographs of him and the young woman caught in bed with him. How stupid he had been, allowing himself to fall for such a guise. The humiliation of pleading with Sir Graham Hall to grant a special permit, so he could save his career. What was he going to do?

Whilst he was contemplating his uncertain future, several wards away Dr Hewitt was paged to go immediately to the Chief Executive's office. He was initially annoyed by the request. He still had over half of his rounds to perform and was already running late. He walked into the reception area where Professor Guy was waiting for him. 'Come in, Dr Hewitt. I'm sorry for taking you away from your busy schedule, but it's urgent.'

Once they were sitting down, Professor Guy said, 'Dr Hewitt, one of your patients is Jason Moore, the MP.'

'Yes, that's right.'

'The police need to speak to him urgently.'

'Out of the question. He needs at least three days of peace and definitely no stress. I've even objected strongly to the presence of the police outside his room. The man attempted to take his own life and it makes no difference to me if he's committed any crime or not. He's my patient and he's only just regained consciousness today. Sorry, Professor. No deal.'

'I thought you would say that. And, for what it's worth, so would I. Unfortunately, I have been instructed by the highest of authorities that Mr Moore must be spoken to by the police.'

'What highest authority are you talking about?'

'The Minister for the National Health Service and the Home Secretary to begin with.'

'Christ. What's he done?'

'Can't tell you. Don't even know myself. Only that he presents a possible threat to national security.'

'We don't have much choice do we, then?'

'Not really.'

'I want to be present when they talk to him. He is my patient after all. Security or not.'

'Sorry. That won't happen either. They will speak to him tonight with a doctor from the security services and if they're satisfied he's well enough, they're going to take him away.'

'Bloody hell. It really is 1984.'

'I'm afraid you're right. Needless to say, they reminded me to tell you, we are both subject to the Official Secrets Act. In fact, they were quite forcibly of that. You're right, it is Orwellian.'

'That may be the case, Professor, but you and I are bound by more than any Act of Parliament, the Hippocratic Oath.'

'Well said, Dr Hewitt, but that won't change a thing I'm afraid.'

45

At the same Jason Moore was returning to this world, DS Morley was about to leave his. He'd just settled back into his large office chair, preparing to check a number of case files awaiting prosecution, when he was summoned by the Superintendent to his office. Announcing the summons to his staff, he said, 'Just going upstairs to see Mr Boring. If I'm not back in ten minutes, for God's sake one of you ring his office and make an excuse to get me out of there.'

They smiled. One of them shouted, 'Shall I ring you to say the results from the pox clinic have arrived?'

'Ten minutes, gentlemen, or it's a big hat[9] for all of you.'

He shoved his chair to one side and sauntered out of his office. He climbed the old wooden stairs, approached the door marked 'Superintendent Operations,' knocked and entered. 'What is it, boss?'

As he spoke he noticed two other people in the room, a man and a young woman. The woman was at least ten years younger than himself, pretty looking, and completely unknown to him. His mind began to wander uncontrollably. Is she coming to work with us? Is she one of these rapid promotion candidates or, worse, from the social services?

She stepped forward. 'Are you Detective Sergeant George Morley?'

'Yes, I am, my dear. Who are you?'

'My name is DCI Hall. I am arresting you for bribery and corruption, aiding and abetting another to commit blackmail, and

---

[9] Return to uniform duties.

176

suspicion of murder.' She continued to caution him as his jaw dropped. After finishing, she asked, 'Do you wish to make a reply before your interview?'

'You must be bloody joking. DCI at your age? And a woman too.'

Yvonne refused to rise to the bait. With a completely expressionless face she ignored his rudeness, but reflected inwardly, 'Not a good start, you bent bastard.' The other officer moved forward and without any hesitation grabbed both his wrists and placed a pair of handcuffs on them, leaving his arms in front of him.

Yvonne said, 'Listen to me, George Morley. You are being taken away from here to another place for questioning. I have the authority from the Deputy Commissioner himself when I tell you that if you attempt to struggle or to inform anyone of your detention from this moment forward, you will be kept away from any contact with the outside world until this investigation has been completed. Do you understand me?'

'No comment.'

She turned to the Superintendent. 'Sir, I would like you to sound the fire alarm. I don't care if it's not practice day. Get everyone out of this station into the rendezvous point in the rear yard, including any prisoners. I want this place deserted when we take our prisoner out of the side door. No one is to see us leave.'

'As you wish Chief Inspector.'

He left the room. DS Morley chuckled. 'Do you think I'm going out of the nick without putting up a struggle?'

'Frankly, Morley, I don't give a shit.'

'What are you going to do? Hit me?'

'No, of course not. But he might.'

Her colleague had remained quiet throughout. He stepped forward and whispered in Morley's ear, 'She's a lady and a boss lady at that. She lives by the rule book. But I don't. And nothing will give me more pleasure than giving you the biggest shit kicking of your life. When we leave this office, I promise you'll be over my shoulder, you fat bastard, if you make any sound. Your call.'

DS Morley recognised the threat. He instinctively knew the officer was more than capable of carrying it out. His mind began to shut down, realising how serious his position was. He started formulating a simple strategy. Keep quiet until they had shown their hand. Ignore any threats of false evidence, getting the sack or even imprisonment. They would probably talk about his relationships with Alex Gilmour and possibly Max Campbell. But there was nothing definite to connect them all together. He had always been an advocate of 'no cough, no job'. Provided he kept to a story he was safe. After all, they would have to prove these offences, and although very serious, that would require a greater degree of proof.

Five minutes later the fire bell rang and the sound of heavy boots was heard everywhere. The Superintendent's office was on the first floor. When all human movement ceased, they left the building via the side entrance into the parking area reserved for visitors, on the opposite side of the building to where the head count for all personnel and prisoners was taking place.

Yvonne led, whilst DS Morley was frog-marched unceremoniously to a plain white Ford Transit van, parked and with its engine running. The two men stepped inside through the rear doors, and Yvonne secured the lock. She walked to the front and jumped in, alongside two other colleagues, John and Phil. They smiled at each other before Phil drove away into the mid-afternoon traffic.

The journey took nearly an hour. No one spoke. Phil reversed the van into a courtyard and parked up. He opened the two rear doors to find DS Morley hunched up against the side of the wire cage. He appeared to have a slightly swollen lip and the relief on his face at seeing Phil was palpable. The officer next to him looked vaguely out past Phil towards the high wooden gates behind him. Phil smiled but said nothing.

Morley stepped out of the van into the bright sunlight. When his eyes became customised, he noticed they were in a courtyard approximately the size of a tennis court, surrounded by a high stone wall. Turning his head, he saw a large L-shaped red brick house with small windows and no curtains, looking empty and uninviting. Yvonne approached him. 'Welcome to your new home for the time being,' but before he could reply, she turned and walked towards a green wooden door. He felt a sudden firm prod in his back and quickly followed her.

They entered a kitchen. It had been untouched for decades, with broken cream wooden cupboard doors surrounding an old chipped Belfast sink. A black cooking range, with cobwebs stretching across its small hatches, stood on a red tiled floor. The room smelt of dampness and stale air. They continued into the hallway and turned left.

He saw Yvonne disappear down a flight of stone steps and hesitated. 'Where are you taking me? If I'm under arrest, I should be in a police station, not here.'

He felt another prod in his back. 'Get down there, before you slip and fall.'

He became anxious. Why was he here? What were they going to do with him? Hell. Were they real police officers? Never seen any of them before. He now felt a twinge of fear.

He followed Yvonne into a cellar measuring fifteen feet square. There was a wooden table with two chairs, a single bed and a sink in the corner. Under the sink stood a bucket with a towel laid on top. A simple utilitarian plywood wardrobe stood in the other corner, its wide-open door revealing some items of clothing. There was no natural light. Illumination came from a flickering double neon tube that made a low continuous buzz.

He stood motionless in the centre of the cellar, looking at the layout. But before he could open his mouth, the door closed behind him with the sound of heavy sliding bolts, followed by footsteps climbing the stairs. His suspicions became more acute; had he been kidnapped by criminals? He knew it was pointless to shout out any protest. Hopefully, he might convince them he was more valuable if he cooperated with them. He sat on the bed and sighed. Two hours ago, he had been in the office with his team, planning their next operation. Now, he was locked up like a rat in a cage. What was going to happen to him?

Meanwhile, Yvonne, Phil and John returned to London in an unmarked police car. Phil drove all the way and dropped John off at his home first.

'Coming for a drink?'

Yvonne sighed. 'No, thanks, I've got some things to catch up with in the office.'

'Things to do too,' said Phil, 'but give my love to Charlie.'

As John opened the passenger door, Yvonne said, 'Oh, John, nearly forgot. Here's some copies of photographs taken a few years ago of Max Campbell. There's some for Phil too.'

John put them in his pocket before the car sped away into the night traffic.

46

Jason Moore was making plans for the future. He remembered the letter and photographs received in the mail at his constituency office and the debacle of the meeting with Sir Graham Hall. The stupidity of asking him to grant a special permit and the miserable failed attempt at his life. The future was now clear; he would resign his seat from Parliament due to his poor health and buy a small country house in Normandy. He could afford to spend the rest of his life there on his savings and modest pension. With a new start in France, he would reinvent himself and try to forget his premature departure from public service. Hopefully, with the passage of time, people would forget the impending scandalous headlines in the newspapers. Perhaps he could even repair the fractious relationship he had with his estranged children.

As he was calculating the monetary conversion of pounds sterling into French francs, he saw two male nurses enter the room. One of them said, 'Hello, Mr Moore, we've come to transfer you to another unit.'

'Where's that?'

'Another hospital, nearby. Don't worry we'll look after you.'

He noticed the plain clothes policeman had gone and there were no other familiar medical staff present. Feeling a little nervous, he asked, 'Where's Dr Hewitt.'

'He knows what's happening to you. There's nothing to worry about.'

'I don't like this. You can go away and leave me alone until I've seen…' He felt a slight prick in his right arm and fell into unconsciousness again, his mumblings hardly audible. This allowed the two medical orderlies free access to his bed, medication and personal belongings. Within a minute he had been removed from the room, wheeled through into the adjoining ward where all the beds were hidden behind their closed courtesy curtains, and placed into the lift. They descended into the basement, before quickly transferring into a waiting ambulance.

Throughout the journey Jason Moore's unconsciousness occasionally lifted, when he faintly heard voices and the sound of the ambulance engine and occasionally the indicators. The sedative administered, rendered him immediate loss of consciousness with some slight paralysis. Although there was always a risk, fortunately he was a strong and physically fit man for his age.

As he began to regain his senses he asked, 'Where am I?'

A woman out of his view spoke softly. 'Mr Moore. You are safe. You are being moved from Gloucester Royal Hospital for your own protection. I must assure you, your safety, health and welfare are my only concern. You are presently being transferred to a private medical clinic run by the Ministry of Defence for service men and women injured whilst on active service. There, you will be seen by a senior police officer, DCI Hall. She will explain exactly what's happened and answer any questions you may have.'

He lay back on the trolley bed, wondering what had happened to him in the last few hours. His thoughts were interrupted as the ambulance came to a halt. He heard the back doors open and felt the trolley move backwards. He saw the greying sky above his head, inhaled the cold fresh air before entering a warm building with bright overhead lighting. He was pushed along a corridor before ascending in another lift. After exiting, the trolley came to rest in a private room with two large windows allowing the daylight to stream through. He was lifted onto a bed and tucked between the sheets by two male nurses.

For a few moments he gathered his thoughts and looked around. Sitting in a chair next to his bed was a young woman, dressed in a dark grey suit, with short dark brown hair and piercing eyes. 'Mr Moore. My name is Yvonne Hall and I'm leading a serious investigation into the suspected murders of two women and several cases of blackmail. I'm particularly interested in your involvement with a woman called Vicky Thompson. Do you know her?'

He hesitated and looked away. 'I think I need to see my solicitor.'

'I think you will do, but not just for now. I'm going to ask you again. Do you know a woman called Vicky Thompson?'

'Yes, I did. But it's all over now.'

'Why is that?'

'I don't want to answer any more questions until I've seen my solicitor.'

'I understand your reluctance, Mr Moore, but please listen to what I'm about to tell you. It's very important. You have got yourself mixed up with some serious criminals. I'm satisfied you had no intention of deliberately placing yourself in such a vulnerable position but the truth is, you were lured into a simple honey trap by a young prostitute called Vicky Thompson. You were photographed and videotaped with this woman and later, a journalist called Alex Gilmour approached you about this. Some pressure was then placed on you to obtain a special importation permit, allowing some crops to be brought into the UK for scientific purposes. And that if you arranged this, those photos and videos would be given to you and the story would never see the light of day. How am I doing so far, Mr Moore?'

He looked blankly at Yvonne. His retirement to Normandy looked a long way off for now.

She continued. 'Let me fill you in with a few details you may be unaware of. Firstly, Vicky Thompson is dead. We believe she was murdered, not long after the photos were taken. Secondly, have you any idea why you were approached to get a special importation permit?'

He remained silent.

'No? Well, let me tell you. The crops in question were to be tons of pure cut heroin from Afghanistan, shipped to the UK via Pakistan and Egypt. This was to be bankrolled by organised crime syndicates in Manchester and Liverpool. Have you anything to say now?'

'No. I had no idea of any of that. What do you want from me?'

'Now, that's much better, Mr Moore. I have been authorised by the Home Secretary to tell you, provided you fully cooperate with us in this investigation, you will be placed in the Witness Protection Scheme and your identity and eventual relocation will remain secret for the rest of your life. As you can appreciate, your career as a politician is now effectively over. But you can still regain some dignity and self-respect if you do as we ask of you. I'll let you have some time to reflect.'

As she left the room, he lay on his back and stared up at the ceiling. He weighed up his options. He had studied law long before a life in politics and knew exactly what they were offering him. Turning Queen's Evidence. 'Supergrass' as it was called in Ulster. After mentally exploring all his limited options, he made his decision, conceding he had little choice; the scandal would not only finish his political life immediately, but also leave him exposed to the vengeful force of powerful criminals. He had no choice but to cooperate with the authorities. After all, he passionately still believed in the rule of law.

He lifted his head from the pillow and shouted, 'I want to speak to the policewoman again, please?'

47

George Morley had heard nothing since walking into the brightly lit but sparsely furnished cellar room. He looked at his watch, but it had stopped. He was now both hungry and a little anxious about his immediate future, but above all else, desperate for a cigarette.

He examined the door and tried to quietly open it. It was locked. He covered every inch of the whitewashed walls and ceiling to see if there were any listening devices or cameras. Nothing. He looked in the small wardrobe and discovered a neat pile of underwear and socks, a dozen shirts on hangers; all his size.

As he returned to sit on the bed, he heard the door unlock and open. Standing inside the entrance was the man who had earlier smacked him in the mouth. He was carrying a tray. He bent down and placed it on the concrete floor and began to leave.

Morley stepped forward. 'Please tell me where I am and what's going to happen to me.'

The man completely ignored him, slamming the heavy door behind him. Morley looked at the tray. It contained a plastic jug of water, sandwiches and a bag of plain crisps. No cigarettes.

He picked it up and ate the food quickly. Afterwards, he needed to go to relieve himself and shouted out, 'I need the toilet.' But there was no reply, just silence. His urge became desperate. He looked at the bucket and realised it was the only solution. There was no way out; no escape; it was the lowest moment in his life and his arrogant manner gradually gave way to servitude. The short but harsh incarceration, without any communication, was psychologically breaking down his resistance.

Left alone all night in silence with the door remaining closed, he had no knowledge of what time it was, but guessed he had been over twenty-four hours since he was seized from King's Cross Police Station.

Suddenly, the door opened and a middle-aged man stood in the entrance. He had been one of the escorts from London. 'Good evening, Mr Morley. Do you want to talk to me?'

He stood up from his bed. 'Just tell me where I am and who the hell you are and what the bloody time is.'

'It's six o'clock. Please sit down. We need to talk.'

'Where am I?'

'You're in a safe house where no one will find you. I know you won't believe me, but there's a contract out on you right now. Your partner Max wants you dead.'

'What are you talking about?'

'Now sit down and listen to what I've got to say.'

As they faced each other over the small table, John continued. 'My name is Inspector John Evans. I have very good reason to believe you've colluded with Alex Gilmour and Max Campbell on several times to commit serious criminal offences. For instance, you've been supplying Gilmour with confidential details of men seen in the red-light area of King's Cross and conspiring with him to commit a multitude of offences of blackmail. Furthermore, I suspect you have received bribes from several pimps and also used your position for financial gain, by offering protection to Max Campbell from police interference and prosecution. I believe I have in my possession sufficient evidence to charge you. As you are well aware, an admission is normally the cornerstone to any prosecution. But I can tell you now, Mr Morley, I don't need one from you. In fact, I would like you to deny all the charges facing you. It would allow me the opportunity of telling the jury just what a bent copper you've been. You'll get at least twenty-five years minimum.'

'Let's see your evidence.'

John produced a small pocket-sized tape player from his jacket pocket and placed it on the table. 'Now, you know these men and so you'll be able to recognise their voices better than me as I've yet to have that privilege. Listen to them talking. The first conversation is between Alex and Max, from Alex's phone. The second is between them both together in Max's office at the Caribbean Club and third is a phone call from Max to someone we don't know yet. This last one, you need to listen to carefully, very carefully. This should convince you of the bad company you've been keeping.'

He switched the button to play. Suddenly Morley leant forward, staring at the small device as he listened to the first conversation. *'George is asking some awkward questions that involve you. Can't talk over the phone about it.'*

The second conversation started, *'Hello, Max. Sorry to bother you before you open but it's important. George spoke to me earlier this afternoon and told me about Vicky Thompson and another girl called Julie something...'*

John paused the tape. 'Listen to this.' He pressed the button again. *'"...Morley is a spineless little shit."*

"What's your relationship like with him?"

"It used to be close, but frankly he's now out of his league. If he gets any wind of the Manchester operation, we're both done for."'

John paused it again before continuing. 'After you've listened to this piece, you'll realise why you're here and not out there.' He restarted the tape. *"There's another job. It's the Babylon on your list. I know it's going to be expensive. No concealment this time. Just an unfortunate piece of bad luck. I'll know when it's been done when I read it in the newspapers."*

He sat back and allowed Morley to digest the contents of the tape. Several minutes passed. Silence. Eventually, Morley asked, 'Is that it? Are you trying to frighten me into saying something that will implicate myself with serious crime? If you've got the evidence, charge me. Otherwise, go to hell.'

John slowly stood up. 'Hell is a place where you are right now and it's going to get a great deal hotter. I don't care whatsoever if you agree to help us or deny the charges. What I can promise you is this. You've become involved in matters far above your head. As your friend Alex has pointed out, you're out of your league. Think about this. You are being protected by the state. This safe house belongs to the security services, not the Met. Your miserable arse is just a sideshow; the real action is far away from here. Good evening, Mr Morley, I'm hungry and going back to London to have a lovely tasty Italian dinner with my wife. What are you going to do? Oh yes. You can stop here and think of all the crap mistakes you've made. After all, who really gives a shit about you.'

'What about my family? They'll be wondering where I am. You can't just lock me up here. They're bound to be asking questions.'

'You're right. We have visited your home and spoken to your wife. She's been told you are on secret operations and will be uncontactable for quite some time. Apparently, she didn't appear too distraught whatsoever. In fact, she's going to visit her sister in Cornwall with the girls. As I've just said, it's up to you. You're not going anywhere.'

John walked to the door and closed it without looking back. He ascended the stairs and saw two men in suits wearing security clearance badges on their lapels. He nodded to them. 'Let him stew in his own juice. No contact until you hear otherwise please, gentlemen.' Both were faceless members of an obscure Security Services Unit consisting of twelve men, all with military backgrounds and briefed to keep George Morley safe from any outside interference.

John walked outside towards the Transit van where he saw Phil standing next to the driver's door. 'How's he doing, John?'

'Still behaving like an arrogant bastard. Have you heard anything from Yvonne?'

'Yes. She wants to see us tomorrow morning in her office; it seems there's been some further developments."

48

Through the dwindling evening rush hour traffic, they returned to London. It was nearly ten o'clock when Phil left John outside his home. As John went inside, Charlie was waiting for him. She looked worried.

'What's the matter, darling?'

'Yvonne's been trying to contact you. Can you ring her at her office now?'

'Of course. What's it about?'

'I don't know. But she seemed quite worried. It's not like her.'

'OK. I'll ring her now.'

John placed the call and Yvonne answered it immediately.

'Yvonne. John here. What's happened?'

'It seems the Caribbean burnt down earlier tonight. Apparently, they've found a body in the cellar, but can't confirm who it is, only that it's a man. No jewellery, other than a watch. Clothing too far gone. Face has been badly mutilated. Early indications are we're dealing with a murder and an arson. If it's Max Campbell, our investigation will now centre on Alex Gilmour. The body has been taken to the mortuary for the Home Office forensic scientist, Professor Brown, to examine in the morning. Hopefully we'll have a better idea who it is after then.'

'Yes, I see that. Incidentally, how was Jason Moore?'

'I think he'll come on board. What about Morley?'

'Still holding out. What a nasty piece of work he is. Left him with the 'suits'. What will they do with him?'

'Not too sure. I suspect they'll hold him there for a couple of days, then throw him back into our laps.'

'Typical. Hopefully, he may begin to see some sense by then.'

'Yes, let's hope. Bugger. I nearly forgot to tell you. There was a high-level meeting in Whitehall tonight about the Manchester mob. It has been decided you will place the advert in *The Times* as we previously discussed. Someone has shown some temerity and wants to 'bag' the whole cartel. It seems the Manchester Police have already identified who might be involved. Approval at ministerial level has been given for a full round-the-clock surveillance operation on them.'

'OK. I assume the Post Office box number I leave will be overseen by others?'

'Yes of course. Once you've done it and found what number you've been allocated, let me know.'

'I'll do all that before our meeting in the morning. OK?'

'Yes, of course. Hell, John, look at the time. See you later.'

John replaced the receiver and turned towards the stairs. Charlie was standing in his way, holding a generous measure of whisky. 'Thanks. Just the job.'

49

Max closed the Caribbean early. With his appetite for keeping the club running as a viable business declining, and only ten customers spending little money, he finally lost his patience and announced to those present, he was feeling unwell and closing the club for a few days.

Since his last meeting with Alex Gilmour, Max had begun to reassess his position. He was shocked to hear the bodies of Vicky and Julie had been found in the Thames. He had paid thousands of pounds for their permanent disappearance and disposal. The Irish boys were supposed to be professionals. But what could he do? There was no point in complaining; if he did, he would be found face down in the same river too. In any case, he had already commissioned them to deal with Morley. Although he was both patient and vengeful, any sanctions against them were completely out of his control.

But had he covered his tracks? Neither Morley nor Alex Gilmour knew anything damaging against him about Vicky and Julie, or their disappearances. Only Sammy. And he was completely out of the picture now. His house was clean. Just suspicion; and that never convicted anyone.

He decided once he had been paid for this import permit, he would simply disappear too. Gemma Baldwin would give him the five hundred thousand pounds and Alex was expecting half. He realised the whole amount, together with the hundred and fifty thousand he had accumulated in recent months, would significantly change his life anywhere in the world. Alex had taken little risk in the venture, hiding behind anonymity with Gemma and his other partner, George. No, he wasn't going to get a penny. He could go to hell.

He reached over to pour another rum but the small tumbler slipped through his fingers onto his lap and fell to the floor. He cursed and pushed his chair backwards to reach for the glass. As he lifted it between his thumb and forefinger, something caught his eye. He bent down further and looked again. It was small, round, and black, measuring the size of a small fingernail.

With his previous experience of covert equipment, he knew immediately what this small object was. A sophisticated listening device. He froze, remained still in the awkward posture, unable to move, staring at it without blinking. His mind began to race. How did it get there? Who put it there? How long had it been there? He remembered the conversation he had recently with Alex regarding Vicky's and Julie's disappearances and the Manchester connection, followed by the telephone call regarding the contract on the Babylon.

Hell, this was a game changer. No more Alex or Morley. He needed time to think about his immediate future. He stood up and walked through the front doors into the cool night air. By the time he had walked the short distance to the main road and back, he had decided what to do. It was a risk, but under the circumstances, he had little choice.

He returned to his office and sat down as normal, knowing if he disturbed the bug they would be on to him. If he kept it there, he might be able to feed whoever they were with false information. He checked his watch: one forty-five. Time to lock up and go home. He would carry on doing the same.

After securing the club, he thought about how someone had managed to gain entry. He shone a torch at the old alarm box. He concentrated his gaze and discovered it had been 'foamed'. He walked to his car, unlocked it, got in and drove away in his normal manner. He was taking no chances. He drove directly home and went straight to bed. Except he did not sleep, he made plans.

Six hours later he arose and went for a walk. It was just after ten o'clock in the morning and the streets were busy, with heavy traffic choking any movement. He was rarely awake at this time of the day, let alone outdoors. He continued for twenty minutes, occasionally stopping at shop windows, pretending to look inside, instead looking at the reflections to check if he was being followed. And once he was satisfied he was alone, he stopped at a public telephone box and made a call.

'Gemma. Max Campbell here…'

After a long conversation with Gemma Baldwin, he returned home and began to search quietly for signs of listening devices or cameras. Although he found none, he still took no chances. He went about his daily business as normal. He ate his early evening meal and drove to the Caribbean, again checking for bugs in his Jaguar. He found none.

He unlocked and entered the club as usual and went straight into his office. He shuffled some papers around before going down into the cellar and approaching the false wall where the merchandise was hidden. He opened the door and looked at the racks inside. They were empty; completely empty. He smiled; so far, so good. His arrangements with Gemma earlier to have the drugs removed to another safe place had been accomplished. He climbed the stairs and returned to his office, glancing at his watch. He was expecting a visitor.

Suddenly, he heard the distinctive knock on the front doors. He walked along the corridor and unlocked them, allowing the visitor to enter. Without any conversation, they walked into the office. 'You got the message, Bill?'

'Well who the hell do you think emptied the cellar? Finding somewhere to store them at short notice hasn't been easy. And it's cost a lot of money too! You're in deep shit with the Duchess.'

It had been several months since Bill had come to the club with his boss. He was not a conversationalist, no social skills or manners. He was an archetypal thug, who could only be trusted to carry out the simplest of tasks, with little or no initiative. He had been a serving soldier before his dishonourable discharge. Although his Court Martial failed to prove the more serious offences of torturing suspected members of the Provisional IRA, they recognised his behaviour was too unbalanced for him to remain in the armed forces.

Max replied, 'I need to show you something in the cellar that you missed.'

'Like what! We took everything with us. What the hell are you talking about?'

Max gestured with his hand towards the entrance to the cellar steps. Bill shrugged and mumbled, 'She's not going to be well pleased with you in Manchester.' As he descended the steps Max made his move. Resting on a ledge above the doorway was an iron wrench. He grabbed it with his right hand and in one swift downward stroke hit Bill on the back of his skull. Although a fatal blow, Bill managed to half turn around and bring his hand up to protect himself. But it was too late. Max hit him again. Blood suddenly spurted upwards. Bill fell to his knees, looking directly at Max with an expression of surprise and anger. He attempted to say something, but Max hit him hard in the face, causing his teeth to shatter and tearing much of his jaw away. He slumped to his knees and finally fell backwards onto the ground.

Max had accomplished the first stage of his plan.

He stood over the body and continued mutilating the face, destroying all dental features. He searched the lifeless body for a wallet and any other identifiable items, including two rings and a gold necklace. After removing these, Max placed his beloved Rolex watch on Bill's left wrist before finally stripping the body and piling the blood-soaked clothes, together with his own, in the centre of the room. As he threw them all together he felt for Bill's wallet and removed it from his jacket. Clutching it in his bloody hand, he ran naked back upstairs to the toilets where he washed and changed into fresh clothes, previously left there.

He placed the bloody wallet inside his own pocket and collected three large cans of petrol from the main dance hall area where he poured the contents of one over the wooden floor. He took another can and doused the furniture in his office. Finally, he descended into the cellar and emptied the final can over Bill's body and the wooden racking running the whole length of the room. As he walked back up the stairs he stopped on the fifth step, lit a small rag and threw it back down towards the racking. It immediately ignited, engulfing the whole room. He ran upstairs and straight out through the front doors, picking up a large suitcase on the way, making sure the door key was still in the lock on the inside. He walked past his new Jaguar car without a glance towards the main road, turned left and caught a bus into the centre of London. On the upper deck, he looked over his shoulder, noticing smoke drifting across the skyline before the double decker passed a block of flats. His life had now changed forever.

The second phase of his plan was now complete.

He booked into a modest three-star hotel, registering in the name of Jimmy Banks, and unpacked. He lay on the grubby bed and reflected on recent events. He placed his hand in his jacket pocket and took out Bill's wallet. It was still damp with blood. He examined its contents: driving licence, credit cards, casino memberships. Tucked away, folded into eight, was a photocopy page showing the dimensions of two wooden boxes, one much larger than the other. He noticed the larger measured three yards square and two yards high, whilst the smaller one obviously fitted inside it. On the reverse side, in handwriting, he read 'proposed measurements of the crates for the transportation of crops as requested. KD Brothers Ltd (Joiners) Karachi.'

Max stared at the paper. Clearly, Gemma had been more serious about her intentions to import heroin from Pakistan than she had implied. It appeared arrangements were at an advanced stage, awaiting the issue of the special permit. He refolded the page and placed it in his own wallet; the remainder would be destroyed the next day.

This could change his future plans for the better. He needed to tweak them a little more. Perhaps a valuable ace up his sleeve, or rather, now in his wallet.

50

John and Phil sat in Yvonne's office waiting for to finish her telephone call. She was talking the Professor Brown. 'That's interesting. We'll follow that up immediately. Well, thanks once again, Professor. Bye.'

She hung up, turned her attention to them. 'Well, that's a mixed bag. There's no doubt the fire in the Caribbean was set deliberately and the body found in the cellar was killed before being burnt. There's no sign of smoke in the lungs. The professor can confirm it was a male, between twenty and forty-five years old and roughly five foot nine tall. All the outer tissue has vanished, burnt away. And the head, especially the facial features, had undergone several serious traumas, consistent with repeated violent blows with a blunt instrument. There were no other visible signs of violence on the rest of the body. The professor said he had seen this type of MO before, where the killer wants to conceal the identity of the victim through dental records. Yet he recovered a watch from his radius bone, just above the left wrist. Not just any watch, but a bloody Rolex. Apparently, information from customers of the club suggest Max Campbell had a Rolex matching this one.'

John and Phil looked at each other. They shook their heads simultaneously. Yvonne looked at them. 'What's the matter with you two?'

John replied, 'It stinks, Yvonne. Someone's deliberately destroying the identity of another, then placing a big fat clue to tempt us down some rabbit hole. For what it's worth, I suspect the owner of this watch is the killer.'

'Fully agree, John,' said Phil. 'If this Rolex definitely belongs to Campbell, we've found our murderer.

'Don't let's get carried away with ourselves. Even if what you say is true, we still have to find him and prove he did this.'

'All my money is on Campbell,' said John. 'If he's killed someone and made it look like it's him, he must be hiding something.'

Yvonne hesitated, then continued. 'Commander Higgins believes it is Max Campbell. He's received information from the Manchester Police that Campbell had fallen out of favour with the Manchurian mob and became a liability. Other than that, the investigation team is keeping very quiet and telling us nothing.'

John nodded. 'That's not surprising, under the circumstances. It's too big an operation to spoil and you know as well as I do, some coppers have big mouths.'

Yvonne nodded and shrugged in agreement. 'Changing the subject, John, did you place the advert in *The Times* this morning?'

'Yes, I've written it all down here for you.' He pushed the note towards her. It read

Pakistani grains and pulses ready for research. Reply PO Box N1-3546

'Good, I'll take care of that. I've used these before because they're discreet with no interference from anywhere.'

John asked, 'What do you want Phil and me to do now?'

'I would like you to go and see Jason Moore. Apparently, he's very keen to speak to us. If he accepts the Witness Protection package, I want him to work with us and play his role. I'm particularly keen on him seeing Gilmour again. Obviously, he'll be wired, but he must convince him the permit may be granted but he still needs all the damaging material returning to him. On reflection, it shouldn't take too much acting. After all, he really does want the photos and video, plus the fact he's a politician. However, you must tell him before he accepts, the Prime Minister expects him to resign his parliamentary seat before the next general election, citing ill health.'

'I expect he's already worked out his political career is over.'

Phil interrupted, cynically saying, 'How sad. Just allows someone else to fill his seat and eat from the trough called the public purse.

Politicians: don't trust any of them.'

'Keep your radical views under control, Phil. We need him with us on this. Anyway, I've got a job I know you're going to love.'

'I promise I'll be the height of discretion, now bugger off, Chief Inspector.'

'Insubordination, Mr Smith.'

They smiled at each other. 'Will you go and see Morley? Nothing physical please, just remind him of his precarious position and that we're actually protecting him. He'll be interested in hearing about his friend Max, even if we believe he may still be alive.'

'My pleasure.'

'Incidentally, Phil, your snooping kit and telephone tap have been authorised by the Commander. We need to monitor the recordings. Can we please use your equipment now?'

'The 'kit', as you put it, is all in my van, parked near Gilmour's place. Am I going to get any compensation for all this, especially since I lost some of it in the Caribbean?'

'Yes, I've already sorted that out. The Commander has also authorised three hundred pounds per day, backdated from the moment you unlawfully installed it. That should also cover your losses.'

'Thank you. That'll do nicely. Here's the keys; make sure I get it all back in working order.'

'Gilmour is now under twenty-four-hour surveillance. I'm anticipating he will trying to contact Jason Moore soon, now the advert has been published. Whether the fire at the Caribbean will spook him, I'm not sure. That's why it's important to check his every move.'

'Only time will tell,' said John.

'OK, gentlemen. Let's meet up later and discuss our progress.'

'The George at eight tomorrow night?' asked John

'The George,' replied Yvonne and Phil in unison.

51

Alex Gilmour was alarmed when he saw the morning's headlines: 'Nightclub burnt down – body found inside.' The details were a little sketchy and only vaguely factual. The club was definitely the Caribbean and the police were anxious to speak to the owner Mr Maxwell Campbell. They were reticent about confirming whether the body was his, but disclosed they were treating the incident as murder and arson.

Where did this leave him now? It was all too coincidental. Had his partnership with Max and the Manchester criminals come to the notice of others? He needed to speak to his friend George Morley urgently; he would know what was happening. He picked up the telephone and called him at his office.

'Hello. King's Cross Vice Squad.'

'Hi. Is DS Morley there please?'

'No, sorry. He's out of town on a major inquiry. Can't tell you any more, I don't know myself. None of us do.'

'Any idea how long he's going to be away?'

'No. Sorry. Can I ask who's calling?'

He hung up. Now he was paranoid. That was not like George, being absent from his beloved Vice Squad. His life was entirely centred around the job. He had no interest in other matters, no ambition or desire to assist with other investigations. This was a ruse. He would try to contact him at home.

The telephone rang out for over two minutes, unanswered, before he hung up. He was now close to panic. Where the hell was he?

He slumped back into his chair, considering his next move. Suddenly he was startled by the telephone ringing in his lap. He quickly picked up the receiver. 'Hello.'

'No talking. Meet me at S.M. Great North Road noon. Come alone.' The caller hung up before he could reply. Who was it? Was it Max? If it was, what did he mean? Why was he so abrupt and talking in code?

He looked at the telephone and immediately understood what it all meant. The telephone had been compromised. But were there any other devices? He looked around the room, careful not to disturb anything. He noticed a fly sitting on top of the bookcase. Nothing unusual with that, or was there?

He picked it up and immediately dropped it to the floor. Heavy and metallic, this was no living or dead creature. It was an electronic device with a fine antenna. He realised the significance of the rendezvous spoken in code but where was SM on the Great North Road? He found the road atlas directly in front of him and took it to the toilet. He considered that had not been bugged, but he checked it closely, just in case. He looked at his watch: ten thirty. The caller mentioned noon on the Great North Road. That would suggest not too far away from where he was.

With his finger, he followed the Great North Road out of London, until it changed to the A1. Then he saw it. SM stood for South Mimms, a service station, north of London, close to the nearly completed M25 orbital motorway, less than twenty miles from where he was.

Suspecting he was being watched, he walked out of his front door towards the Angel Underground station. Without looking back, he flagged down a taxi and travelled to King's Cross Underground station, where he caught the Tube to Edgware, making several changes on the same line in an attempt to shake any followers. On exiting at Edgware, he hired a taxi and arrived at South Mimms at eleven fifty-five.

It was a relatively new building, comprising a mixture of fast food franchises, with a large car park to the rear. The site was an historic trading place between the agricultural northern Home Counties and the rapidly expanding industrial London. But with the extensive motorway construction linking the A1 and the M1 with the London orbital, South Mimms had become a busy commercial transport hub.

Alex walked towards the main entrance. The car park was a hive of activity, with vehicles of all descriptions arriving or leaving and pedestrians milling around the take away food outlets and stalls.

He entered the main reception area and looked around. After several minutes, he had still failed to recognise anyone and so he sat close to the entrance with a cup of coffee. He glanced at the clock – twelve fifteen – and looked again towards the main doorway. There, dressed in a dark blue coat with a red scarf, he saw a familiar face. Max.

Without any contact Max looked at him and walked back outside. Alex put his empty cup down and waited a minute before following him into the car park. He looked around, but Max had disappeared without trace. All the parked cars were unoccupied. He continued along the front edge of the building and turned the corner. Then he saw him standing next to a waiting taxi.

'Get in, Alex,' he said.

'I thought you were—'

'Never mind that. Let's get out of here now.'

The taxi pulled away. Max instructed the driver, 'Just go north, please, for a few miles. I'll tell you when to stop.' Alex was about to speak, when he saw a note passed to him on his lap. He looked down and read, 'Don't speak. Just follow me. I'll explain later.'

They nodded to each other and continued northwards on the A1 in silence. Three miles further on, the road broadened out into a newly constructed dual carriageway where the speed limit increased to seventy miles per hour. Max turned his head and peered through the rear window, then asked the driver, 'Will you pull up under this next bridge, please?'

'I'm not supposed to park here on the hard shoulder.'

'Don't worry, put your hazard lights on and stop here. I'll make it worth your while.'

The driver signalled as the taxi left the nearside lane and entered the breakdown area below the bridge. Max leant forward and passed the driver fifty pounds before opening the back door closest to the grassy verge. He turned to Alex. 'Follow me.'

As they left the taxi, Max looked carefully at the approaching traffic. Once it had passed, he prodded Alex in the ribs and sprinted up the embankment next to the bridge. Alex followed him at a slower pace until he reached the top. He saw that the bridge crossing the dual carriageway serviced a quiet country lane between two local villages. Max walked to a Vauxhall saloon car that was parked on the lane, unlocked it and started the engine, summoning Alex to join him. Seconds later, they were travelling along the lane, heading north west towards St Albans. Once again, they remained silent.

Close to the centre of St Albans lay a mid-Victorian public baths, built by the corporation for the benefit of its residents. In recent years, it had fallen short of its original splendour, with many of its wall and floor tiles broken or missing. Its showpiece was the wrought-iron balcony surrounding the swimming pool but this had been declared unsafe after a health and safety inspection and closed off to the public. The baths were commercially failing and a drain on the council's budget. The only part of the baths making any degree of profit were the old steam baths, recently renamed the Turkish Lagoon.

Max parked the Vauxhall in the baths' rear car park. Together they went in and approached the receptionist. Max said, 'Two for the Turkish baths, please.' Without looking up from the book she was obviously more interested in, she took his money, pressed the ticket machine and handed over two large white towels bearing the council logo. With the towels tucked under their arms, they descended the stone staircase and walked to the changing room.

Five minutes later they entered the main hot pool. There was no one else there. Max jumped into the hot water and waved to Alex to join him. Once they were standing up to their chests in water, Max finally broke his silence. 'Alex, we've been rumbled. I found the Caribbean bugged and I suspect your place has been visited too.'

'Yes, it has. When I received your call this morning, I knew something was wrong. I had a quick look around and found a metallic device in the shape of a fly, sat in my bookcase. Hell, Max, what's happening?'

'Someone is trying to keep a close eye on us. I suspect it's the cops but I'm not too sure.'

'Who else could it be?'

'Think about it Alex, if it is the cops, why haven't they arrested us?'

'I don't know.'

'Our choices are limited now. We can disappear and go on the run or we can hand ourselves in.'

'That doesn't seem to be much choice to me, Max.'

'I agree.'

'Anyway, I thought you were dead. The newspapers think you are.'

'Yes. I read that too.'

After a pause, Max said, 'Let me tell you something. When I realised the club was compromised, I called Gemma Baldwin from a public pay phone. Obviously, I didn't tell her about the bugs, otherwise she would've pulled out of the deal completely. I told her I was being threatened by my old partner Sammy Clarke. Of course, she was not too pleased, but I now know why she's the boss of the syndicate up there in Manchester: she's really very clever. All the merchandise I was keeping at the club was to be removed.'

'What merchandise?'

'You don't need to know about that, Alex. So far as you're concerned, we're dealing with herbs and medications. Anyway, she sent me a nasty piece of work called Bill. On her instructions, he was to deal with Sammy, leave him in the cellar and burn the club down to the ground. The police would think it's me for the time being, a victim of murder and arson. I've no doubt they'll eventually establish it's not me, but hopefully I'll be long gone by then.'

'What!'

'Yes, I know, it's a bit drastic. But things didn't quite go to plan. Sammy got wind of Bill's intentions and shot him at point-blank range in the head. Fortunately, I was able to grab Sammy and disarm him.'

'What happened then?'

'I had no choice, Alex. I shot him.'

'Bloody hell, Max, you've murdered someone!'

'I know, Alex, I'm not proud of it. But what else could I do? He was going to spoil all our plans.'

'What did you do with him?'

'I'm afraid Sammy is now resting with all the other rubbish at the bottom of the Thames. I've got to lie low for the time being, but me and Gemma Baldwin need you to help us.'

'How?'

'Well, she rang me again at my cheap hotel this morning, telling me to get a copy of The Times. It seems our friendly MP Mr Moore has placed the advert. The application for the special permit may be granted after all.'

'Really?'

'Yes. So, we want you to carry on as normal. Go home as if nothing's happened. Of course, your phone and house are probably being monitored, but we have an opportunity of feeding false information to whoever they are.'

'What about Jason Moore?'

'I want you to contact him as we arranged and collect the application forms for this special permit from him. Give him all the photos and video, then let me have the forms as soon as possible. If he tries to double-cross us, I've kept copies just in case.'

'Do you think it's safe?'

'As I've said, if it's the cops listening in, they would have locked us up before now.'

'Yes, but there's something else you should know, Sergeant Morley has disappeared off the face of the earth. I tried to contact him this morning, after you rang me, but his mates in the Vice Squad said he was out of town on a secret inquiry. Max, it's all bollocks. Whoever's bugged our places has kidnapped George as well.'

'You're right. But who? Surely the cops aren't playing it that dirty. They're governed by regulations and all that crap.'

They both stared at an attendant who had entered the pool area. A large man of many proportions dressed in only a towel wrapped around his enormous waist and loose fitting flip-flop sandals. He shuffled towards them. 'Who's first please?' Max climbed out of the hot pool first and disappeared into the massage room, where the friendly giant manipulated his neck and back muscles before scrubbing his skin clean. Several minutes later, Alex followed.

Afterwards, in the municipal café next door, they drank their disgusting coffee. Max said, 'This is the hotel I'm staying at for the next few days. Ask for Jimmy Banks. If I'm not there, leave a message saying you're Graham Downs and a contact number that can't be traced. If I need to speak to you, I'll ring your number from a public box. It will ring three times only. You will then contact me on this number. Obviously, continue to ring anyone else with your home phone. However, I'll want you to make two calls to your local travel agent. The first one, use your home phone to enquire into a trip to Athens. But the second must be made on a secure line. Book an open ticket for six months to Cairo, in my name as well. I'll give you the money for that now. Once the permit has been finally issued, Mrs Baldwin will deposit the half million into my bank in the Bahamas. It should take less than twenty-four hours. You must give me details of your offshore bank as well. Now, Alex, this is important: once you've got the permit from him, you must place it in a security locker at King Cross railway station and leave the key with Benny, the paper seller outside, you can't miss him. He's a small guy with a filthy flat cap. Always wears an identical scarf. You can't miss him, he stands in the main entrance and has the loudest voice of any newspaper seller in London. Once you've done this, you must let me know straight away; that's really important. After that, Mrs Baldwin will get things started from her end.

'Why Egypt?'

'Because I need to get out of the country. We'll just leave it at that.'

'Do you think we're going to succeed in all of this, Max?'

'Yes, I do. We're the only two that knows what's really happening. Mrs Baldwin has no knowledge, so let's keep it that way. I've told her I was having trouble with my old partner, Sammy Clarke, so that's why Bill was sent down to sort him out. Unfortunately, it didn't go to plan, so I'll have some explaining to do when I go up to Manchester. That's why it's vital I take the permit with me. Have you got anyone in mind Alex to complete the application?'

'Yes. It's a guy who can't resist cash and he's desperate for some.'

'Can we trust him?'

'Definitely, he's fallen so far down from grace, he'll do pretty much anything to make some money.'

'Good. We're going to have to register a company at Companies House. I'm not bothered what it's called, I'll leave that to your friend. However, this is also important: I want him to go through the paperwork thoroughly. If there's any chance of disguising the cargo before it arrives at the Pakistani ports, I want to know. Here's five thousand pounds if he can identify such a loophole. Otherwise make it three thousand. Are you clear about that?'

'Yes, but why?'

'Never mind that Alex. Listen, we can do this. The stakes are massive and when we pull this off, we're set up for life. But we must be on our guard at all times. OK?'

'Yes, you're right. Will you take me back to London now, please?'

'Of course. Don't worry, Alex, we're nearly there.' Max passed a brown paper package to him 'There's ten thousand cash. That should cover everything for the time being. OK?'

'OK, Max. I trust you.'

'Good man, I trust you too my friend,' he replied, feeling a twinge of sweet revenge.

52

The two detectives assigned to the lead surveillance vehicle, call sign mobile 1, saw their target Alex Gilmour leave his house, knowing he had received a telephone call from an unidentified male. Operating on a secure radio channel, they were linked to the control room and four other mobile units. Collectively, there were three double crewed cars and a single motorcyclist. The coded message from the unknown caller was *'No talking. Meet me at SM Great North Road noon. Come alone.'*

The officer in charge quickly identified the destination. South Mimms on the A1. Mobiles 2 and 3 were immediately dispatched there, whilst the motorcyclist was to remain close to the lead car in case the information was a decoy. They successfully followed the target to King's Cross Underground station where he boarded a Tube, but lost him four stops north, when he quickly sprinted off the carriage onto the platform through the closing doors. However, when he reappeared at South Mimms the surveillance operation became live again. One team posed as customers in the main reception area, whilst the second sat in their car, in readiness to follow on the A1. But they were unprepared when the target left the main building and walked into the rear car park and met another man before being driven away in a taxi, travelling north.

With some delay, the two mobiles eventually negotiated the traffic merging onto the busy road in their pursuit, but as they caught up with the taxi they were astonished to see it pull into the hard shoulder, under a bridge, and the two men jump out and scramble up the embankment and disappear out of sight.

The operation was immediately aborted.

53

John drove down the leafy avenue approaching the Ministry of Defence hospital, Holden Hall. His appointment with Jason Moore had been hastily arranged through both the civil and military authorities. Temporary passes and security papers were issued, allowing access to the secure wing of the hospital. As he parked his car, he stopped to admire the woodland bordering the sweeping meadow in the shallow valley below. The autumn sun shone on the landscape, picking out the various brown and red leaves desperately clinging to their mother trees. He drew in a deep breath of fresh air and contemplated the interview ahead.

He turned towards the entrance, admiring the old building. Holden Hall had been built in the early nineteenth century, originally the country seat of the Earl of Avon, who gambled and drank all his fortune away before emigrating to America to seek another. He was never seen again.

John entered the main lobby. It was enormous, with multi-coloured mosaic tiled floors, marble columns stretching up towards a large dome that supported dozens of skylight windows around its circumference. John smiled and thought of the cost and maintenance. He continued towards the reception area, where he saw two male nurses talking behind a glass surrounded counter.

Once John had shown his papers, one of them invited him to accompany him along the corridor towards the rear of the building. Once through the next set of oak swing doors, John immediately knew he was in a hospital. The smell. This part of the building was modern: a recently added extension to the old house, with all the facilities of a major functioning NHS hospital. They continued along the lengthy windowed corridors linking various battle trauma wards until they finally arrived at the Post Traumatic Stress Disorder Unit.

John entered through a secure door where he was greeted by the duty doctor. 'Good morning. Are you Mr Evans from the Metropolitan Police?'

'Good morning. Yes, I am.'

'My name is Doctor Simms, Major Simms with the Medical Corp. I've been expecting you. Would you mind signing the visitors' book?'

'Sure.'

'Mr Moore has been transferred into our care for his own protection, following a request from the Home Office.'

'Yes, that's right. I've come to interview him. Is he fit and well enough for me to do this?'

'Of course. In fact, I believe he is anxious to talk with the authorities, so come this way, please.'

They continued through the ward, where some of the side rooms had patients lying in their beds or sitting reading papers. The doctor whispered, 'They're all soldiers, casualties from Northern Ireland. It's a million miles from where those poor lads have been.'

John was shocked to see their ages. Just young men, some even teenagers, lost in their own bodies, looking so vulnerable. He counted fourteen men before they entered another secure unit. Outside an unmarked room sat a soldier, a corporal in the Military Police, who sprang to his feet, replacing the red cap on his head.

'Corporal, this is Inspector Evans. He has come to speak to Mr Moore. Is he ready to see our guest?'

'Yes, sir.' The soldier looked straight ahead, past John, as he stood to attention.

'Good. Mr Evans, please step inside. Remember, Mr Moore is effectively detained here under the Mental Health Act, until we get the green light from above. Therefore, his accommodation is secure and his movements restricted. The Corporal will be outside at all times. Let him know if you want anything such as refreshments or when you're ready to leave. I think that's about it. Good luck.'

They shook hands before the Corporal unlocked the metal door. John stepped into a self-contained flat, whereupon a voice said,

'Hello. Who's that?'

'Mr Jason Moore?'

A well-set man, about ten years older than John, came into the hallway. 'Yes, I am. May I ask who you are?'

'My name is Inspector John Evans. I'm here on behalf of the Metropolitan Police and I would like to discuss with you how we can get you out of here, back into the real world, so you can carry on with the rest of your life. Interested?'

'I certainly am. But I've already spoken to a policewoman.'

'Yes, I know. She's DCI Hall, my boss, that's why I'm here. Will you help us?'

'Yes, but why do I sense there's a catch?'

'Mr Moore, there's always a catch; a price to pay. But for you, I believe it's the best deal under the circumstances. Let's sit down and talk.'

'OK. I think I know what you're going to ask of me.'

After three hours of countless cups of coffee and sandwiches, a deal was struck. John wrote the contract out, together with Moore's statement of his involvement with Vicky Thompson, the communication with Alex Gilmour and the subsequent request made to Sir Graham Hall in the granting of a special import permit from Pakistan.

Jason Moore agreed to cooperate on all matters. On a temporary basis, he would return to Whitehall and continue in the same role he had previously done. However, all his authorities had been rescinded and his movement would be monitored by the DTI and the police. John had asked if he originally believed that the intended crops for scientific research imported from Pakistan for medical purposes were genuine. He did. Yet he conceded it was a little unusual and perhaps some pharmaceutical company would possibly stand to benefit. Stupidly, he was only focussed on protecting his career and the destruction of the compromising images. Since his previous meeting with Yvonne, he had reflected much and made his decisions. He recognised his blind ambition to succeed and the sheer naivety of believing Vicky could be attracted to an older man. But his biggest blunder was allowing himself to be duped by Alex Gilmour into applying for a special permit. Now he was aware of the suspected connection between Gilmour and a drugs syndicate in the north, he was more than willing to help John with any task they asked of him, saying, 'I'll help you in any way I can.'

John smiled. 'Well, that's fortunate, because I've just placed the message in *The Times* on your behalf. I'll be expecting Gilmour to be in touch. Did he mention to you how he would do this?'

'Not really, but he does know where I work and my office phone number.'

'Right. Mr Moore, I've been authorised to release you from this hospital today and take you back to London. You must acknowledge the conditions of this. Basically, we're placing our trust in you to do the right thing. I'll take you straight home to your London flat, but tomorrow you must go into your office as though nothing has happened. Naturally, you'll be asked why you were absent. Just tell everyone you were feeling under the weather and needed some rest. The only person in your Department that knows what's really happening is Sir Graham Hall.'

'What happens if he starts sanctioning me as soon as I walk in?'

'He won't. He'll probably ignore you. Remember again, your role at the Ministry has disappeared other than this operation. Once we've completed this, you'll be allowed to resign for medical reasons, enjoy your pension and keep your reputation intact.'

'I understand.'

Eventually, John went to the door and shouted for the guard. Seconds later, both men left the confined area and walked back along the empty corridors, past the wards, into the main reception area. John signed them out in the visitors' book, returning his passes and security papers. Together, they stepped outside into the cool night air, leaving Holden Hall without looking back. Sitting in the car, Jason Moore said, 'Hell, I never knew this place existed. It looks exquisite, but I never want to see it ever again.'

John nodded in agreement and drove along the tree-lined avenue back towards the main entrance, through the guarded barriers, turning left towards London.

54

Whilst John was having a productive day with Jason Moore, Phil was not so lucky with his. The meeting with George Morley started badly and soon deteriorated into an exchange of insults.

'I'm not talking to you or any other bastard,' shouted Morley.

'Listen to me, you little shit. You're a disgrace to the Service and going down for the rest of your life unless you start co-operating with me,' retorted Phil.

Although incarcerated for nearly two days, denied access to any contact with the outside world, even a solicitor, Morley knew he was being held in custody by some legal authority, not kidnapped by criminals as he'd earlier feared. Eventually, they would either have to charge or release him. Hoping for the latter, he was confident Alex would already be making representations to a lawyer, if not the Police Commissioner himself. If he remained in denial, dismissing the onslaught of threats made against him, he might prevail.

Phil left the room. He was becoming really annoyed with Morley, feeling out of his depth and losing all patience to continue. He was on the verge of returning to London when 'a suit' approached him and indicated the telephone receiver lying on its side on the table. He walked into the small windowless room and picked it up. 'Phil Smith.'

'Phil, it's Yvonne here. We don't need Morley now; Jason Moore is going to work with us. For what it's worth, he's more reliable. Also, I've spoken with the Prosecution's office. They've examined the evidence we've collected so far and are satisfied there's a prima facie case against Morley.'

'Really?'

'Yes, bring him back to London. Take him to King's Cross Police Station and charge the bugger. I shall have the paperwork ready for him by then. How long will it take you?'

'I'll be there in an hour.'

'Good. Don't say anything to him, just take him straight into the Charge Room. I want to be there to see his face.'

'Nice one, Yvonne. I'll go and get him now.'

He turned to the security man. 'I've got to take him to London now. Will you accompany us, please?'

'Yes, I'll get his things and bring him through to the back yard.'

'Thanks.'

Five minutes later George Morley was escorted through the back door, handcuffed to his escort. He looked a little subdued after his earlier outbursts, but as they sat in the back of the unmarked police car, the 'suit' gave him a faint wink. Phil drove out of the back yard and directly to London. Morley asked them a couple of times where they were taking him, but both ignored him. The journey lasted a little over an hour and as the car swung into the rear yard of King's Cross Police Station, his arrogant smile dropped as he recognised exactly where he was. For the first time, he realised the seriousness of his circumstances.

They entered through the rear doors, reserved for prisoners, and walked directly into the Charge Room. Waiting for them were Commander Higgins and DCI Hall. Morley stopped dead in his tracks and closed his eyes. He knew exactly what was going to happen next.

Before he could compose himself, she stepped forward with the familiar pink copy of the charge sheet. After cautioning him, she charged him with six offences of bribery and corruption, two of blackmail and one of conspiracy with others to supply large quantities of a class A drug, namely heroin. His face drained of all colour; all his self-assurance now gone. After reading all the charges, she invited him to reply. He simply shook his head.

As he was being led way to be searched and placed into police custody, Yvonne whispered to him, 'Got you. Believe me there are plenty of other charges to follow. You had your chance to help us. It's too late now.'

55

Jason Moore MP walked through the main entrance to the Ministry buildings carrying his briefcase and umbrella. His professional demeanour concealed his acceptance that this was for a limited time; he was now paying the price for his past mistakes. As he walked towards the back staircase, a junior secretary said, 'Hello Mr Moore, haven't seen you for a few weeks.'

'No. Felt a little unwell. Had a short break and now I'm fine, ready for all the hard work ahead.'

'Very good. Look after yourself.'

He ascended the wide stone staircase to the second floor and entered his office. It had changed. In fact, he checked the name plate on the door to confirm he was in the right office. Yes, as before it read 'Jason Moore MP'. All the furniture had been removed other than a small desk and an easy chair. The telephone, filing cabinets and his diary were missing, but on the desk he saw a note. It read:

Please come and see me as soon as you arrive. Sir Graham Hall.

He folded the note and made his way back to the first floor, going directly to his secretary's office. 'Good morning, Jane. Is Sir Graham in, please?'

'Yes. I'll go and check if he's free to see you.'

Jane had worked in the Department for over thirty years, a consummate civil servant, serving many Permanent Under-Secretaries. She knew everything that happened in the DTI and clearly by the tone of her voice and body language had been privy to his recent debacle. She soon returned. 'Sir Graham will see you now, Mr Moore.'

He entered the large oak-panelled office. Unlike his office, this was opulent, with original oil paintings of portraits of past Presidents of the Board of Trade, spanning over two hundred years. Special hand-crafted book cases stood against three of the walls, whilst the fourth had two enormous windows, stretching from the ceiling to the floor, overlooking Whitehall. In one corner, set at an angle, stood an enormous oak bureau desk, where Sir Graham Hall sat. He looked up from the files placed before him and gestured at Jason to sit down.

As they faced each other, Sir Graham said, 'Mr Moore. I'm pleased you have made a full recovery and that you have decided to cooperate with the authorities. I commend you for that. However, the fact remains you allowed poor judgement in your personal life to overspill into your professional one. You must have been naive to believe I would have recommended a special permit for the importation of crops for scientific research, especially from Pakistan or anywhere on the Indian sub-continent, without a thorough vetting.'

'You're right, Sir Graham. I've been stupid. But before I resign from the Government, I wish to address some of my mistakes. I assume you know I'm working closely with the police?'

'Yes, of course. I'm the only person in the Department who is aware of your circumstances and imminent departure from political life. I have assured the Prime Minister we shall work together with the Police in an attempt to bring to justice, those who wish to flood our street with drugs. Are we as one with this Mr Moore?'

'Yes, sir. You have my word on that.'

Sir Graham reached over towards a large brown envelope and pushed it towards him. 'Open it. Inside, you'll find the draft special permit with all the necessary application forms and papers required to complete it. You will pass these to your contact and give them seven days to complete them. These details include the full description of the crops for import and the scientific analysis required, including their methodology and intended outcomes. It's all jargon to me, but it is the normal process we adopt. The most important documents we're interested in are the transit arrangements: the place of export, their transit route and port of entry into the UK. We shall insist the crops or whatever are contained in the designated crates and will be secured by the UK Government Bond Seal. It's imperative we make the whole process appear bureaucratic; red-tape is like bullshit, it baffles brains.'

'I understand, Sir Graham. I'll expect a visit or some type of communication soon, especially since the message was published in *The Times* yesterday.'

'I agree. You must let me know of any developments.'

'I shall, sir.'

'Good. That'll be all for now, Mr Moore.'

As Jason turned towards the door, Sir Graham continued, 'Mr Moore, if you play your role as you have promised, you can leave this Department with your good reputation untarnished.'

'Thank you, sir.'

Jason returned to his sparsely furnished office and read the explanatory letter and the thirty-four-page application document. The name clearly typed on all the forms showed him as the executive officer in charge of the application process. It was all there. All he had to do now was wait.

He looked at his watch: twelve twenty. It was lunch time. He placed the papers in his briefcase and decided to visit the Peel, a bar regularly patronised by other politicians, civil servants and members of the press. Perhaps he would see Gilmour there. But as he descended the steps outside the front of the main entrance, he heard a familiar voice behind him. Gilmour had found him instead.

'Hello, Mr Moore. I believe you have placed a message in *The Times* yesterday?'

'Yes, that's right.'

'Shall we go for some refreshments where we can talk more privately.'

'I was on my way to the Peel.'

'No. That's a little too public for me. Besides, we don't want anyone you know interrupting our meeting. Do we?'

'Where do you suggest?'

'There's a nice little Italian bistro along here. We can talk there.'

'Fair enough. Let's go.'

Ten minutes later they were sitting opposite each other in a small booth, ordering a bottle of Chianti and a light lunch. Alex started the conversation.

'Have you anything for me, Mr Moore?'

'Yes, I do. Do you have something for me?'

'Yes.'

'Let's talk then.'

Jason opened his briefcase, took out the envelope and placed it on the table. Alex picked it up, unfolded the flap and looked at the documents inside. 'Are all the necessary papers here?'

'They are. You must complete them within seven days. Your client will need to seek professional advice to fulfil all the criteria, especially the scientific research. That includes what methods they intend to use, where the crops and laboratory will be housed together with all security arrangements. Details of their transit, from export to import, are paramount. Once the crops have arrived at the laboratory, they must be examined by an authorised agent immediately after the seal is broken.'

'There's a lot to do here.'

'Of course. These permits are not commonly issued. Provided you complete these forms to a satisfactory standard, they should withstand ministerial scrutiny.'

'Who will scrutinise this application?'

'I will.'

'Very good. I shall take these with me but there may be some gaps. I trust you to fill them in for us, if we can't.'

'Yes, but don't make it too obvious.'

Alex smiled and opened his case. He placed the envelope inside and took out another. He handed it over.

'Mr Moore, these are all the photos of your night with the young lady. My client wants you to have them as a token of his intention to honour his side of the bargain. They contain the negatives. Obviously, the video will remain in his possession until the permit has been issued.'

'You know, Mr Gilmour, I may have been a little indiscreet and showed poor judgement. But you are a slime ball. You know this is downright blackmail. Just tell your client, if he doesn't let me have the video, I shall not hesitate in going to the police and reporting you both in all this.'

'Is that right, Mr Moore?'

'Oh yes. I can rebuild my life again after the scandal and live abroad quite easily whilst you two languish in Her Majesty's Prison. I'll get you your damn permit, but don't think about asking me again for any more favours. Post the papers back directly to me, the address is on the envelope. Send it recorded delivery. It'll take me about three days to push it through all the various channels. I'll meet you here on the fourth day after delivery. Make sure you bring me that video.'

'I shan't argue with you. I shall bring the video with me. Just make sure you have the permit.'

Alex stood immediately and walked out of the restaurant, making no attempt to pay for his meal and wine. Jason Moore felt he had played his part well, not wanting to make the application a foregone conclusion. Throwing in some insults towards the end seemed natural, especially when he meant every word of them. He opened the envelope and quickly thumbed through the images. It was definitely him; the scar tissue around his neck and shoulders gave him away immediately. He put them in his briefcase and summoned the waiter for the bill.

Thirty minutes later he was sitting in front of Sir Graham Hall, reporting back to him on the meeting. 'Well done, Mr Moore. You appear to have played your role well. You will now go home until further notice. I shall contact you when the papers have been completed and the permit is issued. You will come back here to collect it and meet Alex Gilmour again. But this time you'll be wired and kept under surveillance. Any questions?'

Jason looked at Sir Graham, realising it was hopeless discussing any future with the Department. Even the Prime Minister had abandoned him, probably already notified his Constituency Board for de-selection. He knew at that moment it was all over. Time to make new plans. Regretfully, he replied, 'No, Sir Graham. I'll be at home waiting for your call.'

56

Alex Gilmour returned home and packed a suitcase. He knew he was constantly under surveillance, and as he walked out of his house he noticed a parked van with silver-tinted rear windows facing towards him. He approached it. There were no occupants in the front. He knocked on the side panel and shouted, 'I'm going on holiday to Cornwall, staying at the Crown Hotel, Truro. I'll be there until next Sunday.'

He walked towards the Underground and disappeared down the steps. The two plain clothes detectives in the van were completely taken by surprise, bewildered about what their next move should be. Eventually, they radioed their controller to report what had happened. Five minutes later, they were stood down and the operation cancelled. The Devon and Cornwall Crime Squad were asked to verify if Gilmour did arrive at the Crown Hotel.

But he had made alternative plans. By deliberately showing his hand, he had anticipated the police would be in turmoil, allowing him to slip away to make enquiries into who would be best qualified to complete the application forms for the special permit.

By late afternoon he had arrived at Brighton by train and booked into a modest bed and breakfast near the Pavilion. He had travelled there to speak to an old acquaintance, Miles Willis, a retired merchant banker who had barely survived a major scandal involving insider trading on the Stock Market several years previously. Although Alex had discovered damning evidence to expose him, he had applied the Badger Game, whereby Miles had 'donated' a cheque to his private account, allowing the affair to disappear without trace.

Alex now needed him to complete the application forms. He soon located his address in the telephone directory and was pleasantly surprised to discover it was close to where he was staying. He unpacked his suitcase, left the B&B, carrying his briefcase, and walked the short distance along the seafront until he found the block of flats he was seeking. He climbed the shallow stone steps to the front door and peered at the list of names and flats. There it was: M. Willis Flat 8.

He pressed the bell and waited. Seconds later a voice speaking through the intercom said, 'Hello. Who is this, please?'

'Miles. It's Alex Gilmour here. I'm sorry to bother you, but I've got something really important to talk to you about.'

'Hell, Gilmour, you're the last person in the world I want to talk to. Go to Hell.'

'Miles. You have the opportunity of making a lot of money, if you help me fill some forms in. That's all. Nothing else.'

'Go away, or I'll call the police.'

'Would you like to make five thousand pounds in a day, without moving from your sofa? It's all legitimate. I need a hand to fill in an application profile for an import permit. It'll be a piece of cake for you.'

The door buzzer sounded loudly. 'Come up. I'm on the third floor.'

Alex smiled as he pushed the door open and entered a hallway. He walked across the shiny black and white floor tiles to the old lift where he opened a metal scissor door and pressed the third-floor button. A few moments later he saw Miles Willis waiting for him outside the flat. He was a small man: only just over five feet high, now approaching seventy years old and dressed in a grubby house coat, smoking a cigarette. His general appearance was dirty and unkempt. Alex had not seen him for six years since he resigned from the board of directors. His fall from grace was spectacular. Forced to sell his opulent detached house by the Thames in Henley and gleaming new Rolls Royce he had scurried down to the south coast, retiring to Brighton. Clearly, his health had taken a downward spiral too.

'Good evening, Miles. How are you?' asked Alex.

'Cut the crap out, Gilmour. I'm only seeing you 'cos I've fallen on hard times and I need some cash. What's this all about?'

'Are you going to invite me in or are we going to talk business out here on the landing?'

Miles shrugged in contempt. 'Come in then.'

Alex followed him inside. The first shock was the smell: stale tobacco and rotting food. The place was strewn with empty milk bottles and ashtrays over spilling with cigarette ends. Trays with uneaten food covered the sideboard and coffee tables. The dirty curtains were fully closed, barring any natural light or fresh air from penetrating inside. The room was dimly lit by a single electric light bulb, hanging from a once finely ornate ceiling rose. Alex hesitated before sitting down on the heavily stained chair opposite Miles.

He handed over the package. 'Miles, can you complete this portfolio of applications for me, please? You will understand all the necessary details required.'

Miles glanced at the brown package before looking briefly back at his unwelcome visitor. Slowly, he opened the envelope and spilled the contents onto his lap. As the papers scattered onto his dirty trousers he began to quickly flick through the forms. After several minutes he placed them neatly in a pile on the seat cushion next to him.

'Yes, I can do those, but why are you applying for a special permit? All these crops can be easily sourced from Europe. Why Pakistan?'

'I am prepared to pay five thousand pounds for you to complete these forms. Part of that fee is not to ask any questions. Are you interested?'

Miles re-examined the documents. 'Yes. Leave them with me. I've got to do some research to identify Government-licensed laboratories and their area of expertise. I've completed these forms before. Are you aware of Article 7 Shipment Return, paragraph 3, subsection b in this application?'

'No. Why?'

'Most people ignore this. In simple terms, it allows a sister company to operate alongside the main company, without it being mentioned on the permit itself. All the subsidiary requires is the export licence number granted to the major permit holder. Don't ask me why, it's just a loophole, occasionally used by arms dealers, where the destinations within the UK for the research vary.'

'Are you sure?'

'Yes of course I'm sure. Do you think I'm a bloody idiot?'

'No. Just asking that's all.'

'I'll need to register a limited company for you. This will take three days.'

'Can you register me this sister company that won't show on the applications forms?'

'Yes. But what are you up to, Gilmour?'

'Just do it, Miles.'

'What names do you want me to record at Companies House?'

'The main company will be Crops Research UK Ltd and its sister…' he hesitated, thinking of a name that was pertinent to Max, '…Phoenix Laboratories UK Ltd.'

'Come back then with the cash. No cheques, Gilmour, just cash.'

Alex nodded. 'I'll be back in three days' time, in the afternoon, with the money. Make sure everything is ready.'

Without any further delay, he quickly made his way to the door, leaving before the feeling of nausea became too unbearable. Miles remained seated, not wishing to extend any courtesy, concentrating on the paperwork. Alex stepped outside and deeply inhaled the fresh sea air, then immediately made his way to the nearby public telephone box to call Max in London.

He related the meeting with Jason Moore and his visit to his contact in Brighton, especially the anomaly regarding a sister company, in which additional goods could be concealed within the appropriate documentation. Max asked him repeatedly about this little-known clause after which he praised him. 'Good work, Alex, I need to some homework on this at the public library.'

'OK, I should have the application all completed and returned to me in three days' time. Once I've done that, I'll see Jason Moore the following day and get the ball rolling. Hopefully, we should take possession of the permit within the week.'

'Fantastic. You've done well, Alex. We should get paid very soon.'

'Can't wait. I'll speak later before I return to London.'

Max replaced the receiver. This latest news relating to a sister company seemed too good to be true. If, however, Alex was right, he could stand to make far more than the half a million promised by Gemma Baldwin. If he had the opportunity of skimming some of the drugs in Pakistan and bringing them back into the UK without her knowledge, using this ghost company, the rewards would be staggering.

But to succeed in this unexpected windfall there was definitely no place for Alex Gilmour.

57

John entered the George to find Phil and Yvonne sitting in the far corner. They appeared to be in serious conversation.

'Hi John' Yvonne said, shuffling along the leather bench seat to make room for him. 'Listen, both of you, there have been some developments. The Greater Manchester Police have identified and targeted a well known criminal in cahoots with Campbell and Gilmour. Apparently, it's a woman called Gemma Baldwin who's a major player in the North West and runs a syndicate since her husband's untimely and suspicious death last year. Although she has no previous convictions, her associates are deadly and violent psychopaths, heavily involved with drugs, prostitution and extortion in the Manchester area. I can now tell you that the bait has been taken. Jason Moore met with Gilmour today and went to Brighton with the application forms, where he visited a Miles Willis, a disgraced merchant trader who has an expertise in these matters.'

'How do we know this?' asked Phil.

'He was followed. Now that leads me on to a disturbing development. Gilmour has sussed out he's being watched. He slipped the surveillance team two days ago after meeting someone at the South Mimms services on the Great North Road. They were unable to identify the other person, but I know who I'd put my pension on.'

'Max Campbell.' replied John.

'Yes, just like you suspected. The forensic pathologists have not been able to identify the body in the cellar but it makes sense to me; he deliberately mutilated the body and poured fuel onto it to disfigure it so much in order to give him more time. It all makes sense.'

'Yes,' agreed John.

'Unfortunately, Commander Higgins doesn't see it that way. He believes Gilmour double-crossed Max Campbell, killed him in the Caribbean, set it on fire, and is now dealing directly with the Manchester mob.'

'I don't think Gilmour's in that league,' John said, 'He's not that ruthless. I believe Max is still alive and using Alex to get the permit. What I find a little worrying is that if they know they are being watched, why haven't they fled. I think they have some contingency plan. We don't know whether that includes this woman Baldwin or not. Why should they touch this permit if they know it's been compromised?'

'That's exactly what I believe too' exclaimed Yvonne.

'Clearly the authorities have decided to run with the idea of granting this permit in order to capture the main players when this large consignment of drugs lands on our shores. These people are no fools. If they suspect they are being watched, they'll disappear without trace. No, something's not right. Have you spoken to Commander Higgins about this?'

'Yes, I've told him of my suspicions about the burnt body. And if Max Campbell is still alive, that changes everything. But he and the rest of the Command team believe Gilmour is working directly with Gemma Baldwin. They'll import the drugs using this permit and probably abandon Gilmour to his own fate before they arrive here in the UK.'

'But if the permit has been compromised, they won't touch it with a barge pole.'

'I know, Phil. But they won't listen.'

John sat back and drank his beer, concentrating. The others had seen this thought process before, so they remained silent. Eventually he said, 'Yvonne, can you get me the exact copies of the application forms Jason Moore gave to Gilmour?'

'Yes, I believe so. Why?'

'The answer we're looking for may be in there. Try and get them to me as soon as possible.'

'OK. I'll speak to my Dad tonight; he'll get them for me tomorrow. Shall I drop them round to your place tomorrow night?'

'Might as well. And bring a bottle.'

He looked at Phil. 'I suppose you want to come and have a free dinner too?'

'Thought you'd never ask.'

58

It had been three days since his last visit when Alex rang the bell. Now contemplating the imminent unpleasantness of both the stinking flat and its occupant, Miles Willis, he took a deep breath and waited for the reply.

'Who is it?' came a metallic voice through the intercom.

'It's Alex.'

The door buzzed, and he went inside. As he stepped out onto the third floor, Miles was waiting for him in the hallway, holding the envelope. 'Have you got the money?'

'Yes, but I need to have a look at the paperwork first.'

Miles handed him the envelope but still held it tightly by the corner. 'Let's see the money first.'

'Don't you trust me?'

'You're lower than a snake's belly. No, I don't trust you for one minute.'

Alex took a small package from his jacket pocket and opened it. Miles grabbed it and let go of the envelope. Both men examined their respective contents. Before Alex had got beyond the third page of the forms, Miles had counted the money. He said, 'That Article 7 Shipment Return, paragraph 3, subsection b should be useful,' then he turned and walked quickly away, returning to his disgusting flat and slamming the door behind him.

Alex continued checking the completed forms as he descended the stairs. He flicked through to the section Miles had just mentioned and froze. He read it again and stared out of the window towards the sea. This was a game changer. He remained still for a further five minutes before finally descending into the main hallway below. He examined the rest of the file until he was satisfied it had been completed correctly. Miles had been very competent, with all the pertinent areas adequately endorsed and evidenced. Of course, most of the contents were fictitious. But any failing sections would be corrected by Jason Moore personally. All he needed to do now was to contact Max and leave the forms addressed to Jason Moore at the front reception of the DTI offices in Whitehall.

Within two hours from leaving Brighton, he had accomplished this; leaving a message with the paperwork about their subsequent meeting the following day at the Italian bistro at noon.

59

Sir Graham Hall was notified at home of the developments, then placed a call to Jason Moore. They spoke for twenty minutes. The written permit would be placed on Jason's desk when he arrived at his office tomorrow. Soon afterwards, he would be visited by someone from the security services who would place a wire inside his shirt. Conversation between him and Gilmour were to be kept to a minimum. Once the permit had been presented to Gilmour, he was to return to the Ministry immediately.

*

The following day, after Jason Moore collected the permit and wire, he entered the restaurant, as arranged, and saw Alex Gilmour at the same table, drinking a glass of red wine. He sat down opposite him and handed over the thin brown envelope. Gilmour opened it and took out three papers. The first simply stated 'Temporary Special Import Permit (Scientific Research)' whilst the other two explained the terms and conditions. Gilmour smiled, and without looking up he handed a plain video cassette to Jason. 'It's all in there. There are no copies. It's not in my client's interest to double-cross you. He also said it was a pleasure doing business with you.'

Forgetting Sir Graham's last instructions, Jason leant forward and said, 'Bugger off, you parasite. I hope someday you and your cronies will pay some day for all the heartache you've caused.' He stood and left, without looking back. He had performed his last task. Now he was retired, his career in public service as a politician over.

Meanwhile, Alex was elated. He had achieved his goal. Now it was down to Max to deliver his reward. After consuming the whole bottle of wine, he asked for the telephone to be brought to his table.

He called Max. The telephone rang twice before it connected. No voice, just slight breathing. Alex said, 'I have a message for Graham Downs. The papers will be deposited at King's Cross as arranged and the key left with Benny.' The call was cut, the line emitting a continuous tone. Replacing the receiver, he sat back in his seat and closed his eyes as the waiter removed the telephone. A sense of pure euphoria swept throughout his body. He had nearly completed his part of the deal. Now he could plan his future; he was on the brink of fabulous wealth.

Ten minutes later he left the restaurant and hailed a black taxi and travelled to King's Cross station. After paying the driver he entered through the main entrance and went directly to the row of security lockers. Before placing the papers inside the locker, he attached a note to the front of the file, 'Have another look at Article 7 Shipment Return, paragraph 3, subsection b.' He closed the metal door and locked it securely.

He walked back through the main entrance and saw the newspaper vendor sitting against the hoardings behind a makeshift counter piled up with dozens of papers and magazines. He was an elderly man in his seventies, wearing a flat cap and matching scarf, a cigarette dangling from his lower lip. His voice bellowed 'Post' across the concourse. Alex approached him and asked, 'Benny?'

'Yes, mate. What can I do for you?'

'I've got a key for someone to collect from you later.'

'Don't worry, mate, I've been expecting you. Leave it with me.'

Alex handed him the small chrome key, wrapped in a twenty-pound note.

Benny touched the side of his cap and smiled. 'God bless you, guv.'

Alex walked towards the taxi stand and approached the front vehicle. He opened the rear door and got in. He was about to tell the driver his destination when both rear doors opened wide simultaneously, revealing two large men in suits. One of them said, 'Alex Gilmour. You are being arrested on suspicion of blackmail and the importation of class A drugs. Come this way.'

Alex Gilmour looked shocked. 'What the hell do you think you're doing?' But he was unable to protest any further; a rough hand grabbed his shoulder as he was unceremoniously dragged him from the taxi and escorted to a nearby car. He was virtually thrown into the rear seat and a blanket thrown over his head. He felt excruciating pains in both his neck and back; someone was deliberately squeezing several body pressure points. Although several commuters stopped to look on in surprise, no one questioned the men, assuming they were the police arresting a dangerous criminal. Alex's breathing became restricted.

The car pulled out into the heavy traffic. Several times he attempted to ask them where he was being taken but could only manage muffled grunts. His mind was racing. What did the police know? He would remain silent until he saw his solicitor. Tell them nothing.

Eventually, after what appeared an eternity, the car stopped. With its engine cut, everything went eerily quiet. The pressure of the man restraining him relaxed and the blanket was removed. 'Get out,' a coarse Irish accent commanded.

Gilmour stepped from the car and immediately saw they were not at a police station but instead in a large wood. A deep sense of fear overcame him. He immediately recognised the treachery; he had been betrayed by Max. After all the work he had accomplished for him in the past few days, this was how he was to be rewarded. He was pushed roughly towards the base of a large ash tree that had started shedding its foliage. A yellow leaf slowly drifted downwards and gently rested on his shoulder. He focussed on its delicate stem and the browning veins in its form; it was so surreal. It was the last image he ever saw as the bullet pierced his temple and shattered his skull. Without feeling any pain, he died before his limp body reached the soft leaf-covered ground.

60

Within a few hours of Alex's life coming to a violent end, a happier occasion was taking place in North London. John welcomed Yvonne and Phil into his home.

After finishing their meal, Yvonne said, 'Here you are John, my father has sent you the exact copies of the application forms given to Gilmour.' She passed the envelope over, spilling the contents onto the table. A quick glance made him frown. He was surprised at the amount of detail contained in the forms, especially the terms and conditions.

'I'll need to examine these more closely on my own. It may be a long shot, but I'll go through them later. Anyway, what else has been happening?'

'Quite a lot really. It would seem Gilmour has now disappeared again. We think he's arranging to leave the country and travel to Greece. The team managed to tap into a phone call he made from the restaurant after his meeting with Jason Moore. Whoever he spoke to told him to take the permit and leave it inside a security locker inside King's Cross railway station. Another surveillance team was tasked to swoop and pick him up as soon as he'd done this, but they missed him. But that's not too catastrophic; we can pick him up later. It's the identity of the collector that's the main objective. An observation point has been set up inside a store room directly opposite the lockers, supported by others inside the station and covering all the exits.'

'Has anyone been to collect it yet?' asked Phil.

'No. They're still staking it out. It could be ages'

'Hell, that'll be costing a pretty penny' said John.

'Apparently, the Home Secretary had taken a personal interest, so funding won't be any problem He's very anxious that whoever collects the permit must be kept under continuous surveillance until the cargo arrives back in the UK.'

'Who do they suspect will collect the permit?' asked John.

'They're not saying, but the Command Team still think it will be someone from Manchester. I'm sure they all believe Max Campbell is dead.'

'But we all think different, don't we?' said John.

'Bloody right' replied Phil.

Yvonne continued, 'Yes we do. But leaving that to one side, there's something else. I've been instructed to interview Morley tomorrow, with no deals on the table. He can talk to me if he wants. Otherwise he can take his chances at Crown Court.'

'But that's against the rules now he's been charged, isn't it? asked John.

'Not really. I've got other matters to put to him unconnected with his charges. Remember, we've got the backing of the Government security agencies and when it gets to Court, they'll play the 'in camera' card; not in the public interest and all that.'

Phil smiled. 'Like it.'

'But seriously, we must now build up a prosecution case against all of them. For a start, there's the suspicious deaths of Vicky Thompson and Julie Brecon, the unidentified body in the cellar and a host of blackmail charges. And that's not counting the possible importation of vast quantities of class A drugs. No, we've got our work cut out.

John added 'Yes we do. We also need to apply to the local Magistrates' Court for search warrants for Gilmour's, Campbell's and Morley's home addresses. We've must collect all the available evidence before their interviews.'

They nodded their heads in agreement.

After dinner they relaxed, spoke no more of their investigations and reminisced about their past and future aspirations. Yvonne saw how fortunate John and Charlie were, and once again felt envious. Phil's future was simple: retire, travel and utterly spoil his grandchildren.

61

Max was a man with a strong sense of self-preservation, both cunning and resourceful, never flinching for a moment from destroying the lives of others for his own gain or advancement.

He had deliberately sacrificed Alex, a liability who had served his purpose. But the whole enterprise depended on the next stage.

The collection of the special permit was crucial to his plans, even though it was compromised and fake. He had anticipated the authorities would be watching whoever collected the key from Benny and the papers in the locker at King's Cross station. He also knew the consignment travelling from Pakistan to the UK would be closely monitored. Yet, out of this hopelessness, he saw an opportunity to become extremely rich. It just required normal human nature to come into play and, of course, luck. In fact, a great deal of it. But the rewards were potentially staggering.

His first move was to change his appearance. In the past, the Caribbean had occasionally hosted a West Indian Drag Queen night in support of local community charities. It was all very amateurish, but it generated much hilarity, with many of the locals often challenging their friends and neighbours to dress as drag queens and appear on stage, dancing to their favourite reggae tracks. It was all in good fun and the club's takings were healthy. Unfortunately, the police raided the club one night and threatened Max with the revocation of his club licence. According to the licensing justices, the club required a special entertainment licence for such events and those came with stringent conditions and at a considerable cost. The drag queen nights ended abruptly.

However, whilst tidying the stock room, he had recently

discovered a large canvas bag containing a woman's black afro wig, long black coat, knee-length skirt and a pair low-heeled boots. He also found a small bag of makeup tucked in a pocket. He had recovered all these items from the club before setting it on fire. This was also part of his plan and serve as an outlandish and daring deception.

During the past few days, whilst waiting for Alex to sort the permit out, he had practised using the makeup and wig. Standing in front of the full-length mirror he felt only slightly confident he could pass as a young black woman, but hoped the dimly lit railway station at night would be enough to dupe the police. They would be looking for a man. He practised walking across the room, pulling the coat collar up beneath his chin, covering his neck. The black wig covered his forehead and the sides of his face. He applied the red lipstick and smiled enough to show his brilliant white teeth. It was the best he could do.

He went to check out of the small hotel where he had registered as James Green, not Graham Downs. He knew the police would be monitoring all of Alex's telephone calls wherever he placed them from and checking all the hotels and various bed and breakfasts in the Greater London area. Carrying his large suitcase, he entered the lobby where the woman receptionist put on a brave face. She had seen this type of cross-dressing behaviour before. 'Everyone to his own, or in this case, her own taste,' she mused to herself.

He walked outside into the cool autumn evening. Perfect. He hailed a taxi to King's Cross, speaking in a ridiculous high-pitched tone. The driver smiled and again saw through the facade immediately. As they approached the station he cheekily said, 'Here you are, my darling. I bet those lovely legs of yours go right up to your bollocks.'

Max ignored him, throwing a ten pound note over his shoulder before getting out with his suitcase. The boots were pinching his feet and his stride was unnatural. He slowed down to a stroll and approached the newspaper seller. Suspecting he was being watched only served to increase his dilemma. He could feel his heart beating in his chest. Yet, perversely, at that exact moment he had never felt more alive in all his life. He leant over towards the old man. 'Benny, sell me the *Evening News* and put the key inside.'

Benny looked at him. 'Bloody hell, Max. You look a bit different.'

'Just do as I ask, Benny. The Babylon are watching me.'

'Here you go, madam. Goodnight.'

Max took the newspaper and handed Benny a twenty-pound note before walking away, entering the station through the main entrance. Benny smiled again. This had been a good day, making forty pounds in a couple of hours for just looking after a small key. He could afford to call in at the Skinners Arms on his way home. After all, his wife Mabel would only take it from him and put in her secret jar; their holiday savings, kept under the vegetable rack in the outside larder.

Max made his way towards the lockers. He stopped some fifty yards away and looked for the obvious signs of surveillance posts. He immediately saw the disused stock and luggage room with dirty windows facing directly onto them. Instinctively, he knew the Babylon were watching from within.

His aim was to collect the permit from the locker, but he needed a serious decoy to avoid being seen. Again, this was all part of his plan. He strolled over to the fire hydrant hanging on the brick wall next to the public lavatories. Above the length of heavy-duty hose, inside a small glass box, was the fire alarm, designed to activate instantly once the small window was broken. He stood nearby and waited for the public-address system to announce the arrival of the next trains.

It was a short wait. He seized the moment. Whilst the station reverberated to the noise from the PA system and passengers hurried past, he smashed the fire alarm glass and casually sauntered away towards the toilets. As the announcement finished, the fire alarm was audible, causing people to stop and look in all directions. Suddenly a porter arrived and started sounding his whistle and shouting, 'Ladies and gentlemen, please make your way to the exits.'

The area in front of the lockers immediately became congested with commuters arriving for their homeward journeys and those now wishing to leave. For a moment there was utter chaos and confusion. Max dashed for the locker, knowing exactly which one to unlock. It was next to the ground. As he stooped down, completely hidden, he opened the door and snatched the papers from inside. As the crowd continued to pass, he stood up and mingled with them as they all made their way towards the exit.

Gradually the crowd dissipated, leaving the surveillance team peering anxiously through the dirty windows. They were mortified to see the locker door swinging wide open and the papers gone. Although their role was not to interfere, it was nevertheless crucial for them to establish the identity of the collector. Only yards away from their target, they had spectacularly failed their brief.

Meanwhile, Max was in a taxi, clutching the file and travelling to the nearby Victoria Central coach station. After paying the cab driver for the fifteen-minute ride, he slipped into the parking area behind the station and in the shadows, quickly changed into his normal casual clothes, discarding the drag queen attire in a nearby empty bin. He returned to the main bus station and bought a single ticket to Manchester Central coach station.

He walked over to the National Express coach where he placed his suitcase in the hold and boarded through the front door. Almost immediately the coach pulled out of the terminus into the evening rush hour traffic. Sitting back, still feeling the adrenalin coursing through his veins, Max opened the file and immediately noticed the note Alex had written: 'Have another look at Article 7 Shipment Return, paragraph 3, subsection b.' He had photocopied the original application form and the terms and conditions it referred to. But Max had already thoroughly researched this anomaly and discovered the opportunity to make a vast fortune.

According to the small print, additional goods, such as equipment and documents, could be imported separately under the protection of the parent company but they were not subject to the security seal. They could accompany the primary cargo, but there was no necessity to display any special identification labels. It would simply resemble normal imported goods. Max was gambling a great deal on the authorities concentrating on the other containers and ignoring any smaller insignificant crate included in the main shipment. It was the biggest gamble of his life. So far.

He removed the covering note and ripped it into small pieces, scattering it on the coach floor. He glanced at the permit. It had been granted to Crops Research UK Ltd. Once again, Alex had been thorough. He had attached a sheet of paper detailing a sister company, Phoenix Laboratories UK Ltd. He smiled. The irony linking the Caribbean, now reduced to ashes, with his new enterprise had not been wasted. Both companies had been registered in London with addresses in the East End.

Four hours later, the coach swung into the Manchester Central coach station. Max looked at his watch: ten thirty. He collected his case from the hold and walked to the public telephone booths and placed a call to Gemma Baldwin's house. Unable to speak to her, he was instructed to remain where he was.

This was the first time he had visited Manchester. In fact, it was the furthest north he had ever travelled. He noticed people's accents were different and it seemed much colder and less inviting. He was a stranger in a large city, feeling completely out of his depth, alone and in unfamiliar surroundings. But he had a plan and needed to prepare himself for worse to come. Above all else he needed to keep his nerve.

62

When the debacle surrounding the collection at King's Cross was reported, John was even more convinced Max Campbell was still alive. There had been no significant evidence gleaned by the surveillance team. The video footage shot from the observation point showed a mass of commuters hurriedly walking past the lockers. Once they had cleared, the locker was left wide open and its contents removed. The audio even picked up the angry voice of one of the operatives muttering, 'It's like bloody Mother Hubbard's cupboard.'

They were trawling through all the images inside King's Cross and of people purchasing papers from the newspaper vendor. He was known locally as Benny Johnson, a petty criminal with a criminal record stretching over forty years. He was considered an unlikely suspect and would never cooperate with the investigation anyway.

Miles Willis's attitude was in stark contrast. Once the Regional Crime Squad detectives informed him of Gilmour's criminal involvement and imminent prosecution, he willingly told them about the application forms, especially mentioning Article 7 Shipment Return, paragraph 3, subsection b. He smugly predicted no permit would now be granted and conveniently failed to mention the exact fee paid to him for his services.

Unfortunately, the officers failed to mention this in their crime report, even though it was clearly recorded in Willis's statement.

At John's request, Yvonne arranged a meeting for him to see her father, Sir Graham Hall, at Westminster, where they could discuss the application procedure for the special permit.

*

Shortly after nine o'clock the following morning, John was politely ushered into his office. 'Sit down, John. I've heard a great deal about you from my daughter over the years. You certainly made an impression on her, so it's good to finally meet you. How may I be of assistance?'

'Thank you for seeing me, Sir Graham. As you know the permit has been collected by our friends and we are now playing a waiting game. Can you explain to me how the permit will be monitored from Pakistan, on transit through the Mediterranean and its final debarkation in the UK? And there's another matter that gives me some concern. The terms and conditions of the packaging. Perhaps we can discuss them later?'

'Of course. The permit has been issued to a company called Crops Research UK Ltd, based here in London. As you know, it's bogus, the address is apparently an end terrace house in the East End. Companies House records only show scant details of its directors; all fictional.'

'OK.'

'Moving on. This permit allows the holder to store in a thirty-foot container crops and their roots, together with any flowers or seeds. These will be held in three separate wooden crates, all sealed and secured. They'll be inspected by the Pakistani authorities, overseen by nominated members from the British Consulate in Islamabad at the point of departure, which will probably be Karachi Port. Once this has been completed, the crates will be re-sealed, locked and placed in the container. This will remain in a restricted and secure unit, similar to a bonded warehouse, before being hoisted into the ship's hold. It will remain on board ship until it arrives in the UK, probably Southampton. That can change, depending on the weather. If the ship misses its allotted day of arrival, it may be diverted to London or even Immingham near Hull. It will leave Pakistani sovereign waters, sail around the Horn of Africa, up the Red Sea and enter the Suez Canal. It will leave the canal at Port Said after refuelling and sail directly to Southampton via Gibraltar. Once it has docked, the container will be taken from the ship and moved into the main bondage hangar where the seals will be inspected. Provided they have not been tampered with, the container will be ready for collection by the permit holder. In normal circumstances, the container would be sent directly onwards to the science laboratories for research, but we know this is not the case with this one. I'm not privy to what arrangements the authorities are putting in place, but I suspect they will make their arrests once the criminals have shown their hands.'

'That's useful to know. So if the container has been tampered with in any way, it will be opened in the port.'

'On the dockside, I would think.'

'Is there any other way that illegal goods could be brought into the UK under the terms and conditions of this permit, Sir Graham?'

'Not that I'm aware of. They will be inspected before they leave port and kept under lock and key until they arrive. When the container is in the hold, only the captain and the first officer have the keys. In any case, as I've just said, the seal is meticulously scrutinised on arrival here in the UK.'

John leant forward. 'I can't help worrying about this, Sir Graham. Something's not right. The person who I believe collected the permit from King's Cross last night knows we're on to them. What use would it be attempting to bring in vast quantities of heroin if they knew the permit was compromised? And the logistics, not to mention the cost, within Afghanistan and Pakistan would be enormous. So why would they risk all that investment? Do we trust the Pakistani authorities?'

'That's interesting. Obviously, I can't vouch entirely for them but remember, our team from the British Consulate will be in attendance when the contents are inspected and sealed up.'

'Yes, I realise that. But something's not right. Apparently, the Command Team running this operation don't share my pessimism; they are convinced the container will be full of Class A drugs and are busy organising the 'sting operation' once they have identified the port of entry.'

'I'm sorry. I wish I could help you further, John. If I come across any more information, I'll obviously be in touch.'

'Thank you for your time anyway, Sir Graham.'

Both men stood and shook hands, and as John left, Sir Graham asked, 'John, would you and your wife care to come and stay with me for a weekend in the country, when this is all over?'

'It would be my pleasure.'

'Good. I'll invite Yvonne too, if she can spare us her valuable time.'

John left the building with a better understanding of the permit procedure. Yet it posed a larger dilemma. If Max Campbell knew the container would be inspected before the shipment left harbour, how did he intend to ship the drugs back to the UK? It made no sense. What was he missing?

63

Through the Manchester rain, a familiar Mercedes came into view and parked on the opposite side to the coach station. Two flashes of its headlights confirmed the arrival of the Mancunian gang. Max picked up his suitcase and walked towards the car. As he approached, two men stepped out, one opened the rear door. 'Welcome to Manchester, Mr Campbell. The boss is keen to see you straight away.'

The streets were now empty of traffic. And it continued to rain. The car soon accelerated as it travelled out of the city, leaving the drab urban industrial buildings behind. The countryside opened up, but the darkness and heavy rain blanked out the landscape ahead.

There was no conversation throughout the forty-minute journey before the car eventually swung into a long drive, leaving the country lane. The Mercedes approached two large metal gates, slowing down as they automatically opened. Suddenly, the headlights swept across the façade of a large modern house with a central columned arched porch supporting a two-storey panoramic window. Max had not seen a house like it before. He was impressed.

As he got out of the Mercedes, another man approached. 'This way, Mr Campbell' he said, gesturing towards the front door where yet another man, dressed as a butler, stood waiting.

'Please come this way, Mrs Baldwin wants to see you now.'

Max had no opportunity to look at the opulent surroundings as he followed the butler into a lounge where a large log fire burnt, its flames flickering against the colourful tiled surround. Brass wall lamps shone directly above an assortment of original oil paintings, hanging in various wall recesses. Everywhere there was exquisite antique furniture. Facing the fire were two luxurious large brown leather sofas. Sitting in one was Gemma Baldwin. Strewn in front of her, across the carpet, were dozens of papers. She looked up.

'Max. Come and sit down. Why didn't you give me more notice you were coming?'

'I'm sorry about that, Gemma. But much has happened in the past few days.'

'Would you like a drink?'

'A large rum if you have one.'

She looked towards the man in the doorway and nodded. He disappeared and returned almost immediately with the drink. As he took the glass, she said, 'Go on, Max, I'm listening.'

'First of all, I've got the permit here. It's all in order and ready to use. There were a few complications with the initial application forms but they've all been sorted out. We can now go ahead with importing the goods from Pakistan without any hindrance with the drugs agencies, police or customs. Unfortunately, there have been some problems on the way. I've dealt with them, but you should know what's happened.'

'Good. I don't like secrets between partners. Tell me what's happened.'

'As I mentioned when I last phoned you, my old partner Sammy Clarke attempted to muscle in on our business dealings and spoil any chance of us working with each other in the future. So you sent Bill down to the Caribbean to fix him. However, when he was in the cellar, Sammy shot him in the head. I've no idea why he suspected Bill was going to kill him or where he got the gun from, but that's what happened. I rushed him and managed to grab the gun from his hand. We looked at each other for a second and then I shot him.'

Gemma was staring at Max with her piercing eyes. Bill was her most trusted lieutenant. She had been concerned when he had failed to return and was planning to send a search party to locate him. Concealing her alarm, she said, 'Carry on, Max.'

'I left Sammy where he lay.' He hesitated. 'I'm sorry about this Gemma. I know you're not going to like this, but I put Bill in the boot of my car and drove him to Dartford on the Thames, next to the new bridge. There, I placed him inside a blanket, weighed him down a little, and slipped him into the river, letting the tide take him out into the estuary. I then returned to the club and did as you suggested, burnt it down.'

'Was the merchandise affected?'

'No, that was removed by your boys before this happened. I'm really sorry about Bill but I didn't count on Sammy doing that.'

'You underestimated him, Max. You should never do that.'

'I know. Can we still progress with our enterprise or do you want to leave it?'

'I'm not sure, Max. I need to sleep on it; it's late. We've arranged a room for you here, so I'll see you at nine thirty for breakfast in the dining room.'

Max stood and walked towards the door, where his suitcase lay. He stooped down and opened the side pocket, taking out the permit and its accompanying papers. He returned to Gemma. 'Here are the papers anyway. We'll talk about them in the morning. Good night.'

She did not reply. Underneath her composure, she was seething with rage, feeling acutely uneasy about Bill's death. He was a professional, always aware of his surroundings, and he possessed a sixth sense for potential danger. She had heavily relied on his skills for her own personal safety and often, to her annoyance, argued with her about any threats, real or imaginary. She always bowed to his good judgement, completely trusting him with her life. But now he was apparently somewhere in a watery grave in the Thames Estuary. Could she really place the same trust in Max?

She glanced at the permit and took it bed with her.

Meanwhile, Max lay on his bed, unable to sleep. His mind was racing with all the events that had occurred during the past few days. Whilst he felt invigorated by the sense of danger and betrayal, he knew he was riding his luck. Everything now depended on Gemma agreeing to the enterprise and allowing him to go out to Pakistan to oversee the shipment. If she declined, his insurance was the half a million. If she failed to deliver either of these options, he was finished. Even if she spared his life, his future was bleak; no business, limited funds, effectively on the run from the police for the rest of his days and definitely no friends.

*

He awoke the following morning after a troubled night's sleep.

How was she going to react? He peered out of the bedroom window at rolling countryside stretching into the far hills, surrounded by tall trees and woodland shrubs. It had finally stopped raining but the vista was completely alien to his normal surroundings. He was a 'city' man, having seen little greenery other than Hyde Park. He glanced at his watch; a cheap replica of his cherished Rolex last placed on Bill's wrist. It was five past nine.

After a quick shower, he dressed and went downstairs as the hallway grandfather clock struck nine thirty. A voice from behind said, 'This way, Mr Campbell.' He turned around and followed the butler across the hallway into a large room, where in the centre stood a long polished table with seating for twenty. Gemma was facing him from the far end.

'Come and sit down here next to me, Max.'

She pointed to the adjacent chair and returned her gaze to the assorted papers in front of her. 'Just give me a moment, I need to look at these right now. If you want coffee or tea with your breakfast, just tell Peter.'

On cue, Peter entered the room and took Max's order, a plain omelette with black coffee. Before he returned she placed her spectacles down on the table.

'OK, Max. I've had time to think about all this. I'm very upset that Bill is no longer with us and particularly in the way you disposed of him afterwards. Nevertheless, I can see now you had little choice. Moving on to the permit. I've read the documentation and see the enterprise has some merit. But I still have some reservations. A couple of days ago, I received a telex communication from one of my business associates I sent out to Pakistan. He's made a preliminary costing. Even using our regular sources, the quantities we're asking for would cost me in excess of three million pounds. I fully appreciate this can be multiplied tenfold once we have it here in the UK, but the fact remains, it's an enormous outlay for me to make with only a small guarantee of success. The odds are too high, Max.'

'I understand your concern, Gemma, but what can I do to try and convince you more that this is a great opportunity of making an enormous fortune?'

'I've given that some thought too, Max. So this is what I propose. I want you to fly out there and meet up with Afzal Jamali. He's our main man who organises the buying and movement of our merchandise. He will overlook the arrangements for the collection and transport of the goods to the port of departure and ensure the security is not breached. Your role will be to ensure the free passage of them through the docks to the warehouse prior to embarkation. And once the cargo has landed and been safely collected here in the UK, then I'll give you your fee.'

'But that's not what we agreed originally, Gemma.'

'I know, Max. But that's what the deal is now.'

Max facial features changed; he appeared disappointed and angry. He remained silent for a moment before replying, 'But, Gemma, I was expecting my money from you now.'

'I know you were. But things have changed. I was going to send Bill out to Pakistan to supervise the deal but now he's dead. You're going to have to go instead. There's no one else. It's down to you, or the deal is off.'

Max stared at her, his mind drifting towards the contingency plan he had formulated: setting up another sister company to the one shown on her permit. It was all now fitting into place. With some convincing hesitation, he replied, 'If you need me to go out there, I have little choice. But you must know, I've also invested a great deal of money already in the enterprise to get that piece of paper.'

'How much, Max?'

Without changing expression, he lied. 'Twenty thousand pounds.'

'OK. In a gesture of good faith, I'll transfer half of that into your overseas account now.'

He was about to object when he saw her cold eyes focussing on him. Speaking through her thin lips, she continued, 'That's the end of the matter. You're going to be driven from here down to Harwich, where you will cross the channel into Holland, take a short train ride to Schiphol Airport and board a plane for Islamabad. We can't risk you flying from Manchester or London.'

But I don't have a passport.'

'Don't worry about that, I've arranged for one to be made. We need to photograph you before you leave here. You will be assuming a new identity. It will be all processed and couriered down to Harwich in time for you to cross the North Sea, together with sufficient funds for your trip. Once in Pakistan, you will be met there by Afzal Jamali and he'll tell you what's happening. I know you're not happy, but my decision is final on this matter. You will get your money when I get my merchandise. You will take the permit with you and after liaising with Afzal, supervise the packing and transport of our goods before the container leaves Karachi Port. You will do this Max. So goodbye and good luck. I hope to see you on your return with the shipment, safe and sound.'

Two men immediately walked into the room. One indicated with his head to Max that the meeting was over and to accompany him. He was the same man who had welcomed him to Manchester the previous night. As Max walked into the hallway, he was ushered into a small room where he was asked to sit down in front of a white wall and face a static camera on a tripod. Two portrait passport-sized photographs were taken. Within seconds he was back on his feet, re-entering the hallway, where another man summoned him to the front door. He was holding his suitcase. Before leaving, Max looked back towards the dining room door, but it was firmly closed. If his plan succeeded, that would be last time he ever saw her. She had taken the bait. He walked out into the sunny Cheshire air, concealing a wry smile. He was on his way.

Max sat in the rear seat of the brand-new Range Rover as it gently accelerated along the driveway towards the outside world. It was going to be a long and silent journey down to Harwich.

*

Several uncomfortable hours later, the Range Rover approached the entrance to Harwich Docks. The driver pulled off the main road and parked next to a mobile café advertising 'last decent breakfast for a long time'. The driver grunted. 'This is as far as we go. Can you see that motorcyclist over there?' He pointed towards a man in black leathers, wearing a helmet that covered his face, sitting astride a large motor cycle. 'Go and see him.'

As Max stepped out of the car, holding his suitcase, the Range Rover pulled away at speed. He approached the motorcyclist who simply held out a small plastic carrier bag; no conversation was offered. Once he had taken it, the rider sped off in the same direction as the others.

Max went into the café and ordered a coffee and toast. Unsurprisingly he was the only customer. He sat at the far corner table and whilst waiting for his toast, opened the bag and removed a

British passport. Amazingly his photo was there in the front, with the name of Joel Richardson, same date of birth but born in Birmingham. According to the inside pages, he had travelled extensively throughout Asia, especially Pakistan and India. His recorded occupation was agricultural researcher. He removed all the contents of the bag, including two bundles of different currencies, two thousand pounds in sterling and five thousand US dollars. Pinned to these was an open return ticket from Schiphol to Islamabad.

He left the café without drinking the coffee and walked towards the nearby ticket office; the ferry sailed in two hours. After purchasing his ticket, he went through Passport Control, where the smartly dressed officer took little notice of him. His passport was stamped and within five minutes he was sitting in the ship's main lounge, looking out towards the open sea.

He knew all his plans were coming to fruition. Gemma had reacted just how he intended, especially about the untimely death of her close bodyguard Bill, whom she had intended to send out to Pakistan to oversee the packaging and transport of the goods before they arrived at Karachi. Perfect.

He relaxed further into his seat and dared to close his eyes. He was on his way. His spirits lifted. Those late and rushed plans he was forced to make might just succeed. So far, so good.

64

After being remanded into custody to Paddington Green Police Station, the past twenty-four hours had been the most miserable in George Morley's life. Now deserted of his self-assured manner, he knew he was in trouble. Serious trouble. He had only been given access to his solicitor. Any contact with the outside world had been forbidden, fearing he would likely interfere with witnesses and impede the investigation.

He wondered why his family had made no effort to contact to him, nor his old friend Alex Gilmour. Where was Alex? Now alone and isolated, he was a broken man, alone with an uncertain future, facing a later remand in custody to Wormwood Scrubs. And that was dangerous; bent ex-cops were reviled amongst fellow prison inmates, often attracting merciless attacks.

As he sat on the edge of his austere bed, facing the opposite wall of his cell, he heard the metal door lock turn. Looking up, he saw Yvonne and John at the open doorway. He placed his head in his hands. 'What do you want?'

'George Morley, as you might remember, my name is DCI Hall and this Inspector Evans. We want to talk you about a number of different serious issues not related to those you have already been charged with. Do you understand?'

'Is there any deal on the table, if I cooperate?'

'I can't make any promises, Mr Morley, but obviously the courts will take that into consideration. Please follow us to the interview room next door where we can talk further.'

He stood up and followed them out from the cell, down a short corridor to the interview room. After they had sat down, Yvonne said, 'I must caution you first before I ask any further questions. We shall be recording the interview contemporaneously.'

He simply nodded, thinking he knew the procedure of interviewing under caution better that she did. After all, he was doing this when she was still in high school. Bloody upstart, she should be at home doing the cleaning. But he was in custody, on remand and she represented the new 'modern policing'. But what the hell, his career was definitely over, so why should he care. There was only one objective now: self-preservation.

For nearly an hour he kept asking for a deal before answering any further questions, making it difficult for Yvonne and John to progress. He remained silent throughout with only the occasional 'no comment'.

As lunchtime approached, Yvonne was about to suspend the interview when she heard a knock on the door. She looked towards the small window and saw a young detective summoning her outside. Turning to George Morley, she said, 'I shall speak to you later this afternoon.' He shrugged, stood up and was escorted by a uniformed officer back to his cell. The detective entered the room and closed the door behind him.

'Ma'am, I'm sorry for interrupting your interview but something important has turned up and you need to know, before you continue any further.'

'What is it?'

'A couple of hours ago, an elderly couple were walking their dog in Epping Forest when they found a body of a man, with severe gunshot head wounds. The local CID attended and declared it a murder scene. A quick search of the clothing revealed his identity. It's Alex Gilmour. SOCO team believe it has all the hallmarks of a professional execution.'

She turned to John. 'OK. What do you think, John?'

He spoke to the detective, 'I want you contact SOCO. I know they'll have already photographed the body in situ. Tell them to get some copies sent to us here, straightaway? I've got an idea.'

'I'll do it now, sir.' He disappeared towards the Control Room and forwarded John's request. Within two minutes he returned, 'Ma'am, they've already done that and are now developing the negatives. They should be here with your photographs within the hour.'

'Excellent.' She turned to John. 'What have you got in mind?'

'When these photos arrive, I want to interview Morley on my own. Have you any objections?'

'I'm not happy about that. Why?'

'Just trust me, Yvonne. I need about ten minutes alone with him. I'll tell you why when we've finished.'

'Very well. But it sounds very ominous.'

*

After lunch, George Morley was returned to the interview room. John walked in alone with a large yellow folder and placed it on the table in front of him. 'Mr Morley. You and I are old school, but that's where the similarities stop. I know what you've been up to for many years whilst running the Vice Squad. In fact, in the past few weeks I've spent a great deal of time studying you, even had a trip out to Spain to see your old friend Barry Taylor. He told me about your earlier days and of your corrupt practice of passing details of innocent men to Alex Gilmour who had been caught in the King's Cross red-light area. He even explained to me why he had resigned from the Met; but let's leave that for the moment. Let's just say, he doesn't have a very high opinion of you right now.'

Morley looked at John and then turned away. Clearly, he was surprised about his trip to Spain.

'Anyway, I want to show you something, but before I do, just think about your present position. Your old pal Alex had an unhealthy friendship with Max Campbell, as you did. Fortunately for you, you got arrested. You know your life was in danger because you heard the recording of the telephone call Max made to some unidentified killers. I just want you to look at these photographs. They were taken by SOCO two hours ago. You'll also know they are genuine.'

John opened the folder and slid the set of large colour photographs towards Morley. The first image depicted the extreme trauma of the gunshot wound to a man's head. The next image, taken from the opposite side of the head, clearly showed the partial facial features of his dead friend, Alex. As he continued gazing at the others, John said, 'I'm going to leave you alone with theses for a few minutes to reflect on where we go from here. After all, you know very well there's no hiding place in jail.'

Ten minutes later Yvonne and John returned. They were surprised to see George Morley openly sobbing. After allowing several minutes of silence, he looked up and stared directly into John's eyes. 'I'll tell you exactly what's happened. That bastard Max is going to pay for all this.'

65

The Greater Manchester Police had struggled to place a tap on Gemma Baldwin's telephone. The surveillance operation on her movements and those of her associates had been an unmitigated disaster. She rarely left her mansion, set in twelve acres of parkland and heavily guarded by cameras and intruder alarms. Further security was provided by intermittent floodlights and sensors placed strategically along the whole perimeter of the gardens, the main gateway and the doorways leading into the house. The entire estate was patrolled by teams of staff for twenty-four hours a day. According to one officer observing her protection, she was shielded from intrusion better than the Prime Minister.

However, the movement of the Mercedes from there to Manchester Central coach station had not gone unnoticed. Unfortunately, traffic had been light to non-existent, giving little cover for the pursuit vehicles. As the Mercedes stopped near the coach station, a surveillance officer was able to take three photographs using a night intensifier and powerful zoom lens before their stationary vehicle became too suspicious. Later that evening, the images were developed but the use of the zoom lens, together with the rush to take the shots, had left them grainy and slightly out of focus. However, the final photograph was better, showing a black male, in his mid-twenties, dressed in a long dark coat and carrying a suitcase, approaching the Mercedes.

These images were sent immediately to Yvonne for her attention. The following day she showed them to George Morley, who without hesitation positively identified the figure. 'That's definitely that double-crossing bastard Campbell. No doubt about it.'

John's suspicions were now confirmed. Max Campbell was still alive.

Yet when Yvonne passed this information on to Commander Higgins, he dismissed the development, saying, 'It's an old ploy, Yvonne. It's one criminal playing the other one off. Max Campbell is dead, lying on a slab in the mortuary, killed by the Manchester mob. Why would he deliberately burn his own place down and turn his back on a lucrative lifestyle? No, he must have done something to betray their trust. Probably tampered with their drugs for his own advantage. And for your information, the Command Team share my sentiments too.'

When John heard this, he sarcastically said, 'All those senior officers are blinkered, not wanting to rock the boat. Of course they will all agree with the Commander, it makes for an easy life. Why can't they show some initiative and keep an open mind?'

'Hell, John, I need a drink. Let's meet up with Phil in the George.'

Later, in the George, after Phil had joined them, they discussed their position with the investigation, convinced even more that Max was still very much alive and one step ahead of them. But they'd run out of ideas. There was little else to do other than wait until the cargo appeared at a port in Pakistan, probably Karachi, where the permit would be presented. Meanwhile, they had to be patient.

Finally, Yvonne announced, 'We all know from previous experience, most protracted investigations have a lull before a breakthrough occurs. Unfortunately, this is ours. I'm sorry to tell you both but I've no alternative but to stand you down until we hear of any further developments.'

66

As Max stepped out of the plane at Islamabad, it was hot and raining heavily. It was called the 'retreat monsoon'. The effect of the humidity was immediate, and the hot sticky air blew strange aromas he had never smelt before. Although only dressed in a short-sleeved shirt and thin trousers, he was drenched with perspiration by the time he reached the arrivals lounge. There, the efficient air conditioning changed one discomfort for another. The perspiration quickly cooled, acting like a refrigeration process. This was the familiar daily pattern he would come to accept: hot outside, cold air conditioning indoors.

His appearance before Passport Control attracted more attention than his departure from the UK. He was initially questioned about the reason for his visit, but the production of Her Majesty's Government special export permit changed everything. His passport was duly stamped, unchecked, accompanied by a salute. He was courteously waved through the gate without any further hindrance.

He collected his suitcase and continued towards the exit, where he saw a man holding a card with the name 'Mr Joel Richardson'. He approached the stranger. 'Hello. Are you Afzal Jamali?'

'Yes. You must be Mr Richardson. I've been expecting you. Let me give you a hand with your case. I've got you booked into the Serena Hotel. We'll take my car.'

'Thanks.'

*

Thirty minutes later, Max settled into the luxury suite overlooking the noisy frenetic urban landscape, where the traffic pollution partially shrouded the distant skyline. Without any sleep for nearly twenty-four hours, he needed to rest. He showered and went to bed. Mercifully, Afzal Jamali had left him at the reception desk and arranged to return the following day at lunchtime. He glanced at his cheap watch. It was 11.43 a.m. UK time. The hotel clock showed 3.43 p.m.

He lay on the bed and slowly drifted away into a deep sleep.

*

The following morning, he was woken by the telephone ringing next to his bed. He woke up with a start, disorientated, unsure of his surroundings. He picked up the receiver and a voice said, 'Mr Richardson?'

'Who?' he replied.

'Mr Richardson. This is Abdul on the reception desk. You have a visitor. May I tell him you will join him in the guest lounge?'

Max quickly gathered his thoughts. 'Yes, I'll be down to see him in twenty minutes.'

'Very good, sir.'

He checked the clock. It was now noon. He had slept for nearly twenty hours without any disturbances. He felt refreshed and invigorated as he showered, dressed and descended the hotel stairs into the lounge. Through the large glass doors, he saw a beautiful lush tropical garden, with several water fountains connecting to a central pond. Sitting near the pond, in a large wicker chair, drinking a cup of tea, was Afzal Jamali.

Max approached and said politely, 'Hello, Mr Jamali. I'm sorry for keeping you waiting but I've never slept so well in my whole life. I think it must have been the flying and recent business commitments that exhausted me.'

'There's no need to apologise, Mr Richardson, and please call me Afzal.'

'Thank you. Please call me Joel.'

'I'd rather call you Mr Richardson if you don't mind? I feel more comfortable with that.'

'OK.'

'Mr Richardson, we have much to talk about, let's go somewhere where it's quiet.'

'I understand. Do you have anywhere in mind?'

He looked straight ahead and nodded. 'Yes, the garden is the perfect place. I've taken the liberty of having a table and chairs set amongst the trees, in the shade. It's very private there and we won't be disturbed other than when they bring us refreshments and food. I've conducted much business here in the past. It's safe.'

'Good, lead the way.'

Set in idyllic surroundings under the canopy of the trees, the men sat facing each other, drinking tea and eating light refreshments. To an observer, they were two professional men discussing a trade deal or other commercial enterprise, quietly haggling over their individual needs and costs. But their discussion had a deadly nature. Max was astounded at the quantities of heroin Afzal had arranged to be transported from the various provinces in Afghanistan and the logistical problems of paying the Taliban for safe passage across the border into Pakistan. The price had recently spiked, owing to the upsurge of violence following the Russian occupation of Afghanistan, now in its fourth year. All the monetary deals and bribes were handled by Afzal Jamali.

According to Afzal, the drugs would be collected from all their suppliers and stored in a disused warehouse called Grant Mills, set on the outskirts of Karachi. The timeframe for all the drugs to arrive at Grant Mills was three weeks. There, on site, three large special wooden crates were to be constructed like Russian dolls, each crate hold a smaller unit inside, where the drugs would be finally stored. These in turn would be completely concealed inside the larger ones, surrounded by tightly packed maize crops.

After leaving Grant Mills they were to be transported to the docks and presented, along with the special export permit, to the Pakistani authorities and the British Consulate for inspection. This was the most critical and delicate part of the whole operation; the bribing of the Pakistani officials was crucial.

If successful, they would be locked and sealed before being moved to the bonded warehouse. There, they would be placed together inside a large metal container ready for shipment. Max's actual involvement was minimal.

He was very impressed with Afzal's planning. He was only expected to oversee the securing of the heroin inside the wooden crates before accompanying them to Karachi Port. It was there where he took all the risk.

After two hours, the meeting was over. Max returned to his room. Although it was three weeks before he was expected to oversee the packing, there was a great deal for him to organise. Karachi was over a thousand miles away and he needed to go there without delay or attracting any attention to make his own plans for the next stage.

67

To avoid any unnecessary attention from Afzal Jamali, Max informed the hotel receptionist the following morning he was taking a tour, visiting Lahore in the Punjab for a few days. His true destination was much further. Karachi.

The train from Islamabad to Karachi was like no journey Max had ever undertaken. Beforehand, the receptionist had given him some useful advice about travelling on public transport: douse some aftershave on a cotton handkerchief and avoid touching sticky surfaces, especially handrails. Personal hygiene for the majority of Pakistanis fell far short of most Europeans.

Thirty minutes later, Max still held is handkerchief to his nose camouflaging the smell, but by now both arms became weary from the strain. With more passengers sitting precariously on the roofs above than those ticket-paying travellers inside, the train sped across the hot dusty plains southwards towards its destination.

Although he was dark-skinned like most of the passengers, as an Afro-West Indian he still attracted the attention of most on board. He peered outside at the monotonous flat countryside stretching into the far distance, trying to count down the gruelling twelve-hour journey. Fortunately, as the train progressed towards Karachi, the number of passengers gradually dwindled, allowing him some limited freedom of movement.

Finally, after what seemed like an eternity, Max stepped off the train onto the bustling platform at Karachi Central railway station, walked out of the exit and approached the nearby taxi rank. His intention was to make his way to the Grant Mills mentioned by Afzal

Jamali, find an acceptable hotel and locate a local carpenter. This part of his plan had to be completed within ten days, before returning to Islamabad on the stinking train. He spoke to several drivers before one of them agreed on a price of twelve hundred rupees to drive him to the suburb where Grant Mills was located and on to a local hotel.

This journey took under an hour. The taxi pulled into the front yard close to a crumbling red brick two-storey warehouse. He asked the driver to remain there before taking him to a hotel he might recommend. Max walked further into the yard and looked closely at the building. Its twisted rusted corrugated tin roof and boarded-up windows stretching down both sides bore witness to a once thriving enterprise, now decaying and falling into utter ruin. In fact, the whole area was derelict and devoid of human activity. It was a perfect location for storing and packing narcotics.

Grant Mills was similar in size to the Caribbean Club; not too big but spacious enough to store large quantities of drugs. The security of the building had yet to be arranged, with the first shipment not expected to arrive for another five to six days. This gave him ample time.

He pulled at a loosely fitting window board and peered inside. The warehouse was entirely empty, with a concrete floor and iron chain pulleys attached to overhead steel girders. No doubt these would be used to hoist the crates when necessary. Afzal Jamali had chosen a good location. He let go of the loose board so it sprang back onto its frame and returned to the taxi. He had seen all he wanted to.

The hotel the taxi driver recommended was in fact just a short walk away. He presented his passport to the receptionist who appeared surprised at see a foreign visitor. 'Welcome to the Hotel Imperial, Mr Richardson. How long do you intend to stop with us, sir?'

'Perhaps just a day or two. It depends on business.'

'Very good, sir. I'll show you to your room now.'

'Thank you. Before you do that, can you tell me where the nearest reputable carpenter is from here?'

'Let me think. Oh yes. Mr Hussain runs a small business just a few blocks away from here. Would you like me to contact him for you and ask him to come and see you here?'

'Yes, please. First thing in the morning.'

'Certainly. This way to your room, sir.'

The state of the room was far from perfect but a marked improvement on the filthy train. He took room service to eat his dinner and retired to bed, anticipating a busy day the next day.

*

He woke to the horrendous sound of rain crashing down on the metal roof above before wildly cascading over his window onto the pavement below. His view outside was restricted, like looking through a waterfall from behind. Yet he could see the street was deluged with water spilling from all the surrounding buildings. To his surprise, people were going about their business as normal completely ignoring the weather. The thick blue exhaust fumes from the traffic only added to the miserable view.

He dressed and went downstairs to see whatever breakfast had to offer. After discovering the menu consisted of battered spicy cauliflower heads, rice and soup, he played safe and requested tea and plain nan bread only. He lacked any appetite after the previous day's ordeal. However, as he was leaving the dining room, the receptionist approached him. 'Mr Richardson?'

'Yes.'

'Sir, Mr Hussain is waiting to see you in the main entrance. Please follow me.'

In the visitors' area sat a middle-aged man of slight build, wearing a white cotton coat over baggy trousers and loose leather sandals. Max said, 'Mr Hussain. Good morning. I wonder if I could speak to you in private. I have a business proposition for you that requires your immediate attention. Are you interested?'

'Yes, but that depends on what you want and how much you are prepared to pay.'

'I understand, Mr Hussain. What I require is this.' Max handed over a plan of the construction with exact measurements and dimensions, including the materials required. After studying the paper for several minutes, Mr Hussain agreed to undertake the contract, including the price and the timeframe involved. Max paid him two thousand rupees in cash, with a further two thousand on completion, provided he kept the works completely secret. The construction was to remain hidden until he received notification from Max alone. Afterwards, he would be given further instructions about where it was to be delivered. They shook on the deal.

Max returned to his room and packed, checked out of the Imperial Hotel and caught a taxi back to Karachi Central railway station. There, he purchased a return ticket back to Islamabad and bought several English language newspapers to keep him occupied and distracted from the hellish train ride that lay ahead.

Several hours into his journey he opened one of the newspapers, the *Daily Times*. On page five there was a small article titled 'Journalist found murdered in Epping Forest, London'. He read on. The journalist was named as Alex Gilmour. He was famous for investigating the activities of people, often in the public eye, who had used the services of those involved in the sex trade. Reliable sources suggested his murder showed all the signs of a professional assassination, hallmarks of the organised criminal underworld. The police were appealing for witnesses or victims who had any information relating to past threats of blackmail involving Gilmour or anyone else. All reports would be dealt with in the strictest of confidence.

Max made a note of the date. Three days ago. He shook his head in dismay. He had specifically instructed the Irish boys to ensure the body was concealed permanently, yet once again they had failed. Bungling amateur assassins. Unfortunately, the fee had been paid and Alex was now recorded as a murder victim instead of a 'missing person'. Now he needed to be extra vigilant. After this enterprise, he would disappear and no one in the world would be any the wiser. His thoughts turned to DS Morley. Now Alex's body had been discovered, the bent cop would certainly point the finger of suspicion at him. His plans to return to the UK would require some changes. But at least he was forewarned.

The return journey was a marked improvement on the first. The carriages were less than half occupied and the heat more tolerable due to unseasonably low humidity. The locomotive finally pulled into Islamabad Central station at an hour early.

Following a short taxi ride, he arrived back at the Serena Hotel, collected his keys and retired to his room, feeling dirty, exhausted and hungry. Filled with a sense of accomplishment, he soon fell into a deep sleep.

The next stage in his plan was about to unfold. He must be prepared.

68

Two days after returning to the Serena, Max received a telephone call from Afzal Jamali. 'Can we meet in the lounge in an hour, Mr Richardson?'

'Yes. I'll see you then.'

*

Sitting in the same seats as before in the private gardens, Afzal Jamali said, 'Mr Richardson, our plans for the final movements of our merchandise to arrive at Karachi are nearly complete. I believe we should fly down there the day after tomorrow to organise the secure packaging of the three large crates we've had built.'

'OK. What do these crates look like?'

Afzal removed a paper from his case. Immediately Max recognised it. 'Thank God' he thought to himself. It was exactly the same as the copy tucked away in his suitcase upstairs. He leant over and pretended he was interested in the design and construction.

'As you can see, Mr Richardson, all the merchandise will be divided into three. Each load will be housed inside each of one of the smaller crates. Once the contents have been placed inside, these crates in turn will be lowered into the larger outer crates, completely hiding them. The gaps between the inner and outer crates will be stuffed tightly with maize crops and other packaging materials.'

'That looks good. Someone has worked this out well.'

'Yes, there are two brothers in Karachi who specialise in "special packaging", if you know what I mean, Mr Richardson.'

'I do. It all looks very impressive. When we go down to Karachi, how long will it take before we present the crates to the port authorities?'

'The next day. That's when you become involved. I will accompany you with the crates to the docks where you will register them, using the special permit to identify their contents. We'll be directed to the secure compound where they will be visually inspected and placed inside the large metal container. This in turn will be sealed by the customs officers.'

'Will they inspect the contents?'

'No. I have made arrangements with one of the officials to safeguard any harsh scrutiny. In any case, your production of the permit should stop them doing that. It would be, how do you say, "not cricket". They will accept the permit at face value then stamp the outside container and place a joint Pakistani and UK Government seal across the two rear doors.'

'How do you know all this?'

'Because, Mr Richardson, I used to work in the import and export trade.'

'Why did you stop doing that?'

He snapped back, 'It no bloody business of yours, Mr Richardson.'

'I apologise. You're right, it has nothing to do with me. Please forgive my rudeness.'

'Very well. Please be ready to leave in two days' time. I will collect you here at ten and drive to the airport. If the flights from Islamabad are on time, we'll be in Karachi before five o clock.'

'Thank you. I'll be ready.'

They nodded to each other, but Max felt he had unintentionally annoyed him, clearly touching a raw nerve. He needed to make amends. He could ill afford to lose his cooperation at this stage.

But he had other business to attend to. After returning to his room, he placed a call to the carpenter, Mr Hussain. In accordance with his instructions, the crate had been constructed exactly to the specifications and was ready for delivery. Max explained he would be returning to Karachi in two days' time, when he would give his final instructions.

He hung up and lay back on the bed. He was nearly there.

69

The plane touched down at four o clock in the afternoon and taxied towards the Karachi main terminal. They had travelled first class. Any previous animosity Afzal had shown to him two days ago had disappeared. Their behaviour towards each other was both friendly and courteous.

Afzal hired a car in the arrivals lounge and they drove to Grant Mills, some five miles away in the run-down industrial quarter, close to the main maritime port. Max convincingly faked surprise when they pulled up outside the old warehouse, but when they stood at the entrance, it had changed considerably inside. It was now a hive of activity, with dozens of men lifting thousands of packets no larger than shoe boxes, wrapping them into polythene bags and packing each one tightly into three wooden crates standing in the centre of the warehouse. Everyone was wearing face masks and gloves. Set aside to these crates were the three larger ones that would conceal them and hold the crops.

'We must stay outside. It's too toxic to go any closer,' said Afzal.

'I realise that. How long will it take them to finish packing all of them together?'

'I have been assured it will all have been completed by tomorrow morning. I've arranged for the crates to be transported to Port Grand in Karachi at noon tomorrow. They should arrive there about an hour later, providing the traffic doesn't get choked up, of course.'

Max looked carefully at the large outer crates. They were enormous. Now a little concerned, he hoped the one Mr Hussain had

ROBERT HENSON

constructed for him matched these, otherwise it would raise suspicion when they were finally placed inside the metal container and sealed. He turned to Afzal. 'When they arrive at the port, where do they go exactly?'

'They will be driven on three separate lorries to the Port Grand main cargo reception area, just outside the security barrier. There, they will be recorded in terms of their contents, weight and destination. The cargo will be assigned to the next available ship, giving port of destination and dates of departure and estimated arrival. It will be at that stage, Mr Richardson, you will present your special permit. This is important. I have dealt with one of the officials, so you should be alright. You will accompany the crates personally to the bonded warehouse, where, as I've just said, they will remain together before they are finally placed inside the large metal container and sealed in accordance with terms of the permit.'

'Will I be on my own at this stage?'

'Yes, you are the holder of the permit, it's a restricted area with no unauthorised personnel allowed. You will answer any questions the authorities may ask. Normally it's just a formality, and when they've finished they'll take a copy of the permit and give you more documentation as they secure the metal container with wire cables stretched across the opening. Finally, they will place a large wax seal across the wires and stamp them together. Once that's been done, you won't see them until they land in the UK. They'll remain there until they're unloaded from the ship and placed onshore in a secure compound. Only the production of the permit in the UK will allow you to take possession of them again. So, once they're on board, you can fly back home.'

'Thanks. That's really helpful. Incidentally, if I'm not needed until tomorrow afternoon, would you mind if I do some last minute shopping before I catch up with you at the docks?'

'Not at all. Would you like me to accompany you? I'll be able to save you some money. Remember, everyone in my country haggles.'

'Thanks for the offer, Afzal, but I think I'd like to explore on my own. Would you mind?'

'Not at all but don't get lost and mind your wallet.'

'Have we finished here now? I really need to make a few calls back home.'

266

'Yes, of course, we'll go to our hotel. It's not far from here.'

For a moment, Max thought they might be going to the Imperial Hotel. The staff would certainly recognise him and thoroughly jeopardise all his plans. Holding his breath, he anxiously waited until the car finally swung into the drive of the Hotel Izmir, completely hidden in the shade behind tall trees. Hiding his considerable relief, Max realised Afzal only stayed in the best hotels. As they entered though the front doors they were met by two porters who grabbed their cases from the boot. Max asked, 'Shall we meet here about noon tomorrow and make our way to the Port Grand main cargo reception?'

'Good idea. Do you want me to arrange your flight back to the UK for tomorrow night?'

'No, thanks. I might decide to fly to Cyprus for a couple of days to see some friends before returning home. The weather there is so much warmer than at home and the shipment will take much longer. As long as I'm back in the UK before it arrives, that's all that matters.'

'Sounds like a good idea.'

They parted and went to their rooms. Afzal took a shower and relaxed on his bed. Max, however, had work to do. His first job was to contact Mr Hussain and arrange for his wooden crate to be delivered to the Port Grand main cargo area the next morning at nine thirty. His instructions were clear; He was to remain there at his place until Max came through. Max would travel with him in his truck to the docks where he would be told where to unload the wooden crate. Then, he would receive the remaining two thousand rupees.

After speaking with Mr Hussain, he set about his second mission. Locate and reserve a table for two at eight that evening, somewhere near to Port Grand. He made some enquiries at the front desk, and the receptionist recommended one of the most popular restaurants in the area, overlooking China Creek, some five hundred yards from the hotel's main entrance. He booked it, then phoned Afzal in his room.

'Hello. I'm sorry to bother you, Afzal, but I was wondering if you would care to join me for dinner tonight? I've been recommended a restaurant called the Red Catch close to the port where we're going tomorrow. It's on China Creek, I believe.'

'Yes, I know it. It is a good restaurant if you like sea food, Mr Richardson.'

'Great. Shall we walk instead of getting a taxi down. I've booked the table for eight.'

'Good idea. I'll see you in the lobby at seven thirty.'

70

Max ate the best food in his life. Although his favourite dish was anything with chicken, he was completely converted to Asian fish cuisine. They drank several glasses of beer and left the restaurant at ten thirty. It was cool still night and Max suggested they walked along the waterfront back to their hotel. With no traffic or pedestrians present, their route took them past China Creek, a large expanse of water between the outer harbour wall and the West Wharf.

Afzal had relaxed after a couple of beers and spoke briefly about his wife and two teenage sons living in Islamabad. He was looking intensely forward to seeing them in two days' time. He described how he would play cricket with them in the local park. He then showed Max several snapshots of his family and he nodded appreciatively, saying 'You must be a very proud man, Afzal. I'm a little envious of you; I don't have any family of my own.'

'Thank you, Mr Richardson, I certainly have been blessed.'

As they walked further along the quayside, Max stopped and looked across the dark stretch of water to their left.

'What is it, Mr Richardson?'

Max pointed into the black abyss. 'Out there. Can you see? There's someone in the water over there.'

Afzal made the fatal mistake of stepping close to the edge. As he half turned around, he felt a sharp pain across his throat. Instinctively he touched it and noticed his hands were drenched in warm blood. He tried to turn further around to look to Max for help but he stumbled forward and then felt another pain in his chest. Through the shock, he saw the knife. But it was too late; all his strength gave way as he collapsed to the ground. His last conscious feeling was his wallet being ripped from his hand as he fell over the edge of the quay. He did not feel the cool water of China Creek as he fell deep into its fathoms and disappeared into oblivion.

Max coldly watched him sink to his doom. Now, with Afzal out of the way, there would be no further interference. His body would float to the surface in the next twenty-four hours but with no documentation on him he would probably remain unidentified, lying in the port mortuary, for several days. A victim of robbery. But by that time, Max would be thousands of miles way.

71

There was no mention of Afzal Jamali at the reception desk when Max checked out of the Hotel Izmir the following morning. He walked out of the main entrance carrying his suitcase and noticed the car hired by Afzal was still parked where he had left it yesterday afternoon. He continued along the driveway until he reached the road, where he stopped a taxi and then travelled to Mr Hussain's workshop.

When he arrived, the carpenter greeted him cheerily. 'Good morning, sir, your crate has been built and is on the back of my truck. Would you like to see it?'

'Yes, please, Mr Hussain.'

Hidden under a dirty green tarpaulin on the flat boards of a twin axle rigid lorry was the wooden crate, strapped down to the floor, an exact replica of the three he had seen in Grant Mills.

'Perfect. Now I want you to drive me to the docks where I'll tell you what to do next.'

'Very good, sir.'

*

Just after eleven thirty they arrived in the main reception cargo parking area. Max said, 'Mr Hussain, I need you to wait here until the arrival of another shipment I'm looking after. It should be here between noon and one o'clock. When it arrives, it will be on three separate lorries. I shall get into the lead vehicle and I want you to follow them into the pound in the port and park up close to them. You must remain inside your cab. On my instructions, you will then unload this crate after the others. But only when I tell you. That's important, do you understand?'

'Yes. I'll do exactly as you wish, Mr Richardson.'

Waiting patiently for the next consignment, Max walked along the quayside, wondering if Afzal's body had surfaced yet. He looked down towards China Creek, some half a mile away; there was no unusual activity, just the normal movement of small marine tugs and barges. He continually stared at his watch, forcing the dial to move faster. Eventually, he heard the sound of heavy lorries approaching and returned to the large parking area in time to see them turning into the main Port Grand reception lorry park.

He walked towards the lead vehicle as the driver jumped down from his cab. Standing in front of Max, he asked, 'Where's Mr Afzal Jamali? He should have been at the warehouse this morning.'

'Haven't you heard? He had to return home urgently. One of his sons has been involved in a cricket accident. He told me to deal with all matters from here.'

'That's not like him to go without speaking to me, he's very thorough about this shipment. Perhaps I should get in touch with my boss.'

'Listen, it's me that has the export permit. We can't afford this shipment to miss the next available tide. You must be aware of the importance of this cargo.'

'Will you take all responsibility then?'

'Yes of course. You did the right thing bringing the three crates here. I'll take care of it from now on. I've got the necessary documents. All I want you to do is to follow me into the restricted area and deposit the crates in the secure warehouse. Once you've done that, return to Grant Mills and clear up any mess. Leave no signs of any recent activity. Do you understand?'

'Yes, sir.'

'Just wait a minute for me here, I need to speak to someone before we go inside.'

Max returned to Mr Hussain. 'Follow the last one of those three trucks and park up nearby, but not too close.'

Mr Hussain nodded and started the engine. Max walked back to the lead lorry and climbed back inside and instructed the driver, 'Go through those gates, please.'

Five minutes later, all four lorries were parked outside the main reception terminal. Max entered and followed the signs saying 'Registration of exports'. There, he found a large office with several empty booths, each with a polished wooden counter. He rang the bell whereupon a young man immediately appeared, dressed in an old worn-out suit and grubby shirt. With a broad smile, he asked, 'Yes, sir. How can I help you?'

Max explained he had four crates of crops for export to the UK. Each crate was covered by a UK Government Special Permit, intended for scientific research purposes, a collaboration between both countries. He then produced two permits. The first named Crops Research UK Ltd and the other, one he had kept secret, Phoenix Laboratories UK Ltd. The clerk examined the papers and stamped them both before taking photocopies for his records.

'The next available ship is the *Helena*. It sails tomorrow and should arrive in the UK twenty-four days later, subject to fair weather conditions. Let's see. Yes. Beginning of December.'

The clerk handed back the papers, including a pass for the restricted area, and explained where to go with the cargo. Within fifteen minutes the four lorries had driven into the secure compound. The first three parked alongside each other. As Max had instructed, the fourth, driven by Mr Hussain, remained some distance away and waited for Max's signal before moving.

The first lorry drove onto a weighbridge and stopped. The gross weight of the vehicle and its load was recorded before an overhead hoist lifted the heavy crate clear and gently lowered it onto a large trailer. The weight of the lorry was taken and deducted from the gross amount, establishing that the crate weighed over six tons. This process was repeated three times.

Max waved the lorries away, and once they were out of sight, he signalled Mr Hussain to deliver his crate. Soon, all four crates were resting on the same large trailer, waiting to be inspected before being towed into the holding area. He walked over to Mr Hussain. 'Thank you. As promised here's two thousand rupees. That completes our business contract.'

'It's been my pleasure, Mr Richardson. Safe journey and may God be with you.'

He jumped back into his cab and drove away, very happy.

Building the wooden crate had been easy. He had skipped on some of the details with the inner crate, especially the quantity of maize in it, but Mr Richardson had shown little concern, even declining to examine his workmanship. So, he smiled broadly and waved to the Englishman as he drove out of the building. He had earnt the equivalent of six months labour in just two days.

Max turned to the crates and walked directly to the first one in line, where he pinned the permit marked Phoenix Laboratories UK Ltd. On the remaining three he pinned the permits for Crops Research UK Ltd. The switch had been made as easy as that.

Within moments, five officials entered the building, some were in uniform but carrying clip boards. He realised this was the most sensitive stage of the whole deception. If this failed, he would spend the rest of his life in a Pakistani jail.

He breathed deeply and stepped forward. One of the officials asked, 'Are you presenting a special permit for these crates?'

'Yes, I am.' Pointing to the first one he said, 'This crate will be covered by one permit and the other three by another.'

'Why two separate permits?'

'I realise it appears unusual, but the main research company is Crops Research UK Ltd and its sister company is called Phoenix Laboratories UK Ltd. The main bulk of the crops are for scientific research and are contained in the last three crates. However, the first crate only holds the machinery used to source the crops. The two laboratories are closely connected but not located geographically near to each other in the UK. When we originally applied for the permit, we asked for another to be granted to overcome this matter. It makes it more logistically viable when they all dock at Southampton.'

Two of the officials examined the permits carefully, whilst another jumped onto the trailer and looked at the three crates assigned to Crops Research UK Ltd.

'So what exactly are in these three?'

'They are entirely filled with maize, harvested from over fifty areas and districts in your country. They have been carefully identified and cross-referenced and should not be disturbed. However, if you would like to open them, obviously you are entitled to do so.'

But before they had time to ask any further questions, another uniformed official joined them and without consulting his colleagues shouted, 'Get these through to the compound. If they've got the necessary paperwork move them through now.' He then approached Max and smiled. 'You can leave these here. Your papers are in order.'

Max concluded the man had obviously been bribed. 'Thank you. Would you be able to place the first single crate marked Phoenix Laboratories separately in the hold? I don't want to get it mixed up with the other three when it's unloaded. Having them transported to the wrong laboratories would be a nightmare.'

'Of course. We'll leave the single one back until later today. By that time, there'll be hundreds of other cargo containers separating them.'

'Thanks.'

They shook hands and the officials moved their attention on to other loads waiting their inspection. With one stroke, Max had singled out the lead crate and substituted it for Mr Hussain's, lying fourth in the line. He now walked slowly towards the large open doors and closed his eyes. His body ached from the stress of the past ten minutes. He returned to the main office and caught a taxi to Karachi International airport where he purchased a flight to Cairo.

His last task in Pakistan was to send Gemma Baldwin a public telegram: 'CROPS ON WAY. HELENA ARRIVE SOUTHAMPTON EARLY DECEMBER. JOEL RICHARDSON.'

72

Max had always planned it this way. He would return to the UK about the same time as the shipment arrived at Southampton, but through another port of entry. Hull.

He knew the police would be waiting to seize the three crates marked for Crops Research UK Ltd, but banked on them not expecting a fourth one. The identity of Phoenix Laboratories UK Ltd had only been known to Alex Gilmore and no one else. Or had it? The person Alex had hired to complete the application forms was unknown to him; could that be the weak link? Perhaps. With hindsight, he should have dealt that issue too, along with Alex.

After a short holiday in Egypt, he would return to the UK, going back through Europe. He anticipated all hell on earth would be unleashed when Gemma Baldwin realised she'd been duped by him.

Following an eight-hour flight from Karachi, Max landed at Cairo International Airport and booked into the Hilton. He stretched out on his bed, reflecting on how he had arrived at this point in his life. Many people had lost their lives for him to be there. Max was utterly incapable of holding any normal relationship with any other human being, a man without conscience who slept soundly in his bed. And that night was no exception.

73

It was three weeks later, just after breakfast, when John received an unexpected visitor at his front door.

'Good morning, John. Sorry to call so early without phoning first but a couple of important things have turned up.'

'Come in, Yvonne. Coffee?'

'Please. It's started. The special permit was produced in the port of Karachi four days ago. My father contacted me earlier this morning. According to him, there are three large wooden crates on board a cargo freighter called the *Helena* that sailed out of Port Grand Karachi three days ago, bound for Southampton. Its estimated arrival date is first or second of December, in four weeks' time.'

'Are we certain these crates are on board?'

'Yes. There all designated to—'

'Crops Research UK Ltd' he replied.

'Yes.'

'Yvonne, it stinks. Whoever arranged this permit through Jason Moore knows it's compromised. With Alex Gilmour dead and George Morley now co-operating with us, I still think it's our old friend Max Campbell. Has the forensic pathologist made any further progress with the body in the cellar?'

'No, they're still running tests.'

'Well, let's put it this way. There is no evidence to support Max being dead. Is there?'

'None.'

'Have Hampshire Police been notified about the imminent arrival of the cargo?'

'Yes. Plans are already well in advance.'

'Does Gemma Baldwin know the drugs are on their way?'

'According to our informants, she received a telegram from Karachi through British Telecom to the effect that the crops were on their way. Naming the ship as Helena and their place and date of docking as early December in Southampton. Interestingly it was signed off by a Joel Richardson.'

'So, we all know the cargo is on its way. Have we any idea who this Joel Richardson is?'

'No, there's little to go on. There's certainly no trace on PNC or local records office.'

'What about sending the Karachi port authority a photograph of Campbell; see if they recognise him as this Richardson?'

'Already done that. We should get a reply in the next couple of days.'

'What's happening with Baldwin?'

'There appears to have been some activity at her house. Three suspected major drug dealers from Liverpool, Newcastle and Glasgow have been meeting there. The intelligence suggests she has been fronting a syndicate to finance the operation. It must be costing them millions.'

John looked at the photograph of Max Campbell. 'Baldwin and all her cronies will go ballistic when they realised they've been sold a pup. I've no doubt the syndicate will hold her responsible and demand their money back at least. As for Max – well, he's going to be the most wanted man in Western Europe.'

She nodded. 'Then I suppose we can only wait until the cargo arrives in Southampton.'

She stood to leave. 'Hell, I nearly forgot to tell you the second piece of news. Gilmour's solicitor has contacted us about a letter left in his possession. It was written by Gilmour and marked 'Only to be opened on my death or unexplained disappearance.' Apparently, he admits to his involvement with the Jason Moore and Gordon Black affairs and points the finger of blame directly at Max Campbell. He mentions the suspicious disappearances of Vicky Thompson and Julie Brecon and Max's partnership with Gemma Baldwin too. I've arranged for a copy to be sent to my office. As you know, it's not exactly the definition of a 'dying declaration' but it's useful evidence to place before Campbell when he's finally arrested.'

'Yes. It just confirms our suspicions. What does the Commander think?'

'His exact words were "I'll leave that with you." He's too interested in the final cargo.'

'Then it's all down to us, Yvonne.'

'Looks like it, John.'

74

Gemma Baldwin had never completely trusted Max, especially since her trusted bodyguard and confidante Bill had died in suspicious circumstances. She knew he was far more aware of his personal safety than anyone and furthermore, acutely aware of outside surveillance. Billy was an ex-soldier, trained in personal protection. In him she had complete trust. Unlike Max.

On Bill's advice, she had refused to pay Max regarding the special permit. He had warned her 'too good to be true', and wholly discouraged her from taking any further part in it. She recalled him saying to her, 'Why risk everything when we've now got a toe-hold in London? Gemma, leave it well alone.' But she had ignored his pleas and now those last words came to haunt her, just because the potential rewards were out of this world.

Since his death, she had decided to spread the risk of the enterprise by sharing it with her competitors, offering them an opportunity of a lifetime, a chance to import vast quantities of high-grade heroin into the UK under the very noses of the authorities. She had clearly expressed her concerns about the risks to them, but in the end they had become enthusiastic. All were gamblers by nature, willing to participate in a chance to make a fortune. For a modest investment, the rewards were staggeringly attractive. Over a two-day meeting in Manchester, the syndicate of four, including herself, had formulated some costings. If each party were to contribute nearly one million pounds, their share, according to the present street values, would be converted into forty million pounds each. They had unanimously agreed the distribution would be controlled over a period of two years. This prevented the market from becoming swamped, thus maximising their profits. It was all about supply and demand.

Since the arrival of the telegram from Pakistan from Joel Richardson, activities between the three main parties and Gemma reached fever pitch. Representatives from all parties were busy dashing across the UK, arranging storage facilities and transport. Gemma read the telegram many times. Could it be genuine? Did Max really pull this off? Had she underestimated him?

She had repeatedly attempted to contact Afzal Jamali in Istanbul, but he appeared to have vanished. Her last contact from him had been ten days previously when he confirmed Max had arrived with the necessary permit and was going to oversee the crates being processed at Port Grand Karachi. Everything was going as expected. She had specifically asked Afzal Jamali if he was happy with 'Mr Richardson'. He had reported he was in fact very impressed with Max's attention to detail. But where was Afzal Jamali now? He had failed to contact her about the goods departing Karachi and his contract depended on that. Otherwise he would not receive his final instalment. Once again, she felt uneasy; her instincts gave her cause for concern. She decided to act.

Gemma discussed her misgivings with the other syndicate leaders, warning them to be cautious. Although generally dismissive of her concerns, they agreed on a back-up plan to establish whether their cargo had been compromised. In order to trigger this, she telephoned one of her associates who had good links in the Manchester Asian community; she wanted someone with an investigative background who could fly out immediately to Karachi and make some discreet enquiries.

Within two hours, a man called Mohamed Iqbal had been found.

A meeting was hastily set. Her instructions were clear and precise. Fly out immediately to Islamabad and seek out Afzal Jamali at his last known home address. Otherwise, trace his last movements. If he was unable to find him there, take another flight to Karachi and confirm if he was with Joel Richardson at Port Grand when the crops were inspected and sealed, prior to their export to the UK. Mr Iqbal was promised six thousand pounds plus expenses for his services. Half now, the remainder on his return. His final instructions were also explicit: report daily on his progress without fail.

75

Shortly after midnight, the *Helena* docked at Southampton. It was a wet and foggy night as the she steadily slowed and anchored at Dock 5. Her voyage had been uneventful, with fair weather allowing her to arrive thirty-six hours ahead of schedule. She would remain there until the early shift arrived at five, before her cargo was unloaded from the various holds. A time schedule of twelve hours had been allocated. The port authorities were aware of the police interest and their impending operation within its territory. Much to the authorities' consternation, the police were granted full jurisdiction and access to the restricted areas, including the bonded warehouses.

The operation was codenamed Harvest. Commander Higgins had been appointed in overall command with the support of the Home Office, Hampshire Police, the National Drugs Enforcement Authority, Customs and Excise and a large contingent of Metropolitan Police firearms officers. The decision was made to fix a tracking device to all three wooden crates, drilled into the wooden casings, concealed beneath a strong self-adhesive sticker marked 'Helena Freight'. Each crate would be individually tracked by a dedicated team. It was generally agreed by the Command Team that the three crates would be separated before arriving at their final destinations. The seizure of the crates would be gauged on all the information available at the time: too soon would expose their intentions, whilst too late would be disastrous. Ideally, all would be caught in the act of opening the crates, within a short timeframe. It was imperative, once the gangs and their crates were held, they were effectively quarantined until their respective crime scenes were secured. Containment and isolation were paramount.

Fortunately, Commander Higgins and his team had been aware of the progress of the *Helena*, allowing them ample opportunity to prepare for their reception. Facilities had been arranged for the temporary detention and storage of both prisoners and seized evidence at various locations throughout England and Scotland. These would be activated according to where the arrests and seizures took place. Communications between the teams tracking their respective individual crates would be central to the success of the operation.

On the eve of the docking, shortly after eight o'clock that evening, Yvonne convened a meeting with John and Phil. 'The *Helena* will dock at Southampton within the next few hours and the whole of the port is buzzing with activity. I'm not too happy about how this is going to work out. Commander Higgins and his team are convinced they have all the drugs accounted for. But it's my belief we have missed something out. It could all go pear-shaped. Max Campbell is very conspicuous by his absence.'

John nodded. 'I agree. I've been thinking about a number of things whilst this ship has been sailing. One of them is that I want to talk to this Miles Willis again. He might have something to add to his previous statement. Where is he now?'

'Still in Brighton, I believe.'

'Right. I'm going down there tonight to speak to him.'

'OK. Phil and I will travel directly to Southampton. Perhaps, John, you can come through and meet us at the Major Incident Room, now set up at the central police station?'

'Good, let me see what I can find out in Brighton.'

Phil asked, 'What's my role, Yvonne?'

'You and I are going to be the safety net. I think all the teams are going to disappear down a rabbit hole. I don't want to do the same. If I'm wrong, then we'll take a back seat in all this.'

'I do hope you're right, my girl. Don't want those sycophantic bastards taking all the glory.'

76

As Operation Harvest was implemented, Gemma Baldwin received a message from another associate: 'Helena docking in Southampton tonight'. She immediately called for the syndicate to meet and discuss their position. They convened at a hotel near Manchester Airport and by midday all the syndicate partners were in a large conference room, under strict security behind locked doors. After the room had been double-checked for listening devices and with a small team of guards protecting them, she sat down and faced the three men.

'Gentlemen, the consignment from Pakistan will be arriving at Southampton within the next few hours. As you know, I'm not happy with everything at the moment. I've caused precautionary enquiries to be made at Karachi port to check the packaging of our cargo was exactly to our wishes. Unfortunately, my representative who I sent out there to supervise this has simply disappeared.'

'What the hell to you mean?' asked one of the partners.

'He's failed to return to the UK. So I've sent my own investigator out there to check all this out. Until we've heard from him, I think we should be cautious about our next move until we receive confirmation of what's happened.'

Another asked, 'How long is that going to take?'

'I sent someone out there nearly a week ago. Although he reported back to me yesterday, he's not uncovered anything suspicious yet.'

The third man asked, 'Why should there be any problems, Gemma? Is there anything you haven't told us about?'

Without any sign of hesitation in her tone she replied, 'Of course not.' But she knew if she shared with them her suspicions about Max, they would immediately pull out and force her to pay them damages for their share of the enterprise. This would amount to over two million pounds. A sum she could ill afford.

He continued, 'But Gemma, if we delay collecting the cargo from Southampton, it's going to look odd, and soon it will attract attention. I say we go and collect it. This special permit seems to have worked a treat. Aren't you being too cautious?'

'You might be right. But I still think we should wait until I hear from my man in Pakistan. We should have a more accurate picture in a couple of days.'

The first partner was less courteous. 'Bloody hell, Mrs Baldwin. Why are you stalling now? Are you up to something, lady?'

She quickly regained her composure and curtly replied, 'No, I'm not up to anything. And frankly, I take that as an insult. I think we should wait a little longer but if you are determined to collect the cargo immediately after it lands, I won't stand in your way.'

His reply was equally hostile. 'No, you won't. I've put a million pounds into this deal and I'm going to collect the goods when they arrive. We'll stick to the original plan; get them picked up in the container and take it to Leicester. There, we'll unload the three crates onto separate trucks and take them to our own collection points. That's it, short and simple.'

The other two men nodded in agreement. Gemma raised her hands. 'OK. If that's the decision of you all, we'll go for it. The transport company will be notified of the delivery details and destination. We'll split the crates as you say, but we must agree not to flood the markets and keep to the quotas we decided on, otherwise the price will drop and our investments will plummet. Are we all as one with that?'

'Yes,' they all agreed.

'Unless there are any unforeseen delays or if I hear from my man in Pakistan of any problems, I shall arrange for them to be collected as soon as they arrive. Once I know they've left the docks, you will be contacted so you can make your own arrangements to receive them.'

77

John drove directly to Brighton, arriving at Miles Willis's flat shortly before midnight. After several minutes of failed attempts to contact him by pressing the intercom at the entrance, he managed instead to wake up the old lady who lived in the ground floor flat. When she appeared at the front door, he said, 'Madam, please forgive my intrusion, but I'm a police officer and must speak to Mr Willis urgently.'

'He's not here. Miles has gone away for a few days. He told me it was somewhere in Cornwall. Gone fishing I think.'

'Have you no idea where exactly he's gone to?'

'No. Sorry.'

John showed her his warrant card and asked her to let him inside. 'But he's not here, Officer.'

'Don't worry, Mr Willis is not in any trouble, but he may have vital information concerning a police investigation. Normally, Madam, I would apply for a search warrant from the local magistrate, but frankly, I don't have the time. Will you please allow me to come in and have a look inside his place? Naturally, I would want you to be present at all times. I'm only looking for some papers.'

She shrugged. 'Come in then. I'll get his keys, but don't make a mess.'

He followed her into the stinking flat. He was not prepared for it. Clearly, she was the oblivious to the strong smell of stale smoke, rotting food and foul body odour. The dim lights spared him the true extent of the filthy carpets and furniture. But his attention was immediately drawn to an old writing bureau in the far corner where a multitude of full ashtrays nearly covered the papers strewn across it. John quickly picked through the note pads and loose pages, hoping for anything that Miles Willis may have scribbled down in his attempt to complete the application forms some weeks previously. Nothing obvious. He checked the calendar hanging at an awkward angle on the wall above the desk. Still no indication of his past or present movements.

He made a thorough check of all the rooms but found nothing of significance. He turned to the old lady. 'Are you sure you don't know where Mr Willis has gone in Cornwall?'

She simply shook her head and asked, 'Have you finished here now? It's late and I want to go back to bed.'

'Yes, of course. Thank you for letting me in. When he returns home, will you please ask him to contact me on this number.' He handed her his card.

Now resigned as a fruitless visit, he scanned the main room once more before walking to the door, but as he was about to close it behind him, he caught sight of a dirty overcoat hanging on a hook. He leant forward and searched the pockets. Immediately, he found a crumpled photocopy of a single page stuffed in one of them. He unfolded the sheet. It was page three of a larger document, and a circle hastily drawn around some words: Article 7 Shipment Return, paragraph 3, subsection b.

John's mind started to race. Did it refer to the application? What did it mean? Was it important? He folded the sheet and placed it in his jacket pocket, then faced the woman again. 'I'll take this piece of paper with me. Meanwhile, I'll bid you good night and thank you very much for your assistance.'

He descended the stairs and walked to his car. It was now past one o'clock and mercifully the traffic was quiet, allowing him to make good progress over the seventy miles along the south coast.

*

An hour and a half later he walked into the police station and soon found his colleagues in side room on the second floor, along the corridor from the Major Incident Room. The whole station was bustling with activity, with radio messages and telephones constantly ringing.

John handed the page to Yvonne. 'I found this in Willis's flat; can you get it checked out as soon as possible?'

'Under the circumstances, I'm going to call my father now. He'll be able to pull a few strings, even at this time in the morning.' She went out of the room, leaving them to consider their next move.

Phil sighed. 'Hell, John, we're getting too old for all this.'

'You're right, this is definitely our last job. All I want to do is capture Max Campbell when he finally comes back on our radar.'

'Amen to that. I wonder where the bastard is now.'

78

As Operation Harvest was triggered in Southampton, Max was stirring from his sleep in a small hotel in the Belgian port of Zeebrugge, close to the car ferry terminal for Hull. He had travelled across Europe, mainly by rail, still using the name Joel Richardson. His journey to Belgium from Egypt had taken him through Cyprus, Greece, Italy and France, all timed to return to the UK just after the *Helena* had docked. Whilst in Belgium, he had travelled to Brussels where he managed to transfer fifty thousand pounds from his offshore bank into a 'sleeper' Lloyds Bank account, again using the name J. Richardson. Since leaving the UK, he had altered his appearance. He now sported a closely cropped beard and short hair. He had purchased dark-rimmed spectacles with plain glass lenses in Italy. His general demeanour was that of a casual but smartly dressed professional businessman returning from holiday.

After a small breakfast, he walked to the nearby main municipal library, where he telephoned the port cargo reception at Southampton. He established the ship would be docking that evening and her cargo unloaded into the warehouses tomorrow morning. He knew the police would be waiting to pounce on those who collected the container with the three crates bound for Crops Research UK Ltd, so he deliberately delayed his arrival by twenty-four hours; sufficient time, he believed, to allow the police euphoria to subside. They would discover over six tons of heroin and hopefully capture Gemma Baldwin and her associates. It would be international news and the politicians would be congratulating the authorities on a successful operation. The third crate, containing only maize crops, would be considered a clever ploy to deflect any impromptu searches. And by the time he arrived to collect his crate, the police operation would hopefully be stood down.

He was feeling particularly smug, knowing he would collect enough heroin with a street value worth in excess of twenty million for absolutely nothing. All the major players in the UK would be charged with the mass importation of a Class A drug, carrying a maximum penalty of life imprisonment.

Later that afternoon, he boarded the ferry as a foot passenger and rented a small cabin where he remained hidden throughout the twelve-hour voyage. At six o'clock the next morning he disembarked and walked through a newly constructed building signposted 'Welcome to Hull – Passport Control'. Without any delay, he was ushered straight through the barriers by the customs officers. Within moments, he was standing outside breathing in the fresh damp air of the Humber estuary.

Always surveillance conscious, he carefully scrutinised his surroundings, trying to locate obvious observation points or anyone looking suspicious. He half expected to feel a firm grip on his shoulder. But there was no one there. No buildings or nearby vehicles to hide prying eyes. Just an empty car park with a solitary taxi parked close to the entrance.

He slipped into the back seat, holding his small suitcase. 'Railway station, please.'

By seven o'clock he had purchased a first-class rail ticket to London King's Cross. The train was surprisingly empty of passengers as it travelled south, allowing him to concentrate on his future plans. He had a great deal to consider. Arrangements would need be made to collect the crate marked for Phoenix Laboratories UK Ltd, after the others had been collected and seized. But only after he was satisfied his crate was no longer of police interest.

Meanwhile he required the services of a reputable transport carrier. He also needed to find a secure venue to receive and hold it. Once that had been achieved, he would build up his own temporary distribution network to sell the drugs. After that, he would simply vanish and enjoy the fruits of his deception. His recent visit to Egypt had convinced him Cairo was the perfect destination. However, for the time being he must remain out of view at all costs.

As the train pulled into London, he knew exactly how his final plans would be implemented.

79

The transport manager's instructions were clear, although a little bizarre. Collect three crates labelled 'Crops Research UK Ltd' from Southampton Docks at nine o'clock in the morning and deliver them to their company depot, close to the M1 motorway in Leicestershire. The crates were to be split up into three smaller lorries and driven to Leicester Forest East services, where further instructions about their final destinations would be given to the drivers. Each driver would be offered an attractive bonus for their services.

The weather was miserable and wet as the articulated lorry turned into the main entrance to Southampton Docks. The driver had regularly collected freight from there before. After passing the main reception gate and showing a copy of the special import permit, he was directed to the large secured building signed 'Restricted Area'. He drove through the open gateway to platform F, where the crates were ready for collection.

Before the first crate had been placed onto the trailer platform, Operation Harvest was ramped up to full alert. The three surveillance teams, now on standby, each consisted of six motorcyclists, all supported by dozens of operatives in a multitude of cars and vans, old and new, large and small. Everyone was supplied with the latest up to date personal radios, all connected directly to the Major Incident Room. There, Commander Higgins and his Command Team were visibly excited, confirming with all the team leaders their status and location. He had ignored Yvonne for the past several hours, unaware of her efforts to trace the true meaning of the paper found in Brighton.

Several rooms away, Yvonne found John and Phil and exclaimed 'Listen, you two, I've spoken to my father and he's checked this 'Article 7 Shipment Return, paragraph 3' and discovered something we've all missed. Apparently, where the research destinations within the UK vary, and provided the nature of the cargo is the same, it can be separated from the point of export. Secondly, where there is a subsidiary or sister company to the permit holder, it can be imported under that name, not the primary named business. Therefore, a similar cargo may be on the docks right now, containing tons of drugs we are completely unaware of. I've run a check through Companies House and found another business connected to Crops Research UK Ltd. It's called Phoenix Laboratories UK Ltd. Very apt, considering what happened to Max Campbell's club, don't you think?'

'Bloody hell! Nice work my girl,' said Phil.

John shook his head in disbelief. 'Christ Yvonne, have we checked the consignment listings of the cargo on the *Helena*?'

'Yes. Interestingly, I've discovered on the schedule it's marked "3 plus an additional crate" but without any further reference.'

'So, it could have come ashore with the other three,' Phil said.

'Exactly. And there are over fifteen thousand containers and crates, some of which have already been collected. The rest are now in the main building, which apparently holds over half a million items.'

'Bugger,' said John. 'Needle in a haystack comes to mind. Listen, we need to go down there and check everyone who is turning up to collect anything for Phoenix Laboratories. Have you mentioned this to Commander Higgins?'

'Tried, but he's always been dismissive of our suspicions. He just told me to keep an eye out. That's all.'

John retorted cynically, 'That's called strategic bollocks. Similar to when they say "I hear what you say". It really means they're not taking a blind bit of notice of you. There's an old Yorkshire expression that comes to mind: "Sod 'em. If you want a job doing..." Let's just get on with it ourselves.'

Yvonne smiled. 'OK, John. You're in charge. What are we going to do?'

80

Through the fading daylight it rained continuously during the five-hour journey from Southampton to Leicester. All the police motorcyclists were drenched to the skin whilst their colleagues benefitted from the warmth and protection of their vehicles. The articulated lorry was seen entering the depot lorry park, where three other smaller box rigid-axle goods vehicles were waiting close to the entrance. The forward surveillance team saw a large forklift approach the side of the trailer. The tarpaulin curtain had been drawn back, revealing the three wooden crates. Quickly and without fuss they were unloaded and placed individually in the smaller vehicles and within minutes, set off towards the M1 in convoy.

Commander Higgins gave the order to follow them, but as soon as they separated the secondary surveillance teams would concentrate on their respective targets. Tests were continually made to check the strength of the radio signals transmitted by the trackers affixed to the crates. All were strong.

Within minutes, the vehicles drove into the lorry park at Leicester Forest East services. The drivers parked them up in a line and entered the services building. A surveillance officer saw them approach a man already sitting in the Burger King restaurant. As they approached, he stood up and spoke briefly, before handing each of them a large envelope. The drivers immediately returned to their vehicles and once again, re-joined the motorway in convoy heading north. The Major Incident Room gave instructions for the man in Burger King not to be apprehended, but to monitor his movements.

The lead surveillance team followed the three small lorries for over ninety miles until they reached the M62 trans-Pennine motorway that stretched laterally across the north of England, from Hull in the east to Manchester and Liverpool in the west. As the motorways crossed, the lead vehicle turned east, towards the A1. The second and third turned west towards Manchester. All three surveillance teams now came into play, each following their own targets. Each team had further dedicated support units ready to step in if they believed they had been compromised. Stealth and reacting quickly were the main objectives of the unfolding operation.

Commander Higgins had been plotting the routes, constantly updating the Chief Constables in the areas they were travelling through. Within four hours, the first vehicle was stationary outside a large empty factory in Edinburgh, the second had come to rest in a disused warehouse on the outskirts of Manchester and the third was pulling into a large industrial estate in Speke, near Liverpool. The order to 'contain and observe' was given. This was confirmed by all tactical personnel.

Each location was treated as a major crime scene in its own right and once the decision to engage with the criminals was made, the scene had to be clinically closed down and isolated from any outside interference. Those arrested were to be taken to secret prisoner reception centres, whilst the suspected drugs were all contained by Scenes of Crimes Officers and safely transported to the nearest secure laboratory for forensic analysis.

The first location to come into play was Speke. The target lorry had been parked for only an hour when it was approached by five vehicles – four vans and a Jaguar saloon car. The lorry driver was instructed to remain in the cab whilst the rear doors were opened. The vans all lined up behind with their doors opened wide too. The wooden crate remained in the lorry.

The officers saw two men board the lorry and prise open the top of the crate, exposing a smaller one inside. Several other men then rushed forward and began to quickly remove from the inner crate, several large plastic bags all containing hundreds of small boxes, placing them carefully into the waiting vans.

Silently, the outer cordon of firearms officers completely encircled the scene. Previously, at their briefing, they had been informed that many of these criminals would probably be armed and dangerous. The clearest of all their instructions was simply 'no one must escape'. All officers had enthusiastically volunteered for the operation.

Once the operation code word had been activated, the team of one hundred officers pounced. It was over in seconds. The sheer weight of numbers was overwhelming. Although one produced a knife, he was immediately disarmed and thrown to the concrete ground. Another attempted to produce a pistol but quickly surrendered when a pistol barrel was firmly placed against his head.

Seventeen men were arrested without any injuries to either side. A forensic science team opened one of the sacks stacked inside one of the vans. His initial examination confirmed the consignment was most likely to be in excess of three tons of high-grade heroin. In addition, an assortment of illegal firearms was also recovered. The whole operation had been videotaped. The prisoners were hastily escorted away, including the unsuspecting lorry driver. The drugs were eventually transported to the nearest Home Office Science Laboratory, some nine miles away in Runcorn.

The second location was Edinburgh, where events took on a similar pattern. Twenty men were arrested and the same quantity of high-grade heroin was seized. Hundreds of miles away, in the Southampton Incident Room, Commander Higgins was skipping with joy. Two out of three so far.

However, the team in Manchester was still waiting for some movement.

81

Meanwhile, whilst staking out the main entrance to Southampton Docks, John, Yvonne and Phil were listening to the unfolding events on the police radio. They had been given access to an empty office overlooking the reception gates where they could observe all vehicles entering through the gates. The security guards had been given a photograph of Max Campbell and the details of Phoenix Laboratories. If they saw him or anyone remotely resembling him producing documentation for this company, they were to allow him to enter and report it immediately to them.

But the latest communication from the Manchester operation described it as 'no activity'. John considered the implications. 'Yvonne, if no one turns up to collect the crate in Manchester, I think Gemma Baldwin has been tipped off. We know Max Campbell was communicating with her by offering his compromised information on Jason Moore in order to lever the special permit. So what has happened? Max seems to have disappeared off the face of the world, but I'm convinced he's not far away. If she's been tipped off, then why and by who?'

She replied, 'I've been thinking the same.'

'I think we should go and see Commander Higgins and ask him how long he intends to sit on the Manchester site?'

She stood to leave the room. 'You're bloody right, John. I'm really annoyed with him, if you want to know the truth. He hasn't listened to our suspicions whatsoever. He blindly believes the operation to be a complete success. Well, I'm going to piss on his parade. Phil, will you stay here? John please come with me.'

As she stepped outside, Phil whispered. 'I bloody love that woman. Got more balls than anyone else in the Service. Watch out, Commander Higgins.'

Yvonne was a woman on a mission and desperately wanted to make her point but as she and John walked into the Incident Room, taking a deep breath, she heard a radio message loudly proclaim, 'The Manchester crate is crammed full of crops. The forensic scientist believes it to be maize. We can confirm there are no illegal substances contained within. Repeat, no illegal substances here.'

Commander Higgins turned towards his team. 'What does that mean? Why should they go to all that trouble? Is it just a decoy to distract us from the other two crates?'

Before anyone could answer, Yvonne stepped forward. 'Sir, I have a theory about all this. I think there is another crate full of heroin and it's been swapped for that one in Manchester. Will you allow me to pursue my own investigations into this?'

Looking perplexed, he replied, 'What resources do you require?'

'None. I've got my own team. Give me twenty-four hours and a free hand to sort this out, sir. If it doesn't work, you've still been successful in smashing two of the UK's largest drug gangs. As I see it now, we don't have a great deal of evidence to charge Gemma Baldwin, even if the other gang leaders accuse her of any involvement now they're in custody. But Mr Higgins, don't let's forget Max Campbell. I suspect him of murdering two prostitutes, perhaps a journalist and the unidentified body in the Caribbean Club. Not to mention a multitude of blackmail offences. If my hunch is right, Mrs Baldwin may have some information that will help us convict him.'

'You want to trade with the Devil?'

'If I can convict Campbell, yes, sir, I bloody do.'

'Very well, Yvonne. Twenty-four hours.'

82

Gemma Baldwin sat in the rear seat of her Mercedes saloon outside her house, waiting to hear from her team several miles away in Manchester. Unlike the other syndicates' operatives, they were not convicted criminals; all were ex-military and hand-picked by Bill. She remained uneasy about the rendezvous at Leicester Forest East services on the M1. Too public. However, the location where her crate was to be delivered was carefully chosen as it would be easy to detect any snooping police surveillance teams. As she waited patiently for the signal from her team, she saw her butler run out of the front door, waving his arms. She opened the car door. 'What's the matter, Henry?'

'Mrs Baldwin. There's an urgent telephone call for you from Pakistan.'

Returning to the house, she picked up the receiver. 'Gemma Baldwin.'

'Mrs Baldwin. It's Mohamed Iqbal here. I'm in Karachi. I've found your representative Afzal Jamali, but unfortunately he's been murdered. He was found over three weeks ago in the port dock. According to the police he was stabbed to death. They're treating it as robbery because there was no identification on him and his wallet missing. I'm sorry, Mrs Baldwin, I couldn't find him alive. Do you want me come home now?'

'Yes.'

'I'm sorry I haven't been of much use to you, Mrs Baldwin.'

'Oh yes, you have. You just don't know how much.'

She replaced the receiver and walked into the lounge where she poured a large brandy. The telephone rang again. She went back into the hallway to answer it. 'Yes' she said curtly.

A man's voice quietly said, 'There's a great deal of uniformed activity at the collection point. We're aborting the operation.' Gemma immediately recognised the voice. It was one of her men.

'Affirmative,' she said briefly.

She drank the brandy in one gulp and threw the fine lead crystal glass at the wall, smashing it into hundreds of fragments. 'Max Campbell, you bastard. You're a dead man.' All her doubts were confirmed. Also, the realisation she had lost over a million pounds.

She knew the other syndicate members would have been arrested and the drugs seized, even after she had recommended caution. She faced alienation from the criminal underworld throughout the UK, and undoubtedly a contract would now be placed on her life. For the first time in her life she felt the shudder of vulnerability spread through her body.

She poured another brandy and lit a slim cheroot, peering through the French windows, considering her next move. Her criminal empire was extensive throughout the North West, apart from Merseyside, stretching from Birmingham across the Midlands into the Greater Manchester area. Although she had inherited the 'business' from her father, times had changed. Money from prostitution, extortion and blackmail was still rolling into the coffers, but the real opportunities to make vast fortunes were from supplying controlled substances, especially cocaine and heroin. But this bust had changed everything. The interference by the police would have a catastrophic disruption on the chain of supply, from the growers, manufacturers, the collectors and transporters through to the quality controllers.

Although financially this was a serious setback, her personal standing in the criminal underworld gave her more concern. It was now permanently flawed. Trust had now been broken, with little opportunity of restoring her quickly back to the status quo. Her only chance to regain her authority was to find Max and publically hang him out to dry. This would go some way to restoring her reputation.

Gemma leant forward to make a telephone call, but it rang before she touched the dial. An unknown woman's voice asked, 'Is that Gemma Baldwin?'

'Yes. Who is this?'

'My name is Detective Chief Inspector Hall and I would like to come and see you as soon as possible.'

'Are you coming to arrest me, Chief Inspector?'

'No. If I was, I wouldn't be making this call. I would be speaking to you in your house with your front door off its hinges.'

'What's it about?'

'Good question. I can't talk about it on the phone. I need to talk to you in private.'

'Can I trust you?'

'Mrs Baldwin, you'll never trust me, nor I you. Nevertheless, I do have something important to tell you which I'm sure you'll be interested in.'

'But I'll be talking to you, the enemy.'

'That's interesting too. My boss asked me if I was going to trade with the Devil. I told him I was going to try. Anyway, let's not trade any more insults. Will you let me come and see you tonight?'

Gemma hesitated. Could she trust this unconventional police officer? She was right about one thing: if she strongly suspected her of committing a criminal offence, she would have come through the front door without knocking and placed her in handcuffs. Her curiosity was too strong. 'Very well, Chief Inspector, you can come here but I shall have my solicitor present.'

'No problem. In that case I shall be accompanied by my colleague, Inspector John Evans.'

'OK. When shall I expect you?'

'I'll be travelling from the south coast, so let's say in about four hours depending on the traffic.

Gemma looked at the clock above the fireplace. 'Ten o'clock tonight then.'

'Yes.'

She replaced the receiver. Her mind was spinning with all the events of the past thirty minutes. What did the police want, especially this senior officer?

83

As John drove towards the large wrought-iron gates in the unmarked police car, Yvonne said, 'Who said crime doesn't pay?'

'It's obscene. Are you sure you know what you're doing?'

'Yes, trust me, John, on this one.'

The remote-controlled camera on one of the main gateposts was clearly pointing towards them. The intercom below sounded. 'Who are you?'

John opened the driver's window and shouted, 'Detective Chief Inspector Hall to see Mrs Baldwin.' Without any reply, the gates swung open, revealing the house ahead at the end of the sweeping gravelled drive. He drove slowly towards the front porch and saw in his mirror the gates closing behind them.

'Do you have your white flag?' he asked.

'Something like that. Just remember, please let me call the shots here and please don't say a word.'

'I will, Yvonne. Just be careful.'

As they walked towards the oak front door, it opened and a smartly dressed man appeared. 'Please come this way. Mrs Baldwin will see you in the living room.'

They followed him through the marble-floored hallway into a large room with leather sofas facing an enormous open fire. The aroma of furniture polish and burning wood created a warm and relaxed atmosphere. The lavish décor and antique furniture, together with a host of original paintings, only added to the sumptuous surroundings, emanating both taste and wealth. As they entered, two people stood: a woman in her middle thirties, elegantly dressed, and a man in his fifties, wearing a dark suit, white shirt and plain tie. He looked official.

'You must be Chief Inspector Hall,' she said.

'Yes. And this is my colleague, Inspector Evans. I assume you're Gemma Baldwin?'

'Yes, and this Giles Simpson, my solicitor. I'm not taking any chances.'

All four nodded. Gemma continued, 'Now, what's this all about Chief Inspector?'

Without reply, Yvonne walked towards the French windows. Several moments lapsed before she turned around to face her. 'You have a wonderful garden, Mrs Baldwin. Would you be good enough to show me?'

Gemma looked puzzled. 'Why? It's dark and cold out there.'

'Because what I've got to say to you needs to be in private without any witnesses. Not with your solicitor or my colleague. Just you and me.'

Torn between caution and curiosity, she replied 'Very well, let me get my coat.'

Moments later she returned with a full-length coat. Yvonne looked at it, suspecting it would have cost six months of her salary to buy it. By contrast, she wore a plain dark blue raincoat, off the peg in Marks and Spencer. Gemma opened the door and gestured Yvonne to go first. They walked across the lawn towards a water fountain near a leafless oak tree. Fortunately, the garden lights were illuminated. Beneath the tree stood a wooden bench.

Yvonne suggested, 'Shall we sit here and talk?'

Gemma glanced down. The seat was dirty, with some leaves on it. Yvonne saw her reluctance and removed her wide neck scarf and spread it over the wooden slats.

'There you are, Mrs Baldwin. You won't dirty your coat now.'

She smiled. 'Thank you, Chief Inspector.'

Yvonne smiled back. 'Before I begin, I want you to know that I'm not wired and I have no wish to arrest you or even interview you under caution. I know you are involved in serious crime and have made a great deal of money out of the misery inflicted on others. In short, you represent everything I detest the most in the world. And one day I may meet you again where I will prove all this and you'll go to prison for a long time. However, this evening, I want to call a truce. Please listen carefully. Of course, I require something from you, but before I ask, I want to share this. You and I have two things in common. We both operate in a man's world and must constantly prove ourselves more than them to succeed. The second is our desire to place Max Campbell behind bars for the rest of his life.'

'Why should I be interested in this… Max who?'

'Why indeed. I'll tell you. The crate I believe you were expecting to collect has been seized and examined. It contained maize crops only. No drugs or other substances. Although I could still arrest you on suspicion of conspiring with others to import vast quantities of heroin, I have a more pressing matter to deal with. Max Campbell.'

'How can you connect me to these drugs?'

'Come on, Mrs Baldwin. Don't you think we're aware of the special permit that was obtained by blackmailing the MP Jason Moore? Max was always aware we were onto him. Furthermore, he registered a sister company alongside the one he gave to you. He only gave you the copy of Crops Research UK Ltd. He kept the other to himself. It is called Phoenix Laboratories UK Ltd. That's why I believe he switched one of the crates in Pakistan, which happened by chance to be the one you were expecting to receive. Of course, I can't prove it but just consider this: he will intercept the missing crate when it lands in the UK. In fact, he may even be planning to collect it from the docks right now. Losing all your money is one thing but the thought of Max making a pile of money off your back must be intolerable. I know you're going deny all this, so I won't insult your intelligence by asking, but I have a number of unsolved murders in London which I think he's responsible for. So I need to find him fast.'

Gemma stood up and lit another cheroot, drew heavily on it and stared coldly back at Yvonne. 'How do I know this is all true?'

'I've told you, we know about the permit and the MP. We also know you were using Max's club to store all your narcotics. Incidentally, do you know we found an unrecognisable body of a man in the cellar. It would appear he had been bludgeoned to death before the place was set on fire? We don't know who he is, but the latest post-mortem analysis shows it to be a male in his forties. Any ideas who that might have been?'

Gemma's expression remained unchanged, but her mind went immediately to her close friend Bill who she had sent down to see Max but had never returned. He was forty-three. Max's partner Sammy Clarke was at least twenty years younger. Now she knew what had happened to him.

Yvonne continued, 'Mrs Baldwin, did you send Max to Pakistan? Because if you did, it's my theory he always wanted you to do that. Once out there, he would have been able to manage the swop.'

That last question broke Gemma's calm manner. She swung around towards Yvonne, her eyes full hatred and malice.

'Yes Mrs Baldwin. It's my belief your crate is now with him or it's going to be very soon.'

'The bastard.'

Yvonne stood to face her. 'Tell me everything that you know so I can trace this man. I'll never be able to use this information against you because it's my word against yours. And just for the record, or I should say off the record, I'm stepping so far out of my legal responsibilities, it's actually unlawful. So, as we are both women in a man's world, let's screw this bastard properly. Mrs Baldwin, I must have Max Campbell and you can help me.'

'Look for Joel Richardson. He left the UK about five weeks ago. He was in Karachi a week later. The police are investigating the murder of a man called Afzal Jamali. That's all I can tell you.'

'We know about Joel Richardson. Are you telling me he is Campbell?'

'Yes. But that's all I'm prepared to say Chief Inspector.'

'OK. Just one more question. If you trace him before I do, will you let me know?'

'Chief Inspector, we're powerful women on opposing sides of the fence, and if I hadn't been born into a criminal family, maybe we could have been good friends. Who knows? But I like your honesty and direct manner. So I'll answer your last question without any hesitation. No, I won't let you know if I find him. In fact, you won't even find any remains of this man. My understanding is, the rest of the world believes he's already dead, possibly the unidentified body in the cellar. So, as you know better than me, you can't kill a dead man. Can you?'

Yvonne considered the double jeopardy rule but chose to ignore it. Instead, she looked directly at Gemma, 'No, you can't. But I don't want to be spending a great deal of public money nor my time hunting for someone who's already dead.'

'I'm sorry. I can't help you with that matter. But if I do find out any further information, I promise to let you know. Do you have a confidential line I could contact you on?'

Yvonne took a business card from her coat pocket. 'That number on the bottom is my private line. Please don't give it to anyone else.'

Gemma studied the card closely then looked up. Smiling she said, 'Yvonne, today you have been trading with the Devil.'

'You're right, Gemma. And you've been cosying up with the enemy.'

For a second they stared intently into each other's eyes, unable to blink. Yvonne felt a bolt hit her chest and for that moment, frozen in time, a passion so deep and sexual, she held her breath. Both women were utterly transfixed on each other. But she blinked first, before Gemma burst into an uncontrollable giggle. It was too infectious. Yvonne lost all her inhibitions and together they laughed for over a minute.

It was a wholly unexpected sight for the two men, peering through the French windows. John whispered under his breath, 'My God, what have you done now, my girl?'

Both women regained their composure and returned to the house to join the two bewildered men. Yvonne nodded to John and turned to Gemma. 'Thank you for your time, Mrs Baldwin. I don't think we shall meet again in such cordial circumstances but thanks for your help once again.'

'I would like to say "anytime" Chief Inspector, but you and I know very well that will never happen.'

John and Yvonne walked back to their car and drove through the open front gates in silence.

84

Close to midnight, Max stood outside his house in Clerkenwell having been absent for over six weeks. After checking the neighbourhood, in particular the lines of parked vehicles, he approached the front door and was pleasantly surprised to find the locks had remained unchanged. Without turning the lights on, he entered and immediately noticed the house had been thoroughly searched, the contents of cupboard drawers strewn across the floors in most rooms. He climbed the stairs and went into his bedroom and looked in the wardrobe. Most of his clothes remained neatly on their hangers, whilst some were scattered on the bed. He quickly gathered some of his favourite items and placed them in an empty suitcase.

He moved to the dressing table and peered in the opened drawer and found the fountain pen he had been given by his mother just before she died. He stopped and looked at it closely and closed his eyes. Suddenly the smell of Vicky's perfume filled his nostrils and a flash of guilt pierced his conscience. He immediately suppressed the hurt and dropped the pen to the floor.

After showering in cold water, he lay on the mattress and soon fell asleep.

But his mind was permanently on full alert and he woke early the following morning to the noise of traffic outside. Glancing at his watch – 7.15 a.m. – he saw the winter daylight breaking through the window and quickly dressed. He had much to prepare.

Before leaving, he went into the bathroom and pulled away the screen surrounding the semi-circular bath. Although it had been searched by the police, they had failed to notice the cut-away floorboard under the pipes connected to the taps. Lifting it up, he reached into the void and pulled out a velvet cotton rag. He laid it on the floor in front of him and carefully opened it out. He smiled. It was exactly as he had left it over a year ago: a brand-new Glock pistol carrying seventeen rounds of ammunition. He had purchased the weapon for a thousand pounds, ready for such an occasion. Quickly, he rewrapped the weapon and placed it in his suitcase.

Leaving his house, knowing he would never set foot in it again, he made his way towards the taxi rank two streets away. He caught a taxi to King's Cross railway station, avoiding Benny the paper seller, and bought a single ticket to Newark-on-Trent in Nottinghamshire. An hour and a half later he arrived in the town and booked into a small hotel directly opposite the station. After dropping off his suitcase, he walked into the centre where he found the local estate agents, lining both sides of the main road leading into the market square.

In the second agency he discovered exactly what he was searching for: a small holding consisting of a two-bedroomed cottage with a small barn set in six acres of land. It had been unoccupied for nearly twelve months and was described as 'in need of modernisation'. The old farmer had died, leaving his estate to his estranged daughter, who was hoping for a quick sale. Max had no intention of living there nor of purchasing the property but instead he offered a six-month lease. The original price was dramatically reduced to entice a sale, but Max threatened to walk away from any deal unless they accepted his offer. Reluctantly, the estate agent agreed to a lease for six months plus a six-month security bond. Within two hours he had signed the necessary paperwork, collected the keys and hired a small car. The property was outside a small village called Claypot, close to the Great North Road, between Newark and Grantham.

Max drove the small Ford Fiesta down an unmade road for over three hundred yards, through a large spinney, then turned through an entrance in a high brick wall. Before him lay a private courtyard, completely hidden from view. The name on the side of the cottage read Poacher's Hide. It was perfect. He opened the front door and went in. A quick glance confirmed his suspicions. Clearly it was uninhabitable, but Max was looking for the real reason for leasing the crumbling slum. And there it stood in the back field. A brick barn with a red pantile roof, remarkably in better condition than the cottage.

He managed to open the rickety barn doors and discovered it was dry and roomy, with old wooden storage units. It even boasted a cellar, initially hidden from view beneath a carpet of scattered bundles of hay and tarpaulin sheets. This was the place where he would store the drugs until he was ready to distribute them onto the black market. Meanwhile, he had to organise their transportation from Southampton.

He returned to Newark and went directly to the public library, half an hour before it closed. He searched the national telephone directories for a transport company based in Southampton to collect the crate from the docks. Using a local firm from Newark might attract some unnecessary questions. An outside firm would soon forget the farm.

Fennels Haulage of Southampton was chosen. He made a note of their telephone number and left as the librarian was shutting the doors. He drove directly back to his small and uninviting hotel.

In his sparsely furnished room he placed a call to Fennels, hoping it would still be open. It was. The office manager was both friendly and helpful, agreeing to transport the crate from Southampton Docks to Nottinghamshire once they had received the documentation and fee. Max agreed to travel to the Southampton office now and settle up with them on both counts.

The manager said, 'If you do that, sir, we can have it transported up there later tonight. It's much quieter on the roads for the drivers but it may cost a little more. Otherwise, I'm afraid it will be later next week.'

'Make it tonight. I'll pay the extra charge. I'm setting off now.'

'Very good, sir. What name is it, please?'

'Richardson. Mr Richardson.'

'We'll see you in about four hours then Mr Richardson.'

85

As Max was making his final plans, Yvonne and John decided to remain in Manchester, taking separate rooms within the hospitably suite at police headquarters. Before retiring, Yvonne relayed to John, her conversation with Gemma Baldwin confirming Max's alias was Joel Richardson. Back inside his room, John contacted Phil about this new development. It was now important he and the security officers on the main gates to Southampton Docks were on the lookout for either Campbell or Richardson.

'Got that. I'll let them know. If I need you, I'll ring there.' replied Phil.

'OK Buddy. See you tomorrow.'

However, thirty minutes later, whilst Yvonne and John were asleep, events began to change rapidly.

86

Phil had been observing the gates continuously for over twelve hours, but shortly before midnight he awoke from his doze with the telephone ringing next to his head. A voice announced, 'There's a lorry here from Fennels Haulage of Southampton with a docket from Phoenix Laboratories UK Ltd to collect a crate of crops for a science laboratory in Cambridge. Isn't that the name of the firm you're interested in?'

'Yes. Let them in. Where is it to be collected from?'

'Let me see. Unit 19A in B block. If you come down, I'll you show you where that is.'

'What type of lorry is it?'

'It's a medium-size rigid flat back, with a canvas cover.'

'Thanks. I'll be there in a moment.'

Phil approached the single-storey gatehouse where he saw one of the security men. 'Follow me, sir.'

They walked through the yard stretching for over two hundred yards, passing several massive warehouses, until they entered B block. Phil stopped the guard. 'Tell me where it is from here. I'll go alone.'

'Follow the main passage down the centre until you reach a white wooden office door, turn right and second left. That's where Unit 19 is. Running adjacent is 19A. If you walk quickly you'll be able to hear the forklift driver load the cargo onto the lorry. Good luck.'

'Thanks. Remember, don't stop the lorry when it leaves. That's important. Also, if my colleagues get in touch, tell them exactly what's happened and give this to them.' Phil handed the guard a small but heavy package wrapped in brown paper. 'Make sure they get this. It's a radio receiver. My life may depend on it.'

'I will, sir.'

Phil left him and walked briskly towards the dimly lit warehouse. Just as he caught sight of the white office door, he heard voices coming from the direction of Unit 19A. Keeping to the shadows of the tall rows of stacked cargo crates and pallets, he saw the lorry with its tailgate lowered and two men standing nearby. He heard one of them say, 'Bloody filthy night for deliveries, mate.'

'You're right there. Apparently, it's an urgent order, like all the others. Still, at least I got a good bonus on this one.'

'You're lucky. I get bugger all extra for working nights. I'll get you your load. Give me the docket.' The man took the paper and jumped into a nearby forklift. 'Give us a few minutes. This one is in the next row.'

Phil seized the moment. He approached the lorry from the blind side to where the driver stood and slipped underneath it. Lying on his back, he attached a tracker device to the chassis with a strong magnet and tape, pulling out the small extendable aerial. Finally, he coated it with some wet road dirt. With only seconds to spare, he rolled out from beneath the lorry and hid behind a nearby crate before the warehouseman returned with his forklift, carrying a large wooden crate. Skilfully, he placed it gently onto the lorry.

'There you go, mate. Here's your paperwork, you'll need that to get past the gate.'

The lorry driver took the papers before climbing back into his cab. This gave Phil a few seconds to step up onto the back wheel and haul himself onto the platform and hide under the dirty canvas cover. It was pitch black, cold and wet, offering no comfort. But his main concern was its unknown destination. Fortunately, he was wearing his heavy-duty coat but this gave him little protection from the bitter winter's night as the lorry drove away through the open doors towards the exit gates. Phil curled up as best he could, hoping for three things: the tracker performed correctly, his friends would come to his rescue and the ride would be mercifully short.

Unfortunately, he was wrong on all three counts.

87

As soon as Yvonne and John had left her house, Gemma went on the offensive. Yvonne had shown a little too much of her hand. Assuming the point of entry for the Max's crate would be the same as the other three, she contacted an associate in Southampton and asked him to find an accommodating security guard who could provide important information for a substantial amount of money. Within the hour, she received news that such a guard had agreed to her request. For five hundred pounds, she got details of the haulage company hired to transport goods on behalf of Phoenix Laboratories UK Ltd.

88

Phil was suffering now from his ordeal. He was sitting uncomfortably on the hard wooden boards of the lorry, breathing in the exhaust fumes. His position had already been compromised. The telephone call to the guard holding the package Phil had given him sealed his fate. For his bribe, the guard was told to open it immediately. When he discovered it was a tracker receiver, the caller instructed him to render it useless, without it appearing too obvious. It was rewrapped neatly in the brown paper and he simply dropped it several times on the concrete floor.

His reward was another package. This one contained the five hundred pounds in cash, which he later found strapped to the side of his motorcycle in the car park outside the main gates.

89

As Yvonne drifted into sleep, John felt troubled about his friend Phil. He leant over for the bedside telephone and called the Major Incident Room. Eventually he spoke to the duty detective.

'Good evening. This is Inspector Evans, is Phil Smith there please?'

'No, I'm sorry. I believe he went down to the dock gates some hours ago to check on some collection.'

'Do you have the number for the Gate Security Office there?'

'Just a minute. Yes, here it is.'

Within two minutes John was talking to the guard. 'Hello. I want to speak to Phil Smith. Is he there please?'

'I'm sorry sir. I think he left with the consignment earlier. He gave me a package to hand over to you but I'm really sorry I slipped on the wet ground outside and dropped it on the concrete. It seems to be all smashed up inside. I don't know what to say.'

'Do you have details of the haulage company and its destination?'

'Yes, I got the details but I've no idea of its destination. Let me have a look. Here it is. The company is Fennels Haulage. They're a local business. We see a lot of them here.'

John scribbled down the name, slammed the telephone down and ran next door. Without knocking he entered the room and shouted 'Yvonne, get up. Phil's onto something and we don't know where he is right now.'

'What?' she replied.

'Just get dressed Yvonne. First, we've got to get someone in the

Major Incident Room to visit Fennels Haulage in Southampton to trace the destinations of their jobs tonight.'

As John was making the call from his room, Yvonne ran in 'I don't like this, John. If Phil's on board that lorry and we've lost him, together with the drugs and probably Max Campbell, I'm in deep shit.'

'Stop thinking of yourself Yvonne for Christ's sake.'

'Oh, I'm sorry. You're right. It's a bloody mess and it's all my making. We need to do everything we can to find out where he is. What am I going to do?'

'What exactly did you tell your friend Mrs Baldwin again?'

'My God! John, I told her we knew all about the special permit for Crops Research UK Ltd and Phoenix Laboratories UK Ltd. Christ, she didn't know about the second, did she? What have I done?'

'Showed too much of your bloody slip young lady.'

'Christ, I bet she's arranged for someone down there to keep their eye out for a collection from them. What do I do now John?'

'We're going to go and speak with Mrs Baldwin right now. We don't have enough time to wait for them to make enquiries with Fennels Haulage.'

Yes, you're right. But what happens if she won't talk to us?'

'Bugger that too. I'll break the bloody gates down if I need to. Yvonne, I've never questioned your initiative before, but frankly, you've cocked up this time. You got too close to the Devil and she's burnt your arse. This is what we're going to do.'

90

Whilst Yvonne and John were heading west from Manchester towards Cheshire, Gemma Baldwin's team were travelling south east towards Newark. Her associate in Southampton had visited the offices of Fennels Haulage of Southampton and persuaded the night clerk to furnish him with the destination of the Phoenix Laboratories' shipment. Another five hundred pounds in cash had done the trick.

Meanwhile, Phil was in a serious dilemma. He had attempted on several occasions to abandon his ordeal by escaping from the lorry, but its speed was too fast. Travelling through the night, without any significant traffic, it rarely slowed down to less than thirty miles per hour. The severe chill posed a greater danger than the fumes. Initially, he began to cough, followed by nausea and a sore throat. Then he became light-headed and drifted into sleep, finally falling into semi-consciousness. The lorry continued on its way, the driver listening to his favourite rock band on the ghetto blaster perched on the front dashboard, oblivious to the nature of the consignment he was carrying, or the man lying next to it.

*

Max had quickly returned to Nottinghamshire and was now waiting in the grounds of Poacher's Hide, his car tucked away in the spinney near to the entrance. Sitting on a makeshift bench behind a brick wall, he was only expecting the lorry. But he was taking no chances. If he suspected it was accompanied by other vehicles, he would abort the whole enterprise and speed away in the small car. He would have lost the opportunity of a lifetime to make a fortune but at least he would be alive and free.

The night was pitch black. No moon or nearby street lighting. He was dressed in dark clothing, with the Glock pistol loaded and the extra rounds of ammunition tucked away inside his pocket. Once the goods arrived, he would ask the driver to unload the crate into the barn, and give him a tip, expecting him to promptly leave for his long journey back to Southampton. He looked at his watch. Two thirty.

He first saw headlamps through the trees, followed by the sound of a heavy diesel engine changing gears and the crunching of stones in the drive. Keeping his head just above the top row of bricks, he saw the lorry slow down and come to a halt outside the cottage. A few seconds later the engine stopped and the driver sounded the horn. Max made certain there were no other vehicles following. With the driver's door open and the cab dimly lit, he could see he was alone.

Stepping out from the shadows he shouted, 'Over here.'

The driver turned around in surprise. 'Bloody hell, mate, it's a bit isolated up here.'

'Yes. That's how I like it. Have you got the crate on board?'

'Certainly have. Do you want to see it to make sure?'

'No. But can you reverse your truck down to the barn and unload it inside?'

'OK. Switch some lights on and show me where you want it.'

Max opened the large wooden doors and turned on the two spotlights, illuminating the area just inside the barn. The driver got into the cab and reversed exactly to where Max directed. He jumped back out and began to walk along the length of the lorry, loosening the canvas cover straps away from the platform. As the crate became exposed he attached four chains to the corners of the crate, using the on-board hoist to start winching the load upwards.

As this was happening, Phil regained his wits and instinctively knew he was in serious danger. With all the energy he was able to muster, he rolled off the opposite side of the platform, falling silently onto the wet muddy ground, before crawling to safety behind an old stone water trough.

The driver swung the crate over the side of the lorry and lowered it, placing it six feet inside the barn. Max wanted it further inside but realised that was the limit of the hoist. 'Leave it there, please.'

The driver released the winch and the chains fell from the crate.

Max said, 'That's good. Here's a little extra for your help. I can manage from here, thank you.'

He took the twenty-pound note and smiled. 'Thanks, mate. I'll leave it with you. I'll get off back before the early morning rush hour starts.' He replaced and secured the canvas sheet, climbed back into cab, and drove away back towards the A1. Once Max could no longer hear or see the lorry he returned to the barn and closed the doors behind him. Carrying a powerful torch together with a metal crowbar he began open the wooden crate to inspect the goods inside.

Phil wrapped his coat tightly round his body, but he was cold. Very cold. He was desperate to take shelter out of the cold damp air. He peered over the stone trough towards the barn and saw the flickering torch lights through the gap running along the bottom edge of the badly fitting doors. Cautiously, he approached them and placed an ear against one. He heard the sound of timber breaking under pressure. The crate was being prised open.

He stood back and assessed his position. He was freezing cold and had no idea where he was, nor whether Yvonne and John were on their way. But more importantly; who was inside the barn? Was this really Max and was he alone? He needed to get inside without being discovered. But how?

As his mind cleared, he had an idea. Picking up a sizeable pebble, he threw it onto the barn roof towards the furthest gable end. It landed exactly where he intended, rolling down over the red clay tiles before dropping over the far side. The noise inside stopped. Seconds later the door opened, clearly showing the silhouette of a man. He walked outside and vanished towards the back of the barn. Phil sprang forward and ran inside, past the remnants of the wooden crate, past some storage units and finally into an enclosure where pigs had once been kept in years gone by. He immediately crouched down and waited for the man to return. He did not have to wait long.

91

At three in the morning, John drove up to the entrance to Gemma Baldwin's house. He stood next to the main gate and continually pressed the intercom button. Suddenly a voice shouted through the gates, 'What do you want?'

'My name is Inspector Evans from the Metropolitan Police and I need to speak with Mrs Baldwin on a matter of life and death.'

'Go away and make an appointment to see her tomorrow. Mrs Baldwin doesn't want to be disturbed at this time of night.'

John shouted, 'Listen to me. Show yourself now or I'm going to get really pissed off.'

Two men dressed in camouflage jackets appeared from the darkness.

'We're the police and if you don't let me in right now, I'll call in the Bomb Squad and tell them I've received information there are large quantities of explosives on these premises. They'll love it if you were to bar their entrance. Any excuse to lawfully batter the gates down and trample all over your bodies. Now get these bloody gates open and get that woman out of her warm cosy bed before she's dragged out of it.'

Yvonne looked startled. 'Wow,' she muttered under her breath. She had never witnessed John being so forceful before. But his assertiveness worked. Reluctantly, the men manually opened the gates and waved them through. John and Yvonne drove past them to the front door. To their surprise Gemma Baldwin was standing in the porch, devoid of makeup, wearing a thick dressing gown.

John turned to Yvonne. 'You know what to say to her. Now go and trade with the Devil but never do it again.'

Without replying, she opened the car door and walked directly towards Gemma Baldwin.

'Chief Inspector. This is not funny. What are you doing here?'

'In the back garden, if you please, as we have some serious woman-to-woman talking to do.' She turned towards the garden. 'Come on, Gemma, I don't have much time.'

They sat on the same wooden bench. Gemma said, 'I've lived in this house for four years and never ventured here in the middle of the night before. For Christ's sake, what is it, Chief Inspector? Within twelve hours I'm sitting here on two occasions with the enemy.'

'Shut up, Gemma and listen to me. I know you have arranged to intercept the drugs from Max because I screwed up by telling you of his other bogus company. I don't have time to find out what you have done because one of my colleagues has got himself hidden in the lorry with the crate of drugs. Gemma, I need you to protect him from Max and your team.'

'I don't know what you're talking about.'

'Bollocks. I'm pleading with you. Haven't you lost someone who you respected and admired?'

Gemma thought of Bill. Without replying, she nodded and looked into Yvonne's eyes, recognising the sincerity of her plea. Eventually she whispered, 'Let me have Max.'

Yvonne shuddered. She knew exactly what Gemma was asking for and it tore at every fibre in her body, tempting her to abandon her moral judgement for lawful justice for the life of another. How could she cope with the sheer hypocrisy of agreeing to her demands? She turned. 'Gemma, you're playing the Badger Game with me, aren't you?'

'Yes, Yvonne, I am.'

'Let me have my man back and I promise you I'll call off the hunt for twelve hours. After then all bets are off. Deal?'

'Deal.'

She stood up to leave, but Gemma followed her. 'Yvonne, you're a good woman who looks after her team. Sometimes we have to make decisions and judgements we don't want to. I'm sorry about your man and I'll do everything in my power to help him. I promise.'

'Make sure you do, Gemma, or I'll be coming after you. Twelve hours.'

Yvonne walked through the house and returned to the car. They drove back out through the gates. 'John, please go to the nearest police station. I want to check with the Major Incident Room to see if they've found where that bloody crate has gone to. I've a hunch it's not too far away.'

'How's that?'

'Gemma gave me the impression she could save Phil without too much fuss, so I'm guessing he's somewhere in the north of England.'

They entered the small local police station where they found the night Constable sitting at a desk with his feet up on it. He was fast asleep, snoring and completely unaware of his visitors. Yvonne ignored him, went to the telephone and placed a call to the Incident Room, asking for news of her recent enquiry into the destination the Phoenix Laboratories UK Ltd crate. Eventually, she spoke to the Duty Detective who appeared drowsy like the officer now in front of her. Slowly he muttered, 'Just a moment, Ma'am. Oh yes, we've spoken to the haulage company and established the lorry's destination. I've got the details here.'

'Let me get a pen and paper, I need to write this down.' She leant over the large wooden desk and ripped a sheet from the officer's note pad and scribbled to details down. She said, 'Tell Commander Higgins I believe the third crate has been swapped for the one at this address. We're going to investigate now. If you've heard nothing from us by eight o'clock, warn the locals to attend with some firearms just in case. I don't want anyone else attending now. Leave it with me and Inspector Evans for the moment. Have you got that?'

'Yes, Ma'am.'

She replaced the receiver and looked at the address again. 'Where's that, John?'

He looked at it and shook his head. 'Not a clue.'

Shrugging, he leant over the sleeping Constable and pulled a road atlas from a bookshelf wedged between various thick files and reports. He quickly thumbed through the index and turned to the appropriate page. He pointed to a small hamlet called Claypot, close to the Great North Road between Newark and Grantham. He checked their present position and roughly calculated they were about a hundred miles away. Glancing at his watch it was almost three o'clock. At this time in the morning the journey would take about two hours. 'Let's go. We can't waste a minute.'

Clutching the map, they left the station, slamming the door behind them. The Constable stirred, opened one eye and fell back asleep. They were soon speeding east along the trans-Pennine motorway towards the A1 and the Great North Road in Yorkshire, before turning south towards Newark and Claypot beyond. Where the hell was Poacher's Hide?

But Gemma's men were already two hours ahead.

92

Phil tried desperately to keep still but his shivering increased. He rammed his fist in his mouth to soften the involuntarily guttural sounds he was making. Max returned to the barn. It was at that moment he definitely recognised him from the photograph Yvonne had given him several weeks ago. Although he had grown a beard and his hair was a great deal shorter, there was no doubt it was Max Campbell.

Through the open slats of the disused pig enclosure he could see him standing next to the crate, continuing to forcibly remove the outer wooden casing with the metal crowbar. Eventually it completely fell away, revealing bundles of crops tightly bound into larger clumps. Max removed them with a spade and another smaller wooden crate began to emerge behind them. Soon, the floor was covered with scattered broken timbers and crops. The inner crate measured one yard high and wide by two yards long. Once again, Max set to with the crowbar and began disassembling the inner crate.

After several minutes of prising the timbers apart, Max leant over, picked out a package, walked over to a nearby bench and placed it on top. Phil strained forward to get a better view. He could see that the package, roughly the size of a shoe box, was tightly bound in another polythene bag and fixed with red adhesive tape. Max took out a small penknife and slit the bag, pouring a small amount of light brown powder into a glass tube containing a clear liquid. He waited for several moments before holding it to the light above. Suddenly he shouted, 'Yes.'

But his euphoria lasted only a few seconds. A strange sound came from outside. Instinctively, Max switched the lights off, causing the barn to fall into complete darkness. At that moment, the doors burst open and several figures appeared, silhouetted against the headlights of vehicles outside. All were carrying guns.

Max fell to the floor and put his hand in his jacket, intending to use the Glock, but was prevented from doing so by the weight of a heavy boot stamping firmly on his neck. The cold steel of a gun muzzle pressed painfully against his forehead. 'No Max, or I'll shoot you right here.'

Another figure switched the lights back on. Phil saw eight men dressed in black and khaki combat fatigues with matching balaclavas, all wearing night vision goggles. They carried various military firearms. Phil sighed with relief and broke cover, stood up and shouted, 'Good work, boys. Am I glad to see you.'

Everyone, including Max, was astonished to see him there, casually walking towards them, rubbing his numb legs. But his relief was short-lived. A man sprang towards him and pointed a high calibre rifle into his face. 'Who the hell are you?'

'Phil Smith. Working for the Metropolitan Police. I've been expecting you.'

'I don't think you have. We're not who you think we are. Arms up or I'll shoot you as well.'

Phil's heart sank. As he drew closer to them, he could see they were all wearing different civilian shirts under their military jackets and their boots were either black or brown. He raised his arms and said, 'Shit, should have stayed down.'

'You're right there, mate. Put your arms behind your back and do as you're told, or you're a dead man.'

Phil complied. Once his arms were secured, one of them placed a black hood over his head and frog-marched him out of the barn to a nearby vehicle. Still shivering with cold, he sat in the rear seat, completely in the dark. From underneath the hood he could hear the others talking to Max in a similar manner.

Suddenly there was the piecing sound of a shot followed by a voice shouting, 'Get him.' Three other shots resonated from the barn. Then silence. Another voice shouted, 'Are you OK, Jim?' No reply. Another shot was fired but this was louder, a more powerful gun. Silence again.

The man sitting next to Phil moved and got out of the vehicle, leaving him alone. But he was heavily strapped with plastic cuffs and duct tape, unable to move, even sideways. Yet there was an opportunity to look outside. He leant forwards and placed his head against the back of the driver's seat, managing to wriggle his head and lift the hood sufficiently enough to see the commotion inside the barn. There appeared to be a standoff, with a body lying in the entrance. Phil assumed Max had somehow managed to free himself and shoot one of his captors before being cornered in the enclosure where he had hidden earlier.

Without warning, a massive bang came from the back of the barn. One of the men had lobbed a stun grenade towards Max causing him to stagger out from his cover clutching the sides of his face. The area surrounding him immediately ignited; the dry crops and timbers bursting into flames. Three men rushed forward, grabbed Max and threw him to the floor again. This time he was completely overwhelmed, trussed, gagged and hooded before being roughly bundled into the rear of a nearby Ford Transit van.

Within a minute the fire began to consume the barn. The paramilitaries formed a human chain and began to pass the packages from the crate and throw them to safety near to the parked vehicles. Phil saw one of them split as it fell awkwardly onto the ground. After only a few minutes the men were forced to abandon their efforts, driven back by the flames and unbearable heat. Before the barn completely collapsed and succumbed to the inferno, the three vehicles drove away, with Max, Phil, a wounded colleague and the remains of the heroin on hoard.

93

When John and Yvonne finally arrived at Poacher's Hide it was not what they expected to find. A host of blue lights could be seen long before they left the Great North Road. They all belonged to Fire Service, except for a solitary police patrol car. As they approached Poacher's Hide, Yvonne simply said, 'What the hell…?'

As they pulled up next to the police car they were approached by a Constable who curtly asked, 'Who are you?'

'My name is DCI Hall and this is Inspector Evans from the Met. What's happened here, Officer?'

'Sorry, Ma'am. We got a call about forty minutes ago from a passing motorist who saw the flames from half a mile away.'

With the Constable, Yvonne approached the Fire Officer in charge. 'We have good reason to believe there could have been a large quantity of heroin in these premises, or what's left of it. I don't want to put any of your officers in unnecessary danger.'

'Right. Thanks for that. Under the circumstances I'm withdrawing my staff and will allow a controlled burn. Once I'm satisfied it's safe, we'll check the scene with safety apparatus.'

She turned to the Constable. 'Have you searched the cottage and the surrounding area? I have a colleague who may have been here when this happened.'

'No, Ma'am. I'll do that now. Incidentally, my Detective Inspector is en route, along with SOCO.'

Together they searched the dwelling but found no signs of Phil. Outside, John found some evidence of movement behind a stone water trough; the grass had been recently flattened, consistent with someone crouching behind it. There were several tyre tracks and four ruptured packages containing a light-yellow powder. He summoned Yvonne and the Constable over.

'Look at this. There must be at least ten kilos of heroin here. I reckon something went seriously wrong. They must have been in a hurry.'

Turning to the Constable, John said, 'Officer, this is probably heroin, recently imported into this country and subject to a major inquiry. Your role now is to protect this scene. Forget the fire, this is your priority until the Drugs Squad and forensic arrive. OK?'

'Yes, sir. I'll get some tape from my car.'

'Good man.'

They turned around to watch the barn roof finally cave in, causing sparks and flames to shoot high into the breaking dawn sky. The scene was now one of complete devastation.

John looked at Yvonne. 'We can't do anything here until the Fire Chief has made it safe and SOCO have done their inspection. That's going to take days, so we might as well go to Newark Police Station and call Commander Higgins.'

'You're right. Lord knows what he's going to say.'

*

Half an hour later she made the call. Eventually he answered. 'Yvonne, where are you?'

'Newark Police Station. We've ended up here because—'

'Never mind that. A courier arrived a few minutes ago with a short message addressed to you. I took the liberty of opening it. It reads "Your friend is at Ferry Bridge service station in the gents". What does this mean?'

'Thank you, sir. I'll explain it to you later. I'm going up there now with John Evans; it's about thirty minutes away. I can tell you with some certainty, the fourth crate has been destroyed in a fire up here, along with most of the drugs. But I don't know the whereabouts of Max Campbell yet.'

'Alright. Let me know when you've got more news.'

The Nottinghamshire Police obliged in providing a high-speed vehicle and a driver. Within twenty-five minutes, they turned into

Ferry Bridge service station and all three ran into the gents' toilets, much to the surprise of several lorry drivers, stripped to the waist and washing themselves. John walked along the cubicles until he came to the last one. It was locked. Without hesitation, he knelt down and looked under the door and saw two legs tied at the ankles. He nodded to the uniformed officer who immediately kicked the door open. There, tied with duct tape to the pipes and lavatory seat, was Phil. His head was still inside the black woollen hood. Yvonne yanked it off and stared into his eyes with extreme relief. He was gagged, with tape wrapped around his face. John tore it away and cupped both sides of Phil's head.

'Phil, wake up. We're here now.'

He opened his eyes and whispered, 'About bloody time, too.'

Yvonne smiled and threw her arms around him. 'Hell, Phil, I thought we'd lost you.'

'No chance. But I'm cold and need a hot drink. Get me out of here and I'll tell you what's happened.'

John and the Constable helped him to his feet and walked him unsteadily towards the entrance. One of the drivers said, 'Bloody hell, you can't even go for a piss these days without the coppers watching.' Another joined in, saying, 'This is a gents, love; you're not allowed in here.'

Phil raised his head and groaned. 'Listen, this woman's got more balls than all of us put together.'

*

The services manager was informed of the circumstances and the damage to the door and allowed them to use his office. Phil related the events: his intolerable ride on the back of the lorry, Max opening the heroin bags inside the barn, the raid and his bad decision to show himself. He explained that Max had struggled and resisted them, followed by the fire caused by the stun grenade. He estimated only about ten bags had been recovered and thrown into the waiting vehicles. But Max was definitely taken too.

He was completely blind under the hood but knew they had driven for about half an hour before stopping. Then he smelt something on the hood and passed out. His next recollection was John ripping the tape away from his face.

A knock on the door revealed the manager returning with three large breakfasts and mugs of tea, which they ate and drank with relish. Afterwards, they unanimously agreed it was the best meal they had ever consumed in their lives.

94

Max knew his fate. His mind began to wander back to the early days living in Brixton with his mother. Just the two of them. She was so proud of him for many reasons: polite and courteous to her neighbours, achieving well at school and managing to keep out of trouble, unlike the other kids. He remembered the evening he came home from night school to find her dead on the kitchen floor after she had suffered a catastrophic brain seizure. Suddenly he was on his own without any love or moral compass. No one could take her place. And now he missed her like never before. He whispered to himself, 'I'll be with you soon.'

But he thought of how she would be bitterly disappointed at how things had turned out. He had accomplished a great deal in his early adulthood, owning a successful club and enjoying a standard of living she would be unable to comprehend. How did it come to this? He became greedy and over-confident, taking risks and making too many enemies. Twelve months ago, he had everything. Not now. He hoped the end would be quick and painless.

Suddenly the van stopped. He heard the back doors open then he was dragged roughly out. He stood up and the hood was quickly lifted from his head. The first person he saw was Gemma Baldwin, standing in front of six men carrying weapons. Softly, she said, 'Max, you have cost me over a million pounds and nearly all the drugs have been destroyed. But what I really want to know is, how did you kill Bill? Before you answer this, I must tell you, you're going to die anyway. But if you tell me the truth, you won't suffer. It's up to you. These boys are happy to make it long or short.'

He looked beyond her and noticed a large construction site near to a motorway viaduct. He knew he was going to be put in the thousands of tons of concrete supporting the foundations. He shrugged.

'Gemma, I struck him over the head with a metal bar and left him in the club cellar before I set it on fire. Now will you please put me out of all this?'

'Max you were a fool. You should have kept to the Badger Game; you were a good player at that. But you got too ambitious and tried to muscle into my world. Big mistake. If you had only kept to the original business deal we had and just stored my merchandise, you'd have been a rich young man by now. Bill never trusted you, but I was prepared to give you the benefit of the doubt. Max, you screwed up and cost me dearly. Now it's time to pay.'

She nodded to the man standing behind him and stepped backwards. Max felt and saw nothing; no sound or flashing light. Nothing. As he had predicted, his limp body was dispatched into a newly dug trench where hundreds of tons of wet concrete were to be poured. An unmarked tomb where millions of motorists would travel over, oblivious to the resting place of a man who played the Badger Game and lost.

95

Two days later, the Deputy Commissioner, Sir John Simpson, convened a debrief of Operation Harvest in his office. His only two guests were Commander Jim Higgins and DCI Hall.

'Thank you for coming this morning. I just wanted to know what the latest developments are as the Home Secretary has asked me to see him this afternoon. Jim, tell me the latest.'

'Sir. A total of twenty-seven men have been charged with various offences of importing and supplying Class A drugs under the Misuse of Drugs Act. Nearly a ton of uncut heroin has been seized and three major drug rings neutralised. It's the largest drugs bust in this country's history.'

'Excellent. This has certainly been a good operation and no doubt your career will reflect this in the near future.'

'Thank you, sir.'

He turned to Yvonne. 'And how's the investigation into Max Campbell?'

'I need to talk to you privately about that, sir.'

Both men looked at her then each other. 'If you wish,' said Sir John. He looked at Commander Higgins and nodded. 'Will you give us a minute, Jim, please?'

'Of course, sir.'

He stood up and placed a hand on Yvonne's shoulder, giving her a reassuring wink before leaving. This gave her a mixed message. She felt it patronising and unnecessary. After the door closed behind him, she said, 'Sir John, I feel I need to tender my resignation to you this morning.'

'I beg your pardon. I've read your initial report about Campbell slipping through the net, but you prevented most of the drugs being distributed on our streets and rescued your colleague from harm's way soon afterwards. That was good work, DCI Hall. So why?'

'Sir John, I must confide in you and tell the truth. When I spoke to Gemma Baldwin, I asked her to assist me to find Campbell. She refused to begin with, so in order to convince her further, I told her about the shipment and how it had been compromised for many weeks. We always knew about Crops Research UK Ltd. As this had little effect, I explained how she had been duped by Campbell. Then I made the biggest mistake of my professional life; I told her about the shadow company Phoenix Laboratories UK Ltd that Campbell had set up and the swapping of the crates in Karachi. It was only at this point she confirmed to me his alias was Joel Richardson. But of course, this gave her the opportunity to send her team to nobble the security man on the Docks gate, There, they found the transport company and traced the destination of the delivery. To my shame, I seriously let my colleague Phil Smith down by placing him in harm's way.

'DCI Hall. You're right, that was a big mistake.'

'That's not all, sir. When I found Phil Smith had gone and we had no idea where he was, I went to pieces. Fortunately, John Evans showed true leadership. To be honest, I panicked. I just didn't know what to do next. He came up with the solution. He told me I'd made a grave mistake and suggested I went back to see Gemma Baldwin and tell her about Phil Smith's predicament. So, we dashed back to her place again in the middle of the night. Of course, she denied any involvement with the whole affair but when I pleaded with her to keep Phil safe from danger, she told me simply, 'I want Max then.' My next decision was the hardest I've ever made in my life. I told her I would give her twelve hours to find him, provided Phil was released.'

'You actually said that?'

'Yes, sir. I traded with the Devil; Max Campbell for Phil.'

'So what you're telling me is that you deliberately delayed Max Campbell's arrest in return for Mr Smith's life?'

'Yes, sir, but that's not all.'

'What else, DCI?'

'This morning I received this note, sent to my home address.' She handed him a typed note: *Phoenix Laboratories UK has been liquidated along with its Director – Joel Richardson*

'Do you believe this to be true?'

'Oh Yes, I do. I believe Max Campbell has been killed and we'll never find him alive.'

'Who else knows about all this?'

'Just the three of us. John Evans, me and yourself.'

'No. Let's not forget Gemma Baldwin as well.'

'No sir.'

'So, you have denied us the opportunity of bringing this man to justice. Haven't you?'

'Yes, sir, that's why I can no longer remain in the Service. If you wish to prepare any criminal or disciplinary charges against me, I fully understand.'

Sir John stood and walked over to the window, scanning the roof line of the buildings opposite and beyond. He remained silent for several minutes before returning to his desk. Looking directly at her, noticing her sincere remorse, he said, 'If I ask you this question, will you be truthful?'

'Yes, sir.'

'There can be no mistake, you made a seriously error of judgement here. But if you were faced with the same dilemma again, would your decision be the same?'

Without any hesitation, she said, 'Yes, sir, there are some values I hold that mean more to me than my career. And the life of one of my friends is one of those.'

Sir John sat back into his chair and calmly said, 'DCI Hall, your values do you credit, and I will not be accepting your resignation. Sometimes we make mistakes and must face the consequences. Although I would never publically acknowledge that some lives are more important that others, privately I do share this view. I also believe Mr Smith's well-being outweighs that of a suspected murderer, drug dealer and blackmailer who has caused so much pain and damage to others. We're not in the business of wielding justice, that's for the courts to decide, but under these extreme circumstances you had little choice. It would be easy for others to tell me to throw you to the lions and shout 'the police only look after themselves', but the reality is, we do. Why? Because no one else will. We try our best to keep the peace and protect the public, and frankly, on this occasion I believe we have. The world is a safer place without Max Campbell. Of course, I will vehemently deny this conversation. So, DCI Hall, you will remain in post and if any disciplinary matters arise from this, you will face them head on, according to your conscience.'

She looked at him, shocked. Was the Deputy Commissioner really saying this?

'Do not ever repeat this conversation. You're a damn good officer and the Service needs women like you in the future. Meanwhile, I'm going to return you to the project I asked you to run and look forward to your career advancing further. Good morning, Yvonne.'

96

The following evening Yvonne and Phil arrived at John and Charlie's house. It was the opportunity to meet up perhaps for the last time. Yvonne repeated the conversation she'd had with the Deputy Commissioner and swore everyone to secrecy.

Charlie said, 'Yvonne, that's unnecessary. We all trust each other with our lives, so your career is safe with us forever. We shall never discuss this again. Now let's drink to the future.'

They raised their glasses.

John asked Phil, 'What are you going to do now?'

'Spend all my days spoiling my wonderful grandchildren. No more coppering. Ever.'

'How about you, Yvonne?'

'Carry on catching criminals on the computer. That's the future.'

Phil looked at her and casually retorted, 'Bugger off.' They all giggled and took another drink.

Yvonne turned to John. 'What about you?'

'I'm going to carry on with the two investigations I started before you came back into my life. But there's one important thing that needs to be done very soon.'

Charlie smiled; she knew exactly what he meant.

97

John caught the Tube to Kilburn. Without an appointment, he went to see Albert Jones, the head teacher who had been forced to retire due to malicious rumours and gossip. He knocked on the front door and a distant voice said, 'Come in.'

John entered and saw him lying in a single bed that had been set up in the living room, a small suitcase by the door ready for his imminent departure. Unfortunately, his condition had deteriorated dramatically since John's last visit. Clearly, his life was now ebbing towards its end, with only weeks left. The cancer had almost completed its deadly task. His admission into the local hospice was due the following day.

'Good morning, Mr Jones. Do you remember me?'

'Yes. You're the man from the police who came here a couple of months ago. I'm sorry about this but I'm not very well now.'

'Mr Jones, I made a promise to myself when I left you then. Let me explain. As well as working with the police, I'm also a journalist who investigates those who have been the subject of miscarriages of justice. Although you never appeared in court, you were nevertheless falsely accused of something you had no knowledge of, resulting in your life being irretrievably changed for the worse. I have a copy of a letter, written by myself, which will be published in the national press tomorrow morning, completely exonerating you and others who were victims of false lies and accusations by others. I wanted you to read this before it went to press. Your name has been cleared and your exemplary reputation restored. In addition, I have a letter personally signed by the Commissioner, apologising for the conduct and behaviour of some of his officers that caused you so much distress. One particular officer is now awaiting trial at Crown Court, where all the factors relating to your circumstances and others will be heard.'

John gave him the paper and letter to read. He read them twice again, before looking at John with tears rolling down his drawn cheeks. He whispered, 'Thank you, Mr Evans. That means so much to me, especially now.'

ABOUT THE AUTHOR

Robert Henson served for thirty years in the Police Service and Home Office. After retiring he worked as a freelance training consultant working closely with several Government agencies, teaching the Criminal Law and Investigation Procedures.

He now lives in the country, spending his retirement in tranquillity with his wife and two terriers.

ALSO AVAILABLE ON AMAZON:

A Perilous Last Confession (2019)
Justice For Esther (2019)

Printed in Poland
by Amazon Fulfillment
Poland Sp. z o.o., Wrocław